BADGES OF THE BAYOU

ERIN NICHOLAS

ISBN: 978-1-952280-54-2

Editor: Lindsey Faber

Cover photo: J. Ashley Converse Photography

Cover design: Najla Qamber, Qamber Designs

the series

Badges of the Bayou
Gotta Be Bayou
Bayou With Benefits
Rocked Bayou

*

Connected series...

Boys of the Bayou
My Best Friend's Mardi Gras Wedding
Sweet Home Louisiana
Beauty and the Bayou
Crazy Rich Cajuns
Must Love Alligators
Four Weddings and a Swamp Boat Tour

*

Boys of the Bayou-Gone Wild

Otterly Irresistible
Heavy Petting
Flipping Love You
Sealed With A Kiss
Say It Like You Mane It
Head Over Hooves
Kiss My Giraffe

*

Bad Boys of the Bayou
The Best Bad Boy
Bad Medicine
Bad Influence
Bad Taste In Men
Not Such a Bad Guy
Return of the Bad Boy
Bad Behavior
Got It Bad

*

Boys of the Big Easy
Going Down Easy
Taking It Easy
Eggnog Makes Her Easy
Nice and Easy
Getting Off Easy

ROCKED BAYOU

Ex-bodyguard and moody Irishman, Colin Daly needs three things:

To figure out how to have a real job after his longtime client no longer needs him.

To find some really good Irish whiskey in the land of home-made moonshine.

To stop having dirty dreams every time he hears young, beautiful, recently-discovered-thanks-to-social-media music sensation, Hayden Ross, sing. Which seems to be every time he freaking turns around lately.

But now the new-to-the-spotlight sweetheart is being harassed and needs someone to have her back. And Colin will be damned if he's going to let anyone else take this job. No matter how much being her temporary, very protective pretend boyfriend/roommate/whatever is going to rock his world.

one

IT WAS THREE A.M.

He fucking hated three a.m. phone calls.

Colin fumbled for his phone on the bedside table, knocking a half-empty water bottle and his wallet to the floor in the process.

He actually didn't love any calls after two a.m. and before about five a.m. Nothing good happened between those hours when he was asleep and the people who had this number weren't.

He frowned at his phone. It wasn't ringing. What the fuck? What was that noise then?

He listened for a moment, prying his eyes open. That was definitely a phone.

He looked around. Was he in his own bedroom? He hadn't spent time in too many other bedrooms since coming to Louisiana, but it wasn't absolutely out of the realm of possibility.

Yes, this was his room. He reached for the opposite side of the bed. It was empty. He didn't have a hangover and he didn't remember bringing anyone in here last night, so the phone ringing had to belong to him. Didn't it?

He pushed himself up to sit. Then it came to him. He had Henry's phone. Right. Now he remembered. Henry had just left town a few hours ago, leaving his work phone with Colin. Dammit.

Colin didn't know all of the people who might be calling Henry at three a.m., but he couldn't imagine that it was with good news.

Except that it might be Cian. Cian O'Grady was Henry's best friend and Henry had been Cian's bodyguard for the past ten years. Cian was in line—though fairly far down the line—for the throne of Cara. Yes, the *throne*. Cara was a small island nation south of the Faroe Islands. It had been gifted to Cian's great-great-great-grandfather, an Irish sailor, by the King of Denmark after Cian's ancestor saved the king's life. It was a... wild history. And there was a crazy *present* to go with it. All of the grandchildren of the current king—including Cian—had abdicated the throne and come to the U.S. where they'd lived for the past decade. In spite of his anger over that, the king had insisted all of his grandchildren have bodyguards. So Colin had been assigned to Fiona, Cian's sister, and her daughter Saoirse, while Henry had been assigned to Cian, the young playboy prince.

Cian would absolutely call someone, especially Henry, at three a.m.

If Cian was calling and causing Colin to answer in the middle of the night for something stupid, he was going to get an earful, prince or not.

Colin finally located the offending device on his bedside table on the other side of the lamp. He grabbed it up, swiped across the screen, and held it to his ear. "*What?*"

There was a pause on the other end, then a soft, feminine, definitely-not-Cian voice said, "Henry?"

"No." Henry was supposed to have told his clients that he was going to be out of town. But Colin supposed, given the last-minute flurry around Henry's leaving, someone could have missed the message. "Who's this?" Colin tried to soften his voice.

"I really need to talk to Henry."

Okay, the *really* caught Colin's attention. "He's not here. Who is this?"

"Oh, um..."

If Henry had given this number to a girlfriend, Colin was going to...well, fuck, he wasn't going to do much. Colin was Henry's boss, but Henry knew damned well that Colin would never fire him. Henry was too fucking good. And Colin liked the guy. And trusted him. The trust thing was way more important in their line of work than the liking thing, but it was nice to like the guys he depended on too, he supposed. They'd known each other too damned long for Colin to boot Henry for being stupid about a woman, that was for sure.

Especially one with a soft, husky voice like this one.

But Colin was sure as hell going to chew Henry's ass for handing out his work number for personal reasons.

"Ma'am, Henry isn't reachable. Can I help?" Colin asked, finally managing to make his voice a little less gruff and firm.

"No, I need Henry. Never mind. I'm sorry." She hung up.

Colin pulled the phone back away from his face. Okay, well, that was that. He could set the phone on the table and go back to sleep. Henry's girl would have to pull out her vibrator or find someone else. It wasn't Colin's fault that Henry hadn't given her his personal number. And Henry would have to deal with the fall-out of her realizing that whenever he got back.

But something was bugging him.

3

He was *not* offering to help Henry's three a.m. hook-up with scratching any itches, but...this didn't *feel* right.

And one thing Colin Daly always did was trust his gut.

Dammit. If she *was* a client, he needed to find out who she was. Clients didn't call their bodyguards at three a.m. for no reason.

He tapped back to find her number. She was listed simply as HER. *Real nice, Henry.*

But at the same time, Colin knew it was possible that this client needed to be listed by initials or a pseudonym so that not just anyone could find her name.

Which meant, she wasn't a hook-up.

They were bodyguards. Private security. They took care of people who needed protection. They didn't have any really high-profile clients right now—unless you counted the royalty for Cara, which most people probably wouldn't, considering most people didn't even know the tiny country existed. Additionally, now that Cian's older brother Torin had returned home to take over the throne, his siblings definitely had less pressure on them.

But Colin *wanted* to have high-profile clients. That was the whole point of starting this new company. He, Henry, and Jonah, Torin's ex-bodyguard, were now essentially unemployed, specially trained, not-qualified-or-interested-in-much-else security professionals. Colin needed to build this company up and the client list was important.

Maybe Henry had recently talked to someone who was thinking about hiring private security and she was just getting back to him.

Colin tapped her number and listened to it ring twice.

"Henry?" she answered.

"No. Henry's not available. But I'm happy to help. I'm filling—"

She hung up.

Dammit.

Instead of calling her back again, Colin punched in Henry's personal phone number.

It was nine a.m. in London, and Henry answered with a perky, "Good morning, Boss."

"Who is HER?"

"Her who?"

"You have someone in your phone listed as HER. Who is she?"

Henry paused. "Why?"

"Dammit, Henry, she just called. It's three a.m. here. She's looking for you and won't talk to me. She hung up twice when she found out you're not answering this phone."

Henry muttered a curse. "Hayden Ross. She didn't say why she's calling?"

Hayden Ross. Well...fuck.

Of course, it would be *her*. "She did not," Colin said. "Any idea what's going on?"

Obviously, she needed something. This was a problem on many levels. Hayden Ross wasn't a huge client. Yet. But holy shit, the potential was there.

She was a new, up-and-coming singer-songwriter. She'd been discovered less than a year ago but had blown up quickly on social media. Colin's company had been tapped to provide some additional security for her at a recent show because they had mutual friends.

She was just starting out. She was young. Twenty-three. If she turned into a star, even moderately successful, she could need long-term security.

She was exactly what he was looking for.

The problem with that, however, was he'd immediately felt the need to assign Henry as her primary lead on purpose.

Colin wanted to be the front man for any long-term big clients, but Hayden Ross was special. He'd decided that Henry made the most sense because he was used to staying out late and keeping track of a young extrovert who liked to be out and seen. Hayden wasn't quite a female version of Cian O'Grady, but she had a lot more in common with the partying prince than she did with Cian's older sister Fiona, the animal activist and single mom whom Colin had been protecting for the past decade.

Of course, there was also the not-so-tiny detail that Colin was attracted to her.

Inexplicably more attracted to her than he had been to any woman in recent—or even long-term—memory.

She was young. Much younger than him. Seven years wasn't a lot to some people, but to him, it was. And he'd never felt this kind of chemistry with someone before. He'd met many attractive women. He'd had relationships. He'd felt attraction before. But never like he did with Hayden.

When he'd watched her perform, he'd felt drawn to her and protective of her—as in unable to tear his eyes away and like ripping the heads off any men that got within ten feet of her. Then he'd met her when she was opening for Jason Young, the country music star who was crossing the country on his first tour as a headliner, and when Colin had taken her hand it had felt hard to pull away when the handshake was over.

He felt like a fucking pervy old man.

And he was absolutely *not* okay with that.

So Henry had led her security detail while she was performing with Jason.

Things had gone well and Colin was hoping that when Hayden needed security in the future—hopefully when she signed a recording contract and needed ongoing security with her on a regular basis, which was supposedly due to happen soon—she'd hire them.

"Yeah, I have an idea," Henry answered. "Fuck," he muttered.

"What is it?" Colin demanded.

"She's picked up an...admirer."

Colin scowled. "Henry," he said, his tone full of warning.

"He hasn't done anything. Messages through her public contacts. Just...a lot of them. But we've been on alert for any escalation."

Colin swung his legs over the side of the bed and stood. He crossed to his closet. He needed to get dressed.

"You didn't tell her you were leaving the country?"

"I left her a message."

"She didn't get it."

"Obviously."

Colin jerked a shirt from a hanger and grabbed jeans from his dresser. "You need to call her. Find out where she is. If she's safe, tell her to stay put. If not, get her somewhere safe. Then text me where she's at."

"You're going to her?" Henry asked.

"She's calling you at three a.m. Something happened. I need to at least show up and calm her down."

"Did she sound upset?"

"*Henry*," Colin barked, "She's calling you at three a.m. She's not Cian. She's not calling to tell you some stupid story because she doesn't realize what time it is, or to bounce some dumbass idea off of you just because she can't sleep. Unless you tell me that the two of you are hooking up and it's a booty call, something's going on." Colin stopped and shoved a hand through his hair. He waited a beat. "Are you going to tell me that?"

He wasn't sure what he would do with that information. It

7

wasn't okay that one of his guys would be sleeping with a client or even a potential client. But more specifically, it was not okay that Henry would be sleeping with *Hayden*. That was all kinds of complicated, but he didn't want to delve into it or analyze it further.

Actually, he didn't really *need* to analyze it at all. It was jealousy.

It was also a way to fuck up a huge potential contract.

"No, we're not hooking up," Henry said.

"Then we need to find out where she is and if she's all right. You're across an ocean, and I'm right here. I'm going to go to wherever she is."

"I don't know if you need to. Let me call and see what's going on."

Colin dragged in a breath. "I don't care if she just wants a chocolate milkshake. Ask her if she wants a medium or large and *text me where the fuck she is.*"

Henry was quiet for a second.

Colin ground his teeth together. Then added, "She could be an important client for us."

"Right."

The thing about knowing a guy for ten years was...he also got to know you.

They all wanted an impressive new client. They were *all* focused on landing TBC—The Big Client—the one that would be someone important, would pay the bills, and would make them feel like they were doing something that *mattered*. They'd all gotten close to their past charges. Henry and Cian were best friends and had been for a decade. And everyone knew that losing his twenty-four-seven relationship with the little girl he'd been protecting since birth had been very hard on Colin. Still was. Every day. They *all* wanted TBC, or a group of TBCs, like that again.

But Colin was also overreacting to this phone call from Hayden Ross.

Probably.

But Colin didn't want to talk about that.

So he hung up on Henry.

Colin jerked on his shoes, grabbed his keys off his dresser, yanked open his bedroom door, and stomped down the stairs.

The best way to prove to this woman that they should be the ones she hired was to be there for her when she needed something. No matter what it was.

Was she possibly calling about some stupid diva shit?

Sure. Maybe.

Was he going to be absolutely terrible at putting up with diva behavior?

No question about it. Another fantastic reason for Henry to be the lead with her.

But was Colin going to fucking do it to land the job?

Damn right.

He jerked open the front door and stalked across the porch. He'd start toward New Orleans. By the time Henry texted or called him back, he'd at least be on his way…

He plowed into the person sitting on his top step.

Well, she wasn't exactly sitting. She'd been getting up, probably because she heard the front door open.

But he hadn't seen her and she'd, clearly, expected him to stop.

So when he slammed into her, and they went tumbling down the four porch steps, Colin had no choice but to twist his body to take the brunt of the impact, pulling her into him, cradling her against his torso, wrapping a leg around hers, and curling so he hit the ground with her on top of him.

two

HAYDEN WOULD LIKE to think that anyone being tackled on a dark porch in the middle of the night would scream the way she did.

Besides, that really hurt.

The guy who plowed into her and then sent her tumbling to the ground took most of the impact. It almost seemed that he'd somehow managed to roll them, so he was on the bottom on purpose. But she still felt the jar of hitting hard ground. Not to mention the terror.

Even if she hadn't just had a fucking stalker leave her a teddy bear and roses in front of her apartment door, she'd be afraid right now.

The panic was amplified when he clamped his hand over her mouth to stop the screaming.

"Stop," he said firmly. "Jesus. It's the middle of the night."

She tried to respond. With a big, "Fuck you!" and "I know it's the middle of the night! That's what makes this ten times scarier, you gigantic asshole!"

Of course, with his hand over her face, she couldn't. So instead, she decided to kick him.

That didn't work either. Instead, he simply rolled and pinned her beneath him. Completely.

He was now stretched out on top of her, the hand not on her mouth was clamped around both of her wrists, her arms stretched over her head. He was lying fully on top of her and had one leg somehow twisted around hers so she couldn't move.

She wasn't proud of this. She really should've taken a self-defense class more recently than six years ago. And she should've paid more attention during that self-defense class. And practiced even one move at least once since then.

Of course, she hadn't been expecting to get assaulted sitting on Cian and Henry's front porch.

A sudden horrible thought occurred to her. What if this was the wrong house? *Oh, God, please let this be Cian and Henry's front porch.*

And even if it was... what if *this* was her stalker?

The adrenaline dump into her system had her feeling weak and dizzy suddenly.

Did a guy escalate from teddy bears to murder in the space of an hour or two? She wasn't really a true crime or an unsolved mysteries kind of girl so she couldn't really say. And had there been a time in her life when she would have given a teddy bear to a favorite singer as a sign of devotion? Sure. When she'd been fourteen. Maybe even sixteen. But the guy they *thought* was sending her the creepy messages was *not* sixteen.

Nor was the man lying on top of her at the moment.

She suddenly started thrashing. Not effectively, of course, but she couldn't just lie here. She also tried to scream again. That was just instinct.

The guy's body stiffened, his legs clamping around hers,

his hand pressing more firmly against her mouth, and his grip squeezing her wrists.

"Hayden! Stop!"

She did. For a second. He knew her name.

Of course your stalker knows your name!

She started squirming again.

God, she'd driven *closer* to where her pseudo-stalker lived.

Henry had somehow figured out that the guy was sending his emails from near Autre a lot of the time and based on his actual messages they thought the guy had first seen her performance over at Bad Brews, the bar in the next town over.

No, she didn't want to be closer to *him*, but she definitely wanted to be closer to Henry and Cian.

That's gonna do you a ton of good now that Henry's out of town, Cian's not here, and the guy is lying on top of you!

She thrashed again but fuck, she was getting tired. He was big and heavy and a lot stronger than she was and he was holding her tight, and her damned fight-or-flight instinct seemed to be waning and it *was* the middle of the night and more and more she kind of just wanted to cry.

He was like a solid block of muscle. There wasn't one spot that seemed to yield. Not one squishy area to be found.

She on the other hand had several squishy places. And his hard body seemed to settle against hers quite nicely. Like it probably did against pillows.

We're already to the Stockholm syndrome part, bitch? You're going to start thinking about how your potential stalker fits so nicely against you? Really? Not even gonna wait for the rope or blindfold?

She felt her eyes starting to sting. She was *not* going to cry.

Hayden was sure she'd been lying on the ground for only a few seconds all together, but it felt like an hour.

And yeah, she probably was going to cry.

All she knew for certain was that the guy on top of her was not Henry or Cian.

Maybe it's Jonah.

Oh! Maybe it was Jonah!

Her heart leaped. She didn't know the big, broody American bodyguard that lived with her favorite Brit—okay, Henry was the only Brit she knew—and the Irishman who could always make her laugh, but Jonah was no threat. He was definitely big and solid. And good-looking. She'd probably be okay with being up against his muscles. And a bodyguard like Jonah would have probably heard someone on his front porch and come down to...

Then she froze. There was another guy who lived in the house with Henry and Cian and Jonah.

Colin Daly.

Henry's boss.

The very hot, very frowny, very hot—had she mentioned that?—very Irish bodyguard that she'd only met once.

But he'd made an impression.

Yeah, he was also built like this.

She immediately stopped moving. As in she froze. Went completely still. Also stopped breathing.

"There we go," he said.

Yep. Just a hint of Irish in that voice.

How had she missed that? Oh yeah, terror.

He started to lift his hand from her mouth. "You done screaming?"

Well, fuck.

Of course, she'd made an ass of herself in front of Colin.

She had this impression that Colin, older than the other guys by a few years and definitely the guy in charge, looked at her as a young, Ariana Grande-wanna be, with her head in the clouds, needing protection while she sang and danced on social media and tried to get famous.

Though she wondered if Colin actually knew who Ariana Grande was. He didn't seem the type to know that.

"Hayden?"

Oh yeah, he'd asked her a question.

She nodded.

"Can I let you up?"

Jesus, please let me up.

Now that she knew who he was, she was *very* aware of how big, and hard, and heavy he was. And again, how nicely that hard body fit against her soft one.

She swallowed and nodded again.

He was just starting to ease his body up off of hers. When the front door to the house banged open.

"What the *fuck* is going on?" a deep voice boomed across the front yard.

"Nothing," Colin called to Jonah, pushing himself back to kneel beside her. "It's fine."

Yeah, see, *that* was Jonah. She knew it immediately. Colin was the one who had been *lying on top of her.*

Hayden felt her cheeks heat...okay, her whole body heated. Ugh.

"There was screaming. And you're lying on the ground," the big man on the porch, with the very obviously American accent, pointed out.

Hayden squinted through the darkness. Jonah had his feet braced apart, hands on his hips, standing at the top of the steps where she'd been sitting a few minutes ago.

"Just a little mix-up," Colin said, calmly. "Stay there." He said when Jonah started down the steps. He looked down at Hayden. "Are you alright?"

Was she *alright*? Her heart was still pounding, and she felt shaky and...a little humiliated. And like she was on the verge of having to admit to herself that she had a crush on this guy.

But she was *not* going to do that.

"Yes," she managed.

"I hit you kind of hard."

"You *hit* her?" Jonah demanded, he took another step down.

"Stay. There," Colin said firmly.

Jonah stopped, but Hayden heard him give a little growl even from where she sat on the grass next to the front walk. Wow. So Colin was definitely in charge. But being in charge of men like Jonah was probably not the easiest thing. She knew Henry was the most easy-going of the guys. He'd told her that himself. But even he had a very stubborn, brusque side at times.

"Did you hit your head?" Colin asked.

Hayden had the impression that he was keeping himself from reaching out to her. It was dark, but they were still very close, and the yard had a lamp at the end of the walk. She could see just enough, and *feel* enough, to know that he was holding himself tightly. It was like there was tension in the air between them.

"No." She lifted her hand to her head to be sure. "I...don't think I really hit anything. The impact kind of jarred me but I landed..." She trailed off before she said *on you*. He knew. And Jonah probably didn't need to know. And she didn't need to replay it. Until that moment, it hadn't fully registered but she had a feeling that she was going to be unable to avoid replaying it later.

"I..." Colin cleared his throat. "Sorry about covering your mouth but...the neighbors. I didn't want them to hear you screaming."

Hayden felt her eyes widen. That was *not* dirty. Nothing

about him tackling her, pinning her to the grass, and covering her screams had been dirty. It had been scary as fuck.

But now...

She coughed. "It's okay. I'm fine."

He hesitated as if he was going to say something more, but then decided against it. He pushed himself to his feet, then offered her his hand. "Miss Ross."

She didn't have a lot of choices, so she put her hand in his and let him pull her up.

"So, what's going on?" Jonah asked, his tone less gruff now.

"Well, I assume Miss Ross is here looking for Henry. Henry failed to tell her he wouldn't be here. He also failed to tell me that she might come looking for him."

"He said I could come anytime." She combed her fingers through her hair.

"Of course," Colin said.

His voice was gruff and when she looked up, she felt the impact of meeting his gaze.

The guy was intimidating. Or something. That wasn't quite the right word, but she felt butterflies with him standing so close and looking directly at her.

They'd only met once when they'd first discussed the contract for Henry providing security for her. He'd been all business, asking straightforward questions, taking notes of her answers but also questioning Sabrina Sterling to get a full picture of what Hayden would need.

Sabrina was Hayden's pseudo-agent. Or manager. Or something. Sabrina was the woman who'd heard Hayden singing on a street corner in the French Quarter one night and said, "wow, we need to get you in front of more people". Which had started the whirlwind that had been Hayden's last eight months.

It was all ridiculous. Hayden was just a girl from small-town Louisiana who happened to have a good singing voice that a few people liked and were willing to give money to listen to. For a few weeks, she'd set up on a corner in the French Quarter like so many other musicians and artists did every night and performed for the tourists passing by. It was a part of the culture of the Quarter, very common, expected really. She'd never dreamed it would turn into anything more than a chance to make a few people smile and a few dollars.

It was crazy to her to think that anyone would even go out of their way to listen to her sing, not to mention that anyone would take that to another level and try to hurt her. It was hard to believe that she needed any kind of protection.

Until the creepy messages had started.

She was so glad that Colin had assigned Henry to be her bodyguard. Henry Dean had quickly become one of her best friends. As had Cian O'Grady. It was hard to get to know one of them without the other, and for a girl who had moved away from her family and friends and had felt a little alone over the past few years, Henry and Cian had quickly stolen her heart. Sure, Henry had been paid to hang out with her initially, but their friendship had lasted even after he'd no longer been protecting her for money, and she'd believed him—them— when they'd said she could call or show up on their doorstep anytime.

She also knew that Henry was continuing to monitor her fan messages, even though it was free labor now.

She really wished Henry was here. Colin was making her feel jumpy.

Not in a bad way. Not in the way the teddy bear propped against her apartment door had. Not *at all* in that way.

But she didn't feel warm and like a laugh was about to bubble up at any moment like she did when Henry and Cian were around either.

She felt like...she really wanted him to hug her.

Girl, you need to chill.

Just then a car pulled into the driveway.

She immediately felt the increased tension in Colin's body, and he moved to put himself between her and the car. His big hand settled on her hip as he tucked her directly behind him.

Yeah, Henry had done that a couple of times.

But she'd never felt a hot swirl of awareness twist through her belly when Henry did it.

That is not chill, babe. Not at all.

"Hayden? Colin, what's going on?" Cian asked as the car door slammed.

She blew out a breath and felt the tension ease from Colin's body. He removed his hand and stepped away from her. Was it suddenly cold out here? She sighed. No. No, it was not.

"You tell me," Colin said. "I was on my way to New Orleans to find her."

"Why? She's right here."

"Cian." Colin's tone was touched with exasperation.

Cian's grinning face was the next thing she saw as he drew close and pulled her into a hug. "Hey."

Cian's Irish accent also notably failed to give her any kind of tingle where Colin's had made her actually think the word, *yum.*

"Hey," she said, squeezing him back.

"You okay?"

"Better now."

"Probably a little bruised," Jonah commented from where he'd propped a shoulder against one of the columns on the porch.

Cian immediately frowned. "Bruised? What the fuck? Why are you bruised?"

"Ask Colin," Jonah said.

Even not knowing him well, Hayden could hear the amusement in his voice.

Colin let out a heavy sigh. "Shut the fuck up, Jonah."

"What am I missing?" Cian asked.

"Colin wasn't expecting me. We had a little collision when he came out the door," Hayden told him. "I'm fine."

"Collision?" Cian looked at Colin. "What are you even doing up?"

"I answered Henry's phone when Hayden called."

"She said she hung up then she called me. I told her to stick around and I would be right over."

"It's after three in the morning. Where the fuck have you been?" Colin asked.

"Down at the station with Asher and Beck, *Dad,*" Cian looked at Hayden. "Couple of the local firefighters. We play poker sometimes."

"Shouldn't they be fighting fires?" Colin asked.

"It's actually a really good night when they're *not* fighting fires," Cian said. "A lot of the time, they're just there hanging out, waiting for calls, so we play cards."

"I am really sorry to cause this trouble," Hayden said. "I didn't want to wake everyone up."

"It's Henry's fault," Colin said. "He should've told you he was leaving."

"Yeah. But even if he had, I would've called Cian."

Colin scowled. "I didn't even realize you two knew each other."

Why did he look so pissed about that?

"Henry does *not* get to have fun, especially with beautiful women, without me," Cian said. He put an arm around Hayden's waist and started for the door. "Let's go inside."

"You've had *fun* with her?" Colin asked.

Cian looked over at him and Hayden saw the smirk. Oh,

boy. Cian was a troublemaker. It was as if he couldn't help it. He loved mischief, teasing, joking, flirting. And mouthing off. Oh, man did he love mouthing off.

"Lots of times," he said.

Colin scowled. "I see."

"Do ya?" Cian asked.

"Yeah."

Colin stalked past them to the front door. He jerked it open and went inside.

They all watched him go.

Jonah shook his head as the door shut hard behind Colin. "Well, that was amusing."

"Yeah," Cian agreed.

"It was?" Hayden asked.

"Ruffling Colin's feathers?" Cian said. "*Always*. I fucking live for those moments."

He steered her up the steps and through the front door.

She immediately took a deep breath. She was here. Inside. Safe. She had three guys who would take care of her.

Should she be a badass and not let the creep get to her? Sleep in her own apartment alone? Show him he couldn't scare her?

Maybe.

But she wasn't going to.

She was twenty-three, living on her own in New Orleans except for her grandfather, who didn't remember who she was from one visit to the next, and a handful of friends who were more like friendly acquaintances, and no real ability to defend herself.

Because she never would have imagined she would need to actually *defend* herself.

She'd always just ignored people who said snarky shit or whom she didn't like. She'd always been curvy, bigger than the other girls. She was the musical, artistic middle child in a family of athletes. *Star* athletes. Written-up-in-the-newspaper-record-breaking-recruited-from-all-the-schools star athletes. Three of them. So *obviously*, she'd heard insulting things and been called names and been left out and all of that middle-school and junior-high bullshit. She'd had a crush on a couple of guys who wouldn't ever consider her more than a friend. And *one* asshole who'd actually really hurt her emotionally.

But she'd never felt physically unsafe.

And now she fucking did. And she wasn't going to apologize for being scared about that.

Henry and Cian had said she could call or show up anytime and here she was.

Yeah, three a.m. was a little inconvenient. But so was having a teddy bear, roses, and a letter talking about all the ways her "admirer" wanted to "make her his."

A shudder went through her and Cian looked down as they stepped into the living room. "You cold?"

"Um..." She didn't want to tell him about the teddy bear and note. But she really wanted to tell him about the teddy bear and note. "Not exactly."

Cian stopped next to one of the sofas. There were four. As if each of the men living here needed their own. Luckily the room was enormous. The entire house was, really.

Henry had told her how they'd all pitched in to help add on to the house when they'd first moved to Autre. She suspected that by "helping" he meant the three bodyguards and two princes—yeah, they'd told her all about Cian and his siblings' royal lineage and their history with Henry, Jonah, and Colin—had handed tools to the real construction workers. But he'd seemed proud of it, so she'd just nodded and said, "That's amazing."

Whoever had renovated and added on to the place had made the house, which sprawled across four regular lots, into a mini-palace, with high ceilings, wide spaces, and lots of rooms. Everything from the walls to the flooring had clearly been redone and it was decorated modernly. It was also surprisingly clean and neat considering four bachelors lived here.

"So what happened tonight?" Cian asked. "Did you have a gig?"

She nodded and pulled in a breath. "At Ruby's. Pretty small crowd. Had a drink with the band after. Then headed home. There was a teddy bear outside my door when I got there."

"A teddy bear?"

"Yeah. From...him. With a very graphic note."

Cian, the fun-loving, laid-back playboy, shoved a hand through his hair and muttered a sharp, *"Fuck,"* under his breath before turning and yelling, "Colin! Get down here!"

Hayden gave him a wide-eyed look. "Hey!" she whispered.

"He needs to know."

Colin appeared at the bottom of the steps a moment later. Hayden hadn't even heard his footsteps. He was scowling. And carrying what looked like clothes. "What?"

"Hayden has something to tell you."

Hayden frowned at Cian. "Traitor."

Cian shook his head. "This is a problem, Hayden."

She looked at Jonah. "You can't just handle it?"

Jonah rolled his shoulders back as if he was uncomfortable and tucked his hands into the pockets of the gray sweatpants he was wearing. "He's the boss."

Colin crossed to her, his scowl deepening. He handed her what she realized were pajamas. It was really a pair of thin pajama pants in a pale blue and yellow plaid and a white tank top. "They're Fiona's. You can borrow them."

She knew Fiona was Cian's sister and that she'd lived here with her daughter before they'd moved in with Fiona's fiancé.

"Borrow them?" She took them from him.

"You're staying tonight. Well, the rest of this morning."

He didn't phrase it as a question. It was a statement.

Hayden felt relief rush through her. Of course, she'd expected she was staying. She thought maybe they'd sit around the kitchen table, and she could talk with Cian until the sun came up and she felt a little less creeped out about going home. Or she thought maybe she could curl up on the couch.

This seemed a bit more welcoming and absolutely more comforting.

"Oh, thank you."

When she looked up, her gaze snagged on his and she couldn't look away for a moment. He was studying her intently.

"You're welcome." His voice was low and soft.

And that damned urge to hug him was back.

She could have a hug from Cian right now. He was kind of the huggy type. Hell, Jonah might even hug her. He didn't seem warm and fuzzy, but she was a damsel in distress and all. She had the impression that got all of these guys going and she thought maybe she could get away with it.

Colin Daly on the other hand, did not exactly exude hugger vibes, but he was who she wanted one from.

"What do you need to tell me?"

"Oh that." She glanced at Cian. He looked upset. Worried. Those were things she didn't often associate with Cian O'Grady. He was a good time. Mischievous. Seemingly always balancing just on the safe side of too much. Of course, he also had a personal bodyguard who had been following him around for the past ten years and figuratively—and maybe literally at times—grabbing him by the back of the belt to keep him from toppling into trouble.

Yeah, she knew all of Cian's backstory and his and Henry's history.

She'd had a hard time believing it and thought they were screwing with her the first couple of times they'd told her about Cian being prince of a country she'd never heard of. But she'd done a quick internet search on her phone...and lost the twenty-dollar bet.

"It's just...I..." Why was this hard to say out loud to Colin?

"She has a stalker," Cian finally interjected. "He left her a present tonight at her apartment."

Colin's gaze snapped to hers. She couldn't have described the emotion on his face, exactly, but *rage* seemed close. His jaw was tight and if she thought she'd felt tension in him outside, it was nothing compared to right now.

He sucked in a deep breath through his nose and seemed to be consciously calming himself. Then he reached out and grasped her by her elbows, turned her, and nudged her down onto the couch. Then he pulled an ottoman up in front of her and sat, his knees splayed wide so that hers were between them. He didn't touch her, but he leaned closer, bracing his forearms on his thighs, and pinned her with a gaze. Even though it was stern, she felt like he was *almost* hugging her. He was *around her*. His body was shielding her, his body heat reaching out and warming her. His gaze was stern, but she knew it wasn't because he was upset *with* her. He was concerned. And that emotion also wrapped around her, making her feel safe.

"Do you want to tell me about it, or do you want me to call Henry?"

He was also giving her the option to *not* have to fill him in. She felt some of the stiffness in her body ease.

She wet her lips. "Henry hasn't told you about this?"

"Not until earlier tonight. And not in any detail."

Colin was clearly not happy about that.

"Tell me as much as you're comfortable with. I'll get the rest from him." Colin looked to his right. "*Stop.*"

Hayden glanced in that direction to find Cian and Jonah trying to sneak out of the room.

They both turned back with a sigh.

"What do you know?" Colin asked.

"Probably everything she's going to tell you," Cian said.

Colin focused on Jonah. "Is that true?"

Jonah blew out a breath. "Probably more than Hayden does, but less than Henry."

Colin nodded. Then he pointed to the couch perpendicular to the couch where Hayden was sitting. "Join us, won't you?" Colin asked. But it was clear it was not an invitation so much as it was an order. "Cian, sit," Colin said when the other man hesitated.

With a grumble, Cian dropped down onto the couch next to Hayden. Colin gave him a frown, but said nothing. He turned his focus back on her.

Hayden was sitting on the edge of the cushion. They weren't touching, but Colin's fingers were only a few inches away from hers, and his knees on either side of hers made her feel boxed in. In a good way.

"Are you okay with me here? Like this?" he asked.

She knew he was referring to the way they were sitting. Was she okay? She wanted him *closer*. But she just nodded.

"Are you sure? I can give you space."

She shook her head quickly. "I don't want space. I feel safe here with you guys." She actually had to force her eyes from Colin. It should make sense that she felt safe with Cian and

Jonah. She knew them better. She gave them both small smiles that they returned.

Cian was lounging on the other end of the couch, only a couple of feet from her. She could reach out and touch his leg. Jonah was on the couch perpendicular to them, but his body and just his general presence took up a lot of space. He seemed relaxed, but she knew that he was on alert. He seemed concerned.

Colin took a breath. "Do you want Jonah to fill me in? Do you want to call Henry? Or do you want to tell me?"

"I can tell you what I know. But it sounds like maybe Henry knows more." She shot another glance at Jonah.

He gave her a single nod.

She focused on Colin again.

"If Henry is doing his job, he's done some additional follow-up on whatever is going on," Colin told her. "Want to start?"

She took a breath. "I've been getting messages from a fan. I mean, I get messages from lots of fans. Which is nice." She managed a small smile.

"But there's one that makes you uncomfortable?"

"At first it didn't. His were just like everyone else's. And the thing is, mostly, they still are. There's just a lot of them. He writes me every day."

The wrinkle between Colin's eyebrows deepened slightly. He nodded. "Go on."

"The messages just became more frequent. And longer. It was like he was writing me letters. They're always very complimentary. He's never threatened me. But he asks me out. He wants to date me. Claims he's in love and that he understands me in a way no one else will."

"So, a little excessive," Colin said. His voice sounded tight.

"Definitely. And I have no idea who he is. He's always just

signed it with an X. He's made some references to the fact that he knows that my security team knows about him, but that they're not with me all the time." She felt a shiver go through her.

She was shocked when Colin shifted forward. He had his hands linked but he let the back of one of his hands rest against the side of her knee. The touch grounded her and immediately, the shivers stopped.

"So, he's aware that you have security."

Hayden nodded. She remembered when he first mentioned that and feeling that was a good thing. "I didn't tell Henry about him right away. I was getting messages from him before I even met Henry. He said he had watched me on social media. He started emailing me way back. But I mentioned it to Henry one night in passing, and Henry was concerned."

"Henry's got a good gut. What did he say?"

"He just wanted to see the messages. He read through them all, made me promise to let him know whenever X wrote. Now I always forward them to him. But Henry said that there's nothing illegal about what he's doing. Like I said, he's never threatened me, and for a long time, I didn't feel harassed or anything."

"So, have you ever responded?"

"In the beginning. But when he was writing every day, I felt like it was encouraging him. Then Henry told me absolutely not to respond. We thought maybe he would stop, but it almost seemed to make the emails longer. Like he was really trying to impress upon me how important it was that we communicate."

"And then what? What about tonight?"

"Well—" She shot a glance at Cian.

He gave her a little nod.

"When I got to my apartment tonight, there was a teddy

bear leaning up against the door. And some roses. And a letter."

"A letter? From him?"

Colin's gaze was sharper now, and she could see the muscle in his jaw tighten.

She nodded. "It was a lot like his emails, but..." She took a shaky breath.

"Hayden." Colin's voice was gentle and he pressed his hand against her knee more firmly. "You can tell me, we're here to help."

"It was graphic. It wasn't threatening to hurt me, but it was sexually graphic. He was talking about taking me out on a date and then what would happen afterward."

Colin didn't respond right away. His jaw clenched. Then he pulled in a breath. "Was it handwritten?"

She shook her head. "Printed from a computer."

"Did you bring it with you?"

She shook her head quickly. "I didn't want to touch any of it. It completely freaked me out. I practically ran to my car. I drove to a grocery store that's open twenty-four hours. Then I called Henry. Well you, I guess."

He shifted, now sandwiching her hands between his. It wasn't until then that she realized she'd been shaking.

"That was the perfect thing to do. I'm glad you knew you could come here."

"I didn't know what else to do. It completely freaked me out to think that he knows where I live. I mean even the exact apartment. How did he figure that out?"

She realized she'd been holding that thought, and that question, at bay. But now that it had sunk in, she couldn't stop a myriad of horrible, scary images from flipping through her mind. And all at once, it wasn't just her hands shaking, but her entire body.

The next thing she knew, Colin muttered a curse, shifted forward and scooped her up. He turned and sank onto the couch where she'd been sitting. With her in his lap.

His big arms wrapped around her, pulling her against his chest.

She was not a small woman, and she hadn't spent any time on another person's lap since she'd been a little girl. But damn, this felt good. He hadn't even hesitated to pick her up and he'd done it with seemingly zero effort. She fit against him, perfectly.

Colin was a big guy. Muscled. In shape. Clearly used to being physical—or at least prepared to be physical if needed—in his job. And he'd initiated this. So, what the hell? It was the middle of the night. And she'd been dosed full of adrenaline and fuck it. Cian wasn't the type to judge other people and she didn't really care what Jonah thought.

She snuggled against Colin's chest and let him hold her.

"What do you know?"

Colin's voice rumbled under her ear.

"He didn't bring you in on it because, as she said, the guy hasn't done anything illegal or specifically threatening," Jonah answered.

Oh good, Colin wasn't asking her for any more information.

"That ends now," Colin said firmly. "Go on."

"He can't involve law enforcement," Jonah said. "But he'd like to find the guy. Figure out if he's got a history of this. Maybe find a way to get a message across that he needs to leave Hayden alone."

She felt Colin nod.

She frowned. Henry was a friend. He wasn't being paid anymore. He'd provided some additional security—personal security for *her*—during the rehearsals, performances, and fan meet-and-greets for the two New Orleans shows she'd done with Jason Young. But that had all been at the request of Sabrina Sterling, paid for by Jason's music label, and hadn't been intended to be a long-term thing.

Henry had explained that he and Colin hoped Jason and his label would think of them if his current security detail ever needed replacing. Henry had also not-at-all-subtly hinted that if and when *she* ever needed full-time security, he hoped she would consider hiring them. But at the time it wasn't as if Hayden had written anyone a check. No way could she have afforded that. And she definitely wasn't paying him now.

Still, Henry had insisted he wanted to keep checking over the emails as a friend. She hadn't known he'd intended to *do* anything about them.

"Are there leads?" Colin asked.

"A couple," Jonah said. "He thinks maybe—"

"I'll get that from him," Colin cut in.

Hayden frowned again. He didn't want to know who Henry thought the guy was? Maybe he just wanted to get it straight from Henry so he could ask follow-up questions. *She* didn't want to know who the guy was. At least not at this moment. She was feeling raw. Vulnerable. If she found out the guy was someone she knew from one of her jobs or was a bartender at one of the bars where she loved to perform or something, she was going to be *pissed*. And even more freaked out. Was it someone she talked to all the time? Someone *she'd* started up a friendship with? Someone she saw regularly without even knowing he had a weird obsession with her?

She shuddered and felt Colin's arms tighten around her.

She sucked in a breath. She was okay. She was here. No matter who it was, these guys would take care of her.

Did she feel weak? Nope. This was smart. Some guy wanted to tie her up and fuck her with a dildo he'd *made* just for her.

She cuddled even closer to Colin. She couldn't get much closer but damn, he felt good. Big, warm, safe. Mad. He seemed really mad. On her behalf. She wanted that. Henry had reassured her that he was keeping track of the guy and that he was concerned but also that the guy didn't show signs of escalation or violence. That had made her feel good. Henry's calm presence and smiles had been what she'd needed then.

Now she needed a big, broody, Irishman who was angry *for her.*

"We need to meet tomorrow," Colin said. "I want Henry on a call. Zander Landry. And Carter Shaw."

"Carter's the cop over in Bad, right?" Cian asked.

"Yeah," Jonah confirmed. "Good guy. Anyone else?"

"Spencer Landry."

"Jesus, FBI?" Cian asked.

Hayden perked up a little at that. That sounded more serious.

"More as a consult. A friend," Colin said. "Just want him to weigh in. But if we need to pull him in, I will."

See, *that.* That firm, I'm-going-to-take-care-of-this tone. She fucking loved that.

Hayden didn't know these people the guys were talking about, but she didn't really care. It was amazing to sit here in this room and know that these three men would take care of whatever was going on. She didn't have to keep track.

She couldn't remember the last time she could just sit back and let things happen around her and not worry.

In her family, she was the one who took care of things. She wasn't the oldest, but she was the oldest girl. Her older brother, Jake, was too busy being amazing to really help out or think about other people. He was also four years older than her and eight years older than their twin siblings, so Hayden had become the organizer, the worrier, the one who had to be on top of everything. To just sit back and know that other people were taking care of things was a wonderful kind of bliss.

She wouldn't revel in it forever, but for tonight? Yeah. For sure.

Colin nodded. "Anything to add?"

"Just that I assume she's good to be staying here with us," Cian said, apparently the one Colin had addressed.

There was just a beat, and she felt Colin sigh underneath her ear. "Yeah, she's definitely staying here."

Hayden finally made herself lift her head. "For tonight?"

"For the foreseeable future," Colin told her.

Sitting on his lap, their faces so close together, that firm tone seemed to have an even greater effect than usual. Hayden felt a little shiver go through her that was *not* a bad-freaked-out shiver, and dammit if her nipples didn't tighten.

She didn't really like bossy men. Or so she thought.

"How long will that be?" she asked.

"It depends on how quickly I can figure out who your admirer is and have a word with him."

She felt her eyes widen. That was a really good answer. She could stay here *and* Colin was going to find the guy. She believed that. Even if she hadn't been sitting close enough to see the swirling emotions in the gorgeous green depths of his eyes, she'd believe that he was going to get this done.

Hayden swallowed hard and gave him a little nod. "Okay." She paused, then added, "Thank you."

She was shocked to feel Colin's hand lift to the top of her head and stroke down her hair. "You're safe now. And you'll stay that way."

Her entire body heated. She was pretty sure he noticed that her cheeks got pink.

His gaze dropped to her mouth, and she had to resist the urge to wet her lips. That would've been very obvious. Right?

Or maybe she should've done it. Who knew what Colin's next move would've been? But maybe something good.

Jonah cleared his throat, and she jerked out of the lusty haze that seemed to have enveloped her.

Colin made a strange noise that was a combination of a growl and a sigh and then shifted, standing and setting her on her feet as he stretched to his full height.

"Cian can take you upstairs."

Hayden took a deep breath and looked over at her friend.

Cian was watching her and Colin with a bemused expression.

She nodded. "Okay."

What else was she supposed to say? It's like there were a million things she *should* say and also nothing.

She was perfectly fine with letting Colin Daly call the shots. He was clearly used to it, obviously liked it, and there was no question he was good at it.

She was way too far away from him to actually hear it, but she could've sworn she heard Colin let out a long breath as her foot hit the first step on the way upstairs.

She was not, however, too far away to hear Jonah say, "Seriously, dude?"

And Colin reply, "Just shut up."

three

ZANDER LANDRY WAS KIND of an asshole.

Actually, he wasn't an asshole at all. Zander Landry was one of the best guys Colin knew. He was the cop in Autre. He was also one of the many Landry boys who had grown up and lived in the tiny bayou town. Zander, along with his friends who wore badges, took their job of protecting the little town and all the people who lived there very seriously.

He was a guy after Colin's own heart.

But the fucker had said he was only available to meet if it was before eight a.m.

At least he'd suggested meeting at a coffee shop.

Bad Habit was a twenty-minute drive from Autre, but it meant they could talk about sensitive topics without a chance of being overheard. Well, without *as much* chance of being overheard as they would have in Autre. No one in the Landry family was ever truly alone in Autre.

Bad Habit was also hugely popular for the coffee and pastries they sold. But all Colin needed to know to get him in line was that they offered straight-up double espressos.

Colin was a seven-hours-of-sleep-or-more guy.

He could be adaptable, of course. Lord knew looking after Fiona O'Grady, a feisty animal advocate, had required him to learn to go with the flow and not believe too firmly in things like schedules. But most of his time had been focused on her daughter Saoirse. In spite of the fact that Saoirse was royalty—literally—and Colin was employed by her grandfather who thought she walked on water, Colin had, for the most part, been able to call the shots and make the rules with the little princess.

That was definitely one of the things he missed since losing his job. Now he was working with adults who had opinions and liked to be in charge of their own lives.

Saoirse's Uncle Torin had rescinded his abdication and taken his place as the next in line for the throne, which meant Saoirse was no longer the next direct descendent. In addition, her mother had fallen in love and Saoirse now had a new step-father who was as protective as any paid bodyguard and was, of course, living with them. Saoirse no longer needed a twenty-four-seven bodyguard and her mother and stepfather didn't want it. Fortunately, she now lived in the big house across the backyard from where Colin, Jonah, Cian, and Henry lived so they were close by and could help keep an eye on her. But his twenty-four-seven, decade-long gig had changed almost overnight.

And yeah, he missed it. Missed Saoirse. A lot. It was very much like going from being a full-time dad to a divorced, part-time-custody dad, and he knew he probably hadn't fully dealt with all of those emotions. But what right did he have to have emotions about it anyway? Saoirse wasn't his daughter. And Knox loved Fiona and Saoirse fiercely. Colin couldn't have picked a better guy for them.

Maybe if Colin and Fiona had ever had even an inkling of romantic attraction and he'd thought they could make a real family out of their situation, he might have had a leg to stand on. But they hadn't. Fiona was like a sister to him. He loved her. He cared about her. He wanted her happy. And that meant he wanted her with Knox.

But fuck...she couldn't have just waited another eight years to fall in love? Until Saoirse was eighteen and out on her own and needed a bodyguard to go to college with her or something?

Or Torin couldn't have just continued on as a globetrotting, nerdy professor who didn't want to settle down and didn't believe in the concept of a monarchy? Torin, Fiona, Cian, and their oldest brother, Declan, had all abdicated the throne a decade ago. That had made Saoirse heir-apparent—at least until she was old enough to abdicate herself.

In the first few years, Colin had thought maybe Fiona would fall in love and he'd have to deal with a stepdad in the picture. But after ten years of watching Fiona love animals far more than any human—other than her daughter, of course— he'd started thinking maybe she was just too much of a handful for any man to settle down.

Then Knox had walked in.

Or rather, Fiona had walked into Ellie's bar in Autre. And then Knox had walked in. And...it was all over.

Colin scrubbed a hand over his face as fatigue hit him. It was more than physical fatigue, but he was definitely praying the caffeine would kick in quick. He was a highly trained body-guard who'd spent a decade fingerpainting and baking cookies and telling bedtime stories to his longest and favorite full-time client. A client who had only been up at three a.m. if she'd had a nightmare—which had been rare—and had been easy to put back to sleep.

Saoirse had never had a stalker.

He'd never lost sleep with her the way he had over Hayden Ross last night.

Fuck. He really needed a new job. Maybe one with an old, rich dude who went to bed at ten p.m. and slept through the night. An old, rich dude who just needed Colin to hang out in the background and not be *friends* with him. Colin had enough friends. He really didn't want to get so deeply invested again. That had hurt when it ended.

But dammit, he could not get the feel of holding Hayden Ross in his lap on the couch last night out of his head.

God, she'd felt good.

And she'd needed him.

All of that had been instinct. He'd seen her fear and vulnerability, *felt* it, and had been unable to keep from reaching for her.

He wanted to rip the head off of whoever was sending those emails to her and whoever had dared show up at her door last night.

So much for finding a new client he wouldn't get invested in.

He paid for his coffee and headed for the upper loft of the coffee shop. Apparently, Zander and Knox, Autre's city manager and Zander's favorite coffee buddy, had a regular table up there.

At least he wasn't the only one going on little sleep this morning, Colin thought as he eased himself into a chair next to Jonah.

Jonah looked almost as bad as Colin felt.

It was seven-thirty a.m. Not exactly the ass-crack of dawn. But after being awakened in the middle of the night by the Hayden Ross chaos and then having a hell of a time going back to sleep after he'd tackled her, found that she had a stalker, held her on his lap, and nearly kissed her before sending her to bed just down the hall from his own room, Colin was severely sleep deprived.

Jonah's cup of coffee was three times the size of Colin's. Of course, the other man was probably drinking just regular coffee rather than shots of espresso.

Zander already had his coffee as well. Something that smelled like someone had melted butterscotch candies down in a cup. It even had a swirl of whipped cream on top.

And then there was Henry. He was on the screen on the laptop computer Jonah had brought along, set up so he could see everyone at the table. He also held a cup, but Colin assumed it was tea. He shuddered. Hot tea was disgusting.

What was also disgusting was how bright and chipper Henry looked.

"Well, you all look like hell. Except you, Zander. Good morning."

"Morning, Henry," Zander greeted. He was leaning back casually in his chair.

"I'd be careful," Jonah warned Henry. "You are number one on Colin's shit list."

Henry frowned. "What are you talking about? This is perfect. She's staying with us now. This is the perfect chance to show her that we're ideal for her long-term team. You should be *thrilled* with me right now," he said to Colin.

Carter Shaw, Bad's cop, showed up just then and dropped into a chair across from Colin. "What's goin' on?" He was the only one without coffee.

But his arrival wasn't going to save Henry.

"A *stalker*?" Colin said, leaning close to the computer screen. "Goddamn it, Henry. When were you going to mention that?"

Carter's eyebrows shot up, and he exchanged a glance with Zander. Zander just lifted his cup for a sip.

"Well, I think that's a bit of an exaggeration," Henry said. "And I can handle monitoring the emails."

"He knows where she lives," Colin said, through gritted teeth. "He showed up there last night. That's why she called."

Henry's look of shock quickly morphed into anger then concern. "What happened?" he asked firmly, suddenly all business.

Colin finally took a chance to really look around the table, addressing everyone. "The man who's been sending Hayden Ross fan messages for months, on a daily basis, left a teddy bear, flowers, and a note outside her apartment door last night. This is the first time he's approached her in person. At least with any kind of direct romantic overture. If he's talked to her in person before now, she's not aware of it. We have no idea if he thought that she would be home or not. The note was written on a computer and printed. There was no hand-writing. I sent people to gather the items and dust for prints."

"Is she alright?" Zander asked.

"Shaken up. She didn't touch anything other than the note. Left it all and drove straight to Autre."

Carter nodded. "Smart."

Colin scrubbed a hand over his chest where it felt tight. It had felt tight since he'd heard the word *stalker*.

That wasn't entirely true. It had felt tight since he'd real-ized that the body underneath him on the grass in his front yard was Hayden. But the tightness at hearing she had a stalker was definitely a different kind of tightness.

"Where is she now?" Henry demanded.

"At the house with Cian," Colin said. It wasn't perfect. Cian wasn't a trained bodyguard. But he could use a gun. And knew the way to the hidden safe room in the lower level of the house. And he sure as fuck knew how to call for back-up.

Henry nodded, clearly thinking all those same thoughts.

"After she went upstairs last night, Colin and I checked around the property but didn't find any unusual tracks or signs that anyone followed her to Autre. But who the fuck knows for sure?" Jonah added.

"We don't know for absolute certain that this is the same guy who's been sending her messages." Colin turned his attention to Henry. "I'm having the New Orleans PD scan the letter and send it to me. I'll pass it on to you."

He wasn't sure he would be able to handle reading it if he was being honest. Which was a huge red flag. She was a client. A *potential* client. Someone they'd worked with before who had come to them for help. He needed to be able to look at all of the facts and evidence. But fuck... the idea of another man writing graphic, sexual stuff to Hayden...

His reaction to that was unreasonable and potentially very problematic.

He cut those thoughts off and forced himself to focus. "Since you're the one who's been reading all the emails, maybe you'll have a feel if you think it's the same guy," he said to Henry.

"Did she say anything about the note?"

Colin pulled in a breath.

He was grateful when Jonah said, "It was sexually graphic."

Henry's expression turned even harder. "Fucker."

Colin appreciated the other man's emotion, but he was across an ocean.

"Does that feel like the same guy possibly?" Colin asked.

"It almost has to be," Henry said. "It's not often a guy would just approach someone out of the blue like that without some lead up."

"Unless it's a neighbor with a crush," Carter offered. "Someone in her building who knows where she lives? A coworker who knows her address? Maybe it's not related to her music."

Colin pulled in a breath. Maybe. That didn't make it better. "It's an unwanted advance."

Carter nodded. "I'm with you. Just offering other ideas."

Colin pulled his phone out and jabbed a finger at the screen to open his email. It was too early to hope that he'd have a copy of the letter, wasn't it?

"It should be there," Zander said. "I called a friend a few minutes ago."

Colin looked up at him with a frown. "How did you know?"

"Jonah filled me in while you were getting your coffee."

Sure enough, there was an email with a pdf attachment. He hit forward to send it to Henry. "It's in your email," he told Henry. "Take a look."

"You're not going to?" Henry asked.

"I..." He stopped before he said *can't.* "Trust you."

"Morning, gentlemen."

They all looked up as Spencer Landry joined them.

Colin liked Spencer. He was FBI so he was a straight shooter. He'd also recently brought a woman with him to Autre to keep her safe after she'd had a bomb threat directed toward her.

The woman he'd fallen in love with and was now engaged to and living with in New Orleans.

Colin knew Spencer was protective and serious and ready to kick ass.

"Thanks for coming," Colin told him. Spencer had needed to drive down from the city.

"I owe you," Spencer said, with a simple lift of his shoulder. He pulled another chair up to the table.

Colin had helped provide security for Max, the woman Spencer had been protecting, while they'd worked to find the guy who had threatened her. He'd been happy to do it, of course, but he'd take Spencer up on the IOU.

"And I've got something for you," Spencer said. He leaned over and handed Colin a piece of paper. "Fingerprints."

Colin took it. "Already?"

"I know some people."

Colin looked from him to Zander to Carter then back to Spencer. It was really nice to have local guys on his team. "Thanks."

"Sorry it won't tell you much. There's like nine sets of prints on everything. But at least it narrows things down to nine people."

"It's possible he had someone deliver the stuff to her door," Zander commented.

Fuck. That was possible. The guy still knew where she lived, though.

"So, he's smart. He's already told us he knows she has a security team," Henry commented.

Great. A smart stalker. Colin passed the report over to Zander and Carter. "Recognize any names?"

They both glanced over it, but shook their heads. "No, sorry," Carter said.

"I have a theory that this guy first became obsessed with her in Bad," Henry said.

Colin looked at him, then to Carter, who was frowning.

"Why's that?" Carter asked.

"Hayden's performed at Bad Brews several times," Henry said.

The bar was owned by Marc Sterling, Sabrina's husband. Sabrina was the one who had discovered Hayden, and the bar was where she'd first brought Hayden to perform. It was where most of Hayden's social media posts had come from initially.

"Some things the guy has said in his emails make it sound

like he's seen her perform several times in person. That they've maybe even talked. Then one message referenced something she was wearing. She remembered the outfit from a performance at Bad Brews. She hadn't worn it anywhere else. Another mentioned a song she'd performed for the first time. She's never sung it anywhere else because she sold it shortly after. So, we've assumed he's come into Bad Brews more than once."

Colin frowned. "That helps. The crowds in Bad are smaller than in New Orleans."

"These are all guesses, of course," Henry said. "Don't have any proof. It's just things we've pieced together and my gut. And no one's ever approached her at the bar in a manner that's made her uncomfortable. A few people here and there giving her compliments, but she hasn't even had any guys flirting or asking for her number."

"That's probably because Sabrina has made sure Marc and Luke and Jase and Jackson are around. We don't need paid bodyguards," Carter said with a smirk at Colin and Jonah.

Jonah flipped him off as he lifted his cup again, clearly too tired to *say* much in response.

"You guys pay enough attention that you'd be able to recognize guys showing up there repeatedly?" Colin asked.

Carter nodded. "Yep. We know almost everyone who comes in. Outsiders stand out. They're welcome, of course, but we notice 'em."

"She performs a lot in New Orleans too," Henry said. "If someone showed up there *and* in Bad, he's probably a pretty dedicated fan."

Jonah was nodding. "Yep. We could take photos at a gig in New Orleans, show them to Carter and the guys and see if we get any matches. That would narrow things down quick."

"Makes sense," Carter agreed.

Colin ran a hand through his hair. The rational part of his mind knew that all sounded like a good plan.

But instead of taking her out to more gigs and trying to lure the guy out, getting him closer to her again, Colin wanted to tuck her away and keep her hidden.

Yeah, he wasn't rational when it came to Hayden.

And he barely knew her.

"We also need to monitor to see if he contacts her now after leaving the gifts," Zander said. "I would think he'd want acknowledgement of those from her. And if she says nothing, or even asks him to stop contacting her, that might push him to escalate things. Then maybe we can do something."

"Push him so he harasses her *more*?" Jonah asked with a scowl.

"If you want law enforcement involved officially, he has to *do* something," Carter said.

Zander just nodded.

Jonah looked at Colin and they both looked at Henry. They weren't law enforcement. Not in the way the other men at the table were. They could... color outside the lines a bit.

It might just take talking to the guy to get him to back off.

It might take more.

But they could do something before anything got worse for Hayden.

As soon as they knew who the guy was.

They needed a plan. But probably a plan that the local cops didn't know about. For everyone's peace of mind.

"Okay," Colin said. "I guess we'll let you know when we know more. Thanks for your help."

Zander simply lifted a brow.

Spencer actually laughed. "Yeah, I'll be sitting by my phone waiting for your call."

Colin knew that the other men knew that he and his guys were going to take this into their own hands.

And that they understood.

Colin looked at Zander, Spencer, and Carter. "Thanks for meeting with us." He needed them to get the hell out of here so he could talk to Jonah and Henry alone.

Zander propped an ankle on his opposite knee. "I hope you're not trying to get rid of me. I'm meeting Knox here in a little bit." He looked at his phone, noting the time. "In fact, you all need to get lost."

Carter shook his head and stood. "Well, as someone who has a real job he needs to get back to, I'll see y'all later."

"Thanks, Carter," Colin said sincerely.

The other man gave him a single nod. "Of course. You know where to find me."

Spencer settled back in his chair. He looked over at Zander. "I drove all the way down from New Orleans. I'm not leavin' yet."

"*He* invited you," Zander said, inclining his head toward Colin.

"You're still my favorite cousin," Spencer said.

Zander sighed. But he didn't look like he considered that a compliment, necessarily, but he also didn't seem all that put out. "You're lucky Knox likes you."

"Yeah, I know I'm still gonna feel like a third-wheel for your bro-date," Spencer said. "But you can buy me a cinnamon roll to make up for it."

Colin shook his head. "Guess we're going."

"Take me with you!" Henry said from the computer.

Jonah swept the laptop up. "Of course. You can be *my* bro-date."

Luckily the wi-fi from the coffee shop worked out in the

parking lot and they propped the laptop up on the hood of Colin's truck.

"We need a plan," he said shortly. "I want this guy. ASAP."

"He hasn't threatened her. Maybe if she tells him to back off it will be enough," Jonah said. "We don't have a reason to think he's violent."

"He showed up at her apartment! That mother fucker!" Henry exclaimed.

Jonah reached over and turned the volume down on the computer. Then he grinned at Colin. "Damn. Too bad we don't have a volume button on him all the time."

They could still hear Henry's, "fuck off" though. They hadn't completely muted him.

The thing was, Colin agreed with him.

The guy had made Hayden feel uncomfortable. The gifts had obviously rattled her. If his attention was really just complimentary and made her feel good, it would be one thing. But obviously, the presents at her door had freaked her out. He did not like seeing her scared and he was going to do whatever it took to make her feel safe.

"He knows where she lives. We need to make it clear he is *not* going to show up within one hundred yards of her ever again. We'll make our own fucking restraining order," he said firmly.

All the men were quiet. Henry nodded. It was clear he was upset by this whole thing.

"She needs to stay with us until we figure it out," Henry said. "She's all alone. She doesn't have any family in town except for a grandfather who's in a nursing home. She doesn't have friends who stop over regularly, no roommate. There's nowhere else for her to go where she'll be as safe as she'll be with us."

"And if he's following her, it won't matter," Jonah said. "He'll just follow her to someone else's place."

"She needs to be with us until we can figure this out," Henry repeated.

Colin hated that idea. Because he loved that idea.

He wanted Hayden under his roof. Where he could see her. Take care of her.

Thank God it made sense. He could tell himself he was doing it to prove that he and the guys should be her long-term security detail.

There was no place safer for her to be than in their house. Three of them were trained bodyguards. The house had been designed with the intent of keeping three members of a royal family safe. The security system was the best money could buy.

Plus, he would never sleep well again if he had to wonder and worry about her every night.

"She's potentially a really important client," he said, probably unnecessarily.

"Great reason to keep her with us," Henry said. "We'll keep her safe, show her how we work, that she can trust us, then when the music execs come back to town in a couple of weeks and she signs and is ready for a security detail, we'll obviously be her pick."

Colin frowned. "In a couple of weeks?"

Henry nodded. "Something like that. I talked to Sabrina just last week. They really like her. They want to meet with her when they're back in town." Henry grinned. "Our girl's going to be a star."

Colin clenched his jaw at the *our girl*. He was overreacting to how much the guys seemed to like Hayden. How well they seemed to know her. It was bugging him—how had they gotten so close? And just how close were they?—but it was ridiculous that he cared.

"So she stays with us until we find this guy or the record execs get back."

"Or both," Henry said. "When she signs with the label and they hire us as full-time security, we can move her to a better building, and I can move in. Even if we don't find this guy by then, we'll make sure she's taken care of."

Again, Colin felt his jaw clench. Of course, Henry would move in. Not *with* Hayden. In the apartment next door. That's how it would work. He would be head of her security team. And obviously she and Henry were close. It's what Hayden would want.

It would keep her safe.

That's what *Colin* wanted.

And yes, he definitely wanted her with them until all of that happened.

"Fine," he finally said, acting as if he was making a huge concession.

"When are you getting back here?" Jonah asked Henry.

Henry sighed. "As soon as I can. Things are complicated here."

"Do what you need to," Colin said. He wasn't going to push. Henry would share what he felt they needed to know. "But Hayden obviously trusts you. I think she really wants you here."

Henry nodded. "I know. But she's got you guys. It'll be fine."

Fine. Yeah, Colin wasn't so sure that's how he would describe how things were going to be.

It was just a gut feeling, but *fine* seemed very inadequate for how things were going to be with Hayden under their roof.

And one thing he always trusted was his gut.

four

AS COLIN and Jonah stepped through the front door of the house thirty minutes later, Cian met them in the foyer.

"*Shhh*," he said in a hushed voice.

Colin frowned. "What's going on?"

Cian smiled. "Listen."

What he meant was evident immediately. Hayden was singing. It sounded like she was in the kitchen.

Damn.

She wasn't just good. She made his heart trip.

Colin had experienced his heart tripping in the past. It had always had something to do with Saoirse O'Grady, though. She'd had him wrapped around her little finger since the moment he held her in the hospital after she'd been born. He had been paid to take care of her. Paid to protect her. He'd met her mother while she was still pregnant with Saoirse and had known from that moment on that Saoirse was going to be his primary focus in life.

But the truth was that the moment that little girl opened her eyes and looked at him, he'd been in love.

So, over the next ten years of watching Saoirse grow up and

experience things like her first steps, her first words, learning to read, learning to ride a bike, and developing a love for animals, his heart had tripped and flipped a number of times.

But it had never happened for an adult woman.

Until Hayden Ross belted out an especially sultry note in his kitchen that Friday morning.

He was in so much fucking trouble.

Jonah grinned. "Damn, she's amazing."

Cian put a hand over his heart. "We get a fucking private concert. Someday that girl's gonna win a Grammy and we're going to be able to say she sang for us in our kitchen while making pancakes."

Colin studied the other two men. They were huge fans of Hayden's. It hit him just like Henry's comment earlier about *our girl* had. They believed she was going to be a star. And it wasn't about her being a potential client or being a big paycheck someday. They genuinely loved her voice and knew she had what it took.

He wasn't sure how he felt about that.

He liked it. She deserved a huge fan club, and he was glad he was hanging out with and hiring smart men.

But it also made him jealous as hell.

"Pancakes?" Jonah asked. "Can we go in?"

"I make you guys pancakes all the time," Colin groused. He cooked for them all ninety percent of the time. Well, maybe seventy percent now that they were living in Autre and could go to Ellie's bar whenever they wanted. But he was a damned good cook.

"But you do not sound or look as good as she does doing it," Cian said.

Colin narrowed his eyes. "What is with you and Hayden?"

He shouldn't care. He at least shouldn't ask. These men knew him. He wasn't going to be able to hide if he had feelings for Hayden. And he shouldn't fucking *have* feelings for Hayden. But Cian being close to her was rubbing Colin the wrong way. He needed to at least know what that relationship was really about.

Cian smirked. "What do you mean?"

"How well do you know Hayden? What did you mean last night when you said that you've had fun with her?"

He nodded. "Oh, that."

"Yeah, that," Colin said firmly.

"We're friends. I like her. A lot. She's funny, sweet, and genuine. I fuckin' love hearing her sing and it's like she doesn't even know how good she is. She's just fun to hang out with. And she thinks Henry and I are funny. It's like she soaks up being with us."

Colin rolled his eyes. "So, she has terrible taste?"

Cian laughed. It was nearly impossible to insult the man. "No, it's like she's attention starved or something. I mean, not in a pathetic or desperate way or anything. She just loves hanging out. It's like she just loves to laugh and hear our stupid stories. She doesn't even say much most of the time. She just listens to us being dumbasses and smiles at us like she adores us."

Colin took all of that in. He wasn't sure exactly what it meant, but it seemed like Cian had not slept with Hayden. Which was very important. Cian was not his employee. He could put rules up around Henry and Jonah and how they interacted with Hayden. He had a lot less to say about how Cian O'Grady acted with her. "So you haven't hit on her?"

"I didn't say that. But..." Cian squinted as if thinking hard about something. "Not sure I have. Like we maybe flirted a little bit at first?" He ended that with a question mark as if he wasn't sure. "But it feels more like she's my sister or something. God, she's so much easier to hang with than Fiona. You know I love Fiona, but she's such a constant ball of energy and always lookin' for a fight. Hayden's not constantly trying to make me a better man like Fiona is." He rolled his eyes. "I think Hayden's gorgeous. But there's no spark."

Colin could certainly not say the same. But he was happy that that was Cian's report. "Okay."

"Any specific reason you're asking?"

"She's going to be staying here. With all of us. Just good to know where everybody stands."

"Guess that makes sense," Cian said. "I'm glad she's staying. So where does she stand with you?"

"She's a potential client. We need to keep her safe. And hopefully, she'll hire us full-time when this is over."

"So, this is like a trial run?" Cian asked.

"Something like that."

"Plus, we're keeping a really nice woman safe from a stalker," Jonah pointed out.

Colin sighed. "Of course."

Hayden's voice floated down the hall as she started a new song, and the smell of bacon hit him, and he took a deep breath. Damn. The current location of Heaven might be his kitchen.

Cian grinned. "I am on board with this plan."

Colin led the way down the hallway. The less talking he did with Jonah and Cian, the less chance there was of him saying or revealing something he didn't want to.

The moment he stepped into the kitchen, he realized that Cian had been exactly right. No one had ever looked or sounded as good as Hayden Ross did in his kitchen making pancakes.

And she was singing a cappella. There were no headphones or earbuds to be seen. He didn't recognize the song, which didn't necessarily mean anything. He wasn't a huge radio listener. But he wouldn't be surprised if it was an original or even something she was working on. He'd done a thorough study of her when Sabrina had first approached them about providing security and the idea that it could be an ongoing contract.

Hayden wasn't just a singer. She was a songwriter. She'd written a couple of songs for Sabrina since the women had met. She'd also written one that Jason Young was going to be singing on his tour that might make it on his next album if it was well received.

Cian and Jonah each took a stool at the wide breakfast bar.

Colin watched them, amused. Hayden gave them both a grin and slid plates across the marble countertop before she flipped chocolate chip pancakes onto them. Singing the entire time.

Both men seemed completely enthralled. Almost as if she had enchanted them.

She was clearly not self-conscious about her voice. Or about the fact that she was in her pajamas.

Then Colin frowned.

Those weren't the clothes he'd given her last night.

And they weren't hers. She was wearing a pair of gray sweatpants and a plain maroon t-shirt. That were familiar.

"Why are you wearing Henry's clothes?"

Hayden spun, clearly not having seen him hovering in the kitchen doorway. Her eyes were wide. "I didn't know you were here."

He walked further into the kitchen. "Why are you wearing Henry's clothes?" he asked again.

The sight of her in those clothes made him irrationally annoyed.

She looked down. "Well, I think it's sweet of you to not notice, but obviously Fiona is a lot smaller than me."

Colin took the opportunity to drag his eyes over her body. It hadn't exactly been an invitation, but it seemed a good excuse. Hayden was curvy. Deliciously, gorgeously curvy. She had great breasts, a fantastic ass, and simply lots of surface area to run his hands—and other things, like his tongue—over.

He realized he wasn't supposed to be thinking of her that way, but he'd been unable to rein in his thoughts so far, and at the moment her body was very much the topic of conversation.

Yeah, okay, maybe Fiona's clothes wouldn't have fit Hayden. But he honestly hadn't thought about it last night. He knew Fiona well. He'd spent ten years living with the woman.

And yes, now purposefully comparing the two women, Fiona was much smaller than Hayden. Fiona was quite petite, actually.

He'd been a dumbass thinking that her clothes would fit Hayden.

"You could've told me," he said. "I would've loaned you something."

She laughed. "I assumed you were all asleep and I'd already woken you up once. And Henry's stuff was right there. I don't think he'll mind."

Colin was sure Henry wouldn't. That wasn't the point.

What was the point? Was there a point? The woman had needed different clothes. Bigger clothes. And she'd found some. It was not a big deal. There was no point.

Except for the fact that he hated seeing her in another man's clothes.

Jesus, he was losing it.

"She slept in his bed. I doubt he'll care that she's wearing one of his t-shirts," Cian said, biting into a piece of bacon.

Colin swung to face the other man. "She slept in Henry's room?"

Cian lifted a shoulder, but Colin saw the twinkle in his eye. Bastard.

"Yeah. I guess I could have put her in Torin's old room. But it seemed like she should be in Henry's."

Cian was poking him. Cian did this. Colin knew that. This also shouldn't be something Cian was *able* to poke him about.

Colin took a breath and decided to just ignore the prince. It wasn't easy, but Colin had some practice.

"We'll have Jonah and Cian head over to New Orleans and get your things," Colin said shifting up onto one of the barstools and trying to act casual and not like he was jealous as fuck that she'd slept in another man's bed—even without that other man—and that he had a semi-hard on just from studying her standing in his kitchen in sweatpants and a t-shirt.

Henry was obviously bigger than her, taller and broader , but his clothes still clung to her curves enticingly in a few spots. The pants were way too long, and she had them rolled up. The arms of the t-shirt were too long as well and while it did still cling a bit to her breasts, it was baggier on her. But the pants molded to the globes of her ass and he wanted to squeeze them. Very much. God, he wanted to squeeze them.

"I need my stuff?" she asked.

He pinned her with a direct stare. He was not going to have anyone arguing this with him. "You're staying here. Until we figure out who this guy is and deal with him."

She chewed on her bottom lip. He guessed it would taste like maple syrup. He wanted a taste.

He stoically held her gaze. She *was* staying here. And it wouldn't take much for him to tie her to her bed to get her to stay.

Or his.

"I should go with them, shouldn't I?" she finally asked. "To get my stuff."

"You shouldn't go anywhere near your apartment," Colin said, probably more firmly than he needed to. But he was still apparently operating in overreact-to-everything-about-Hayden mode. "You can give them a list of things you want. I assume you're okay with them going through your stuff?"

She shot the guys a look.

Cian grinned. "If I find anything scandalous in your panty drawer, I promise to keep it a secret."

She laughed. "I don't keep my scandalous stuff in my panty drawer."

"What about your panties?" Cian teased.

"My panties aren't really that scandalous, sorry."

Jesus Christ. Colin wanted to punch Cian just for saying the word panties to Hayden.

The temptation to punch Cian wasn't a brand new urge. It was actually a fairly common one. But Cian talking about panties with Hayden and making her blush and laugh—which she was definitely doing now—made Colin want to punch him even more than he had the time Cian had let Saoirse stay up late watching a documentary about elephant poaching.

She'd sobbed for *hours* and had nightmares for a month.

The kid could watch scary movies and not be affected but tell her a single news story about animals being mistreated and she'd rant for two hours, insist on looking up the addresses of every public official she could possibly write to about the problem, and have a fundraiser planned before she'd even think about eating dinner, doing her homework, or going to bed.

"So where *do* you keep your scandalous things?" Cian asked, wiggling his eyebrows.

"In my bedside table, of course. Within easy reach."

Oh yeah, Colin definitely wanted to punch Cian. Because now he was going to be thinking of Hayden and her bedside table in the bedroom here at this house. Every. Fucking. Night.

Cian nodded. "Excellent answer. Are the extra batteries in there too or are we gonna need to go through the kitchen drawers to be sure we have everything you need?"

"They plug into a USB port to recharge. No batteries needed," Hayden said.

Colin noticed the same word Cian did. Both of their heads came up to look at Hayden at the same time.

"*They*? How many of them do you want me to bring?" Cian asked.

She laughed. And blushed harder. "How long will I be here?" She looked over at Colin with that question.

And everything in him tightened.

He wanted to say, "You're not going to be needing any of that stuff." He also wanted to say, "Bring it all." He wanted to see everything she had.

And he couldn't say *any* of it.

She's twenty-three, for fuck's sake.

She's a client.

She's being stalked.

She's a job.

His dick did *not* care.

He cleared his throat when it was clear everyone was waiting for him to reply. "We're not sure."

"Better bring a couple then," she said.

"Requests?" Cian asked, clearly delighted.

The idea of Cian handling Hayden's vibrators *absolutely* made Colin want to punch him.

"The purple one for sure," she said. "Then you pick the other."

Jesus Christ.

Cian laughed. "Damn, now I wish we *were* sleeping together."

Hayden laughed too.

Okay, so they were joking around about sleeping together. That meant they *weren't*. And wouldn't be. Cian had said he felt she was like a sister.

"Here." Colin abruptly thrust a pen and notepad toward her. "Write down what you want them to get. The *clothes* especially. Other stuff we can replace here if they forget something."

"Yep. Happy to make a run to the sex toy shop," Cian said with a nod.

"Shampoo," Colin gritted out. "Toothbrush. Stuff like that."

"But can you guys grab some of that too?" Hayden asked, bending over the pad of paper. "I really like my shampoo."

"Of course," Jonah told her. "Whatever you need."

"This seems like a lot of trouble for them to go to." She sighed. "With the sun up, I'm feeling a little less freaked out."

Colin frowned, trying to shake the thought that he was glad she was going to have her shampoo here. Her hair had been silky last night, and he could still smell it.

"Don't feel less freaked out," he said sternly. "Be a little scared until we know exactly who this guy is and what's going on, how far he might think to escalate this. The guys will look around while they're there. They can dust for some additional prints, maybe ask the neighbors some questions. Besides, if he happens to be watching your apartment or your building, and he sees a couple of big guys there, he might get the idea that he'll have some trouble if he tries to approach you again."

Her eyes were wide. "You think he might be watching my building or my apartment?"

Colin didn't want to scare her, but... if scaring her a bit kept her safe, then so be it. "We have no idea. We don't know exactly what he wants. If he thinks he's in love with you and wants to date you, that's one thing. Maybe if he's soundly turned down, he'll give up. But if he's somebody who might escalate and wants to do you harm when he doesn't get his way, that's something else."

She pressed her lips together, staring at him, the wheels in her pretty head clearly turning.

"Lighten up," Jonah said around a bite of pancake. "She's gonna be fine. We've got this."

Colin didn't take his eyes off Hayden. "I'd love to lighten up. But I want her safe. She needs to understand what's going on."

She nodded. Then she flipped two pancakes onto a plate and handed it to him.

"Eat up," Cian said. "She can give you a run for your money with pancakes, man,"

Hayden looked at him. "You cook?"

"He does all the cooking," Cian said, nearly finished with his pancakes. "He's awesome."

Hayden was studying Colin. Then she handed him the spatula. "Well, this whole breakfast thing was a sorry for all the trouble last night."

"It wasn't trouble," he told her, making sure his voice was firm but gentle.

She nodded. "Okay. Still, this was my thanks for letting me stay. But if you're the cook, I am happy to turn it over."

"You don't like to cook?" He cut into his pancakes and took a bite. "Because these are delicious."

"Oh, I love to cook. But I love when people cook for me too."

He studied her as he chewed and swallowed. Okay, he was going to cook for her. He loved to cook and suddenly impressing Hayden in the kitchen was a new mission. "Are you a picky eater?"

She laughed and looked down at herself, then back to him. "Um, no."

He narrowed his eyes. In general, she seemed very confident and didn't seem too hung up on her size. She'd talked matter-of-factly about Fiona's clothes being too small. She'd been dancing and singing in his kitchen without any self-consciousness. She was slightly self-deprecating but didn't seem shy. Still, he loved her curves and in that moment he felt the need to make sure she understood that.

"I love to cook," he said. "I had to get good at it when I was taking care of Saoirse. Fiona had crazy hours and I wanted to be sure Saoirse had a schedule and good meals. Then Cian and Henry were around a lot, and Torin and Jonah were in and out, so there were always lots of people to feed. And they all love my food."

Cian and Jonah both nodded around mouthfuls.

He paused and leaned in, making sure she was looking directly at him. "But I'll tell you a secret—there's nothing hotter to a guy who loves to cook than a beautiful woman who appreciates his food."

He ignored the two other men with them. He made sure his voice was low and just gruff enough that she caught the dirty undertone of what he was about to say.

"I'd love to feed you, Hayden."

She seemed to get the message because her cheeks got a little pink.

Would he love to make food for her? Absolutely. Would it be a turn on? Yup.

He had cooked for several women, but it had been a long time. As Saoirse had gotten older, it had been harder and harder to bring women to the house without Saoirse having all kinds of questions.

Long-term, serious relationships were almost impossible. He'd essentially had a daughter. But yet, he hadn't. His situation with Fiona and Saoirse was very unusual and had been hard for women to understand, especially when he hadn't been able to tell them who Fiona and Saoirse really were. That they were royalty had always been kept under wraps.

So, he and Fiona had chosen to play the part of a man and woman who had a child together but had a platonic relationship with one another. Women seemed to think that was cool. At first. But that never lasted long. There was a lot of jealousy and Saoirse always had to come first. She wasn't just a job, she was his heart. When it came to choosing a woman or Saoirse, it was *always* Saoirse.

So he couldn't remember the last time he'd cooked for a woman he was attracted to. He was sure that it had been something fancy and gourmet and probably more to show off and seduce.

With Hayden, he had the urge to make her something traditional and satisfying.

He wanted to make her sweets. Or soup. Or pasta. Something comforting and warm. Something that would make her moan and smile. It wouldn't have to be something fancy or something hard to pronounce. He just wanted it to be something that would make her happy. To make her feel cared for.

What Cian had said earlier about her being alone, away from family and friends, had been niggling at him.

Cooking for her would make him feel the way he felt when he made homemade chicken noodle soup from scratch for Saoirse when she was sick or when he made her favorite mac & cheese when her mom was away on a trip, and Saoirse was missing her.

Hayden wet her lips and continued to stare at him. Then her eyes dropped to his mouth.

Okay, it wasn't exactly how he felt when he cooked for Saoirse.

He wanted to take care of this woman. But he also very much wanted to run his hands all over those glorious curves when she hugged him and told him thank you for dinner.

Jesus Christ, she is too young for you, and she's a potential client, and she's in a very vulnerable state. You need to back off.

"You guys almost done? You need to get her stuff and get me some information," he said, forcing his attention away from Hayden.

Cian was running a finger through the syrup and melted chocolate on his plate and then licking it clean. "Yep. Thanks for breakfast." He gave Hayden a big grin.

She laughed. "You're welcome."

Don't you fucking hug her.

Colin managed to not say it out loud, thankfully.

"Finish your list. We're leaving in five minutes," Jonah said, taking his and Cian's plates to the dishwasher.

Hayden leaned onto her forearms on the counter and started writing on the pad of paper again.

Colin concentrated on finishing his pancakes. And *not* thinking about the baked five-cheese macaroni he made that actually was damned good. Or how much he wanted to walk behind her and check out her ass as she bent over like that.

He also did *not* think about him and Hayden being alone in the house for the next couple of hours while the guys headed to New Orleans.

A noble endeavor that was blown to hell the moment the door closed behind them, and she turned to him and asked, "Would it be okay if I take a shower?"

For just a second Colin looked like she'd slapped him.

Hayden could not get a read on the guy. There were so many mixed signals. One minute he seemed upset and frustrated. Then the next, he was protective and concerned. Then the next, he would smile and nearly knock her on her ass with how hot he was. And then he said stuff about feeding her, and her entire body got hot, and she had no idea what to do.

Now he was looking at her like he wasn't sure what language she had just spoken.

"Colin? Would that be okay?"

"Yeah, of course." He shook his head.

"Are there towels somewhere?" she asked slowly.

"Aye. Come on." Again, his tone switched, and he was now firm.

They started up the steps, him in the lead. Which made everything all better. Climbing the stairs behind him gave her a fabulous view of his ass in those jeans.

At the top, she started to turn left, but he stopped her.

"This way." He turned right.

Henry's room with his en suite bathroom was to the left. Cian's room was also down the hallway in this direction, along with two other rooms she assumed were Jonah's and one that had previously been Cian's brother Torin's room.

"Oh. Um."

Colin kept walking. In the opposite direction.

"Okay, then." She followed Colin because she didn't have a great reason not to.

He led her to the end of the hallway and through a wide arched doorway. This was obviously the part of the house they had added on. The entire house was enormous, but it was clear that they had added a wing onto this end.

They stepped into an area that was lit by a wide skylight at least twenty feet above them. The hardwood floor was covered by a plush rug and there was artwork hanging on the cream-colored walls. She peered at one of the paintings. It was an island. They all were she realized, glancing around. This was an aerial view. The island was lush and green, with sapphire blue water surrounding it on all sides. Other paintings depicted bluffs and mountains. The one directly across from where she stood was of a brightly colored village nestled into a hillside. And the one behind her—she turned to take it in— was of a castle.

They were paintings, so they could have been imaginings, but she had a feeling these were paintings of real places.

Of Cara. It had to be. The island nation Cian and his family were from. Where they were royalty.

Whoa.

Colin continued on to one of four doors that opened off of the wide hallway. He pushed it open and waited for her.

She didn't know why but she felt butterflies kick up in her stomach as she drew closer, then stepped past him.

Into his bedroom.

She swallowed hard. Ah, that was why. The butterflies had known.

"My bathroom is fully stocked," he said. His tone was gruff, and he wasn't looking at her.

"I can't... I mean, I don't need to use yours. I'll be staying here for a while and..."

"Use mine," he said shortly. He opened the closet and reached inside, withdrawing towels and a washcloth." "Until you have your shampoo and everything."

"I could just use what's in the other bathroom."

He turned and finally met her eyes. "Henry's?"

She nodded. "Yeah."

"We'll move you into Fiona's old room when the guys get back with your stuff."

"Oh, I could...stay in Torin's." *Away from you.*

He shook his head. "Cian put you in there, so you were closer to him and Jonah last night, I assume. And..."

She tipped her head as he trailed off. "And?"

"He knew having you sleep in Henry's bed would irritate me."

He met her gaze without blinking as he admitted that.

Well, maybe it wasn't an *admission*. But he wasn't denying Cian's plan to annoy him had worked.

She didn't say anything. Because all she wanted to say was, *Why does me being in another man's bed bother you, Colin?*

"But when we built this part of the house, we put Fiona and Saoirse's rooms down here. Near me."

She looked over her shoulder toward the other doorways in this wing of the house. That made sense, she supposed. They'd want Saoirse near her bodyguard and her mom would want to be near Saoirse. And, of course, they'd given the newer section of the house to the princesses.

"I see."

"So you should be down here. Fiona doesn't need the room anymore. It also has an en suite bathroom. And Henry will be home. Eventually."

"I feel like this is all a bother."

"It's not. I want you in that room," he said firmly. He handed her the towels. "And you using my shower for now."

See, he said stuff like that and it was hard to read him.

Or was it?

Maybe it was just that she wasn't sure she *should* read him.

Surely, he just wanted her closer because he was putting himself in charge of her safety and security.

Was this far more than they'd do for any other girl who sang a few songs in a bar and attracted an ardent admirer?

She frowned for just a second thinking of another girl showing up on their porch in the middle of the night and being taken care of the same way.

She didn't like that.

And that was problematic.

First, she hated the idea of anyone having unwanted attention. But every woman should have three handsome, amazing men there to protect her if that ever happened.

But second, she was *jealous*? Of the *idea* of another woman having Colin's intense protectiveness directed at her? Being cuddled on his lap? Being told he wanted to feed her?

Uh...yeah, she was.

Well...*fuck*.

Hayden swallowed hard and nodded. "Okay. Thanks."

He looked like he wanted to say something more, but instead just gave her a single nod and crossed the room to the door. She watched him go, clutching the towels. She needed some space from him. He was scrambling her brain.

But he paused in the doorway and turned back. "Sorry. The showerhead isn't detachable."

She stared at him. Two seconds later, she realized what he was talking about, and her mouth dropped open, and her cheeks heated.

Yes, she'd talked about vibrators with Cian in the kitchen. And she supposed with Jonah, since he'd been sitting right there.

And Colin had definitely been there.

She'd been painfully aware of that.

Still, she hadn't been able to keep all of the teasing inside. Cian had that effect. He was funny and mischievous, and she liked making him laugh. When she was around Cian and Henry, they brought out a playful side that she hadn't felt in a long time. It was how she felt when she hung out with her younger brother and sister. It made her miss them, but also feel a little less homesick.

Of course she hadn't expected to be joking and talking about vibrators, but she'd gone along with it feeling playful. And there had definitely been something hot about doing it in front of Colin

But now it was just the two of them...

She tried to summon some bravado. She wanted to seem confident. She was aware that he was a few years older than Cian and Henry, and he definitely exuded a certain take-charge, totally competent energy that made him seem even more mature.

There was something about it that made her feel completely safe and happy. And that made her want to knock him off-kilter at the same time.

"Well, dang. Do any of the other bathrooms have that?" she asked.

He didn't smile. "No. But the guys will be back from New Orleans soon enough with your...supplies."

Right. Her supplies.

She hoped that Colin Daly thought about her vibrators. A lot. Later. While he was alone in bed.

There. She'd let herself at least think that full thought without shutting it down. She found this guy extremely attractive and would probably have her own dirty thoughts about him in the next few—okay several—nights. He kept making her pulse race. She wouldn't mind having *some* kind of effect on him.

She nodded. "True. And it's not like I can't make do until they get here, even without a detachable showerhead."

Then she pressed the towels to her chest, turned, and walked into the bathroom, shutting the door behind her.

She slumped against it and took a deep breath. She couldn't believe she had just said that to *him*. She wasn't bold and brazen about sex. She'd had sex exactly two times in her life, and the last time had been nearly three years ago. And neither time had been mind-blowing.

In fact, according to her experience, she actually preferred her vibrators. They worked just fine, were faster, and she didn't have to talk to them afterward. They knew they'd done a good job. They didn't need to be praised.

She wasn't a prude. She loved steamy romance novels, really did have five vibrators, and some of the songs she wrote were pretty sexy.

But she had never stood in a man's bedroom and been flippant about getting herself off in the shower.

Especially not a man like Colin Daly. A big, badass bodyguard seven years her senior who had, no doubt, *a lot* more experience in bedrooms—and probably showers too—than she did.

She really hoped he was gone when she went back out there.

She straightened away from the doorway and looked around, able to actually concentrate on her surroundings without Colin in her space. She honestly couldn't say what his bedroom looked like. But she could have described the exact green of his eyes, the way his beard framed his mouth, how big his hands were especially in comparison to the size of her breasts...

Stop it. The showerhead doesn't detach, remember?

Hayden took a deep breath and looked around.

And holy crap. If the bathroom in Fiona's room was

anything like this, Hayden might just be okay with being stalked.

Everything was tan-colored tile and marble, mahogany wood, and gold fixtures. The whole place was bigger than the kitchen *and* living room of her apartment combined. And they were combined with just a little breakfast bar separating them.

The toilet was in its own little closet off to the side. There were two sinks with an enormous marble counter, even though, apparently, this was just for one guy. The general color scheme was darker than she would have chosen, but it fit Colin. Big, dark, sturdy. He also wasn't a bath guy, evidently. There was no tub. But there was a shower. Like a *shower*. It was huge. Six people could shower at the same time in that thing. And the walls and door were all glass.

She noticed some dials on the wall and walked over to inspect them.

No way. The floor in here was heated.

She was maybe never leaving this room.

She shed her clothes, swept her hair up into a messy bun, secured it with one of the ties she always had in her purse, and padded across the floor to the shower.

She immediately realized why it didn't need to have a detachable showerhead. There were six different showerheads mounted on one wall at different levels. And they were all adjustable.

Then she looked up. She frowned. There was a large gold rectangle above the shower. It had little holes in it like a showerhead but it was nearly as big as the entire floor of the shower.

She reached in and turned the water on.

And her mouth dropped open. Water fell from all the holes above. Like rain.

She studied the knobs, then turned them again.

What?

Now she had a "waterfall" effect.

She turned them again.

Now she had a rainfall and a waterfall from above.

And she hadn't even started on the nozzles on the wall yet.

Yeah, this was possibly going to be the longest shower of her life.

five

WHEN HAYDEN STEPPED out into the bedroom a good forty-five minutes later, she was warm and thoroughly scrubbed and very relaxed. Even though she hadn't been able to actually pleasure herself.

Not for lack of great images—all of which starred Colin Daly—but because she somehow knew when she saw him afterward he would *know*.

That was the weirdest feeling.

They really didn't know each other well at all.

She definitely appreciated his protectiveness. He absolutely made her feel safe. She wanted more cuddling like he'd given her on the couch last night. But she also got the impression that was not a typical move on his part, and she didn't expect it to keep happening.

She stopped in the middle of his bedroom, wrapped in the biggest bath towel she'd ever seen, and looked around.

In the middle of the wall was a bed that she had to believe was bigger than a king. Did they make beds bigger than kings?

It faced the only windows in the room. But they were the only windows needed. They were huge and there were a lot of them. They also looked out the only side of the house where there were no neighbors.

This side of the house faced the Boys of the Bayou Gone Wild Animal Park and Sanctuary.

The park was owned by the Landry family but she knew, again from Cian and Henry, that Fiona had a lot to do with the rescues that called the sanctuary home. It was the entire reason they had all landed in Autre.

Fiona. The princess. The petite woman who rescued animals for a living and who had lived with Colin for ten years.

Hayden was *so* curious about this woman.

Something moved off in the distance and Hayden crossed to the window to peer out.

Okay that couldn't be...

But yes, she was ninety percent sure she was looking at a giraffe.

It was two hundred yards away or so, but that had to be a giraffe. She knew the park had some. She supposed it wasn't impossible. But...wow.

Now she understood the chair that Colin had positioned next to the window. Sure, there was also an enormous bookcase. Maybe he sat here and read. But she'd bet he watched the giraffes too. And...she blinked...yeah, that looked like a zebra.

She was going to have to head over to the park and check things out. Staying in Autre for the foreseeable future suddenly sounded like a great idea.

Hayden turned and checked out the rest of the room.

Two bedside tables—again she felt her cheeks flush thinking about what she'd told Cian and okay, the other guys too, about her bedside tables—huge bed with a thick duvet with a mosaic pattern in various shades of brown, pile of clothes on top of the duvet.

She walked over with a small smile. It was another pair of

sweatpants, and a shirt. Not a t-shirt, but a Henley, in a light blue.

She picked it up and held it to her nose, breathing deeply.

These were Colin's clothes. They smelled exactly like him. Which meant they were very specifically not Henry's clothes.

He'd said that Cian had put her in Henry's room because it would irritate Colin. She could have chalked that up to Colin not wanting her to be in Henry's way, or staying in someone's room who was still living here and would be coming home soon. Or even that he was concerned Henry's room wouldn't be clean and tidy.

But clearly, he was also bothered by her wearing Henry's clothes. And he'd given her his. That seemed like...something else.

She still had Henry's clothes. She'd slept in them and worn them this morning, but they certainly weren't dirty. She could put them back on to make a point that Colin didn't get to decide what she wore.

But...this was kind of sweet. And they definitely smelled great. And she kind of wanted to wear his clothes.

That was stupid.

But it was true.

Maybe he was trying to take care of her. She was a guest, and he was trying to make sure she was comfortable. Maybe he'd thought she'd want to get out of the clothes she'd slept in.

Yeah, she wasn't sure that was exactly it. But whatever the reasoning behind it, she felt warm, and her stomach got kind-of flippy.

She dropped the towel and started to get dressed. And realized immediately she'd messed up.

She'd washed her bra and panties out in the sink in the bathroom without thinking about the fact that Cian and Jonah would probably not be back yet with new ones.

She could easily go commando on the bottom, but it was going to be a little more difficult to be discreet without a bra. One of the drawbacks to being large breasted.

With a sigh, she pulled the shirt on, then pulled up the sweats. The shirt definitely covered her, but it was quite obvious she was not wearing a bra.

Okay, well, she just needed another shirt on top, or a hoodie, something a little thicker than the shirt. Layers. Layers would help.

She started to cross to Colin's closet, then hesitated. She knew Henry well enough to not feel bad about going through his closets and dressers, but she wasn't sure she felt that comfortable with Colin.

Actually, she did *not* feel comfortable with Colin. In a delicious way. But not in a go-through-his-drawers way.

She needed to ask.

She drew in a deep breath, crossed the door, pulled it open. But she froze on the threshold when she heard, "Fiona! Don't!"

Fiona? She was here? Now?

"Oh, relax! I'm not going to get in the shower with her!" a woman—obviously Fiona—laughed. "I'm just going to make sure my room is neat and that I haven't left anything here that I might need."

Her voice was getting louder. She was coming up the stairs.

Hayden ducked back into Colin's room and closed the door but didn't fully latch it.

"You haven't lived here in almost a year!" Colin shouted. "You haven't left anything here you need, and your room is fine!"

"Just want to be sure!" She was all the way upstairs now.

Hayden realized she was holding her breath.

Why was she holding her breath? They knew she was here. She was *supposed* to be here.

Because she was a little intimidated by Fiona. At least the *idea* of Fiona. And she wasn't wearing her own clothes. Or any underwear. And she smelled like Colin. And she suddenly felt very vulnerable.

What if Fiona didn't like her?

Why the hell does it matter if Fiona likes you?

She didn't know. But it did.

She peeked out the door to see if Fiona had ducked into her bedroom yet. The bedroom Hayden was very interested in seeing now that she'd seen Colin's. Surely *the princess* would have an amazing bedroom and bath.

But the only thing she saw was a wide chest coming at her.

Colin pulled open the door and crowded through it, backing her up.

"Hey!"

"Good, you're dressed."

"You didn't look like you were about to knock." She crossed her arms over her breasts, very aware of the no bra thing now.

"I..." He paused. Then frowned. "...wasn't going to knock. No."

Her stomach swooped and she ignored it. "What's going on? Why is Fiona here?"

"Because I texted to tell her you'd be staying here. Stupidly. And she's nosy as hell." He shoved a hand through his hair. "I'm sorry."

"Am I supposed to be a secret?"

"No. I'm not sorry for telling her. I'm sorry she's here."

"Why? Will she be mean?"

He laughed. And the sound rocked through Hayden. She stared. Damn. She wanted him to do that some more. And also never again.

"She will not be mean. She'll be...Fiona."

"How so? She'll want to know my whole life story? Give me

the third degree since I'm staying here with her brother and two of her best friends?"

Yes, she knew exactly how Henry felt about Fiona. He loved her almost as much as her own brother did. And just from the conversations she'd had with Cian and Henry, she knew that Colin and Fiona were very close.

"Oh, no, it won't be about you," he said. "I'm certain Henry and Cian have gushed all about you to her."

Hayden felt her brows arch. "They have?"

"They like you. A lot. And they're like puppies—especially Cian. If he's excited about something, everyone knows."

Hayden felt warmth spread through her chest. "Aw. I like them too." The idea that they'd talked to Fiona about her was sweet. Then she frowned. "So why are you worried about Fiona being here?"

He sighed. "She's a lot when you first meet her. And after you get to know her." He rolled his eyes. "And always. She'll tell you all about Saoirse. And Knox. And Ellie. And tigers. And giraffes. And the entire Landry family. And the whole animal park. And…"

Hayden felt her mouth curling up. "And?"

"Me."

She let herself smile fully then. "This is supposed to scare me off?"

"It's a warning. I know you aren't used to having tons of people around and maybe quite that much…energy."

Oh. Henry and Cian had been talking about her to Colin too. "I'm actually one of four kids. I have two younger siblings. Twins. A boy and a girl. I can handle energy."

"Oh." He frowned. "Henry and Cian said you were on your own."

"Here I am," she said with a nod. "I moved to New Orleans to be with my grandpa. He has Alzheimer's." Dammit, her voice caught on that word every damned time she said it. She cleared her throat. "We looked around and found the *best* memory care for him. But it's in New Orleans, which is five hours from home. I was the one who was unattached and didn't have big stuff going on, so I made the move with him. So I have people. Just not right here with me."

"Being an up-and-coming music sensation isn't big stuff?" he asked, his voice gentler now. As was his expression as he studied her.

"I wasn't...that..." She couldn't bring herself to refer to herself that way. That was weird. "...when I came to New Orleans. And I guess my stuff can still kind of happen from anywhere. Everyone else's stuff is different."

"That all makes more sense," he said.

"How so?"

"You're..."

"I'm?" she prodded when he trailed off.

"You're warm. And easy going about the teasing and shenanigans. You put up with Cian and Henry and Jonah like an older sister." He lifted a shoulder. "That fits."

She nodded. "Cian and Henry are...a lot *more*...than my brothers and sister."

Colin gave a soft laugh. "I'm sure they are."

She grinned. "But I love being around them."

"Well, the feeling is obviously mutual."

There was a softness in Colin's expression now. One that she hadn't seen before. One that made her breath snag in her chest.

"Do you feel like a big brother to them?" she asked.

"Yeah." He nodded. "They drive me nuts, but I'd do anything for them."

Her heart squeezed with that. "And Fiona."

"And Fiona," he said.

Hayden's heart squeezed again. But there was a tiny twinge of jealousy with that one. Dammit.

"So I came in to warn you and see if you just wanted to hide out until she's gone." He grimaced. "Though she might just not leave until you come out. She's like that."

"I don't need to hide out," Hayden said. "I want to meet her." That was true.

This woman was Cian's sister. She was important to Henry. And Colin. So Hayden was definitely curious. Fiona headed up missions to rescue domestic and wild animals kept in captivity. She traveled the world. Hell, she was kind of a *princess*. She had not rescinded her abdication but still, she had a fascinating story.

"Okay." Colin seemed hesitant.

"Do you not *want* me to meet her?"

"Well, it's inevitable." He still didn't seem happy about it.

"What's the problem?"

Colin's gaze met hers and he just looked at her for a long moment. Then he said, "She knows me really well."

Hayden nodded. "I'm sure."

"So, she's probably going to be able to tell that I..." He pushed a hand through his hair. "Do not feel brotherly toward you."

Her eyes went wide. "You...don't?"

"Cian and Henry have told me that's how they feel about you. Like friends. And protective brothers." He seemed to lean in closer. "That is not how I feel. And Fiona is going to be able to tell."

Hayden's mouth was dry and her heart was pounding. She had *not* expected this. "Well, you don't really know me. Maybe after a little while, you'll feel brotherly toward me."

"I don't think so." His voice was low.

Her skin felt tingly and hot. "So...that's a problem?" she asked, trying to breathe normally.

That seemed to snap him out of some kind of daze. He leaned back. "With Fiona? Yes. She'll make a big deal out of it. I just want you warned so you don't get uncomfortable. She doesn't really believe in boundaries."

Hayden had no idea what to do with *any* of that. She knew she'd sort through it all later and try to figure it out, wonder about it, second guess it all. And probably still not totally understand what he meant.

She could just ask him, she supposed.

But he was talking about the attraction between them, right? The fact that there was a chemistry that wasn't there between her and Henry or her and Cian. A chemistry that made it hard to think of her like a sister.

That didn't mean anything was going to happen or that things couldn't progress as planned. She was going to stay here until this guy with the emails and teddy bear got the message to back off. That could happen whether she and Colin had chemistry or not.

Finally, she just said, "Got it."

"Okay." He hesitated, then turned toward the door.

"Colin?"

He stopped. "Yeah?"

"I do need one thing."

"Okay."

"A hoodie? Or another shirt? Like a flannel or something?"

He frowned. "Are you cold?"

"No. I'm...braless."

His gaze predictably dropped to her chest, where she still had her arms crossed. "What?"

"I washed my bra out without thinking about the fact that

I don't have a replacement. And I don't really want to meet Fiona flopping around."

He swallowed hard. "Oh."

He didn't move.

"So, do you have a hoodie I can borrow?" she asked.

"Yeah."

He still didn't move. And his eyes were still on her arms. It was as if he was still processing what she'd said.

Or picturing it.

"Colin?" she asked, amused. This guy did not strike her as the type to be easily rattled and she loved that she could do it. And so easily too. She dropped her arms.

He took her in. His gaze heated. But finally, he coughed. "Sure." He crossed to his closet and yanked it open with far more force than was needed. He tossed her a button up chambray shirt. "Will that work?"

"Perfect."

She slid her arms in, which caused the Henley to pull tighter across her chest for a moment. Or two. Or five.

He watched the whole thing.

Her nipples liked the attention. They'd liked everything about how he didn't feel brotherly toward her either. And she was sure that was evident now. But there wasn't much she could do to hide it.

She pulled the shirt together in front and took a breath. "Okay, as good as it gets right now." She did not feel put together enough to meet Fiona, but what the hell?

"You look..." Colin's eyes finally left her breasts. Now they were focused on the ceiling, and he pulled in a deep breath. "...fine," he finished.

Fine?

Well, considering everything about the crazy situation she was currently in, fine was probably pretty good.

Colin caught Fiona right outside her old bedroom. He grabbed her elbow and started for the stairs.

"Hey, what about Hayden?" she asked, looking back over his shoulder.

"She'll be down in a little bit."

"Is she okay?"

He didn't let go of Fiona as they made their way to the first floor. "She's staying with us. And she's not dating any of us. I can't say more but you can put two and two together."

Fiona's eyes widened. "Oh. Okay."

He sighed. "Just cool it, okay?"

She nodded. "Okay."

"Is your room all set up?"

"Yes." She grinned. "She'll love it. I'm head over heels for Knox but damn, I do miss that bedroom."

Colin rolled his eyes. No expense had been spared remodeling this house and the two princesses had gone all out with their wish lists. And Fiona's grandfather's expense account.

"So if you came over to give me a hard time about having a woman staying here, now you know it's not what you were assuming. You can go."

They stepped into the kitchen, and he let go of her arm. Fiona turned and planted her hands on her hips. "Uh...it's *Hayden Ross.* I'm not leaving until I meet her."

He frowned. "You want to meet her?"

"Colin, she's going to be the next Taylor Swift! Of course, I want to meet her. I love her music."

He shook his head. "I know Saoirse sings her stuff all the time, but I just assumed that was Cian's influence."

"It started that way, but I love her too. I'm staying." Fiona crossed her arms now.

Okay, so maybe he'd miscalculated. He'd assumed when he'd texted *someone's going to be staying in your room for a few days. It's not a big deal but thought you should know* Fiona would text back a few annoyingly nosy questions that Colin would dodge, and then she'd drop it.

For some reason he hadn't thought about her asking Cian who their houseguest was. The chances of Cian spilling the beans had been about one hundred percent. Cian understood keeping things under wraps, but he would never consider Fiona someone he needed to keep a secret from.

Fiona had shown up fifteen minutes after she'd texted Cian *who's staying at the house in my old room?*

Colin sighed. "Fine. She wants to meet you too. But try not to...overwhelm her."

Fiona lifted a brow. "Me?"

Colin just snorted. Then he noticed the additions to his kitchen countertop. "What's all this?"

"Oh." Fiona moved toward the grocery bags. "I also need a favor."

It was his turn to cross his arms. "How long have you known about whatever this is and forgot to tell me?"

She bit her bottom lip, and he knew she was trying to figure out how to lie about it.

The answer was, she couldn't. He knew her too well.

"Two weeks. But in my defense," she said quickly, "that big cat rescue last week took two days longer than I'd expected and I was called out last night and just got back."

He shook his head. "I don't work for you anymore."

She batted her eyes. "But it's for Saoirse."

He narrowed his eyes. That was, of course, the sure-fire way to get him to do something. "What is it?"

"You know there were parent-teacher conferences last night and tonight," she said.

He did. Saoirse was coming over here this afternoon because she was getting out of class early because of those conferences and Fiona and Knox were both working. "Okay."

"Well, the parents always bring food in for a potluck to feed the teachers and I signed up to help."

"You don't cook."

"But you do."

"So you signed *me* up."

"I signed *us* up," she said with a smile.

But it still made his chest tight. Saoirse wasn't his daughter. He wasn't attending parent-teacher conferences. Anymore. He used to. He'd go when Fiona couldn't. Sometimes he'd go with her. The school in Florida, where they'd lived before coming to Louisiana, had believed that he was Saoirse's father. It was just easier that way. It gave him the ability to be close to her, get information, and make demands that were sometimes needed to keep her safe.

Working for the king of another country—even if it was a small one with no trade agreements or significant benefits for the US—had its perks when it came to getting permissions and paperwork and things Colin needed to do his job.

"What did you sign *me* up to make?" he asked, annoyed with Fiona.

He knew if he explained how he felt, she'd understand. Hell, she'd probably feel bad. She knew how much he loved Saoirse. She had to know how much he missed her. But he couldn't lay that on her. She'd fallen in love. With a great man. A man who also loved Saoirse deeply. Knox was very good for them, and Colin wasn't about to make any of them feel bad about their new family unit.

"Crawfish beignets." Fiona grimaced.

He stared at her. "What?"

"Yours are so good."

"Well… yeah. But I was expecting cookies. Brownies. Maybe a salad. This is a potluck."

"Right. But people had already signed up for desserts and salads and they needed main dishes and those are easy to eat and…"

"How many?"

"Five dozen."

"No."

"But—"

"No. It's too much. I don't have time for that. I'll make cookies."

"They don't need more cookies."

"No one's gonna die with more cookies."

"I know I messed up not telling you ahead and I messed up not signing up earlier for something easier, but I'd rather *you* think I'm a mess than all the other moms thinking that."

Colin blew out a breath. "I don't think you're a mess. Jesus, I know how you spend your time, Fi."

What Fiona did with her life was amazing. He'd always admired it, even when it had kept her away from her daughter at times. He'd been there. As had Henry, Cian, and Torin and Jonah at times. Saoirse had been very well cared for. She'd never gone without anything—attention, protection, people in the audience cheering her on, help with homework, love and affection. And now that Saoirse was a little older, it was easy to see her mother's influence had been very positive. Saoirse was an animal lover who was confident and fierce, and a strong leader amongst her peers.

He was so fucking proud of her.

"I'm too comfortable thinking that you'll always be there to back me up," Fiona said quietly.

"No," he said sharply. "You're not. I *am* here to back you up. Always."

She looked torn.

This was their dynamic. It had been for ten years. They'd raised a daughter together. No matter what their exact relationship was, no matter how difficult it was to define and explain, they *had* raised an amazing little girl. Together. They were both a part of that. And he knew Fiona appreciated him. Loved him.

"What about a seafood dip?"

They both turned toward the doorway.

Where Hayden stood.

She moved into the room. "You could do a cheesy dip with the crawfish and shrimp and bread or crackers to dip in it. It would still be hot and savory but way easier to make and transport and just as easy to eat."

Colin and Fiona both just stared at her.

Fiona probably because she was a huge fan of Hayden's music.

But Colin was staring because she just looked fucking gorgeous. Wearing *his* clothes. Without a bra.

He couldn't *really* tell. But he knew. He *knew*.

"Oh my God!" Fiona finally said. "Hi!"

Hayden smiled at her. "Hi. I'm Hayden."

"Oh, I know!" Fiona took a step closer. "I'm a huge fan."

Hayden's nose wrinkled. "You are?"

"Of course! I discovered you because of Jason Young. Is that okay to say?"

Hayden laughed, and Colin felt his gut tighten. God, he loved hearing her laugh. In contrast to the scared woman who had shown up on his doorstep last night, he loved seeing her happy and comfortable.

And yes, praised.

Her cheeks were a little pink and her eyes held a touch of wonder. Like she couldn't believe she had fans.

"Of course, that's okay. I guess that's the point of performing with him," Hayden said lightly.

"Well, don't tell him, but I've listened to your stuff way more than I've listened to Jason's now," Fiona said. "And I'm not just saying that."

"Thank you. It's all so crazy," Hayden admitted. "I've always just written and sung for myself and friends and family. I never expected to have a real audience. It still feels a little surreal."

"You better get used to it," Fiona said. "You're going to be *huge*."

Hayden blushed deeper and Colin wanted to cup her cheek, feel that warmer skin, brush his thumb over it, and tell her how damned gorgeous she was. But she was clearly uncomfortable with the praise, so he cleared his throat. "What were you saying about dip?"

"Oh," Hayden shook her head. "Yeah. I just overheard you talking about beignets. And I was thinking that the ingredients for a hot dip would be similar to the filling. Not exact but we could make adjustments. And that would be fast and easy."

"You know how to cook too?" Fiona asked.

"Oh, when it comes to food, I love to shop for it, cook it and eat it. I love it all." Hayden said.

"The dip is actually a great idea," Colin said. He dug into the bags that Fiona had brought over. He pulled out the meat and cheeses, he crossed to the fridge. He had cream cheese and all the spices they would need. He turned back. "Yeah, we have everything. Let's do that."

Fiona beamed at Hayden. "Thank you so much."

Hayden laughed. "When it comes to food, I'm your girl."

Colin carried the additional ingredients over to the counter.

"You might have to run to get crackers," he told Fiona.

She frowned. "I'll try to get them later. Or maybe Knox can. I do need to be at the park for a tour."

"Are you saving that for something special?" Hayden asked, pointing to the loaf of French bread on Colin's counter.

Colin knew exactly what she was thinking. "I can replace it."

"Great." She grabbed it and pulled a knife from his knife block and began slicing.

He lifted his brows and then looked at Fiona. She slid up onto the barstool and grinned.

It looked like Hayden was going to make herself comfortable in his kitchen. And he liked it. Probably too much. He didn't actually share the kitchen easily. Mostly because everybody else was always more in the way than helpful. Maybe Hayden would be the same way, but suddenly he wanted to find out.

"So, do you do something with cooking for a living?" Fiona asked Hayden, reaching out and snagging a piece of Parmesan cheese from the bowl where Colin had dumped the package out. "Like when you're not singing?"

Hayden laughed. "Oh no. It's purely for pleasure."

Colin realized that reacting to this woman even saying the word *pleasure* the way he did was ridiculous.

"You're able to make a living with your singing?" Fiona asked.

Hayden shook her head. "Oh no. Not performing or recording, anyway. I mean, I get paid by the bars where I perform, and I've sold a few songs to other artists, and that's amazing. Of course, the shows with Jason were amazing. But that's all just going into the bank. I'm a music therapist, actually."

She moved around his kitchen opening cupboards.

"To the left of the fridge," he said, knowing she was looking for the olive oil.

She shot him a smile and grabbed the bottle. He handed her a small pastry brush and a bowl, feeling a strange camaraderie in anticipating her needs as they cooked together.

"What's a music therapist?" Fiona asked.

Colin watched Hayden pour oil into the bowl, then handed over a baking sheet.

As she started arranging the small pieces of bread she'd cut, he started mixing up the dip ingredients. But he was grateful the recipe was simple and one he'd done several times because he was hardly paying attention. All of his focus seemed to be on the gorgeous brunette that he kind of wanted to give his Henley and chambray shirt to permanently.

"We use music for therapeutic purposes with a number of different kinds of clients. We work with kids with developmental disabilities and kids and adults with emotional and physical trauma. Music helps them process information differently, or opens them up to receiving new information, or helps them talk about difficult topics.

"Sometimes we help people learn to play instruments with different adaptations. For instance, someone who has had a stroke or some kind of traumatic brain injury, or an amputation will need instruments or music adapted. We have to be creative in really unique ways." She smiled as she brushed oil over the pieces of bread in front of her. "We also work with a lot of adults with mental illness, as well as things like strokes, dementia, Alzheimer's."

Colin heard the little catch in her voice on the word Alzheimer's. She'd told him that her grandfather had it. He looked over. And damn if the urge to hug her didn't get even stronger. She was concentrating on the task in front of her, but he could tell it was as routine to her as his mixing cream cheese, parmesan cheese, and crab meat. She didn't see the bread and oil.

"That's mostly what I do," she went on. "I like working with older adults. That's actually how I found out about music therapy. I was in college, working on a degree in music education, when my grandpa moved into an assisted living facility that had a music therapist. I would go visit him all the time and we would sing together a lot. She heard us a few times and finally approached me one day and asked if I'd ever considered music therapy."

"I know exactly what it's like to see someone in my line of work and just recognize a spark, someone who should be doing the work," Fiona said. "I think that's part of important work—finding more people to carry it on."

Hayden looked up and gave her a sweet smile. "When Grandpa transferred to New Orleans to a memory care unit, I moved too and started the program at Loyola. I just got certified six months ago and I plan to work on my Master's."

"That sounds really rewarding," Fiona said.

"It is," Hayden agreed. "For instance, with Alzheimer's patients, sometimes a favorite song from their past can break through and help them communicate by triggering certain brain centers." She paused. "And even when it doesn't, I think it gives them comfort. Losing memories can be so sad and scary. They're often confused about where they are. Forgetting the people around them and their routines is so disorienting. Hearing familiar songs can ground them and can evoke happy, calming emotions."

Colin realized that he had abandoned mixing and was staring at her. Hayden was glowing talking about her profession. It was clear it meant a lot to her. She was smiling, and yet, he wanted to hug her now too.

Scared, sexy, happy, flirty, shy and humble, sad about her grandfather, proud of her profession—all of these sides of this woman made him want to hold her.

Fuck.

He looked over and caught Fiona watching him. She grinned at him. He frowned at her.

Double fuck.

Finished with the oil, Hayden started reaching for spices from his spice rack and mixing a combination into a small bowl.

Damn, her comfort and competence in the kitchen were attractive. He had no idea that was a turn-on for him but...it definitely was. She didn't measure, she simply poured and sprinkled and pinched, then mixed, even while talking.

"So, is your whole family musical?" Fiona asked, leaning to prop her elbow on the counter in front of her and rest her chin on her hand.

Colin glanced at his friend. She gave him a wink. Okay, he appreciated what she was doing. Sure, she was interested in Hayden too, but her questioning also meant he didn't have to ask.

He'd known Fiona would be able to tell that he had some feelings for Hayden. She wasn't saying anything about it or teasing him—at least not right now—but she was helping him get to know Hayden better.

He had really good friends.

Even when they were being a huge pain in his ass.

He went back to mixing the dip ingredients together so he could transfer them into a baking dish for the oven.

Hayden laughed. "Not really. My family is very athletic." She started sprinkling the mixture of herbs and spices over the bread. "My oldest brother is a star baseball player. He's actually in the minors, on the verge of moving up. My younger brother and sister, twins, are in college now, both playing for their college teams. Baseball and softball. My dad was also a college baseball player and now coaches high school. So our entire family always revolved around sports. Except for me. I mean, I tried, but I sucked—much to my parents' chagrin—and I hated it." She laughed. "I don't really like to sweat."

I bet I could make you like sweating.

The thought snuck up on him and was *not* welcome.

Colin cleared his throat, even though he had not said it out loud.

"You don't suck at music," Colin said. He was as surprised as the women seemed to be that he'd finally spoken. He looked at Hayden and shrugged. "Well, I'm right. Obviously, you're *very* musically talented."

He didn't fully understand it but hearing her talk about not being as talented as her siblings irritated him. It was ridiculous.

"Yeah, I guess, except for that. My grandpa was actually musical. He was the one who taught me to play. The one who is here in New Orleans."

Ah, another puzzle piece clicked into place. Not only had Hayden apparently been the only one *available* to move to New Orleans with her grandfather, but she had probably been close to him growing up if he was the other musical member of the family.

Colin was glad they were here together. If the rest of the family valued baseball over music then fu—Colin cut off the unflattering thought about Hayden's family. He didn't know them, and it wasn't fair to judge them based on what she'd just said. They might be lovely.

But he couldn't completely quash the feeling of protectiveness he felt thinking about her family not fully valuing what was special about her.

They both finished their portion of the food preparation at the same time. They shared a smile, and Colin felt it grab him in the gut. He carried the baking dish of seafood dip while she brought the pan of bread to the oven, and they slid them in to bake.

Fiona jumped off the stool as Colin shut the oven door.

"I should probably get back to work. Thank you so much for covering this for me."

"Do you need me to drop it up at the school?" Colin asked, already knowing the answer.

"Would you?" Fiona asked. "Maybe when you pick up Saoirse?"

"Of course," he said. He would've said of course anyway, but it made sense since he was picking Saoirse up when classes were over around one.

"It was *so* nice to meet you, Hayden," Fiona said.

She came around the end of the breakfast bar, and Colin knew what was coming.

"Would it be okay if I hugged you?" Fiona asked Hayden. "I'm kind of a hugger."

Hayden laughed. "Yes, that would be okay."

Fiona wrapped her arms around Hayden, and when Hayden returned the embrace, something in Colin's chest tightened again.

It wasn't because of anything strange like two women who were important to him forging a friendship. Or that he liked seeing Hayden being appreciated and praised and shown affection. None of that made sense.

Hayden was a hopefully-someday-client. He was on a sort-of job interview here with her. So, yes, he was glad people were being nice to her. That was it. It was as if she had come to his office—if he had an office—and a member of his staff—as if Fiona would ever be a member of his staff—had brought her a cappuccino and told her that her outfit was cute. Sure. It was just like that.

He ran a hand over his face.

This was nothing like any of that.

Good God. She was wearing *his* sweats and shirt. She'd just helped him make food for a potluck at Saoirse's school to make Fiona look good. Fiona had fangirled all over her and uncovered a lot about her past as if *Hayden* had been the one at a job interview.

This just felt like he was really happy to see these two women being friends. And like maybe he could easily imagine them embracing over and over in the future.

Yeah, he was in big trouble.

six

HAYDEN DIDN'T THINK she was ever going to leave
Fiona's room. Or, rather, Fiona's old bedroom. It was absolutely a dream room that Hayden hadn't even realized she'd
ever dreamed of.

But if a princess was going to have a bedroom, it would be
this one.

It was decorated in a light mint green and white with a
deeper teal accent. All of the wood trim and crown moldings
were white. The walls were painted mint green. The thick
plush rug on the hardwood floor was mint green. The duvet on
the four-poster bed with the filmy white canopy over it was
mint green. The fluffy pillows stacked against the headboard
were a mix of white, teal, and mint green. The armchair that
sat next to the gas fireplace for those cool, rainy days in
Louisiana was white with a mint green throw pillow and a
mint green Ottoman as well as a cashmere throw blanket
draped over the back that was a gorgeous teal.

There were tall, white French doors that opened out onto
a balcony that overlooked the animal park. And yes, she
could see giraffes from here as well. In fact, more of them

were out now. Which meant she was right next to Colin's room which, in Hayden's estimation, made this room even more perfect.

The ceiling was high with two slowly circulating ceiling fans, and though she was having a hard time saying exactly which part of the room she liked best, it was a tie between the floor-to-ceiling bookshelves on either side of the French doors and the coffee bar in the corner on the way to the spa-like en suite bathroom.

And truly, the coffee bar might be just slightly ahead. It didn't just have a coffee pot, but a full-blown cappuccino machine, as well as a refrigerator underneath and a small wine rack overhead.

There was also an enormous walk-in closet that could have fit her entire wardrobe as well as all of her siblings' wardrobes. Unfortunately, it was not fully stocked. Nor were the bookshelves. Obviously, Fiona had moved her things out of this house and into Knox's.

The en suite bathroom was just as gorgeous as Colin's. But it was done in lighter colors—more whites, teals, and soft yellows—and Fiona's had the additional perk of having a bathtub. And not just any bathtub, but a gigantic claw footed bathtub. And the bathroom *was* fully stocked. The cabinet over one of the two sinks had bath salts, face scrubs, facemasks, and candles, while the cupboard between the bathtub and the shower was full of the fluffiest towels and washcloths Hayden had ever touched.

And then she found the best part. Probably even better than the coffee bar.

There was a small, built-in dryer that would toss her towel while she showered or bathed so that when she was finished, her towel was fluffy and *warm*.

She'd actually squealed when she'd figured that out.

Hayden was pretty sure she could stay inside this room and not leave. Ever.

Of course, once she was dressed in her own clothing, she got curious.

Specifically, she wondered what Colin was doing.

She didn't like how interested she was in the man, but she couldn't deny it.

So, eventually, she wandered downstairs to see where everyone was and what they were doing. She liked Cian and Jonah a lot too, of course, and she needed to talk to them about the gig she had tonight in New Orleans. She assumed one of them would feel compelled to go with her. Which was fine. Not just because of the stalker but because she always liked their company.

Voices drew her toward the kitchen. But before she stepped inside, she realized that it was Colin and he was talking to a little girl.

Hayden flattened herself against the wall. Not because she didn't want to be seen but because she very much wanted to eavesdrop on this conversation.

That had to be Saoirse he was talking to.

Talk about curiosity. Hayden absolutely wanted to know more about Fiona's daughter. And specifically, witness Colin and Saoirse interacting. Without them knowing they had an audience.

Was it sneaky? Yes. Should she let them know she was there? Probably. Was she going to? In a few minutes.

"I need to talk to you about something," Saoirse said.

"I'm listening."

"I'm talking to you as a friend, not a grown-up."

"I'm a grown-up no matter how I'm listening to you."

Hayden thought she heard the sound of a knife against a

cutting board and figured he was slicing apples or something. Probably an after-school snack.

"You know what I mean. You can't be a grown-up who tells my mom and Knox about this," Saoirse told him.

There was a pause. "I'm not going to like this, am I?" Colin asked.

"This is very serious," the little girl said. "But you don't work for my mom anymore. You're not my bodyguard. But we're still friends, right? I can tell you stuff."

Hayden felt her heart squeeze. There was another long pause and the sound of slicing stopped. Then Colin said, "Of course."

"Stuff I can't tell Knox and Mom?"

"Saoirse, are you in trouble?"

Now Saoirse paused. "What if I am? Would you still keep it a secret?"

Hayden's eyes widened. She was picturing Colin's face. He was studying Saoirse seriously, she knew. He knew this little girl well. Had known her all her life. Literally. There was no way Saoirse would be able to get away with anything with him. Even Hayden felt like *she* couldn't hide anything from him, and he didn't know her the way he knew this girl.

But Colin had a very protective yet soft side. Hayden had seen it herself. How much deeper and stronger was it for this girl?

"I would if it was important to you," he finally said. "I can keep you safe from anything. But you have to know that they want to know things about you because they love you."

"You love me too."

Hayden put her hand to her mouth. Well, she hadn't expected this. She thought she'd hear them joking and teasing. Maybe Colin helping Saoirse with her homework. She hadn't expected to overhear a conversation like this.

"'Course I do, *mo leanbhí*."

Hayden made a note of the phrase that was clearly a term of affection. She had no idea how to spell it, but she wanted to find out what it meant. His accent already made her stomach flip, and calling a little girl by an endearment was sweet even if she couldn't understand it. But if that was some Irish phrase, Hayden's crush was definitely going to deepen.

Maybe she *shouldn't* look it up.

"You love me as much as they do. We've known each other a *long* time," Saoirse went on.

"Where is this going?" Colin asked.

"It's nothing bad. Nothing bad for *me*, anyway."

"Saoirse," Colin's voice held a touch of warning.

"Okay." Saoirse almost sounded annoyed. "I heard Knox and Mom talking about something."

"Okay. What was it?"

"They want to have a baby."

There was a much longer pause this time. Hayden felt her eyes widen.

"Oh." Colin paused again. "Okay. How do you feel about that?"

"I'm worried."

"You know your mom and Knox love you, *a stór*. They'll love you just as much if there's a baby. Having a little brother or sister will be a ton of fun."

Hayden smiled. There was that sweet side she knew she'd overhear. He was really good with this kid. She wasn't sure how she'd known he would be. She'd seen nothing to make her think so, but she'd been sure of it.

"I know that," Saoirse said.

Hayden could practically hear the girl's eyes rolling.

"That's not what I'm worried about. I know they'll still love me. Babies are great. I love all the babies around here."

"Then what are you worried about?" Colin asked.

"I'm worried about the baby not having you."

"What do you mean? The baby won't need me. The baby will technically still be a prince or princess, but since your uncle Torin went home to Cara, everything's changed. You don't have to worry about the baby being safe."

There was a pause and Hayden could picture Colin reaching out to ruffle Saoirse's hair or cup her cheek. She really wished she could *see* them together.

"But even so, I'm right here." His tone was soft and affectionate and reassuring.

Hayden felt a warmth swirl through her. When he talked like that, how could anyone feel anything but fully cared for and safe?

"I'm not going anywhere. I'll help take care of the baby if needed. I'd never let anything happen to *any* of you. And Henry's here. And Jonah."

"No, that's not what I mean," Saoirse said. "I know we're safe. But the baby won't have you like a dad. It won't get to live with you. And spend all the time together like we did."

Oh.

Hayden felt her chest squeeze a little and she put her hand over her heart. This was definitely not what she should be eavesdropping on.

Still, she couldn't make herself leave. This was giving her a lot of insight into Colin and...she liked it. This was a side of him she bet not many people got to experience. Then again, she doubted that he held back when he was around Saoirse, no matter who else was around.

This relationship was so intriguing. Saoirse wasn't his daughter. He'd been her bodyguard, but it seemed like he'd been almost more like a nanny. Her life hadn't been of paparazzi or death threats. He'd lived with Saoirse and Fiona and helped raise her.

Yeah, he hadn't even been like a nanny.

He'd been like her dad.

And now he...was like her dad with partial custody since her mom had remarried. But Saoirse knew he *wasn't* really her dad.

It was so complicated.

Yet, their affection for one another was clear.

It took Colin a second to respond. "The baby won't need me the way you did, Saoirse. Knox will be the baby's father."

"I know," Saoirse almost sounded sad. "The poor thing will only have one dad, instead of two like I do."

"And you think that's a bad thing?"

Hayden thought she heard a new gruffness in Colin's voice.

"Well, obviously. I'm so lucky. I have both you and Knox. The baby will never get to live with you and have all the fun times we did. And get to come over here like this. And now I have Knox. Which is so cool too. The baby will only have him. He's great," Saoirse said. "I love him a ton. But having both of you is super great. What if the baby is sad about it? Or jealous?"

"Well," Colin said. Then stopped and cleared his throat.

Hayden wanted so badly to see his face. She wondered what was going through his mind. This was sweet, and kind of funny. Saoirse wasn't upset about how the baby was going to change her life. She was worried about her younger brother or sister missing out on what she had with Colin. This little girl loved him so much, but so matter-of-factly.

Hayden wanted to see how it affected this big tough, gruff guy.

"Well, I would be happy to have the baby come over here

with you anytime. We can build blanket forts. Read bedtime stories. Have movie marathons. All the stuff that you loved."

Oh, yes, she *really* wanted to see Colin Daly building blanket forts.

Hayden could hear Saoirse's heavy sigh. "I know. It just won't be the same. I got to live with you for ten years. The baby will never have that."

"You know, you're pretty awesome," Colin said.

His voice was thick, and Hayden could tell he was emotional.

"Well, that's because you helped make me awesome. And I'm really lucky that I have you."

"Glad you feel that way. You always have me."

"I know. And you see why I didn't want to say anything to Mom and Knox. They would feel bad."

"I think this would make them feel good. Because you're happy. I mean about me being in your life. And how much you love Knox. And happy about a baby."

"Yeah, but it might make Knox feel bad that his baby's only going to have one dad."

Hayden heard Colin's snort. "Yeah, I guess it might make him feel bad to think that he may not be enough all by himself and that you think it would be better with both of us."

"Right," Saoirse said seriously.

Now Hayden really wanted to meet Knox.

"What are we doing?"

A whispered voice made Hayden jump and she glanced over to see that Cian had snuck up beside her.

"Saoirse's in there with Colin. I didn't want to interrupt," she said, blushing at having been caught eavesdropping.

Cian grinned. He obviously knew what she was doing.

He nodded. "Are you nervous about meeting her? She's kind of a hard ass."

Hayden grinned. "Well, she *is* a princess."

"Aye, the O'Grady family is super intimidating," he said, rolling his eyes.

"Hey, did I tell you that Hayden Ross is here?" Hayden heard Colin ask Saoirse just then.

Oh, he was trying to change the subject.

The next second, there was a loud squeal. "Oh my God!"

Hayden's eyes went wide. Cian laughed.

"Yep, I'm friends with her," Colin said, his tone smug.

"Shut up," Saoirse said. "She's here? Like in the house?"

"Yep. Your mom got to meet her a little bit ago."

"*Shut up.* Do I get to meet her?"

"You know I don't love the 'shut up' stuff," Colin said.

"Sorry, but do I get to meet her, Colin?"

"If you want to."

"*Oh my God.* Do you think she knows anything about wombats?"

Hayden pulled her phone from her pocket and immediately opened an Internet search tab and typed in wombats.

Cian chuckled again. "They're pretty cool," he said softly.

Hayden started looking at facts.

"I really don't know. I'll be honest and say, it wouldn't surprise me," Colin told Saoirse.

Hayden smiled at that. Colin thought that it was possible she could know something about wombats? She wasn't sure why that was complimentary, but it was.

"Well, I hope she doesn't," Saoirse said.

Hayden frowned and stopped swiping. She looked at Cian. He just shrugged. She waited for more information.

"Why is that?" Colin asked.

"Because then I can tell her," Saoirse said. "She is an amazing superstar singer who sings my favorite songs," Saoirse said. "I need to have something to impress her with."

Hayden tucked her phone back into her pocket. Cian laughed softly.

Colin said, "She's going to like you for who you are, *a stór*. You don't have to impress her with your knowledge of wombats."

"No, I need something cool to talk to her about. If she knows a bunch about wombats, maybe she won't know anything about giraffes. Or then she probably won't know anything about penguins if she knows a lot about giraffes and wombats both, right?"

Colin laughed. "You need to relax. She's very nice. She's going to be easy to talk to, no matter how much she knows about animals or not."

Okay, that was definitely a compliment and Hayden felt her chest get warm again. The things this man could do to her so easily should probably concern her.

"Should we go in before the ten-year-old has a stroke?" Cian whispered.

Without waiting for Hayden to respond, he stepped past her and walked into the kitchen. "So, as I was saying, during bushfires, other animals will use the burrows to hide out because they are so huge and deep. So I think they should be the official firehouse animal instead of a dalmatian. Michael says since they're not native to Louisiana, or even North America, it doesn't make sense. But JD and Asher are on my side since we have some right here at the animal park."

Saoirse gasped. "Cian, are you talking about *wombats*?"

He strolled over to the counter. "Oh, hi, Saoirse. Yeah, of course. Don't you think it would be cool to make the wombats the official mascot of the fire department here?"

"Well...yeah."

Hayden was still out of sight. She fought a grin. Clearly, Saoirse was torn between this very exciting new idea about her favorite animal and the idea that Cian was the one blabbing about wombats.

"Who were you talking to?" Saoirse asked her uncle. "Were you on the phone?"

"Oh, no. I was just talking to my new friend Hayden Ross about the wombats."

Saoirse gasped again so loudly that she nearly started to choke.

He was such a jerk. Hayden walked into the kitchen.

"Hi, everybody," Hayden said calmly.

Colin frowned at Cian and slid a glass of something toward Saoirse. Then he met Hayden's eyes.

She tripped over her own feet. Then sighed at herself and continued on into the room.

"Saoirse, this is Hayden. Hayden, this is Saoirse O'Grady. She's Cian's niece, Fiona's daughter," Colin said.

"Hi, Saoirse, it's so nice to meet you. I've heard a lot about you."

The girl was staring at her, her mouth not even moving.

Hayden looked over to Colin, then to Cian. He was grinning as if he'd never seen anything funnier.

"So, what are you two up to?" she asked Colin, trying to make it all less awkward for Saoirse.

"Just chatting over Saoirse's after-school snack," Colin said.

Sure enough, there were carrots and red pepper strips on the cutting board with a bowl of ranch dip in front of the princess.

Saoirse looked at Cian. "What did you tell her about wombats?"

Cian picked up a carrot and shrugged. "Oh, just everything I know. Which is kind of a lot after living with you for a long time."

Saoirse looked crestfallen.

"He's kidding," Hayden said. "He just told me that one thing about the firehouse. We were just getting started." Hayden propped a hip against the counter and reached for a red pepper strip. "I'm *fascinated* by wombats." She thought of the one fact she'd read before she'd heard Saoirse say she hoped Hayden didn't know anything. "I recently found out they're marsupials, like kangaroos. I didn't know that. Now I want to learn everything I can."

"I can teach you," Saoirse said quickly. "I know so much more than Cian. I taught him everything he knows. I'm an expert. They are my favorite animal. If you need to know *anything* about wombats, *pleeeeeease* ask me."

Hayden gave her a huge grin. "You're kidding! That's amazing. I would love to learn about them from you. Cian messes around and teases a lot, and I never know what to believe from him."

Saoirse nodded solemnly. "I know exactly what you mean."

Cian clutched his chest as if mortally wounded. "Wow. Pretty girls comin' at me from all sides."

"There are baby wombats down at the animal park," Saoirse said excitedly, ignoring her uncle. "I can get in to hold them. No one else really gets to. But I can get you behind the scenes."

"I can *totally* get you behind the scenes," Cian said.

Saoirse frowned at him. "You're not supposed to. Not since you tried to get one of the penguin's footprints. Jill is *still* mad at you and made Charlie swear you're banned." Saoirse looked at Hayden. "Jill is the vet who is the penguin expert and she's super protective and Charlie is kind of in charge of the whole place in general and Cian is..." She glanced at him and rolled her eyes. "*Trouble.*"

Hayden tried very hard not to laugh. Saoirse seemed about thirty years old when talking about her youngest uncle.

And she wasn't wrong about him.

"I needed that print," Cian said.

"What for?"

"It was supposed to be in exchange for some very important information I was trying to get," he hedged.

"*Anyway*," Saoirse said. "Behind the scenes normally costs extra. And you still don't really get to go everywhere. But if you're with me, you can go to all the areas." Her enthusiasm quickly morphed her tone back into excited-ten-year-old-girl. "Plus, I can tell you about all the animals. I know more than anybody. My tours are the best ones. And I was thinking that if you wanted to take a tour of the animal park with me and do all the behind-the-scenes stuff, then maybe in exchange, you could give me some guitar and singing lessons."

Hayden found herself completely sucked in by Saoirse's sparkling blue eyes and how genuine she was, and, if she was honest, the fact that the little girl loved Colin and could so easily make him all mushy and soft. She nodded. "That sounds like an amazing deal."

Saoirse was practically bouncing in her seat. "I love to sing. And I have been singing to some of our sick animals. And I really think that it helps them. And some of our really obnoxious animals because sometimes when they come in after they've been rescued, they're really skittish, and they're really wound up and upset, but when I go in and sing to them, it helps calm them down. I think it really helps them. And I think that if I could play the guitar when I sing, it would be even better."

Hayden gave her a huge smile. "I think you're right. I'm a music therapist, and that's pretty much exactly what I do for people. I sing to them when they're sick or when they're upset or anxious. And it helps them. There's no reason to think that it wouldn't work for animals."

Saoirse's eyes got round. "Do you think you could come and sing to the animals with me? We have a sick alpaca, and I think it would really help him to have a professional."

Hayden was completely wrapped up in this little girl. She was an absolute ball of energy and light. Hayden wanted nothing more than to take her hand and go and find the alpacas and spend the rest of her week singing to them all with her guitar. "I would absolutely love that, Saoirse. I can go get my guitar right now. It's upstairs."

Suddenly a man was clearing his throat. Saoirse and Hayden tore their eyes from one another and looked at him.

Colin was watching them with both eyebrows up. "Excuse me, but that isn't going to work."

Hayden frowned. "Why not?"

He gave her a *you should know better* look. "Because you need to stay here at the house right now and work on some things. And Saoirse has some chores to do at the animal park. She can't go see the sick alpaca right now. Griffin and Tori are taking care of him. You know they're doing a good job, *a stór*. Maybe in a day or two, the singing will be fine. But right now, you both have other things to concentrate on."

Right. He didn't want her wandering around Autre when he didn't know where her stalker was.

Hayden took a breath. "Right. I forgot about the...work...I need to get done."

He gave her a grateful look.

She focused on Saoirse again. "I really would love to do that with you, though. Another time?"

Saoirse nodded. "Definitely. Because trust me, you want to learn about wombats from me." She gave her uncle a look. "*Not*

Cian." She focused on Hayden again. "And you definitely want to hold the babies."

Hayden wasn't sure anyone had ever said anything more true. "I *absolutely* want to hold baby wombats."

"Okay, we'll do it soon."

"Definitely."

"Go get your shoes on," Colin told Saoirse. "And grab a bottle of water. Meet me by the front door."

She ran out of the room, and Colin focused on Hayden. "Thank you for going along with that."

"The singing to alpacas or the holding baby wombats? Because I'm fully on board with both of those things."

The corner of his mouth curled up. "The staying here and not doing either of those things right now."

"Oh, that. Yeah. I kind of forgot why I was here, I guess."

"Well, hopefully, it won't be for much longer."

Yeah. Hopefully. So why did the idea of all of that coming to an end make her sad? She'd been here for less than twenty-four hours, and she was ready to move in permanently.

She watched Colin leave the room, then settled down at the table with Cian. "Well, now that the big, bad bodyguard is gone, I have something I need to ask you about," she said.

"Hit me." Cian tossed a baby carrot into his mouth.

"I have a gig tonight at a bar in New Orleans. Will you come with me? I really don't feel like being alone."

He crunched on the carrot, frowning. "You should *definitely* not be alone. But Colin is not going to like that. We'll have to take Jonah with us."

Hayden shrugged. "I'm fine with that. You think Jonah will be?"

Cian nodded. "I'm sure. Maybe we should call Henry and get his input."

Hayden nodded. "I'd love to talk to Henry about it."

"I'll go find Jonah. You call Henry and see what he's doing. We can get on a video call."

"Sounds good."

Fifteen minutes later, Cian and Jonah were back at the table with her, and Henry was on the screen of Cian's laptop.

Cian and Jonah were finishing off the chopped vegetables and ranch dip that Colin had made for Saoirse. Henry was drinking a beer on the back patio of his family's home outside of London. Hayden was drinking a sweet tea and thinking about how much she liked these three men.

"She should definitely go to the bar tonight," Henry said. "But both of you should go with her."

"You don't think it's a problem?" Cian asked. "The guy went to her apartment just last night."

"I actually think that's better," Henry said. "He just escalated his behavior. If we want to find out who he is and what he's *actually* after, she needs to keep showing up at her regular gigs."

"Bait him?" Jonah asked. He didn't seem skeptical. It just seemed he was trying to clarify what Henry was saying.

"No. I mean, yes. Kind of." Henry sighed. "Just let Hayden do her usual thing so that he will show us what *his* thing is. He finally got brave enough to approach her apartment. That means he's ready to take this to the next level. We need to figure out what that means. With her surrounded by protection, of course. And we'll get photos to share with Carter. See if anyone looks familiar to him."

"How do you feel about that?" Cian asked Hayden.

She thought about that. "It's a little creepy. But the idea of him just being out there and not really knowing what he's thinking or going to do next is just as creepy. If you guys are with me, I'll feel safe. And I can't just hide out here. If I'm here and he's just waiting for me to show up again, then we're not getting anywhere."

Henry nodded. "Exactly. It's just a standoff if she's in hiding. I think if she's out, there's a better chance he approaches her, and we can find out who he is and what he wants."

"People do approach her at the bar, though," Cian said. "We might not be able to tell who he is."

It was true that people would often come up to her after a show. And yes, some of them were men. Usually, they were just complimentary. Sometimes they would talk to her and the band. Other times they just wanted to talk to her. Guys asked to buy her drinks and told her how much they loved her performance all the time.

"Well, I have an idea. I thought we would wait until I got back. But actually, it might be better with Jonah," Henry said.

"I'm listening," Jonah said.

"According to his messages, the guy already knows that I'm her security. He probably assumes Cian is as well, since he's seen us both with her. And he's probably observed how we act with her."

"What do you mean?" Jonah asked.

"We're clearly not romantically involved with her," Henry said. "He's never seen either of us kiss her or hold her hand or touch her the way a boyfriend would. So, he's assuming we're both security or just friends."

"But he's never seen Jonah," Cian said, nodding.

"Exactly," Henry said. "One of two things is going to happen if he thinks Hayden has a boyfriend. He's either going to back off because she's now unavailable. Or he's going to get jealous and possessive. If he leaves her alone, great. If he comes out of the shadows, we nail him."

Hayden let all of that spin through her mind. She watched

the other men. Cian was already nodding. A few seconds later, Jonah did as well.

"I like it. Makes sense," Jonah said. "He went from emails to an in-person visit at her apartment, in spite of knowing she had security. We need something more."

"But it's not really a long-term solution, is it?" Hayden asked. "If it works to make him back off, how long do Jonah and I have to pretend to date before we're sure this guy is going to leave me alone for good? What if he continues to watch me, and when Jonah quits showing up with me, he comes back?"

"I'll be honest with you," Henry said. "I do think we need to be prepared for it to take a little while. A few weeks, at least. And Jonah will have to be very convincing. You guys will have to act like you're seriously involved. But I also don't think he's going to back off. I think he's going to get jealous, and I think we're going to find out who he is."

Jonah nodded. "I do too. At least, I think that's the more likely outcome."

"Or he backs off temporarily," Henry said. "But if we keep it going for a few weeks, he'll get tired of it. He'll hate seeing you with someone else when you've been keeping him at arm's length in spite of his *many* messages."

"So Jonah has to really act the part?" Cian asked.

Typically that question from Cian would be a joke, but he was clearly serious. Hayden looked at all three men. They were all taking this seriously, and as freaked out as she was when they talked about this topic, having them figure this out for her made her feel safe and confident.

"I mean, they're going to have to act in love with one another. Lots of touching, kissing, lots of PDA. You guys will have to be convincing," Henry said. "Everyone in the bar will have to believe that you are really into each other. And you'll have to act like it's been going on for a while. It can't seem new."

Hayden and Jonah shared a look.

Jonah was extremely good-looking. It was just a fact. Pretty much any woman would find him attractive. But there was no spark. This was going to require some acting.

"I'm game. Kissing you won't be a hardship," he said, giving her a grin.

"Okay, I'm in," she agreed.

"Absolutely not."

They all turned at once toward the firm, growled words that came from the kitchen doorway. Where Colin stood.

seven

COLIN WAS SCOWLING at them all.

"Oh, boy," Cian said, low enough that only those at the table could hear.

"Hey, boss," Jonah greeted.

"What do you mean absolutely not?" Hayden asked.

"That plan is not happening." He stalked toward the table. "And no more meetings and decisions without me."

"You're pissed we're meeting without you?" Cian asked.

"Aye. Because you clearly come up with terrible ideas without me." Colin wasn't even looking at Hayden.

She frowned at him anyway.

"It's a good idea," Henry argued. "Hayden has a gig tonight. She needs protection. We need to bring this guy out of the shadows. The best way to do that is for him to think she has a boyfriend. But it has to be a serious boyfriend, so he has reason to be concerned and jealous. So it has to be the only guy who hasn't been seen with her before."

Colin put his hands on his hips, glowering at the other men. Finally, his gaze landed on Hayden.

"I agree."

Hayden's brows rose. "You...do?"

"Our job is to keep you safe while you live your normal life," Colin said, his voice strangely calm even though he was still scowling.

Hayden just nodded slowly. That made sense.

Colin didn't look at anyone but her. "You want to perform tonight?"

"Yes."

"You're not scared?"

"I won't be if the guys are with me."

"And you agree to having a fake boyfriend?"

There was a strange challenge in his eyes and tone of voice now.

She lifted a shoulder. "I trust you all. If that's what everyone thinks we need to do, then that's what we need to do."

"Fine." Colin said with a nod. "But Jonah's not doing it."

Henry sighed. "I would do it if I was there. But the guy already knows me anyway. And Cian doesn't have the training."

"That's why *I'm* going to do it."

Hayden blinked up at Colin. He was studying her intently.

He was going to do it?

It being the whole touching-her-a-lot-and-kissing-her thing?

Oh, really?

She had no idea what to say.

"*You're* going to do it?" Henry asked.

"Of course," Colin said.

"Why you?"

"Because I'll be sure to keep it *professional*."

Cian gave a soft snort.

Everyone ignored him. But Hayden certainly made a note of it.

Her heart was pounding in her chest, and her palms felt a little sweaty. She also had a strange tingling sensation at the back of her neck. Colin was going to come along with her tonight to the bar and pretend to be her boyfriend?

She liked the idea. A lot.

It was also potentially bad. She wasn't sure she could pull it off. He made her jumpy. Not a bad way. But in a very not-totally-comfortable-longtime-lover way. Anyone watching them would be able to tell that, if anything, they were newly dating.

That could be problematic.

She still wanted to do it. If it meant Colin would be right next to her, standing close, putting his hands on her, kissing her...

Yeah, her heart was definitely pounding.

She wanted to do this.

"I'm okay with it," she said.

As all the men turned to look at her, she realized she must have blurted that out in the middle of something they were talking about.

She put on some bravado and said, "I just wanted to say that I'm okay with it. As long as I can go to work."

"Where are you performing?" Colin asked.

"Trahan's."

He seemed relieved. "Oh. Good. I know the Trahans well." He looked at Henry. "I can ask Matt to be there, too."

Henry nodded. "I still think Jonah should go."

"I can go too," Cian said. "That will make it seem like things are normal. Even if he just thinks Jonah's a friend, at least Colin is there."

Colin nodded. "Agreed."

"Who's Matt?" Hayden asked.

"A friend. We met through the Trahans," Colin said.

Gabe and Logan Trahan were the owners of the tavern that had been in their family for at least a couple of generations. It sat on a busy corner of the French Quarter in New Orleans and catered to locals and tourists alike. Hayden had, ironically, performed on a street corner just a block up from the tavern before Sabrina had discovered her. Sabrina had introduced Hayden to the brothers months ago, and she'd performed in the tavern a handful of times now. They were great guys, and they paid her well above what she got at a lot of the other spots.

"Matt is ex-Army special forces. He's back in New Orleans now and has helped us out with a few things."

Hayden's eyes widened. "Well, I'm not missing you much at all, Henry."

Henry laughed. "I guess that's the general idea, isn't it? No matter where you are, or what your needs are, we've got you covered."

Hayden smiled and nodded. She knew they were all considering her a pseudo-client. She knew that if she got offered the deal with the label in a couple of weeks as Sabrina expected, Colin and these guys would be the ones everyone would expect her to hire for her security team.

And of course, she would. No one would make her feel safer than these guys.

So tonight, them coming with her and keeping her safe and making her feel comfortable and taken care of was...a job. Or training for a job.

She supposed faking that one of them was her boyfriend was fine since they would all be kind of faking being there because they cared...

Okay, she was being dramatic and a little pathetic now.

She needed some space.

She shoved her chair back and stood. "I'm going upstairs. I need to work on some things for tonight."

Colin looked like he wanted to say something but instead, he stepped back and nodded. "We'll be down here if you need anything."

She slipped past him and started for the stairs.

She'd almost made it when she heard his low voice behind her.

"Hayden."

She sucked in a breath, schooled her features, and turned. "Yeah?"

Colin looked concerned as he strode across the foyer toward her. "Are you okay?"

"Sure."

"You don't seem okay."

She could try to challenge him on the fact that he didn't really know her well enough to know that, but...he did. Somehow. He seemed to be able to read her.

"It's just all...a lot."

"You don't have to go tonight."

"I want to." She wanted to sing. She took a breath. "I don't want to let some creepy stranger dictate what I do. I just don't have a lot of experience being a girlfriend, so I'm worried I might not pull it off."

Colin looked like he was having trouble finding words for a moment.

She liked that. She liked throwing him off balance. He was always so sure, so in charge, so competent. She loved watching him do everything from make a plan with the guys to move around the kitchen. He always knew what he was doing. But making him unsure for a moment, like she wasn't always what he expected, gave her a little thrill.

That was dangerous.

She *really* liked him. She was wildly attracted to him. If he played her boyfriend tonight as competently as he even chopped vegetables, she was in trouble.

"You don't have to do this tonight. Jonah and I can play pretend," she told him.

"No."

That was his entire answer. Along with a scowl, of course.

"Why not?"

"Because I don't want things getting messy."

"Messy? What does that mean?"

"I don't want Jonah falling in love with you. That would complicate things."

Her eyes went wide and she sucked in a little breath. Then she snorted. "That's not going to happen."

"Why wouldn't it happen? You're gorgeous. Kind. Smart. Funny. Talented. Sweet. Why wouldn't they fall for you?"

Hayden knew her eyebrows were nearly in her hairline. He'd just delivered an entire list of compliments to her. Ones that made her stomach feel hot and swirly. And he'd been scowling the entire time.

"They?" she asked.

"Henry and Jonah."

"They don't have those kind of feelings for me."

"Yet."

He was ridiculous. But her stomach still felt swirly. "What about Cian?" she teased, the corner of her mouth curling up even as she fought it.

"Well, Cian is kind of a dumbass," Colin said. "Plus, he's doing his Cinderella thing."

"Cinderella thing?"

"He met a girl a few months ago and found out she gave him a fake name and number. He's been looking for her ever since. Henry can't find her, but Cian can't stop thinking about her and says he won't give up until he finds her. I'm sure that's why he needed the penguin flipper print. He probably made a deal with some guy who convinced him he had information about this mystery girl."

Hayden's eyes were wide, but she nodded. "I guess that *is* kind of like when the prince searches the entire kingdom for the girl who lost the glass slipper." She sighed. "I always thought that was so dumb. Surely more than one woman would have the same shoe size."

Colin actually smiled—kind of—then. "But she also had the matching shoe."

"True. And in Cian's case, he has her bracelet, she has a tattoo he seems to remember very well, and it wasn't a masquerade so he, you know, actually knows what she looks like," Hayden said.

"So, he's told you about her?"

"Yes." Cian told everyone about everything as far as Hayden could tell. He was an open book. "But Henry seems stumped."

"Cian still won't give up."

"It's romantic," Hayden said with a little sigh.

"Yeah." Colin was watching her with a funny expression.

They just stood there, not saying anything for a few heartbeats.

Then he said, "I'm doing this tonight."

He wasn't asking, he was telling. And she was definitely fine with it.

"Okay."

"Okay."

She turned and started for the stairs again.

He didn't stop her.

As Hayden shut the door to Fiona's old bedroom behind

her, crossed to the chair, and sank into it—it was even more comfortable than it looked—she sighed.

This house had everything she wanted in it. The dream bedroom, a gorgeous kitchen, a bunch of guys she'd love to be friends with, and a man that made her heart beat fast. And not just because he was gorgeous and had an Irish accent, but because he was an amazing cook, fantastic friend, was protective and growly, was sweet with the little girl that he'd helped raise, and because he made Hayden feel like she was very much all of those things he'd listed off as reasons Jonah wouldn't be able to help falling in love with her.

Her head fell back against the cushion behind her.

Nope, she never wanted to leave.

Yep, this was definitely the opposite of what she should be feeling right now.

"I'm surprised you're going along with this," Henry said to Colin.

"The primary priority is keeping our clients safe while they do what they want and need to do. If she's going to be a performer, we need to prove to her that we can keep her safe while she's performing. This is perfect. We can't keep her locked up in hiding at the first sign of a threat."

"So this is still about the job?" Henry asked.

"Of course. We can also get the photos we need to send to Carter to see if anyone in Bad recognizes anyone there tonight as men who've frequented Bad Brews during Hayden's shows there."

It was definitely partly about the job.

"It's solving the bigger problem, too," Jonah pointed out.

"It'll be good if we can get this guy to come out of the shadows. We need to deal with him."

Colin nodded. It was that too. It would be even easier if the guy would just step up and say, "Hey, it's me". They wouldn't need the damned photos then.

Of course, he wasn't going to share with the men how all of this was so much more.

Hell, he wasn't sure he was ready to admit to himself how much more this all was.

It *shouldn't* be. How he felt about Hayden was a complication. It was potentially a huge fucking problem.

But the idea of sitting in the bar as the backup while watching Jonah kiss, touch, and play her boyfriend had just been too much.

Fortunately, if he was too distracted to pay attention to any threats around her tonight, he knew these men—with Matt, Logan, and Gabe as additional back-up—would be alert and on top of things.

That was the kicker. He totally trusted these men. He put his trust in Jonah time after time. With his own safety. Even with Fiona and Saoirse's safety at times. Jonah had never let him down.

But with Hayden, *Colin* had to be the one taking care of her.

It wasn't just that the operation had to be right. It was *her*. If someone was going to make her feel safe, calm her, soothe her, put himself between her and danger, it was going to be Colin.

And, of course, if anyone was going to be kissing or touching her, it was going to be him.

But what she'd said in the foyer had rocked him.

I don't have a lot of experience being a girlfriend.

What did that mean? He had to know. If she was inexperienced and needed someone to lead her along, he sure as *hell* wasn't going to leave that to anyone else.

She'd also said she wasn't going to let anyone take performing away from her.

Damn right. He was going to do whatever was necessary to ensure that she was safe and confident when she was on that stage. If that's what she wanted, if that's what she *needed*, then he was going to make it happen.

Even before she'd told him that, he'd been willing to go along with the plan.

But when she'd said that, she'd flipped a switch inside him. No one was going to take any power away from Hayden Ross if he had anything to say about it.

And he had a lot to say about it.

"I'm going to go get a hold of Gabe and Logan and Matt," Colin said, moving toward the door.

"I can handle that," Henry said.

Colin didn't stop. No way was he going to have anyone else set things up for tonight. "I've got it."

"What about Saoirse?" Cian asked.

"She's up at the barns with Fiona," Colin said. Saoirse was fine. He wasn't needed anymore.

He tamped those feelings down quickly. She was with her mother. That was how it should be. If Colin was busy after her chores were finished, there were a dozen people she could hang out with. She'd rather be at the animal park anyway.

Hayden needed him more than Saoirse did.

He needed this job with Hayden *because* Saoirse didn't need him anymore.

This was where his focus should be.

And hell, he was going to get to kiss Hayden Ross tonight.

It was pretty fucking hard to feel bitter about anything with that thought in his head.

By the time they were outside next to the cars ready to leave for Trahan's four hours later, Colin had his plan in place.

It was exactly what needed to happen.

And it was possibly going to kill him.

"You guys go on ahead. Hayden and I need to talk. Besides, we shouldn't all show up at the same time."

Jonah and Cian nodded their agreement and got into Jonah's truck.

After they'd pulled out of the driveway, Colin turned to Hayden. "I thought we should go over how things will go tonight. Make sure we're on the same page."

She tucked her hands into her back pockets, and Colin could no longer ignore how she looked.

Fucking gorgeous.

She was in tight black jeans with black ankle-high boots that had a slight heel. She wore a shiny emerald green top that dipped just enough in the front to hint at cleavage when she stood still and more than hint when she moved in certain ways. Like when she'd bent over to tighten the strap on her boot. And when she'd bent over to pick up her purse.

When she'd bent over to pick up the lipstick she'd dropped, she'd been facing away from him, which solved the looking-down-her-blouse issue. It did not, however, solve the issue of how fantastic her ass looked in those jeans. Or the issue of him finding it impossible to look away. And how much he was looking forward to having an excuse to put his hands all over those curves.

Hayden took a deep breath as she waited for him to explain his plan for the evening, and he was distracted by the way the shiny top caressed her breasts.

He knew the top had tiny spaghetti straps, and the back

dipped low enough that it made him wonder what kind of bra she was wearing. Thankfully, she'd slipped into a short, fitted black leather jacket that covered most of her creamy bare skin, but that silky material still moved over her body as she twisted and bent and, hell, just breathed, in a way that made him want to touch.

He almost laughed out loud at that thought. As if he needed silky material sliding over her curves to make him want to touch.

"Am I supposed to be reading some kind of silent signals here? Because we're definitely going to need to practice those if so. I'm not getting anything," she said.

Well, it was probably good that she couldn't read all the things he was thinking. He shook his head. "No. Sorry. Was just...mentally going over a few things."

Like every curve and dip of her body.

"Okay, so what's the plan?"

Obviously, she was going to let him take the lead. Which was definitely how he preferred things. "First rule, we're going to have to act very close. Like we've been close for a while."

She nodded.

"Like we've been physically intimate," he said to emphasize his point.

She nodded again, seemingly not fazed. "Obviously."

"So we probably should go over some specifics."

"Specifics like what?"

"Like that I need...your consent." So that sounded awkward as fuck out loud.

But again, she barely hesitated. "You have it."

"I haven't even asked you for anything."

She took a step closer. "Colin, I completely trust you. Whatever you need to do, I'm in. You have my consent to do anything."

His body tightened in response to that. There were several things his cock thought he needed to do at least, and the idea of having her all in, just completely trusting him, letting him lead the way.... Jesus. This was dangerous. Having this woman's consent to do whatever he wanted to and with her was like a dream come true and a nightmare all rolled into one.

She. Was. A. Client.

Basically.

Just because she wasn't paying them at the moment, his responsibility was to keep her safe. And he was more or less on a job interview tonight, right?

He took a breath and attempted to pull his shit together. "Okay, that helps. You trusting me is really important. There might be moments where I can only give you instructions without explanation."

"I get that," she said. "I'll cooperate."

"And there might be times I have to just *do* something without any words at all. And...explain later."

She nodded. "Got it."

"So...is there anything you absolutely can't tolerate? Any triggers? Phobias?"

She lifted her brows. "Give me an example."

"Total darkness. Having your face covered. Certain smells. People touching your hair. Anything like that you can think of?"

Hayden was staring at him, but Colin could tell it was not in fear, but fascination. He was grateful that she seemed to be carefully considering what he'd asked. Finally, she shook her head. "I honestly can't think of anything."

"Are you allergic to anything?"

"No. Not that I'm aware of."

"Is there anywhere you don't want me to touch you?"

She didn't even think about that one. "No."

Again, his body reacted. He stubbornly focused on the conversation. "You're sure? No spots that are off-limits? Anywhere you're ticklish?"

"No. I mean, I'm a little ticklish. Like anyone. But there's nowhere that I don't want you to touch me."

His pulse hammered in his veins. He moved in closer. She was going to have to get used to him being close to her. Very close. And this would help emphasize what he was asking about and help him gauge her reactions. He needed to be *sure*. She might be trying to spare his feelings, or she really might not be aware of things that might, in the moment, make her uncomfortable.

"I have to play your boyfriend tonight. Someone who knows you well and who's been close to you. Naked with you. Who's seen and touched and tasted you," he said, letting his voice drop. It wasn't intentional, but he didn't fight it when his voice got husky. "If I touch you and you stiffen up, reflexively pull away, act skittish, and he's watching, he'll notice."

She didn't lean away. In fact, she stepped closer. "Colin, I honestly can't think of a single place where you could touch me that I wouldn't like it."

Damn. His whole body went hot and hard. His chest felt tight. "Hayden," his voice had dropped lower. "You shouldn't say stuff like that."

She frowned slightly. "I shouldn't tell the truth? You're asking me questions, and I'm giving you the answers. I feel completely safe with you. And I'm attracted to you. I realize that we're going to be playing roles tonight, but the idea of you touching me absolutely does not offend me, scare me, or repulse me in *any* way."

He took a step closer. He was now practically on top of her. They were breathing the same air. Air that was heated by both of their bodies. He wasn't touching her, but he might as well have been. He was aware of every breath she took, and that those breaths were a little more uneven than they had been just a moment before, and that they moved that damned silky green material enticingly over her breasts. Her cheeks were pinker than they'd been a moment before as well, and the flush was spreading over the pale skin above her breasts.

He lifted a hand, and with just his index finger, he traced the v at the base of her throat. "I think we need to be *sure*."

Her tongue darted out and wet her lips. "Okay," she said softly.

"If I kiss you in public and it's like kissing your brother, we should know ahead of time," he said, his voice low. "In case we have to act our way through it. It's good to know what to expect."

"That makes total sense," she said. "And we're going to have to do more than kiss in public, right?"

Holy shit, this was a bad idea. But he asked, "What did you have in mind?"

"I mean, I'd expect a boyfriend that's...how did you put it?...seen, touched, and tasted me..."

Colin's cock pressed against his zipper, totally into this conversation.

"...would at least have his hands on me in a bar, right? His hand up under the back of my shirt, his hands in my hair, hand on my ass, that kind of stuff."

He lifted a brow. "You sound like you have some experience." And he wanted to kill every single one of the guys who'd ever touched any part of this woman.

Yeah, he was doing a great job being totally professional.

And they hadn't even left the driveway.

She laughed lightly. "I've spent time in *a lot* of bars, looking out over crowds of people from the stage."

His brows pulled together now. "You *haven't* had a man's hands all over you in a bar?"

She shook her head. "Not like that. I've had a couple of boyfriends who were really nice and touched me in private. And a couple of dates who got a little handsy while we were out, but I wasn't attracted, so it was creepy, and I pushed them away. Never a guy who I *wanted* to touch me, who was also so into me he couldn't keep his hands to himself in public."

Colin felt his body move into hers without even thinking about it. He backed her up against his truck. "That's the craziest fucking thing I've ever heard."

She laughed breathlessly, her hands coming up to his chest instinctively as his palms settled on her hips. But she wasn't pushing him away.

"It is?" she asked.

"A guy was given permission to get this close to you and he *didn't* put his hands on you? You've been with some real idiots, Ms. Ross."

The smile she gave him was bright and sweet...but there was a mischievous, sexy-as-hell edge to it that had Colin groaning inwardly. He'd just given her an admission that she could use against him.

He really hoped she would.

"Maybe," she said. "Or maybe it's not as fun as it looks."

His gaze dropped to her mouth. Oh, it was definitely going to be fun. Like never-get-over-it fun. "I think how fun public displays of affection are depend a lot on how fun the *private* displays of affection are," he said.

He was very aware that his hands were still resting on her hips and that hers were on his chest. They were belly to belly, and he felt every inch of his body straining to be against every inch of hers.

Now her gaze was on *his* mouth. "That makes sense."

"The fun of the public stuff is the teasing and tempting, the barely holding back, knowing it can only go so far. And remembering other times when it went further." He lifted one hand and stroked it over her hair from the crown of her head to the ends where the waves fell against the middle of her back. "And working up to later, when it can go further again."

Her hair was silky and warm, the way he'd imagine the fabric of her shirt would be if he ran his hand over it, rubbing it against her skin. He slid his hand up under her hair, threading his fingers into the thickness at the base of her skull, resting his palm against her head. Then he tipped her head back slightly, meeting her eyes.

"Knowing that even though you have to be good at the moment, someone is thinking about how bad he can make you, how much he wants you, how gorgeous and sexy you are every minute you're together, and even when he's doing something as simple as having a drink, or a conversation with someone else, or listening to music, or walking down a damned street, you're on his mind, teasing and tempting him." He squeezed her hip and leaned into her, pressing his cock against her.

He enjoyed her little gasp far too much.

"And every touch. Every kiss—" He leaned in, coasting his lips over her jaw. "Every dirty word—" His lips trailed over her cheek to her ear. "—is just worshipping you over the course of hours the way you deserve because when he has you alone, naked, in his bed, he can't possibly slow down and take enough time because he wants you too damned much."

"Holy. Crap," she whispered.

Then he had to kiss her.

It was for the job.

He turned his head and captured her lips.

And the second she sighed and arched closer, her fists

clutching at the front of his shirt, he went ahead and admitted that was a total fucking lie.

His hand moved from her hip to her ass, where he gratefully, *finally*, squeezed and brought her up more firmly against his aching cock.

God, she felt amazing.

Her arms stole around his neck, and she went up on tiptoe to get closer. Their tongues stroked, the kiss hot and deep almost immediately.

She ran her hands from his neck to his shoulders to his back, dragging her fingertips down the muscles on either side of his spine. She gave a little moan and then her hands dipped under the bottom edge of his shirt. Her hot hands connected with his bare skin, and he gave a low growl. As she stroked up his ribs on either side, Colin lost his hold on the tiny shred of control he'd been clinging to.

He pulled his hands from her ass and hair, shoving the jacket off her shoulders. She moved her hands only long enough to let it drop to the ground before returning them to his abs. His muscles jumped under her touch as she stroked them. She moaned into his mouth as she ran her fingertips over the ridges.

His hand stole under the bottom edge of her shirt in the back, stroking up the smooth, silky skin. He encountered the strap of a bra, answering that question. He followed the slip of fabric up over her shoulder, then hooked a finger under what turned out to be a clear bra strap. Taking it and the strap of her top with it, he pulled them down her shoulder as his mouth moved along her jaw, down her neck, over her shoulder, then to the now exposed upper curve of her breast.

Her skin was so fucking soft. She smelled amazing. And he wanted to scoop her up, feel her legs clamp around his waist, settling her hot center against his cock, as he carried her back inside.

Or he could just press her into the side of his truck.

He just needed to be *against* her. Around her. Inside her.

Fuck...wherever they were going. He didn't remember at the moment. And he sure as hell didn't care.

"God, Hayden, you taste so good. Feel so good."

"Same," she said breathlessly, letting her head fall back. Her long hair brushed the back of his other hand where he held her.

That hand stole around her waist and up to cup her breast as he dragged his lips across her collarbone. He cupped her breast, his thumb running across the nipple that was hard behind the silky green material that had been taunting him. Yep, it moved deliciously across her skin, just as he'd imagined.

"Colin," she gasped.

He could listen to that over and over again.

She was gripping the waistband of his jeans now as if that was all that was holding her up.

"You're so fucking sweet," he growled against the front of her throat. "I want to taste every inch of you. I'll bet it gets even sweeter from here."

"God. I—"

She was interrupted by the shrill sound of her cell phone ringing.

Colin jerked back, lifting his head.

Reality crashed back in as the phone rang again. He sucked in a deep breath as their hands fell away from each other's bodies.

She stared up at him, breathing hard, her eyes wide.

"Sorry," he bit out.

"You better not be." She gave him a frown as she bent to pick up her purse and dug for her phone. "What?" she asked whoever was on the other end. She paused. "Yes. Just running a little behind." She paused again and met Colin's gaze. "We're on our way."

Colin shoved a hand through his hair. "Fuck," he said, at a loss for any other appropriate response. She'd said he'd better not be sorry.

And looking at her now, her hair tousled from his fingers, her lips pink from his kisses, her slipping her straps back into place from where he'd pulled them down, he felt...not sorry.

"What are you upset about?" she asked, returning her phone to her purse. She bent to pick up her jacket and slipped it back on, then ran her fingers through her hair.

"That got a little out of hand."

"We established ahead of time that you have my consent. We were preparing for tonight." She met his gaze directly. "And I think it's safe to say that I'm not going to be pulling away or flinching when you get close tonight."

Damn, he liked her. The thought seemed to come out of nowhere. It wasn't a startling revelation. He wasn't surprised. It was just an odd moment for it to hit him. She looked sexy as fuck. Her hair was still mussed, her lipstick was smudged, her cheeks were flushed, and her nipples were still hard behind that damned thin silky green top.

But in addition to how much he *wanted* her, yeah, he liked this woman a lot.

"Yeah, I think we're going to be okay," he finally said.

She gave him a little smile. "Do you think it will add to the effect if you're wearing my lipstick, or do you want to wipe that off?"

She also wasn't embarrassed by what had just happened. That was good. Because what just happened...was definitely going to happen again.

eight

THE FIRST TIME Hayden had ever gotten on stage to sing, it had felt purely selfish. She'd gotten up at a high school talent show. She hadn't been on the list. She'd been at the show because her little sister had been performing a dance number with three of her friends and Hayden had helped them with their costumes.

The contest was being held on the same stage where all three of her siblings had received several awards. It was where her older brother, Jake, had sat behind a table with their parents flanking him and signed his college commitment to play baseball at LSU, his dream school.

Her parents had been there. Her grandparents had been there. Her siblings had been there. And she'd just thought *fuck it*.

She'd walked out from behind the curtain during a lull between contestants due to an issue with a couple of trained cats, headed straight for the microphone, and launched into an acapella version of "Fallin'" by Alicia Keyes.

The place had been silent when she'd finished. Stunned. Amazed.

Then they'd applauded. Loudly.

Afterward, many people had gushed about how good she'd been.

Her family had assumed she'd been asked to fill in the gap while the errant cats were rounded up.

Still, it had felt pretty good.

Now, every time she got on stage, she felt like she was sneaking up there. Like maybe everyone was showing up for the cats, but they were also going to accidentally hear her and maybe be delightfully surprised.

And then...every time magic happened. Not only did she get to stay for more than one number, but she looked out over the audience and did not see stunned expressions. She saw happy, excited faces who were smiling and singing along. And afterward people did come up to her. And they didn't say things like, "I had no idea you could sing," or "thanks for helping out like that," or "your sister's costume was so pretty!" Instead, they said, "you're amazing!" and "I love your stuff," and "can I have your autograph?"

Over the last eight months, people had started showing up *to see her* on purpose.

Most of the people who came to see her perform didn't even know she had siblings.

Sure, a few of them had Googled her and knew that her brother Jake was in the minors and the twins played for their colleges and Jared was on the brink of breaking the records Jake had set, but people didn't show up to hear her sing because of Jake or Jared.

It turned out that *her music* helped other people. It made them smile. It helped them escape for a minute, or an evening. Maybe it made them think of a happier time and remember something good. Maybe it gave them the courage to ask someone to dance. Maybe it just gave them a minute to feel a part of something, connected to other people, whether it was friends or strangers.

When Sabrina Sterling had first approached Hayden after hearing her sing on a French Quarter street corner and asked if she could buy Hayden a cup of coffee, Hayden had felt a swoop of butterflies in her stomach.

Sabrina had approached her, on purpose, while Hayden had been singing.

Sabrina had been walking by with her husband. Hayden had noticed them. She'd always looked around, noticed the people who watched her even if they didn't stop, definitely noticed those who did stop, and remembered those who stayed for more than one song and who chatted with her for a bit. Sabrina had been walking by, had stopped, stared, crossed the street, and stayed for five songs.

Hayden had also taken note of the way Sabrina's husband had watched her—with a loving, slightly bemused expression, standing back and just coming along for coffee, but not saying much.

And after only twenty minutes of talking, Hayden had known she'd found a soulmate of sorts in Sabrina Sterling.

Then Sabrina had introduced Hayden to more musicians. Like the Locals, the band Sabrina performed with—not coincidentally—locally, and James Reynaud, a New Orleans firefighter who moonlighted as a jazz pianist. He played with one band in particular on weekends, and they'd been happy to let Hayden sing with them whenever she wanted to.

The chemistry with all of them had been immediate and she'd been performing in Bad with Sabrina and with James in New Orleans regularly ever since.

James and the guys were with her tonight at Trahan's, and it was a thrill as usual. Her skin felt tingly, her blood was pumping, and her heart felt bigger in her chest.

But it was all amplified tonight. Like everything had been turned up several notches.

Because Colin Daly was across the room, leaning on the bar, a glass of something forgotten by his elbow, his dark eyes on her as if he couldn't look away.

When he'd walked out of the house dressed in black boots, jeans, and a fitted black t-shirt instead of his usual button-downs, she'd been afraid her tongue was hanging out. She knew the outfit was supposed to look "casual" and un-body-guard-like.

But Colin Daly pulling off casual was like asking a panther to look like a golden retriever. A panther might be able to lounge around in the sun, but it would never be able to get rid of that I'm-the-top-of-the-food-chain air.

It was really no wonder she'd kissed him like he was a giant piece of chocolate cheesecake, and she hadn't eaten in a month.

The man looked that delicious. He also felt, smelled, and sounded that delicious.

Yeah, she'd tasted Colin Daly.

Maybe not in all the ways that wonderfully dirty phrase sounded but she'd gotten a taste, and she wanted more.

And now, with the adrenaline of performing rushing through her, Hayden felt the most intense high she'd ever felt performing. And that included when she'd been on the big stage in New Orleans with Jason Young.

She could only imagine what sex with Colin could do if just kissing him made her feel like this.

She would really like to find out.

Sure, this was kind of a job to him. She'd basically pushed herself onto him by showing up on his porch. He was a friend of a friend or the boss of a friend or something.

But nothing about that driveway kiss had felt fake or like

he was doing a job. He hadn't been forced to kiss her. Sure, they'd been talking about how that would help their whole role-playing tonight, but it had escalated quickly.

She wasn't the most experienced when it came to men. She was the first to admit that. But there was no faking all of that. If Colin went around kissing all women like that, the streets of Autre, Louisiana, would be lined with women's panties.

That, of course, made her wonder about the other women Colin had been with, which made her frown. Not what she should be doing while waiting to start the next song.

She pushed all of that away, mostly, and focused on her bandmates.

"You sound amazing tonight," James told her, handing her another water bottle to replace the one she'd emptied during the first set.

"Thanks. I feel good tonight."

James laughed. "Yeah. I noticed."

She gave him a look. "What's that mean?"

"Um, I've noticed Mr. Feel Good Tonight watching you. As has everyone else in this bar," James said, inclining his head toward where Colin was leaning on the bar.

Cian was sitting on a stool just to Colin's left but Colin never looked at the other man, even when they spoke. Jonah had chosen a table across the room, near the front doors.

They'd called Colin while he and Hayden were in the truck still driving to New Orleans. Jonah and Cian had decided to arrive at the bar separately, parking several blocks away and walking from different directions, pretending not to be together. That way Jonah could observe the room from another angle.

Their friend Matt was behind the bar. He was a friend of the Trahans, and Logan and Gabe had no trouble letting him help serve drinks. It gave Matt a chance to interact with most of the patrons, especially any single guys or even small groups of guys, they decided.

Logan, Gabe, and James had also been given the heads up about Hayden having a not-welcome admirer that might show up tonight, so they were keeping their eyes on the crowd as well.

"Come on," she said with a laugh. "He's not *that* noticeable."

"Uh, Hayden, that guy is making it very clear to everyone else that you are very taken."

She looked over at Colin again. "You think so?"

James laughed. "As one of the men in the room, I promise you, his vibes are very don't-even-think-about-it."

"You're married."

"Colin doesn't care. He's covering his bases."

She lowered her voice. "You know he's just faking it. My secret admirer brought a teddy bear to my apartment. Creeped me out. Colin is trying to convince him I have a boyfriend, so he backs off."

"Fuck," James said, with a frown. "They said you had a guy giving you too much attention. I didn't know he'd showed up at your place."

She nodded.

"You know I'm just a phone call away, right? Even if I'm on duty, call. I'll come or send someone."

She smiled. She did know that, actually. James was awesome. She also wouldn't hesitate to call the police. She was *not* shy about getting help. "You're the best."

He frowned. "Well, I mean it." He glanced over at Colin. "And, uh...how do you feel about *him*?"

"Colin? Um, I feel..." She could feel her cheeks heating. "Um." She wet her lips. "Fine. I feel fine about him."

James grinned and gave her a wink, clearly reading more than "fine" in her answer. "Good. Because he's not faking."

"But...he is."

"No. I mean, he's putting it out there for everyone for a purpose maybe, but that she's-mine stuff? That's real. Trust me." James tapped her on the end of her nose. "And it's about time someone made you look like that."

Hayden lifted a hand to her cheek. "Like what?"

"Like you want to be his." James winked at her again, then moved back to his piano as the rest of the band started taking their places.

Hayden looked back at Colin. His gaze was still on her. And she *felt it*. Not just the weight of his stare, but the *she's mine*.

Damn.

She pressed a hand against her stomach.

Yeah, she wanted that.

But first, she had to somehow remember how to sing songs that she'd sung easily a hundred times each.

"Show time," Jonah said in her ear.

"Yep," was Colin's simple reply.

The guys had given her an earpiece too, so she could follow any instructions they needed to give her. Of course, she hadn't put it in until she was leaving the stage.

But now "the show" was moving from the stage to the main part of the bar. They were going to really put this fake-boyfriend thing to the test.

The butterflies kicked up in Hayden's stomach and she took a deep breath as she headed toward Colin and Cian.

"Great show," Cian said with a grin, sliding off his stool to give her a hug.

"Thanks." She squeezed him back.

Colin didn't move.

"Hey." She gave him a smile and then greeted Matt with a smile as well as he pushed a glass of water and her usual post-performance shot across the bar.

She gave them all a little toast, then tipped it back, swallowing the very strong shot that tasted like orange and reminded her of her grandpa. She opened her water bottle, then turned to Colin as she lifted it.

But the bottle didn't even meet her lips.

Colin's hand was on the back of her hair, but instead of his fingers in her hair like in the driveway, this time he simply gathered her hair in his fist in a sort of ponytail, tipped her head back, and covered her mouth with his.

She melted into the kiss. She'd wanted his mouth back on hers ever since he'd pulled away in the driveway.

He kissed her thoroughly. There wasn't a single person in the bar who would've thought they were just friends. His tongue licked along her bottom lip, and she gave a small moan that only he would've heard. Or maybe in the noisy room he just felt it.

Her hand gripped his bicep and allowed her to press closer. She opened her mouth under his, and his tongue slid against hers. She could taste the whiskey he'd been drinking, though she was sure that he'd only been sipping and that he was fully sober.

After a few seconds, she heard Jonah in her ear. "Okay, we've got the point."

Colin lifted his head, staring down at her. "Orange," he said huskily.

She nodded. "Grand Marnier and tequila. It's called an Alice in Wonderland here."

"Why that shot?" He still hadn't let go of her.

140

"My grandpa. He always drank Grand Marnier. When I was a kid, he'd give me orange soda to drink with him. Reminds me of him."

Colin's gaze dropped to her mouth. He leaned in and kissed her again, this time softly. But his tongue stroked over her lips again before he lifted his head. "Delicious."

Hayden felt the warm tingles rush from her head to her toes. Of course, there were certain areas in between where they settled in particular. This guy was potent. Far more so than any shot anyone could have mixed up behind the bar.

"Okay, so we've been watching everyone in here tonight. There are a few guys who've been here the whole time. All of them, of course, mesmerized by Hayden," Jonah said in their ears.

"Maybe one more than everyone else," Cian's dry reply came.

Colin didn't even blink. One corner of his mouth tipped up. "I'm good at my job."

There were soft snorts in the earpieces and she smiled as well. She liked the idea that maybe not all of this was fake.

Part of it was what James had said. He didn't know Colin, hadn't seen them interact before tonight in the bar, yet he sensed something between them, even from across the room. She loved that.

Was she a romantic? Yes. Did she like the idea that she and Colin had stumbled across each other's paths but had chemistry that was too much to ignore? Yes. Was she totally fine with this particular set of circumstances throwing them together and that something deeper would develop from it? Also yes.

One thing she knew for sure about life, you never knew what curveballs were coming. You had to be ready to roll with it and adjust on the fly. If Colin Daly was a curveball in her life, she was very ready to adjust.

She cuddled closer to him. Hey, a girl would have to be crazy to not want to be up against this guy, and she had a very good excuse. He didn't move back, of course. They'd practiced being close to one another, so neither of them would flinch or stiffen. She slid her arm around his waist, and his arm draped over her shoulders. She lifted her water bottle to her lips and took a long drink. "Now what?" she asked after she'd swallowed.

The question wasn't for anyone in particular.

"Now you and Colin keep that up, and we see who reacts," Matt said. He was behind them but was washing glasses, not looking at them.

"I'm taking photos," Jonah said.

"We've also got video running on the security system," Matt said. "We can review it later."

Hayden focused on Colin since there was nowhere she'd rather look.

"What did you think of the show?"

"You are sexy as fuck, and if there's anybody in here who doesn't want you, I'd be shocked," he said easily.

She looked at him in surprise. "Really?"

"If the guy who's following you *is* here, he's going to want to get close to you. And seeing you here with another guy is absolutely going to work." He didn't seem happy, in spite of that being the exact plan for the night. "So we're going to cuddle for a little bit and then I'm going to leave you alone. We're going to see if anyone approaches."

"Leave me alone?" she asked, her fingers fisting his shirt at his side. "I don't want you to leave me alone."

She meant that on a number of levels. She wanted to stay

close to Colin. She also did *not* want to be unprotected in this bar.

"Just for a few minutes. I'll go to the bathroom or something." Again, he did not look happy.

"We've got your back," Jonah said. "There's nothing to worry about. Just stay close to the bar where Matt is."

"Hey, I'm here too," Cian said from his stool.

"Yeah, I know," Jonah said placatingly.

Hayden knew that Matt had been special forces in the Army. He could probably kill a guy just by looking at him. Still, it was Colin that she wanted close. She tightened her arm around him. "Can't we do this another way?"

He stroked his hand down her back. "Wish we could. But the sooner we get him front and center the better." His hand continued down her back until it rested on her butt. He gave her a little squeeze. "Though there are some definite perks to dragging this out."

He was trying to lighten the tone. She looked up at him with a smile, letting him. In part because she appreciated it. And, in part because she sensed that Colin Daly was not exactly the comic relief in typical circumstances, and she enjoyed the effort.

"Agreed," she told him. "If the guy doesn't show up tonight, we should probably keep doing this."

"Actually, we will *have to* keep doing this if he doesn't show up," Jonah said.

The flirting with the other guys listening was a little disconcerting. Still, Hayden said, "Or I mean, I guess we could do it even if he does show up."

She felt Colin's hand squeeze again. That was at least something the other guys wouldn't know about.

"I'd love to see you perform again," he said.

Yeah, she hadn't been talking about him watching her perform. But he knew that.

"Well, I guess if there's a chance this is the only night for this, then I should take advantage of it," she said, turning to face him fully.

For just a second, he looked puzzled. But then she put a hand on the back of his neck and pulled him down. His mouth covered hers without hesitation. Maybe he felt the same way. This was a very good excuse to kiss one another, and neither of them had to come up with any kind of reasoning.

"Damn, I like a girl who can be direct," Cian said in their ears.

Hayden ignored him. Colin, thankfully, did as well. His hands went to her hips, bringing her up against him, and he deepened the kiss. Tongues tangled, and her hand slid under the back edge of his shirt and onto the hard, hot, bare muscles of his back. She loved the way they bunched under her touch.

Jonah cleared his throat in their earpieces. "We need to move this along."

"Don't want him to get antsy," Matt agreed. "But I hate to interrupt."

Colin lifted his head but seemed reluctant. He looked at her for a long moment. "Okay. Just a few minutes," he said. She could tell he was trying to be reassuring. He brushed her hair back away from her face and tucked a strand behind her ear. "You'll be okay. We've got you."

Looking into his eyes, she felt completely confident. These men would do whatever was required to protect her. Particularly this one. There was something about the way Colin looked at her that made her feel...treasured. She truly felt as if he would do absolutely anything it took to keep her safe.

She wet her lips, then nodded. "Okay. What do I do?"

"Stay here. Matt can get you another drink. Just wait for

me. Talk to whoever comes up to you. Be normal, approachable, friendly. No reason to be suspicious of anyone. We don't know if he's even here. The guys will watch every interaction. If anything seems off, Matt is right there."

She nodded. "Got it."

He reached up and cupped her face and leaned in to kiss her one more time. It was sweet and hot. She wanted so many more of those.

"Be right back," he said softly.

He stepped away and moved around the edge of the bar toward the back of the room where the restrooms were located.

Hayden took a breath and looked at Matt. "Rum and Coke," she said. "Please."

"You got it." He mixed the drink and slid the glass to her.

She took a sip. It was very light on the rum, and she appreciated it.

It only took twenty seconds for someone to come up to her.

"Excuse me," the man said.

She turned. The guy had dark hair and was clean shaven. He was probably in his early thirties. He didn't look familiar to her at all. "Hi."

"Hi," he laughed nervously. "I just wanted to say I really enjoyed your performance. I didn't think your boyfriend would appreciate me saying that, so I wanted to come over while he was gone."

She smiled. "Thanks. I appreciate that. Have you heard me perform before?"

"Yeah. I heard you with Jason Young. I went to the show because of him," the guy confessed, looking a little sheepish.

She laughed. "That's okay. That's the point of being an opening act. You hope to get discovered by new people who've come for the main act."

"Well, it worked," he said. "I looked you up afterward and have watched a lot of your stuff online since then. But this is *really* cool seeing you in a smaller place. I didn't know you'd be here tonight."

She studied him. She couldn't tell if he was lying or not. But he said it very easily and naturally. She'd let the other guys worry about if he seemed genuine or not. "Well, that's amazing. Thanks a lot."

"You bet. Look forward to seeing you again sometime."

"What's your name?" she asked quickly as he turned to leave.

"Oh. Casey."

"Hi, Casey." She put her hand out. "I'm Hayden."

"Yeah, I know." He laughed but took her hand.

He moved off without even asking for an autograph. Again, she didn't know if that was strange or not.

She looked at Matt, but he failed to make eye contact with her.

Right. They weren't in cahoots.

She picked up her glass and took a longer drink this time.

"Ms. Ross?" This time it was a woman's voice.

Hayden turned to find a woman and two guys smiling nervously. "Hi."

"Oh my God, hi. It's so nice to meet you. I mean, is that okay? Is it okay to come talk to you?"

Hayden laughed and nodded. "Totally okay. Thanks for coming over."

"I'm a huge fan. I was so excited when I saw you were going to be here tonight," the girl gushed. The guys were standing behind her. Not exactly bored, but not engaged. "I follow you all over social media."

Hayden had posted on her social media that she'd be at Trahan's a few days ago. Before the teddy bear incident. She hadn't updated anything today so this girl would have had to make a note of it and remember. That was nice.

"You've seen me before?" Hayden asked. Was she being too forward?

"Tons of times. I've seen you down in Bad a few times. One of my friends is from a town near there and she's a huge fan of Jason Young's and she got hooked on Sabrina Sterling and The Locals, and then you. She showed me some of your stuff and now we go to Bad whenever you perform." The girl tucked her hair behind her ear, giggling nervously. "I've just never been brave enough to come up to you before. But Brody said I totally should." She shot a glance at one of the guys with her. "My friend, Annie, will be *so* jealous."

Hayden appreciated her enthusiasm. "Well, I'm so glad you came over." She smiled at Brody. "Thanks for talking her into it." He blushed slightly. Hayden reached for two napkins and grabbed a pen lying on top of a credit card receipt Matt hadn't collected yet. She scrawled her name across both napkins and handed them to the girl. "Give one to Annie. And thanks for following me."

The girl's eyes got huge as she clutched the napkins into her chest. "Oh my God. Thank you so much."

"What's *your* name?"

"Stacy. And this is Brody and Charlie."

"Nice to meet you guys."

Brody blushed again and gave her a smile and a, "thanks, you too". But Charlie clearly didn't care at all.

"Okay, well, we'll see you. Thanks again," Stacy said, almost tripping over her feet as she turned to leave.

Hayden felt her nerves settle a little. And she reached for her water this time.

"Hi, Hayden."

She turned. This guy looked vaguely familiar. "Hi."

"Great show. I love when you cover Miranda Lambert."

She straightened slightly. She often covered Miranda but not at every show. And she hadn't done a Miranda cover at the Jason Young concert. "You've seen my show before?"

"Of course. I'm huge fan."

"Thank you. I appreciate it."

"My name's Dan." The man moved a little closer. "Can I buy you a drink?"

Had he not seen her with Colin? Or did he just not care?

"Oh boy. Here we go," Cian said in her ear.

"You think this is him?" Jonah asked.

"I have no idea. But I was hoping somebody would ruffle Colin. He's not going to like this."

"Maybe we should get rid of him before Colin comes back." Jonah said.

"Please don't," Cian said.

"Actually, I'm here with someone," Hayden told Dan quickly, before Jonah could get involved.

Dan looked around. "I don't see anybody."

"He's just in the bathroom. Have you been here all night?" There was no way this guy had been here and not noticed Colin. Maybe he was fishing for information but there was also no way he could have mistaken Colin for anything other than her boyfriend.

"He should know better than to leave you alone," Dan said, moving even closer.

"Oh, fuck," Jonah said.

Matt moved closer to Hayden's end of the bar. Cian straightened slightly on his stool.

"Don't worry. He's around whenever I need him," Hayden said.

"But he hasn't been around much," Dan said. "I've never seen him with you before."

Okay, yeah, clearly Dan had been to more than just a few shows then. That was good information for the guys to have. She should keep Dan talking. Probably.

"You've been paying attention," Hayden worked to act friendly, even intrigued by Dan's interest. She propped an elbow on the bar and twirled a strand of hair around her finger.

"Of course. I saw you sing the very first time you ever performed in Bad."

"Really? Are you from there?"

"Nearby. Couldn't believe it when you walked through the door. Took my breath away."

That was a pretty good line. "You've never come over and talked to me before."

"I've never seen you here with a boyfriend before. I've seen you hang out with a few guys. I assumed they were either security, or just friends. Maybe part of your management."

"You couldn't talk to me when they were around?"

"I was traveling a lot for work. Wasn't really in the place where I could start a relationship. But I thought I had time."

Okay, that was pretty direct. He hadn't approached her because he wasn't in a place to start a *relationship*? Meaning that he thought they could have a relationship if he *had* approached her? But he hadn't been worried that she would have any other offers in the meantime. Nice.

"I see," she said, unsure what else she was supposed to say.

"Take it easy. Just be friendly. We're right here," Jonah said softly in her ear.

Hayden forced herself to take a deep breath. She really wished Colin would come back.

Then it occurred to her that he had to be overhearing all of this. He still had his earpiece in even if he was in another room.

She breathed deeply again. "Well, I'm glad you came to see

me tonight," she said to Dan. That was a comment that could be taken in a couple of ways. One, that she was just appreciating a fan's attention. But it was something a guy could take as an opening, too.

"I am too," Dan said. He leaned in. "So how about that drink?"

"It's not him, you guys," Jonah said.

Hayden worked to not react to that sudden statement.

"Henry just texted," Jonah continued. "He's been monitoring the email account. X just emailed a minute ago at the same time this guy was talking to her. Can't be him."

Hayden wasn't sure what to do with that information, exactly. So Dan wasn't the guy. But he was still obviously into her and trying to make a move here.

"Her answer's no."

Hayden almost sagged with relief when she heard Colin's voice behind her.

Dan straightened, frowning. "I didn't hear her say it."

Colin's body was against her back, his heat seeping into her. He put a big hand on the back of her neck.

"Hayden?" he said roughly. "Would you like to have a drink with this man?"

"No," she said. "I'm great with what I have."

Dan frowned at her. "Well, I'll be around, so when he moves on, let me know."

Colin kept his hand on her but stepped to her side. "What the fuck does that mean?"

"That I'm a true fan. I'm not just passing through."

Colin took the tiniest step forward and his voice was deep and low and menacing when he said, "You need to stop coming to her shows."

"Are you threatening me?"

"Aye, I am," Colin said calmly.

"You can't keep me from a public place."

"No. But I can make you regret going there."

Dan's eyes flickered to Hayden then back to Colin. "I don't think her followers would like knowing her boyfriend treated one of her true fans this way."

"I'm guessing most of them won't like that a fan is harassing her and talking trash about the guy who's obviously in love with her."

"Is that what they'll think?" Dan challenged.

Cian leaned in, waggling his phone. "I promise I can get to the fan forums faster than you can."

Dan scowled at him. "Whatever." Then he turned and stalked out of the bar.

Hayden watched him go. No one said anything for a few seconds. Then she looked up at Colin, "I think maybe that got a little out of hand."

He nodded. "Yeah."

That was it. Just a "yeah".

Cian chuckled. "I loved every second of it."

"You love that I have a stalker *and* now a guy who's going to go online and tell my fans that my boyfriend freaked out on him?"

"Freaked out on him?" Colin asked, turning back to the bar. He didn't, however, take his hand off of her. "Now *that's* over-stating."

"Well I mean, that wasn't freaking out compared to how some people do it," Cian agreed. "But for you? Mr. Calm and Cool? Mr. Decorum? You threatened a guy with bodily harm, just for wanting to buy Hayden a drink."

"I didn't specifically say bodily harm."

Cian laughed. "Okay. Still..."

"And he didn't just want to buy her a drink. He was calling

151

our relationship into question. Making it sound like I'm just messing around with her."

Hayden looked up at him. "You mean the fake relationship that literally just started a few hours ago? Yeah, how silly of him."

Colin looked down at her. "That doesn't mean we're just messing around."

Her eyes went wide.

Jonah cleared his throat. "Hello? Her *actual* stalker sent an email just a few minutes ago. Focus, people."

"What did it say?" Colin asked crossly.

He was studying the room, his hot, heavy hand still resting on the back of her neck, and Hayden loved having it there. Talking about the creep made her feel cold. Especially after Dan. He wasn't the guy, but he'd made it feel more real.

"He was obviously here tonight. Possibly still is. He knows what she's wearing, all the songs she sang and in what order, how many drinks she's had, and he knows she's with you," Jonah reported.

Colin moved in closer to her, though Hayden would've thought that was impossible. The press of his body against hers, positioning himself between her and the rest of the room, was incredibly comforting.

"We'll go over the surveillance tapes," Jonah said. "I'm guessing he's still here."

"Why is that?" Cian asked.

"He's feeling slighted. Hurt. Not angry," Jonah said. "He's probably still wanting to watch Hayden, be close to her. But he's intimidated by Colin. He's also feeling jealous and like this is all horribly unfair. He's given her all this attention, been loyal to her, has given her gifts. But she's here with someone else, rubbing it in his face."

Hayden chose not to study the room and left it to the guys.

Jonah spoke as if he had some kind of experience and training in profiling or something. This was way outside of her expertise.

But Dan's comment about her fans niggled. As did Cian's comment about getting to the fan forums first. She pulled out her phone and started scrolling through social media.

She searched for her name and found a few photos from the evening posted from inside Trahan's. There were selfies, as well as shots of her on stage. There were comments under the photos from people jealous of those at the show, people wishing they'd known about it, people saying things like *I love her* and *she looks gorgeous*, and *oh my God*.

Then there were photos from after the show. Photos of her kissing Colin.

She couldn't believe she hadn't thought of this before. Of course, there were fans in the building. Obviously. These weren't just people. These were *fans*. People who would notice her making out with a hot guy and *care*. God, she was so not used to being important to total strangers. It was so weird that people she didn't even know cared about her music, not to mention other things going on in her life.

There were far more of the photos of her with Colin than there were of the performance.

And she and Colin did look hot.

He was kissing her as if he was about to strip her clothes off and back her up against the wall.

These were candid photos, but the chemistry was dripping from them. She wanted to screenshot several of them herself. Underneath there were already hundreds of comments.

Oh my God, who is that?

Holy. Shit.

You go, girl.

Who's the guy?

And eggplant emojis, fire emojis, and lots of heart eyes.

But mostly eggplants.

There were also several with crying face emojis because they were hoping for her and Jason Young to get together. Never mind that Jason was engaged.

But yeah, *this* was how she would expect her fans to react when she *thought* about it. When she thought about how *she* felt as a fan. They would be happy. They would be curious. For sure, but they would think Colin was hot and be totally into her having a guy like that all over her.

So one comment in particular really stood out.

WHORE. In capital letters.

Also the username 128cb7. Not a person's name, no photo, just letters and numbers.

And that one word.

A few people had responded defending her, but the person had not posted any further.

Hayden went through and clicked the heart on several of the comments. She responded to a couple with simple heart eyes and a few teasing remarks like *it's going to be a good weekend* and *oops, forgot we were in public.*

But under the *WHORE* comment, she wrote a little more.

If you mean I'm easy for him, yeah, guess so. I swear, as soon as he said my name, I was a goner.

She wasn't lying. When Colin had her pinned to the ground in the front yard and said her name, she'd felt the butterflies. That had been the beginning of her trusting him, liking him, wanting him.

If you want something to happen, you have to make it happen. She finished the comment and hit send.

She took a deep breath.

Just last night she'd been scared and worried. Now she was feeling confident and ready to face this guy.

Colin, Jonah, Matt, Henry, and Cian were definitely doing their jobs. They were making her feel safe. She was going about her usual activities with confidence because they had her back. And she was ready to end this thing with X. He was messing with her emotions, her routine, her *life*. If he was here, she wanted him to come up to her.

No more of this hiding, sending her emails signed X, using usernames that were just letters and numbers.

This was bullshit.

If he was mad, jealous, whatever, he didn't get to hide in the shadows and call her a whore.

He could walk up to her in this bar like Dan had done, like Stacy had done, like Casey had done. Sure, Dan had gotten shot down, but he'd tried.

Okay, he'd gotten physically threatened too, but still...

If X wanted her attention, he needed to come and get it.

nine

THE CREEP'S reply came in under a minute.

Wow, that really is easy. He just has to say your name and you fuck him? Nice.

Okay, so her comment could have been worded better.

Well, have YOU ever actually said anything to me? she replied. She needed to push this guy and find out what she could about him.

Him: *I've said a lot. You know me well.*

Hayden: *No one I know well would call me a whore.*

Him: *Maybe I shouldn't have said that.*

Hayden: *Maybe you should apologize. The next time you see me. In person. Not behind a keyboard.*

"Hayden, stop," Jonah said in her ear.

"What's going on?" Colin immediately shifted, looking down at her.

"She's talking with him online. In the comments on a forum."

Colin was suddenly in her face. "Now?"

She nodded. "If he's here, I want him to show himself."

Colin studied her for a long moment. "Do you think he is?"

"This is the easiest way to find out. But you need to give me some space."

It was clear he didn't like it. But after a moment, he nodded. "Go to the restroom. Maybe he'll follow."

"Colin—" Jonah started.

"We'll be right here," Colin said. "But she can call some shots."

Wow. She appreciated that.

"Dammit," Jonah muttered.

"Do you actually want to talk to this guy?" Cian asked her.

"Yes. I want to get a look at him. I want to know who he is," she said, irritated. "I hate how he's making me feel. I want this done."

"No one in the room is giving me vibes," Matt said. "There are people on their phones, but none of the guys seem especially agitated or anything."

"Agreed," Jonah said.

"All the more reason to see if I can get him to come to me," Hayden said. She met Colin's eyes. "You need to be out of the way."

He nodded.

"But I want you close."

His eyes flared with a mix of emotions. He nodded again.

"Tell me what to do," she said.

There was definite heat in his gaze as he squeezed her neck, then dropped his hand. He lowered his head, closer to her ear. "I'm going out the front. When I'm sure he's not following me, I'll go around back, come in through the kitchen, and go into the women's restroom. I'll be in one of the stalls. You come in. We'll see if he follows you."

"I'll..." She felt her cheeks burning.

"What?"

"I just..." She leaned in closer to Colin. "I do actually need to pee." Then she realized even whispering to him, the other guys could hear in the earpieces.

He cupped her cheek with a small smile. "You don't have to come into the same stall with me."

"But you'll...hear."

He kissed her mouth, hard and hot. "It'll be okay."

She believed him. Even about stupid things like peeing with him in the stall next to her. She shook her head. She was really gone for this guy. That could end up being a problem. But at the moment she had other things to focus on. She took a deep breath and slid off the stool as Colin backed up.

"See you soon," he said.

She nodded.

He turned and headed for the front of the restaurant, stepping out onto the sidewalk, and turning left, the direction he'd have to go to get back to the car. If X had been watching or following them, he would know that.

Now Hayden had to assume that whoever he was, he'd be watching her, not Colin. She smoothed her hands down the front of her shirt, then tipped back the rest of her drink, and returned the glass to the bar. "Thanks. I guess we're heading out," she said to Matt.

"No problem, Ms. Ross. We've got your tab covered."

"Thanks." She knew Matt didn't mean that just her tab was covered.

Her back was covered.

She was going to be fine.

"I'm here," Colin said in her earpiece.

She let out a breath. "Good."

She started for the bathrooms. She stepped through the doorway that led to the back hallway. To the right was the kitchen. To the left were the two restrooms and then, at the end of the hallway that was only about a hundred feet long, a door led out to a back alleyway.

"Hey," she said softly as she stepped inside the ladies' room.

"Hey," Colin replied, amusement in his tone.

He was in the last stall, closest to the wall and window.

She slid into the first stall, putting two between them, shutting and locking the door behind her.

There was a pause. "You can go," he said. It sounded like he was trying not to laugh.

She let out a little chuckle. "God. This embarrassing."

"Yeah. Sometimes this work isn't glamorous. I was thinking though, you could sing while you go."

She laughed. "That's a good idea actually."

"Hayden," he said as she lifted her shirt to reach for the button on her jeans.

"Yeah?"

"Take your earpiece out. The other guys don't need to hear."

She blushed hotly. No, Jonah, Cian, and Matt did not need to hear the sound of her peeing.

She pulled the earpiece out, flipped the little switch on the side, then stuffed it into her pocket. She started humming as she pushed her pants down. Then she sat and launched into an acapella version of Kelsea Ballerini's "Hole in the Bottle".

She heard Colin chuckle. She had no idea if he actually knew the song, but the lyrics were funny even if this was the first time he'd heard them. And the acoustics in here were great.

She finished and flushed, pulling her clothes back into place, but kept singing even as she stepped out into the main part of the bathroom and washed her hands.

She finished the song and waited a few seconds. "Okay, now what?" she asked.

"You wait a little bit. Check your makeup and hair. And stop talking to me. If he hears from outside, he won't come in."

Right. She ran her fingers through her hair, blotted her face, and reapplied her lipstick.

She liked the way she looked. Her cheeks were a little pink, thinking about why her lipstick was gone.

Then she turned and leaned against the counter.

"Guess I was wrong," she whispered. "I don't think he's coming. I'm going back out front."

"Ready to go home?" he asked softly.

She didn't know if it was because they were closed in the bathroom together or because of the whispering but this felt strangely intimate.

Of course, it might've been because she had peed next to him.

"Yeah. It's been a long night."

"Tell me when you get back up to the bar. I'll go out the back and come around front for you."

"Okay. See you soon."

She straightened and pulled the door open, stepping out into the hallway.

As soon as the door shut behind her, a strong arm wrapped around her waist, a hand covered her mouth, and she was pressed into the dark corner past the restrooms near the back door.

"Hey, Hayden."

The voice wasn't familiar. The gruffness in part because he was talking quietly

but this was definitely not Colin, Jonah, Cian, or Matt.

What the fuck?

This had to be *him*. He hadn't followed her into the bathroom, but he'd been waiting for her.

Her heart was hammering, adrenaline coursing through her body but she reminded herself that this was what she wanted. And that Colin was just behind her.

"I said your name to you in person, I guess I get to fuck you now, right?"

She stiffened. He knew what she'd written online. It was definitely him.

She had to see his face.

There was no way he was going to rape her in the hallway. Colin was going to be out any second. But this guy could drag her out the back door. Thankfully, she was not a lightweight. He was going to have to work for it.

She tried to twist in his grasp, but the arm around her waist tightened.

She made note of the fact that he was big enough to wrap his arm all the way around her and he was tall enough that when she brought her head back quickly, she only connected with his sternum.

He shook her. "I'm not worried about this guy, you know. I've known you a lot longer than he has."

She couldn't talk with the way he was covering her mouth. Hayden squirmed in his arms again, but he had her arms trapped against her body. She thought fast. She lifted her boot, glad she'd worn ones with a heel, and rammed it back against the front of his leg.

He yelped in surprise and pain. It was enough to make him loosen his hold and she was able to push her ass into him, while digging her elbow into his side and turning.

She wasn't prepared for the slap across the face, though. The blow stung and she tasted blood from where her bottom lip hit her teeth. But she tossed her hair back and swung with her fingers curled so that her nails would meet his face first.

In the dimly lit space, she couldn't see what she connected with but she felt the hair of a beard that would, unfortunately, mostly protect him from her nails. He grabbed her wrist, pressing it against the wall.

"Now be nice, Hayden."

"Fuck you."

"You said you wanted me to come talk to you."

"This is assault, not talking."

"I was just getting started."

She pulled her other arm back, knowing that she wouldn't be able to deliver any real force with her left, but wanting to distract him.

It worked. He grabbed that wrist and pressed it to the wall as well, but that gave her a chance to bring her knee up hard and fast between his legs.

She connected with his balls, and he doubled over immediately with a yelp.

The ladies' room door started to open—*Colin!*—and he suddenly jerked upright, then dove toward the back door.

Hayden lunged for the restroom door.

She nearly whacked Colin in the face with it as she tumbled through. He took one look at her and pulled her inside, slamming the door behind her and locking it. "What the fuck happened?"

"He grabbed me in the hall."

His expression was instantly enraged. He started to pull on the door handle, but she clutched at his arm. "No! Don't leave me."

"Jonah! Matt!" Colin barked. "Back hallway. He approached."

"He went out the back door," Hayden managed. She was

aware that she'd started to shake. The aftereffects of adrenaline dumping into her system, she knew.

"No one went back there!" Cian practically shouted.

"He came in the back door?" Jonah asked.

"Couldn't. It's locked from the outside," Matt said.

"Doesn't matter. Find him," Colin said shortly.

Then Colin's full attention was on her. His arms were around her and he pulled her up against his chest. His hand went to her head, stroking over her hair. "I'm here, *cailín*. I'm here."

She could feel his heart thundering in her ear, and his breathing was ragged. His entire body was tense.

"He was out there waiting. He grabbed me from behind."

Colin muttered a curse in Irish and she could feel the anger vibrating through his body.

"Did he hurt you?"

She decided not to lie to him. What was the point? He'd see her lip. "He slapped me. My lip's bleeding."

Colin pulled back with a jerk, his eyes scanning her face. He cupped her face in his hands. "Jesus, Hayden."

"I'm okay."

"Mother fucking son of a bitch." His thumb grazed gently over her lip in spite of his clear rage. "I'm going to kill that bastard."

"I'm okay," she repeated.

"I don't care. He touched you."

That sent a warm shaft of...*something* through her. His protectiveness made her feel warm, but it also made her...hot. She knew that Jonah, Matt, Cian, and Henry would be upset when they knew what had happened, but there was something more with Colin.

"I think I scratched his cheek. I tried anyway. And I kneed him in the balls. Then he ran out the back door."

Colin gathered her hair in his hand and then tugged on the ponytail, tipping her head back further. Now he was looking directly into her eyes. "Good girl."

"It was him, I'm sure of it."

Colin nodded as if he completely believed her. "What did he say?"

"That now that he'd said my name, he could fuck me. Just like we were talking about in the comments in the forum."

Colin's body went completely still.

She went on anyway. "He said he didn't care about the guy who was with me tonight because he knew you were new. He'd never seen you with me before. Something about him and me having a longer relationship."

"What did he look like?" Colin was talking through a visibly tight jaw.

She sighed. "He was wearing a ball cap. He was taller than me. Quite a bit. Bigger too. He is able to wrap his arms all the way around me and trap my arms against my side. Really strong. But otherwise, I didn't get a good look at his face."

"Beard?"

Hayden nodded. "Yes. Short."

"White? Black?"

"White. Louisiana accent."

"Okay. That helps."

She laughed, humorlessly. "Yeah, a tall white guy with a beard, and a Louisiana accent. He'll definitely stand out down here."

Colin took her face in his hands again, his thumbs resting at the corners of her mouth. "We'll get him."

"I believe you," she said softly, meaning it.

He swallowed hard. "I should have come right out after you. I told Matt to tell me when he saw you back up front."

"No," she shook her head. "This plan worked exactly the way we needed it to. We wanted him to come up to me."

"He hurt you." Colin's voice was dangerously low.

"Not really. I'll be okay."

"Hayden..." He sucked in a deep breath. "This kills me. Maybe I'm not thinking, planning, clearly with you. I can't stand that someone...you...that I wasn't there."

She pressed closer, wrapping her arms around his waist. "But you were there. You were the first place I wanted to go. Not just away from him, not just into the closest room, but to you." Her voice got softer. "I wanted to get to you."

Then she did the only thing that she really could—she rose onto tiptoe and pressed her lips to his. She felt the cut on her lip, but she didn't care. She *needed* this kiss.

His fingers slid into her hair, holding her still as he kissed her. It was gentle, but there was definitely a hunger behind it.

She arched closer with a little whimper.

He lifted his head. "Hayden." His voice was gruff and full of need.

Her entire body heated, and her nipples beaded.

"I wasn't lying when I said that all it took was you saying my name to make me willing to do anything...for you...with you."

They stared at each other for five seconds.

Then suddenly their mouths crashed together, and their hands were everywhere. Hayden didn't even feel the sting of the cut on her lip now as Colin's mouth moved over hers.

Her hands were under his shirt, stroking over hot, bare skin, relishing the bunching of muscles and the growl that came from deep in his chest.

He shoved her jacket to the floor, running his hands over her arms and upper back then sliding under the edge of her shirt, his big palms gliding over her bare skin, stroking up and down her spine.

She moved her mouth from his, over his jaw, down his throat, pulling another low deep, hungry growl from him that shot heat and need straight to her clit.

He backed her up until she was pressed against the bathroom door. He filled one hand with her breast, kneading her and running his thumb over the hardened tip, making pleasure ripple through her entire body from that one tiny spot.

She arched closer with a whimper, wanting his bare hands on her bare skin. As if reading her mind, he hooked a finger under both straps on her shoulder and pulled them down her arm, exposing her breast. He cupped her bare flesh, her nipple pressing into his palm, heat zinging straight to her clit. He plucked and tugged. "Fuck, Hayden."

Her head fell back against the door, and she struggled to pull in a deep breath. "Oh my God, yes, Colin."

He dipped his knees, putting his mouth against her breast, kissing his way to the center, then swirling his tongue around her nipple, before sucking. Her fingers curled into his back as she gasped.

Then he was pushing her top up to bunch below her breasts as he dragged his mouth over the silky material to her bare belly, kissing his way to the top of her jeans. It wasn't far to go. These jeans were high rise. She *hated* low rise jeans.

He unbuttoned the top button and lowered the zipper, following the exposed skin to the top of her silk panties. She sucked her stomach in, but not because this was her least favorite part of her body. But because his hot, hungry mouth on her simply took her breath away.

Her fingers threaded through his hair as he kissed along the top lacy edge that rested at her belly button. Yeah, no bikini panties for her either.

Colin didn't seem to notice or care about her jeans or her panties. He just wanted them out of the way. He pulled the panties down too, kissing to the top of her mound.

She was so hot, so wet, on edge, and so—

Suddenly there was a loud bang on the other side of the door, as if someone had dropped a metal tray.

Colin froze.

Hayden groaned.

He moved his hands to grip both of her hips, his forehead resting against her stomach.

They both stayed like that for a few seconds, sucking in air.

Finally, he looked up at her.

It might've been the sexiest thing she'd ever seen—Colin Daly on his knees in front of her with that hungry, hot look in his eyes.

"We can't do this here," he said.

"I kind of have no idea where I am right now...for some reason." She gave him a smile.

He pulled in a breath. "I am not doing this in a public restroom of a bar."

He kissed her stomach, then rose to his feet. He dragged her top and bra back into place, covering her breasts as she redid the zipper and button on her jeans.

Honestly, she couldn't believe she had even done *that* much. She wasn't a huge fan of her stomach and certainly not of having it touched and kissed. But she'd been so wrapped up in everything she would have let Colin do anything to any part of her.

He didn't step back, but he said, "This is all an adrenaline reaction. It's a mix of shock and fear and misplaced gratitude."

"You're feeling grateful to me for something?" she quipped, running her hand through her hair. She knew what he was actually talking about, of course.

"You're feeling grateful to me."

She rolled her eyes and pushed him back. "I don't really see how *you* going down on *me* is a sign of me being grateful to you." She took another deep breath. "I mean, afterward probably. But you didn't get that far."

He looked surprised at her sassiness. "The kissing. The letting me put you up against the door. The rest of it was…"

She lifted an eyebrow, waiting for him to continue.

"Chemistry that got out of hand."

"Right," she said. Then she lifted her hand to his lips. She dragged her thumb across the bottom one, wiping the lipstick off. "That seems to keep happening to us."

He didn't say anything to that. And a moment later, he pressed a finger to his ear. "Yeah."

His earpiece.

Oh my God…the guys had just heard all of that.

Her face suddenly felt *very* hot.

But fuck. If she'd had her earpiece in, the guys would've heard everything that had happened in the hallway.

She dug in her pocket, pulled the tiny device out, turned it on, and stuck it into her ear.

"Son of a bitch. Nothing," Matt said just as she tuned in.

She was going to guess that they hadn't been able to find the guy.

Great.

"The only good news is Henry's on his way home. He gets on a flight tomorrow morning." Jonah said. "I'll send photos to Carter tonight."

"I'm taking Hayden home," Colin said. "You guys hang back. See if anyone follows us."

"You got it."

"I'll go over tapes," Matt said.

"White guy, tall, beard, well-built," Colin said, watching

Hayden. "That'll at least rule a few people out."

Twenty minutes later, they were on the highway back to Autre.

They weren't speaking, and Hayden was okay with it. She was tired, but also strangely restless.

Everything felt so out of her control. She *hated* that feeling.

She was used to being the one that took care of things. That had been her role in her family forever. While her family focused on her older brother's athletic pursuits, she'd been in charge of making sure things ran smoothly for the twins. Then, when they'd started playing ball too, she'd been essential in keeping everything running since everything was then doubled and meant two different directions.

Then when her grandpa got sick, everything felt out of control. There were more questions than answers. More *I'm sorry*s than actual solutions. So, Hayden had taken it upon herself to do whatever she could.

She'd moved. She'd used her degree in a way that made her feel she was helping. She was his advocate even when he didn't know her name. She went to the doctor's appointments. She read, and researched, and asked questions. She felt as in control as she could.

When she'd been offered a chance to perform her music for larger audiences in bars and make a little money, she'd taken it. She loved the idea of having something that made her special. That let her stand out a little. But when Sabrina had said that she might have a real chance at a recording contract and that Jason Young's label wanted to talk to her in a couple of weeks, she'd hesitated. The contract would give her a bigger audience. It would put more money behind her and give her more exposure. But it would also give other people a say in where she performed, when she performed, how she looked, and what she did with her music.

And then she'd ended up with a "fan" who was messing with her life—changing where she was living, how she was coming and going from gigs, changing how she *went to the bathroom at the bar.*

And she'd ended up on the porch of a guy who was messing with her...libido.

She was going to say libido. That was probably safer than admitting that Colin was messing with anything more than that. Like her heart.

And those last two things had taken less than forty-eight hours.

Most of it had been in less than twenty-four.

She studied the scenery passing her window.

Autre was about twenty miles from New Orleans. Some of the drive was wide-open space, but a lot of it was dotted in lights and there was plenty of traffic on the main road before they turned off to take the final five miles or so into the small town.

Hayden was aware of how uncommon it was for her to have someone else driving her. She very rarely was the passenger. That seemed like a great metaphor for her life, as a matter of fact. But damn...she liked it.

It was nice to not be in charge every freaking minute.

They finally pulled up to the house and Colin turned the truck off. But when she started to get out of the cab, he put a hand on her thigh.

She looked back.

"Wait," he said. "I need Jonah and Cian to be sure no one followed. And they'll go in first."

Right. Stalker.

She just nodded and settled back in her seat. Colin removed his hand.

And they sat quietly, not talking, a weird tension between them.

Jonah and Cian rolled in behind them about fifteen minutes later.

Colin checked his phone as a text came in. "No one followed." They watched the other men enter the house, lights going on in various rooms as they moved through.

Finally, Colin's phone lit up with another text.

"All clear," he said.

Hayden just nodded and got out of the truck. He was right behind her as she climbed the front steps and went into the house. She really didn't know what else to do. She paused at the bottom of the stairs leading up to the second floor. "Thanks for tonight," she said. That sounded so stupid.

"'Course. I'm sorry that—"

She stopped him with her hand up. "You did your job. I wanted to perform, you made that possible. There was a man there. He wanted to... I don't know, do things I didn't want him to do, and he didn't get to because you guys were there."

He nodded. "Yeah."

She looked at him for a long moment. Not sure what to say or if she should say anything at all. Finally, she just settled for, "Goodnight."

"Goodnight, Hayden."

Yeah, when he said her name, it was different than when anyone else did. And for a second it seemed that he'd very much done it on purpose.

She went up to her new room, showered, put on pajamas, got into bed, and pulled up a book on her phone to try to read. It was always a little hard to unwind after shows, so she had a routine.

But it wasn't working tonight. She was wound up. And it had nothing to do with the performance. Or even X.

And she had a feeling there was only one way to actually deal with it.

Head on.

She leaned over and opened the bedside table. Cian, being Cian, actually had brought her vibrators. And he'd brought all of them rather than just two.

She pulled the purple one out.

She glanced at the door. She should probably go lock it. But who was going to come in? Colin was the only one who would dare. And if he walked in while she was...well, she wouldn't really mind at all.

Hayden lay back against the pillows and turned the vibrator on to setting one.

She closed her eyes and pictured Colin. Then she thought about the way he'd kissed her in the driveway. The way he'd watched her when she'd been on stage. The way he'd kissed her when she'd come off stage. She trailed the vibrator over her breast, on top of her pajamas, teasing her nipple as she remembered the way his hand, then his mouth had felt there. The vibrations caused ripples of sensation to slide through her belly to her clit. She trailed the vibration down her stomach, recalling the feel of his beard against her belly and...

There was a soft knock on her door and she sucked in a quick breath as the vibrator fell to the duvet.

She hit the off button, then scrambled off the bed and went to the door. She pulled it open, realizing that she was breathing a little fast.

It was Cian on the other side.

He lifted a brow. "You could *try* to hide that you're disappointed to see me."

She puffed out a breath, blowing the hair out of her face. "Sorry."

"I'm going to pretend that you were just about to fall

asleep rather than hoping for someone else."

"Thanks," she said instead of denying what he'd guessed.

"Are you okay?"

"Yes. Mostly."

"We're just making sure that you're not too shaken up."

"We?"

"Aye. *I* would've just texted you." He gave her a knowing smile.

She crossed her arms. "Someone sent you?"

"Yeah. Not that I'm not concerned. But like I said, I would've texted or called. And I know you would've called me if you needed me."

So Colin had sent him to check on her. Dammit. Why hadn't Colin come? "Well, I'm mostly okay. Not sure if I can sleep yet because I haven't tried. If I can't, I'm not sure that it will be because of the guy in the bar, though."

"At least not the creepy guy whose name you don't know," Cian said with a small smile.

"I'm pretty obvious, huh?"

He glanced toward Colin's doorway. "You both are." He gave her a wink, then tucked his hands into his pockets, turned, and sauntered down the hallway toward his own room.

Hayden looked at Colin's doorway for a long moment. Then she shut her door, turned, and leaned against it.

He'd sent Cian to check on her. And she was sure Cian was worried about her too and would have checked on her. They were friends, after all.

But Cian wasn't overprotective of her.

She looked toward the bed where her vibrator was lying on the duvet.

Screw this. She opened her door, took a deep breath, walked across the small foyer to Colin's door, and knocked.

ten

THERE WAS NO ANSWER. She'd taken Cian's glance toward Colin's door as an indication that he was inside. But maybe not. Or maybe he was in the shower.

Her body reacted to that idea. Could she slip inside and join him? What would he do? She wasn't sure he would exactly *welcome* her. But she wasn't at all sure that he would push her away either. He'd probably tell her it was a bad idea. He'd probably try to resist for a moment. But then she remembered him pushing her jacket off and pulling her top down and sucking on her nipple. Her entire body went hot. She wasn't so sure he'd push her away. She lifted her hand to knock again.

But just then, the door swung open.

Colin stood staring at her.

His hair was tousled, and he was wearing only pajama pants. They were slung low on his hips as if he'd pulled them on quickly. His cheeks were slightly flushed, and he was breathing a little fast.

And, most notably of all, he was hard. His erection was obvious behind the thin navy-blue pants.

She let her gaze drag over him slowly. Twice. She had no choice. It was like her eyes moved on their own.

"What are you doing?" he asked, his voice tight but husky.

"Well, I was getting ready to masturbate. But then I thought maybe you were doing the same, so I figured I'd come down here and see what you thought of just helping each other out."

His eyes went wide, then narrowed. But they were hot.

"Hayden." His voice was almost strangled.

"Just being honest."

She had an inkling that that was exactly what he'd been doing. She hoped to God he'd been thinking about her.

"I sent Cian to check on you."

"Yeah. He did. But I was hoping it would be you."

"Is that how you answered the door?" Now he let his gaze track over her. Her short, thin, silky shorts, the matching tank top, the lack of a bra.

"Yeah. This is what I was wearing."

"He saw you like that? No robe? Nothing?"

"Nope. I mean yes. This is how he saw me."

"I don't like other men seeing you like that."

"Then you should have been the one to come check on me."

"I knew what would happen if I did."

"Me too." She tipped her head. "Does that mean you're a chicken?"

"More like...a crow."

She let out a soft laugh. She might've expected him to say a bird of prey. "A crow?"

"One of the smartest birds."

"Meaning you were *very* sure of what would happen."

"Aye, Hayden, I was very sure of what would happen."

His use of her name had tingles skittering across her skin. "Let me guess, you think it's a bad idea."

"Tonight was emotional. A lot of adrenaline. How you're feeling is—"

"Stop telling me how I feel," she cut him off, planting her hands on her hips. She made note of the way his gaze dropped to her breasts again before bouncing back to her face. Her nipples hardened in response. She did nothing to cover them. "How I'm feeling about you has nothing to do with the other guy tonight. Or me being afraid. Or adrenaline. Or gratitude."

"I know you think that."

"Okay." She took a deep breath. She dropped her hands and shrugged. "Maybe this is a little about him. And the fact that he's taking away so much of my control and power." She frowned and stepped forward. "He's inserting himself into my life uninvited and *unwanted*. He's changed where I live, he's changing my routines, he's on my mind. He's making himself a part of my life, and I want nothing to do with him. I'm sick of it, already. Don't let him take this away from me too."

Colin sucked in a breath through his nose. "That's not what this is."

"Colin, I want you." She took another small step. Now her toes were right on the threshold of his doorway. "I wanted you before the bar tonight. I would want you even if he had never sent me a single email. Even if he didn't know my name. When you touch me, I go up in flames. I want your hands on me. I want your mouth on me."

Colin's breathing was ragged, and his hands were balled into fists. His eyes were hot, and he definitely wasn't moving away from her.

She took another step closer. Across the threshold. Officially into his room. She was directly in front of him now. Her voice dropped. "I want to be against you. I want you around me, on top of me, inside me. And that has nothing to do with anyone else. If you want to say no for other reasons, then say no. But if you say no to me because of him, then he *is* taking that from me." She wet her lips. "Don't let him do that."

Colin stared at her for several beats. Then he reached out, grabbed her wrist, and pulled her the rest of the way into his room.

⸙

This was possibly the worst idea he'd ever had.

But if he was going to fuck everything up, he was going to fuck it up big.

If he was going to lose the chance at a long-term contract with Hayden, then he was going to do it big. And hot, and hard, and all damned night long.

Colin shut the door and pushed Hayden up against it. He pressed her into the wood, her wrist still in his hand, holding her still. He leaned in and put his mouth against her ear, breathing in her scent. Then he said huskily, "Last chance to leave this room without the hardest orgasm of your life."

She laughed, the sound husky, her breath hot against his neck. "So not the way to get me to say no."

"Good. Because I think if you said no, I would die."

"You really do want to do this?" she asked.

"So fucking much, I almost can't breathe."

She ran her hands up his chest to the back of his neck, linking them behind his head. "Thank God."

He cupped her face, dragging his thumb along her jaw. Then he touched the little cut on her lip. Fuck. She was so goddamned beautiful. He'd never wanted a woman like this. He ran his hand down her neck, over her shoulder, then down her side to her hip, where he squeezed. "You need to understand, I think this is probably a bad idea. And I never make bad decisions."

"Does that mean you're making an exception for me?"

"Exactly."

"So you're going to regret it?"

"Maybe. But not as much as I'll regret never having you."

She arched into him. "I can live with that."

"You need to know something else," he said. She needed to understand what this was going to be.

"Okay."

"I'm going to be possessive as fuck. I already feel that way about you. If I take you to bed, you're mine. I will not share. It will be very hard to get rid of me. I will try to take care of you in every way I can. That all means that I could become a huge pain in your ass."

She looked up at him, studying him closely. Good. He welcomed that. He was entirely serious. She needed to know that giving herself to him like this meant she was signing up for more than a one-night thing.

"How come you don't already have a girlfriend? If that's the kind of guy you are?"

"I didn't say that was the kind of guy I am." He'd *never* been like this with anyone else. And he hadn't even seen her naked yet. "I said all of that is what *this* is going to be."

"I don't understand."

"I don't either entirely. It's just...you."

She pressed her lips together and seemed to be thinking that over.

He liked that. He needed to know she was taking this seriously. The burning *need* he had for this woman, and the fact that it had come on so quickly, was something *he* was taking very seriously. If she didn't want him, and all the intensity and possessiveness that came with him, then she needed to leave. Now.

"I'm never attracted to men this quickly," she finally said.

"Never this intensely. In fact, I haven't thought about romance or dating in a really long time. I have a lot of responsibilities, people who need me and depend on me. Having a guy in my life who would need time and attention and energy just has not been something I've wanted to do." She took a breath.

Colin let her process all of it, staying quiet and still, though a part of him wanted to beg her to take this on. To take *him* on.

"But with you...it doesn't feel that way. You make me feel... like having you around would be *easier*, not harder. That you would take care of me too. That you would make everything feel better. That you would definitely take up space in my head, and you would take time and energy, but it would...be time and energy I'd *want* to give. I actually feel *more* energized when I'm around you. You make me feel better. Lighter." She frowned and shook her head as if a little confused. "We barely know each other, but I feel this pull to be closer to you all the time. No matter how good and happy I feel around the other guys, no matter how safe and supported they make me feel, I always would rather be with *you*."

Colin finally spoke. "Am I opening the door...or locking it?"

She leaned away from the door, and he let her, giving her a few inches of space. She turned and lifted her hand.

Then *she* locked the door.

Heat and desire pounded through him. He wanted this woman in a way he couldn't explain. Being upfront with her about how he was feeling was the only way he could do this. Yes, he was intense. About work. About his friendships. About Saoirse. But he'd never been intense about a woman.

Maybe he'd never been in a place where he could be. That was possible. He'd never been fully single before now. He had been, technically, of course, but Saoirse had always been a consideration before. He hadn't been in charge of where he lived, his schedule, or his priorities. So maybe this was timing.

But that didn't feel like all this was. Hayden was different. Special. He wanted to take care of her, and yet she didn't feel helpless. She didn't feel like she needed him.

She *wanted* him.

Intensely. It was her intensity that matched his. She seemed sweet, but she also seemed to give her whole heart to what she cared about. That's what he needed. Someone who could take him and his life on. Completely.

She would let him be what he needed to be—protective, possessive, fully honest with his words and actions—but she would tell him everything she was thinking and feeling as well. The combination of Hayden's vulnerability and feistiness drew him.

He wanted to wrap her up and take care of her while cheering her on.

Taking her to bed would be the same way.

He was going to fully take care of her, while making sure she was with him every step of the way.

He stepped back, taking her in. She looked so fucking sexy. The pajamas were nothing. They covered her, but every curve was on display. Her nipples were hard behind the thin cotton, and the silky material of her shorts would have surely showed panty lines if she had any on.

There were no panty lines.

"Strip," he said.

Heat flared in her eyes, but she didn't hesitate. She pushed her shorts to the floor first, kicking them to the side.

Her thighs were thick and full, curving into the gorgeous hips he loved to grip and squeeze. He was barely able to pull his eyes away from the apex of her thighs, a place he tended to dive in and spend a lot of time when she pulled the tank up over her head and tossed it to the side as well.

Hips, tummy, breasts—it was all on display for him. She

stood with one foot on top of the other, her hands gripping into fists, then relaxing, then gripping again at her sides as if she was trying to stand still but was feeling jumpy. Her hair hung over her shoulders, the tips brushing the tops of her breasts. The single lamp beside his bed lit the room in a soft golden light, and her skin glowed.

She looked like a Greek sex goddess.

And he was ready to be on his knees worshipping her.

"Bed," he said shortly. In part because he wasn't sure he could string more than a word or two together at a time. But also because he wanted to see just how submissive this woman would be before she started pushing back.

She looked him over.

"Okay, but you better lose those pants before you come near that mattress."

She started for the bed, her hips swaying, her breasts bouncing softly, and Colin realized that if he had finished jerking off before she'd come to his door, he might've been better off.

He was on edge, and even the *sight* of her was pushing him almost to the brink.

As she started to climb up onto the bed, he made a mental note to text the guys to let them know that neither he nor Hayden was going to be available before noon tomorrow.

He had a lot to do to and with this woman tonight, and it was going to take them well into the early morning hours.

He watched her climb up onto the mattress, her gorgeous ass swaying as she did so. She started to lie down, but he stopped her.

"Wait."

He crossed swiftly to the bed. She stopped on all fours, looking over her shoulder at him. It might've been the sexiest thing he'd ever seen. He ran a big hand up over the curve of one cheek to the middle of her back. She arched and gave a little moan, much like a cat being petted.

"Do you know how fucking gorgeous you are?" he asked.

Her hair was falling over her face. "You make me feel gorgeous."

"I have no idea where to even start with you," he said, realizing his voice was unusually gruff.

"Anywhere," she said, pressing her ass back into his hand.

He squeezed, then ran it up and over the curve again. "This is even better than what I was imagining."

She looked back at him again. "So you *were* thinking of me?"

He moved in behind her, cupping both ass cheeks now, with his hands. He pressed into her, his pants still in the way, letting her feel how hard he was. "It wasn't the first time either."

Her head fell forward, and she groaned. "That's so hot."

"You want to watch?"

Her head came up, and she looked back. "*Yes.*"

He chuckled. "Gladly. Sometime. Need to touch you first."

She pressed back against him. "Please. All over."

He flipped her to her back, loving how her body bounced, and how great she looked spread out on his sheets. "Oh, yeah," he praised. "This. All of this."

Colin pushed his pants to the floor and let her take him in for the first time. Her eyes were wide and hungry as they roamed over his body. They lingered on his cock. She wet her lips and he groaned.

"Oh yeah, that too," he promised.

She propped up on her elbows. "I don't know if I'm any good at it. Haven't done it that much."

"You will be good at it."

"You'll teach me?"

"We're going to know everything about how to pleasure each other by the time that door opens tomorrow," he told her, fisting his cock and giving it a long stroke.

Again, she wet her lips. "Oh my God, this is amazing."

He loved that she wasn't trying to hide her body. She wasn't even blushing. Her cheeks were flushed, but he knew that was from lust.

"You're not a virgin?" he asked, putting one knee up on the mattress next to her knees. He hated the idea of any other man with her, but she didn't act like a virgin and that was probably for the best, considering the things he wanted to do to her.

She shook her head. "No. But it's never been great. And it's been a while."

"Excellent answers."

She lifted a brow. "It's excellent that I've had bad sex?"

"I'm an asshole if I say aye, but...aye."

She huffed out a soft laugh. "As long as you correct that."

"Oh, *cailín*, I'm going to correct it so well, you won't remember anyone else's name."

He assumed she didn't know what *cailín* meant. Literally, it was the word 'girl' in Irish. It could also be a first name. But it was often used as a term of endearment and affectionately used for women who were more girlfriends. He'd never used it before, yet it had just tumbled out with Hayden.

She seemed to sense the feelings behind it, because her expression was soft and she pulled her lower lip between her teeth as she watched him, clearly turned on.

He crawled up until he was braced over her on hands and knees. "I hope you don't have anywhere you need to be in the morning."

"If I do, I expect by the time you're done with me, I won't be able to remember it either."

He lowered himself, so his mouth was against hers. "That was the right response."

Then he kissed her, deep, hot, and thoroughly. His tongue stroked every corner of her mouth. He drank her in. She was sweet and responsive, meeting his tongue stroke for stroke, and he would never get enough of kissing her. Just kissing her. He could do this for hours.

But then her arms went around his neck, and her body pressed up against his, and he realized that he had so many more things to do. He ran his mouth down her neck, kissing and sucking gently until he got to her collarbone. He lifted a hand to cup one of her generous breasts, running his thumb over the tip. He loved the sounds she made when he played with her breasts. He plucked and tugged on one nipple until her hips were bucking against his.

"Colin, yes."

He lowered his mouth to that nipple and started sucking. Running his hand down over her belly to her pussy, he teased the outer folds, then circled over her clit gently. The way she gasped, however, sounded as if he'd plunged deep.

"So needy," he said softly. "So hungry."

"Yes. Need you."

He loved her wanting him like this. He eased his finger into her. Jesus, she was tight. His cock twitched thinking about the grip her pussy would have on him. He stroked in and out just to his second knuckle and she was gasping.

"You were going to get yourself off thinking of me?" he asked.

"I had my vibrator on."

He lifted his head. "When?"

"When Cian came to the door."

Colin stopped his finger moving. "Did he hear?"

Her eyes fluttered open. "I don't think so. I'd just gotten started."

He slid his finger deeper, their eyes locked. "If he had heard, whose name would you have been calling?"

Her knees shifted apart, and she arched up closer to his hand, his finger sliding deeper. "Yours. Just like last night."

He pressed deeper. "You touched yourself last night thinking of me?"

She nodded. "Yes."

He pulled out, then added a second finger, stroking deep and slow. "In this dirty vision, was your vibrator my tongue, my fingers, or my cock?"

"Your cock," she said breathlessly. "

"We just went straight at it, then?"

She nodded.

"That's not what you're going to get tonight, *cailín*."

"No?"

Colin knew exactly where he wanted to start now. He pulled his fingers out and lifted them to his mouth, letting her watch him lick them clean.

"Oh, there's so much before that." He lay back against the pillows, pulling her over on top of him. She straddled his stomach, his cock nudging against her ass.

Her eyes were wide. "I don't love being on top."

"Why not?" His hands gripped her hips, and he moved her up his torso.

Her hands went to the pillow on either side of his head causing her breasts to swing closer to his mouth. He took advantage, licking his tongue over one nipple and pulling it into his mouth.

She gasped, and he felt her thighs tighten around his ribs.

"It's not the most flattering," she managed.

"You're fucking gorgeous. In any position. Every position. And I intend to have you in them all," he told her firmly.

"But in this position, you can see everything."

He nodded. "Exactly." He urged her to sit up.

He filled both hands with her breasts, plucking and teasing her nipples. They were darker pink now and there was a pretty flush climbing up her chest to her throat. She tipped her head back, her hair falling down her back.

His gaze roamed over her body. Her ribs, belly, and where her pussy was hot and wet against his stomach. "Damn, *cailín*, this is what I'm going to think about next time I'm jerking off."

Her head came up and he could tell she was going to protest, so he tugged on one nipple harder as he dropped his hand to the spot where she straddled him.

"Aye," he said, before she could say anything. His thumb found her clit. He pressed. "Lean back." He slid his knees up and she leaned back, resting against them.

Oh, fuck yes. He could see all the gorgeous pink between her legs. He circled her clit and felt her thighs tighten around him again.

"I could make you come just like this. Your sweet stickiness all over my stomach."

She lifted her hands to cover her face as she laughed. "Oh my God."

"Look at me, Hayden," he said firmly, circling her clit, and pinching a nipple.

She dropped her hands with a gasp. Her gaze locked on his.

"You are everything. You're so fucking hot. I want *all* of you. Do you understand?"

She swallowed.

"Hayden, I am going to know every inch of your body. We're going to be as intimate as two people can be. Say, *I know you want me.*"

She took a deep breath. She was slick and wet. He could feel her body trembling. He could send her over the edge right now. He could fuck her in eight different positions. But he had to hear her say that she knew how much he wanted her.

He stopped moving both hands. "Now, *cailín*. Say it."

She swallowed again. "I know you want me."

He took her hips and started to pull her up his body.

She seemed to immediately understand where this was going.

"Like this?" she asked, digging her knees into the mattress.

"Like this," he said firmly, his hands cupping her ass.

"Are you sure?"

"Goddammit, Hayden, grab onto my headboard, and let me eat your pussy." He pulled her the rest of the way, bringing her knees over his shoulders, until her pussy was against his mouth.

She had no choice but to grip his headboard, so her nose wouldn't smash into his wall.

"Colin!"

But he licked against her clit, then pulled her into his mouth, and the next noise she made was one of a combination of a moan, gasp, and, if he didn't know better, a prayer.

"Colin-holy-oh-my-God-yes."

"That's my girl," he praised, licking her again, his fingers digging into her ass to hold her against his mouth.

"That's...oh, my God... so good."

"Fuck yeah, it is." He licked her hard, then sucked. "You're the best thing I've ever tasted, Hayden."

"I just...Colin!"

That was exactly what he wanted—his name being chanted, over and over, by this woman while he brought her over the edge.

He pulled her closer to his mouth, but he could feel that

she was holding herself up.

He swatted her ass lightly and she gasped. "Colin!"

"Quit bracing yourself," he told her. "Sit down."

"I can't *sit down*," she protested. "I'm too heavy."

"Sit. On. My. Face. Hayden," he said, pulling her fully onto his mouth and sucking hard on her clit.

She cried out, and after only a moment of him holding her in place, he felt her pressing closer and moving against his tongue, riding him.

There we fucking go.

He continued to eat at her until she finally came, crying his name.

"Oh, *God*, yes, Colin! Oh, *yes!*"

Fuck. That was the best thing he'd ever heard. He flipped her to her back, bracing himself over her, kissing her deeply, making her taste what he'd just feasted on.

She wrapped her arms and legs around him, holding him close, her body hot, soft, and still trembling.

"I want the taste of you on my tongue every night," he told her gruffly, his cock resting against the hot wetness he'd helped create.

"I had no idea that would be so...amazing," she said, running her hand over his cheek, looking at him with eyes filled with lust and wonder.

"I've barely even gotten started with you," he said, running a hand down to palm one breast. "I need to fuck you."

"Yes. God, please."

He rolled away, reaching for the bedside table. She clutched at his shoulders.

"Condom," he said.

She let go, and he grabbed several packets, scattering them across the bed.

She laughed. "I'm going to be sore tomorrow, aren't I?"

"You're not going to take a step without thinking of me," he agreed, unapologetically.

She didn't protest. She watched him roll a condom on, her gaze hungry. He was so hard, it was nearly painful.

He braced himself above her. "I have so many ways I want you, but this first time, I just need to drive deep. I'm so fucking desperate for you, *cailín*."

"God, yes. Whatever you want."

Yeah, he really liked that too. Almost too much. His cock pulsed as he positioned himself between her thighs.

He took one leg and wrapped it around his waist, hitching her thigh high, spreading her out. Then he eased in.

He tried to take it slow, but he needed her so badly and she was so slick and hot, that he slid into her tight heat in one thrust. He paused. They were both breathing hard.

"Holy shit, Hayden."

"I know. Oh, my God, Colin. You feel so good."

"Fucking heaven." He rested his forehead against hers. *You cannot just pound into her. You cannot just pound into her. You cannot just pound into her.* His body did not want to listen. Everything in him screamed, *Fuck her. Now. Hard.*

"Colin?" she asked after a few seconds of him not moving.

"Yeah?" His voice sounded hoarse.

"You okay?"

"Nope."

"Oh." She sounded worried.

"I'm about to lose my soul. I'm just preparing."

There was a beat, then he felt her smile. He lifted his head.

"I promise to take care of it," she said softly.

Jesus. He was falling in love with this girl. Already. This easily. Fuck.

He leaned in and kissed her. It was deep, and hot, but sweet too. He was buried balls deep. He could still taste her on his tongue. He'd never been this hard in his life. But it was the sweetest kiss of his life.

He lifted his head. "You ready?"

She nodded. "Beyond."

Yeah. Him too.

He pulled out, then thrust back in, slow and easy.

Her body clutched at him, her pussy milking him, her breasts cushioning his chest, her sweet scent surrounding him, her hair spread across his sheets, her leg wrapped around him, holding him close. Colin never wanted this to end.

And slow and easy lasted for three more strokes.

Soon his thrusts were coming hard, fast, and deep. Hayden was gripping his back, her neck arched, his name coming in between her *oh, yeses,* and the *please, mores.* He scooped a hand under her ass, tipping her pelvis just right so he could rub her clit, and hit her G-spot. He filled her fully, but she took every inch. Every hard, thick, thrusting inch.

"Good girl," he told her roughly, one arm braced on the bed beside her hip. "You take me perfectly, Hayden. God, you were made for me."

She whimpered, her pussy tightening around him.

"That's right," he said. "That's it. You're so good, baby."

She tightened again and her heel dug into his butt.

"Fuck, Hayden. Take me all the way. This cock is all yours. Give me your pussy. Give me all of you."

Her muscles clenched harder, and he felt her breathing change.

"I want you to come, Hayden. I want you to coat my cock. I want you to give me everything."

"Oh God," she moaned.

"Pinch your nipple," he told her, moving his hand between them and circling her clit with his thumb. "I want your orgasm, *cailín.* I want to feel it. Milk me, Hayden, fuck me."

She lifted her hips as she tugged on her nipple. He circled her clit faster and felt her climax begin.

"That's it. That's my girl."

Then it hit. She shot up and over the peak, crying out.

"Colin! Oh yes! Colin!"

He leaned in, kissing her deeply. Then he pulled back and, finally, pounded into her. And she took every single thrust.

His climax hit hard, rushing over him, tightening everything, then exploding. He continued to pump his hips for several seconds, the waves of pleasure going on and on.

Finally, he slowed, then stopped, breathing hard, holding himself over her, just staring down at her.

She was pink. All over. She was breathing hard too. They were both sweaty.

And clearly, a little stunned.

He shook his head.

"What?" she asked, an almost shy smile teasing the corner of her mouth.

"You're...extraordinary."

Her smile was full-blown, bright, and it hit him directly in the chest, then seemed to soak in and wrap itself around his heart.

He felt warm and happy and light.

Colin lowered himself to the mattress beside her, gathering her against him.

Then he took a deep breath. A deep, very satisfied breath.

The most satisfied breath he'd taken since he'd realized that he was no longer needed in Saoirse's life. Or really anyone's life.

He cuddled Hayden close and ran a hand up and down her back.

Damn.

And they were just getting started.

eleven

OH, hell no.

Colin's eyes opened as he reached across his bed and felt...nothing.

He scowled and looked at the empty bed next to him. The covers were thrown back. The pillow still had an indentation in it. But the sheets were cold.

No. He was *not* going to wake up in bed alone after fucking and falling asleep with Hayden. Then waking her up and fucking her again. And again.

Absolutely not.

He threw the covers back, pulled on sweatpants and a t-shirt, and went stomping out of his room.

He intended to find his woman and fuck her, then feed her. Or maybe he'd feed her first. Either way, Hayden was coming back to his bed. Now that he'd had her, he wasn't sure he was ever going to get enough.

The first floor of the house was quiet, though. Frustrated, he looked out to the driveway and found all the vehicles accounted for. So she was here somewhere. Then he heard voices outside. He stepped through the back door to the yard.

Finding her underneath another man was definitely not what he'd been expecting.

Jonah climbed off of her and offered her a hand up. Pulling her to her feet, he said, "So if he comes up behind you like that, you'll want to step back and twist."

"Okay, got it." She brushed her hair back from her face. "Let's go again."

What they were doing was obvious immediately. Jonah was teaching Hayden self-defense moves.

Part of Colin wanted to stomp out into the yard and carry her back to bed. But something made him pause. They hadn't noticed him yet, so he crossed his arms and propped his hip against the porch railing, settling in to watch for a bit.

Jonah took her through a few more moves, coaching her patiently. She executed them well, but without the smoothness and confidence she needed. She would need a lot more practice. Still, Jonah praised her.

"Good. Good. That was better. We need to go over this several more times," he told her. "And there's a lot more. These are the basics, though."

"He taught Saoirse to shoot, too," Cian said from where he was sitting on the stone wall that circled the patio. "Archery, too. But that probably won't do you much good."

Hayden propped her hands on her hips. "Archery sounds cool, though."

Jonah chuckled. "I'll teach you all of it if you want. But we're starting with the stuff that's most helpful first."

"Shooting him could be very helpful," Cian said darkly.

"Just getting away from him is the most helpful," Jonah told Cian firmly. Then he looked at Hayden. "Though I promise you, if you do shoot him, no one will *ever* find that body."

Her eyes widened.

Colin almost chuckled. And it wasn't because he thought it

was funny. It was because she didn't realize that Jonah was only one of *many* who would help dispose of any dead bodies she produced in self-defense. Or even not-so-self-defense. She now had a posse of people who would dig a hole for her without question.

Hayden was frowning now. "I hate the idea of carrying a gun."

Jonah put a hand on her shoulder. "I know. I hate that it's even something you have to think about. And there are lots of other ways to keep yourself safe. We're going to go over everything. And we're going to just do our damnedest to be sure you're never alone. But I don't ever want you to feel helpless."

Hayden covered Jonah's hand with hers. "Thank you. You guys make me feel so much better."

Jonah looked almost proud of that.

The entire scene warmed Colin's heart, even as everything from the night before at the bar played through his mind.

These men really cared about Hayden. Colin had known that, but last night he'd seen more than them just enjoying her singing or laughing with her and teasing her. They'd been worried about her and furious that someone had assaulted her. He'd been almost relieved that Jonah hadn't been able to catch up with her attacker. It could have gotten out of hand. Jonah hadn't been pursuing the man in the name of his job as a security professional. He'd been going after someone who'd hurt a friend. He might have overdone his retaliation if he'd found the guy.

Another thought hit Colin right on the heels of that.

These guys needed someone like Hayden in their lives.

Someone to take care of, who would love and appreciate them back. Someone who would take all their protectiveness and give it back to them on another, softer, sweeter level.

Someone like...Saoirse.

Not in the little girl, like-a-daughter sense. Saoirse had never really been like a daughter to the other men. She'd been more like a little sister.

And when Colin had lost Saoirse, Jonah and Henry had to. Cian too, though, as her uncle, he had some assurance that she'd always be a part of his life in some capacity.

She was still part of all of their lives right now, but not at all in the way she had been before. And, as far as Jonah, Henry, and Colin were concerned, there were no guarantees they'd always be included. They weren't blood related.

Not having her around twenty-four-seven, not living with them, not a part of their lives in the same way, had left a hole in their hearts too.

Colin had been her primary caregiver, but Jonah, Cian, Henry, and Torin had all been a part of her life. Torin had helped with her schoolwork, Cian had been one of her best playmates, and Jonah and Henry had taught her self-defense, shooting, horseback riding, and, yes, archery.

And lots of other things. They'd read to her. Baked cookies with her. Played with animals from puppies and kittens to giraffes and tigers with her.

And they'd watched her try new things, learn new things, succeed and fail. They'd shown up to programs and recitals, accompanied her on trips, and gone with her to everything from movies to shopping sprees to swimming lessons to Disney World a million times.

Colin had needed to physically restrain Henry from driving to pick her up from summer camp when she'd been seven and called them homesick. One of her most prized possessions was a framed photo of her with all "her guys" sitting on Santa's lap at the mall one year. Okay, she was on Santa's lap and the guys were gathered around Santa, looking ridiculous but happy to make Saoirse happy. They'd all enjoyed it as much as she had.

Saoirse spoke three languages fluently, had traveled extensively, knew more about world history than many college students, and knew more about world politics and international affairs than she probably wanted to. She was very well-rounded, and it was in large part because of these men.

Colin hadn't really thought about how much they must miss her.

Hayden was filling in a gap for them as well. She was giving them someone to protect and teach and was bringing some softer feminine energy into the house again.

And it had been forty-eight hours. It was amazing to him how much energy and light and warmth Hayden Ross brought with her.

Dammit. He really was falling for her.

"Okay, let's go again. I'm going to come up behind you and grab you. You're going to try to flip me. Even if you can't..."

Colin didn't hear the rest of what Jonah was saying.

As much as he loved these men and understood that they cared about Hayden, suddenly, he needed a lot of her energy, light, and warmth himself. Up close and personal. Right now.

He came down the steps and across the yard.

All three of them turned to look at him.

Obviously, they were expecting him to say something.

He didn't. He went right up to Hayden, bent, hoisted her over his shoulder, turned, and headed back to the house.

"Colin!" she exclaimed.

He still didn't say anything. He just settled one hand on her ass.

He heard the other men chuckling behind him.

"Guess we'll save the rest of the lesson till later," Jonah called.

Hayden giggled. "Guess so."

Colin carried her inside and straight up the stairs to his bedroom. He strode through, kicked the door shut behind him, and dumped her on the bed.

She smiled up at him. "Good morning."

"Not good." He reached over his shoulder, grabbed a handful of his shirt, and yanked it over his head. Her eyes widened as he continued to strip. "I woke up without you in the bed beside me."

She licked her lips as he got naked. Then he reached for her shoes.

"I woke up early and went downstairs for coffee. The guys offered to teach me self-defense."

He pulled her shoes and socks off, tossed them over his shoulder, then hooked his thumbs in the top of her yoga pants. He searched for the top of her panties as well, but didn't feel them. He pulled the soft, black material down and found that there were no panties.

He lifted a brow. "Where are your panties, Hayden?"

"I didn't put any on." She swallowed. Probably because his eyes narrowed. "I thought I'd be coming right back upstairs."

He stripped her yoga pants off.

"You don't go out of my room without panties and a bra. There are three other men living here."

She nodded. "Okay."

He ran both hands up the insides of her thighs.

"I don't like waking up and finding you with other men," he said, trying to sound angry. He wasn't, of course. Well, he hadn't liked waking up without her, but he wasn't upset about how she'd been spending her time.

His friends were like brothers to him. And they loved her. She loved them. That warmed him. He needed them to all care about each other. Those men would protect her. They'd make her laugh. She'd take care of them and make them laugh. It was all good. Very good.

But he knew she liked him bossy and gruff.

She shifted her legs on top of the duvet, and his eyes went immediately to her sweet pussy. He could still taste her from last night, and he wanted more.

He reached for her shirt, taking it up over her head. She reached for her bra. As soon as she was naked, she sat up, but he had a better idea than just fucking her missionary style on the bed. He tugged her to standing, then scooped his hands under her ass and lifted her. Her legs went around his waist, and he sealed his mouth to hers. They kissed long and deep.

By the time she lifted her head, he'd carried her into the bathroom.

"What are we doing?"

"Shower. I just got up, and you've worked out."

"Oh, I thought we were going to have sex. We can shower after that."

He set her down outside the glass shower door and reached in to turn on the water. "We are going to have sex, Hayden."

He nudged her inside the shower.

The water was the perfect temperature, but she shivered as the water hit her, and he knew it was from desire. He watched the water spilling over her smooth, creamy skin, and he lifted his hands, running them over her slick shoulders and down her arms.

"I thought about waking you up," she told him, her hands on his chest.

"You are always welcome to do that," he told her.

"Well, I kept you up late." She gave him a mischievous smile. "So, I thought I should let you sleep."

He loved this sexy, playful side.

"You chose incorrectly," he said, frowning. Still attempting to seem upset. "So now you have to make it up to me."

"Gosh, how will I do that?" She widened her eyes as if she was actually concerned.

"On your knees."

Now, her eyes widened for real. She looked down. His cock was already hard and thick.

She wet her lips.

He nodded. "Exactly."

She went to her knees without a further word. He gathered her wet hair back, holding it in a ponytail at the back of her head. Her hands held the back of his thighs, and she just studied him.

He gave her a moment, letting her check out his size and girth. He didn't know how experienced she was with this. Last night she'd said she didn't think she was good at it. He didn't know if that was from lack of practice or a past lover's report. Or perhaps a lot of past lovers' reports. But he didn't care. She was going to be good at this for him. He'd help her along until she was.

"Open," he said, taking his cock in hand. He stroked up and down in front of her face, slowly, squeezing slightly.

Hayden Ross on her knees in front of him, wet and glistening, her mouth open, waiting for him, was one of the hottest things he'd ever seen. This wasn't going to last long.

"This first time, I'm not going to come in your mouth. But you're going to suck me until I'm ready. Then I'm going to come all over your gorgeous tits," he told her. "But we'll get to everything else. Eventually."

She nodded, breathing faster now.

He traced her lips with the head of his cock. As if on instinct, her tongue darted out to lick his tip.

He groaned. "That's right, *cailín*. That's right."

She extended more of her tongue, and he slid against it, heat and lust pouring through him just from that simple touch.

"Now, close your lips around me."

She did, and he slid in and out of the O she made with her mouth.

Even this was fucking Heaven. He didn't need her to do anything more. That was what was amazing. He held the back of her head while he braced his other hand on the wall over her. He locked his knees so they wouldn't get weak. That's what this woman did to him.

He slid in a little further. He had no idea how much of him she could take, and he wasn't going to push her. Over time they would learn one another. He'd take this slow.

"Suck a little," he told her.

She did, and he wobbled slightly.

She looked up at him through her lashes, as if she noticed. His vixen was getting confident already.

"Take more," he said, gruffly, pressing further into her mouth. She opened a little wider, taking him further in, then closed her lips around him tightly, sucking and sliding along his length.

He gave her only shallow thrusts, and she took as much as he'd give, sucking and humming with pleasure.

Holy shit. There were certainly women who knew more about blow jobs than Hayden did, but he'd never had a better one.

He was already climbing toward climax, and he realized that it only had a little to do with the physical act and so much more to do with who this woman was and how he felt about her.

"I'm getting close, Hayden," he told her, tightening his hand in her hair. "When I tell you, I want you to pull back."

She nodded her understanding.

He picked up the pace slightly, thrusting still shallowly but quicker, as he felt his orgasm tightening at the base of his spine and his balls.

Then it was upon him. "Now," he ordered, tugging on her hair.

She let him go with a pop, and he took his shaft in hand, stroking hard as he came over her chest and breasts. The sight was again one of the hottest things he'd ever seen. He hauled her to her feet and sealed his mouth over hers, stroking his tongue deep.

She clung to him, kissing him back hotly, clearly turned on.

He set her back, studying her. He lifted a hand, tracing a finger through his come and swirling it over her nipple. "Holy shit."

"Colin," she said, her voice needy.

"You need something, *cailín*?"

She nodded. "Please."

He knew exactly what to do. He turned her, pressing his front to her back, sliding his hand down over her stomach and into her folds. He teased her clit, then pressed two fingers deep into her hot, tight pussy.

She groaned. "Yes, Colin."

He walked her forward toward one of the water jets on the wall.

"Let's get you some relief," he said against her ear.

He positioned her in front of the jet and then reached out to make sure it was pointing just where he wanted it. He lifted one of her legs, spreading her in front of the stream of water. He kept his fingers in her pussy, thrusting as the water hit her clit.

She gasped, her hands holding onto his forearms, digging in.

"That's my girl," he said against her ear.

He lifted his other hand and played with her nipple, tugging and squeezing. He felt her climax coming on quickly and continued to thrust in and out, quickening his pace as he felt her nearing the peak.

Within just a few seconds, she shot over the edge.

"Oh my God! Colin!"

As the waves crashed over her, he turned her, kissing her deeply as he pressed her against the wall.

"You're the hottest fucking thing," he praised. "I want you so fucking much. All the time." He knew he should take the chance to soap them both up and wash their hair, but he couldn't. He shut the water off, scooped her up in his arms, and carried her out to the bed.

"Hands and knees," he ordered.

He was hard for her again, and as soon as she was in position, he rolled on a condom and thrust deep. She cried out, her pussy still sensitive and hot from the orgasm she'd just had. He reached around and played with her clit, and soon they were both going over the edge again.

Breathing hard, he moved up onto the bed, spooning her and pulling her back against him.

"We're getting the duvet all wet," she said.

He reached for the edge and flipped it over the top of them. "Do not care."

"You know, you're not really giving me a good reason not to continue waking up exactly the way I did today."

He reached down and pinched her ass. "I want you in this bed when I wake up."

"But then I don't get thrown over your shoulder and fucked in the shower."

"Who said that? I'll gladly fuck you wherever you want me to, whenever you want me to."

She rolled back and looked up at him. "Well, that would be anywhere, anytime."

He grinned down at her. "Glad we're on that same page."

They cuddled and talked about nothing in particular for twenty minutes. Then they were back in the shower together, and this time they managed to use soap and shampoo. Of course, he couldn't resist taking her up against the wall before they got out.

But when they finally emerged from the bedroom washed, dry, dressed, and very satisfied, they were both grinning like idiots.

"I need to go to the nursing home for a little while today," she told him as they descended the stairs in search of some breakfast.

"To see your grandpa?"

"That and to work. I have a music class to lead."

Colin nodded. "I'll go with you."

She stopped on the third step from the bottom. "Really?"

"We can't let you go out by yourself until we find this guy," he reminded her. He reached out to tuck a strand of hair behind her ear. "And I'd love to meet your grandpa. I'd love to see you doing your music therapy. Can't think of a better way to spend my day."

She gave him a soft smile and it was very difficult for him not to throw her over his shoulder again and go right back upstairs.

She seemed to read something in his face, and she continued the rest of the way down the stairs with a giggle. "We can't keep doing that."

"The fuck we can't," he growled.

She started for the kitchen. "I will say I really love this side of you."

"Good thing. You're going to be seeing a lot of it."

twelve

AS THEY APPROACHED the doors to the nursing home, Hayden took a deep breath and blew it out. Then another.

"Are you nervous?"

She looked up at Colin. She wasn't used to someone being here with her. Or lots of places with her. Or paying attention to things like her *breathing*.

She shrugged. "I just...get a little worked up. I never know what to expect when I come visit him. His days and moods vary."

"What stage is he?"

"You know the stages?"

Colin paused just a moment, then he shifted her guitar case to his other hand and reached to link his fingers with hers. "I've done some reading over the last couple days."

Her eyes widened. "Because of my grandpa?"

"Because of you."

Her heart flipped over in her chest. He'd done some reading about Alzheimer's because of her. Because she had a grandfather with it.

She didn't know what to think about this guy.

Of course, *she'd* looked up facts about Cara and the royal family. So she supposed maybe it made sense.

She frowned a second later.

No, none of this made sense. She barely knew the guy. Yet she had the distinct feeling she was falling head over heels for him.

"He's in the moderate stage. Has been for a while. Of course, that's the stage that lasts for years in most cases and has the most variations."

"Does he know you?" Colin asked it gently.

Hayden took a breath. "Not anymore. He recognizes my name. He'll talk about me. But he doesn't recognize *me*."

Colin squeezed her fingers. "I'm sorry."

Her throat got tight as it always did when she thought about it. "Thank you."

"How long has it been since he recognized you on your visits?"

"It happened slowly. For a while it was just every once in a while. But it's been about six months since he's really remembered. For a bit, he would think I was my mom. Even though my sister looks more like her than I do. Sometimes he would think I was my grandma." She smiled softly at that. "Then when I came, he would look at me and I could tell he knew that he knew me, but he just couldn't come up with any of our names." She swallowed. "But honestly, it's been about two months since I've seen even that recognition." She hadn't said that out loud to anyone. She hadn't admitted that to her family. It would devastate them. "I haven't been able to tell my mom or grandma that," she confessed. "They aren't able to get down here to see him very often. I'm the one who visits and keeps up with things and then gives them reports."

"Do you keep the reports upbeat and sunny?" Colin guessed.

"And I feel bad about it," she said with a nod. "I feel guilty all the time, though. I don't know if I should be telling them the truth or if it's okay to be sugarcoating things. They're so far away that I wonder what good it would do to upset them with the reality. They can't come more often and there's nothing they can do about any of it anyway. No one can fix this. I know they would just sit at home and worry and feel terrible. And what good does that do? But then I wonder if it's right to let them think everything is fine too. When they do come next time, they're going to be shocked by the decline."

Colin lifted her hand to his lips and pressed a kiss to her knuckles. "I don't think there's a right or wrong way to do this, Hayden. It's not your job to know how everyone will feel and react to everything or to protect them from everything, is it?"

She studied him. That was interesting, coming from a man who seemed to believe that it *was* his job to protect the people around him from everything. And no, she didn't think Colin only physically protected the people he loved.

She took a deep breath. "Kind of. I've always been the one who thought ahead to what everyone needed. And I am protecting them. Or trying to. And I think deep down, they know that I'm lying to them. I don't think anyone's actually in denial. They know he's not going to get better. And they know I'm here taking care of the hard stuff. And they know that I don't want them to feel bad. So I think they all kind of know that I'm not telling them everything."

"What do you mean you thought ahead to what everyone needed?"

"When my brothers and sister were growing up they played ball."

"Baseball and softball," Colin said. "They were big stars."

"Are," she corrected. "My older brother, Jake, is in the minors now waiting for his shot. Everyone thinks he'll be called up soon. Jared and Hailey are in college and are the MVPs of their teams."

Colin didn't roll his eyes, but she could sense that he wanted to. "Okay."

"They've been playing since they were little. And with the three of them going in different directions, they kept my parents really busy. Mom and Dad both worked—Dad's a coach so he had his practices and games too—so I helped out. I did a lot of cooking and laundry. I did meal planning, packed lots of travel bags, went to doctor's appointments, and planned lots of team parties. That kind of stuff."

He looked down at her, understanding on his face. "No wonder you could just jump in when Saoirse needed something for school."

She grinned and nodded. "That was a piece of cake. Throw me a challenge sometime. Like a whole class holiday party in under twenty-four hours. Then you'll really see my skills."

Immediately Hayden felt her cheeks heat. That had sounded a little like she was fishing to be hanging around for the next holiday. And maybe a little flirtatious when discussing skills...

"Oh, I've already been impressed with your skills," Colin said, his voice a little husky. "Definitely want to see more."

Okay, maybe the flirting wasn't so bad.

But then he was frowning. "But now you're taking care of the hard stuff with your grandpa? On your own?"

She nodded. "I'm his medical and financial power of attorney. If the nursing home or anyone needs anything or if anything happens, they call me. I go to the doctor with him. And I deal with the times when he has outbursts or when he wants to call home or when he won't cooperate with the staff."

"How often does that happen?"

She lifted a shoulder. "Actually, that's been a couple of months too. He used to call me periodically in the middle of the night, demanding I come and get him and take him home. He'd also refuse to shower for the staff. He'd accuse staff members of stealing from him." She sighed. "All kinds of things." She shook her head. "But it's been a while. They've adjusted his meds a little and..." She swallowed. "He's declined a little too. He's not as combative."

Colin stopped in front of the doors and tugged her to the side. He studied her face for a moment. "You really are alone here." It wasn't really a question.

She'd told him this. "My family's about five hours away."

"I know. I just... It's not just the distance. You're shouldering all of this on your own. You didn't tell your family about any of the outbursts or combativeness either, did you?"

Hayden's eyes widened. Even remembering them made her sad and exhausted. She *never* could have told her mom and grandmother about those. "That would've been horrible. My grandmother would have been heartbroken. My mother would have been so stressed."

"So, they just think he's mostly happy and everything's fine?"

"They know that he's sick and that his memory is failing and that his physical decline is slow, but sure. But they prefer to think of him the way they last saw him. Where he remembered everybody, and he was able to talk about the old days. His short-term memory was a problem then, but he could still talk about past Christmases, and taking us fishing, and my siblings playing ball, and fixing up old cars with my uncle."

"And now?"

Hayden pressed her lips together and shook her head. "Not as much."

Colin lifted his hand to the back of her head and pulled her in, pressing her forehead against his chest. He stroked his hand over her hair, and she felt his lips on the top of her head. "I'm so fucking sorry, *mo grá*."

She pulled in a deep breath, taking in his scent at the same time.

She'd looked up *cailín* and *a stór*, two terms Colin had used for her and Saoirse. *Cailín* was "girl" but it was used as an endearment with girlfriends often. When she'd read that, she'd felt warm and tingly, especially remembering the sexy gruffness in his voice when he said it, and the circumstances they'd been in when he'd used it. *A stór* was "dear" and his soft affection, both in his voice and his eyes when he used it for Saoirse also made sense. Now she was going to have to look up *mo grá*. But the *way* he said it already told her it was said with fondness, and holy crap, she needed that so much right now.

She put her arms around him and squeezed.

"Thank you, Colin."

She often breathed deep when she was here. It was the way to hold back the tears. She loved the work that she did here. She knew it was important. She knew that she brought joy to these people's lives. It helped with their memories. It helped stimulate their brains and brought them happiness. That included her grandfather. Music was a way they could still bond.

But this deep breath was different. This had Colin in it. She felt his sympathy. But it didn't feel like he was pitying her. It felt like he wanted to help her. And he was. His warmth, his strength, just that he was here.

"Of course," he said gruffly.

She looked up at him. "I mean, I know you had to. It's your job and I'm in danger and all of that." She blushed. It was stupid to be thanking him for coming.

Although it *wasn't* his job. She wasn't paying him. Hell, he was still auditioning for a maybe someday job.

She didn't know for sure the record label was going to offer her a deal. What if they didn't? What if Sabrina had gotten her hopes up? What if Henry had gotten his and Colin's and Jonah's hopes up? What if it all fell through after they'd given her all of...this? Their time and help and friendship?

Dammit. This all felt very tangled up.

But Colin gave her a smile. "I'm not here for that. I mean, I am, but I could've sent Jonah if it was just that. Or I could've had Matt come over and meet you. I just... I wanted to be the one."

Her throat tightened again but she didn't feel sad in this moment. She lifted up on her tiptoes and pressed her lips to his. "I'm glad."

They both left it at that. He looked at her for another long moment. Then he simply pulled the door open and ushered her inside.

They approached the front desk and the receptionist Morgan lifted her head and greeted them with a smile. Then her eyes widened. As did her smile. She looked Colin over from head to toe. "Well, hi. Welcome."

Hayden gave her a look. What the hell? She was definitely checking Colin out. But Morgan didn't notice Hayden's look. Because she hadn't taken her eyes off of Colin yet.

"Hey, Morgan, this is Colin. We're here for the music class."

Morgan turned the clipboard around and pushed it toward Colin. "Nice to meet you. Just need you to sign in with your name and number, please."

Hayden's eyebrows climbed. Morgan didn't need his phone number. What would that be for?

Colin nodded. "You can just use Hayden's phone number. If you need to get a hold of me, you can easily find me with her."

He scrawled his name across the board, then put his arm around Hayden, tucking her up against his side.

Her heart squeezed. So, he'd realized Morgan was flirting with him too.

"Is Grandpa in the common room?" Hayden asked, slipping her arm around him.

Morgan finally met her gaze. She grinned as if to say, *hey, worth a shot.* "Yeah. He's having a pretty good day."

"Great. We'll visit with him first. The group will start at three."

Morgan smiled. "I'll tell Lisa."

Hayden linked her fingers with Colin's and led him down the hall. "During the day, they try to have everyone out of their room and participating in activities. Even during non-structured time, they encourage residents to spend time in the common rooms, reading, or doing puzzles, or watching television. It helps them to socialize and gives them routine and the stimulation helps them sleep better at night."

"I read about that. Different facilities have different philosophies about routines though, right?"

Hayden nodded. "Some let the residents just do their own thing. If they sleep during the day and are up at night, they accommodate that. Others try to keep everyone on a more typical schedule. Others do a hybrid model."

She keyed in the code that would let them through the locked doors to the common room in the memory care unit. For the residents' safety, the doors were kept locked, so no one wandered into unsupervised areas or out of the building. But the memory care unit was large, with high ceilings, lots of windows, and wide spaces along with an inner courtyard with a smoothly paved path lined with plants, flowers, and bird feeders where they were free to walk and sit outside whenever they wanted to, so they had plenty of room to move and wander as they needed to.

"Is the music therapy part of their daily routine or only when you come?" Colin asked.

"They have music time every day, but it's not always a formal session with a music therapist like today. I come twice a week. On the other days, the staff leads the sessions. We use songs they probably know. Sometimes just hearing a song can help stimulate memories and we get them talking about those memories or their feelings. Sometimes we get them singing along. We also try to use repetitive motions and incorporate exercise. Sometimes we even get them to play instruments along with us. It's amazing what they retain in their deep memories. For instance, my grandpa was a guitarist and when I come to see him, he'll often play with me. He taught me to play piano too. The motions and the rhythms are really ingrained."

"The human mind is fascinating."

She nodded with a smile. "I agree." She located her grandfather across the wide-open room.

The room had a high vaulted ceiling and was lined with windows on two sides, making it bright and sunny. It was filled with multiple tables that were used for a variety of activities. Several were occupied, while other residents sat in chairs around the television or near the windows like her grandfather.

As they started across the room, a large golden lab came ambling over to greet them.

"Hi, Ben." Hayden went down onto one knee to give the dog some love.

Colin knelt next to her, reaching to stroke the dog's head. "Ben?"

She grinned. "Ben lives here. Lots of places have live-in

pets. Ben's been here for ten years. My grandpa loves him. He had a dog like Ben growing up. Most days Grandpa thinks Ben is his dog, Scooter."

"Hey, Ben," Colin said, his voice low and gentle as he stroked the dog's face. Ben leaned into the touch.

Hayden didn't blame him.

"You like dogs?"

Colin laughed. "Absolutely. All animals. Living with Fiona and Saoirse, it was kind of a requirement. I've been around a lot of interesting, unique ones, but nothing beats a great dog."

"You don't have one, though."

He shook his head. "I'm still kind of settling in. This is the first time that I've actually been able to make those kinds of decisions for myself."

She frowned. "Really? They wouldn't let you have a dog?"

He lifted a shoulder. "I mean, probably. It's just that I've spent so many years thinking about what's best for Saoirse and what she wanted, I never really thought about having something of my own."

Hayden frowned. Colin's past ten years had been so strange. The guy's entire world had revolved around that little girl. Her mother, too, of course, to some extent. But all of his decisions, his choices, everything he'd done, had taken Saoirse into consideration. It had been his job. He'd understood it when he'd signed on, of course. And clearly he'd loved it. But it was...weird.

"Well, what about now? You should get one," Hayden said.

"I can't really until I know what my next job is. I might be traveling a lot. It depends on my next client," he said. He gave her a long look.

Right. Because it might be her. And she would be touring the country.

Well, she'd let him have a dog.

213

But if it wasn't her...if the record label didn't offer her a contract...who would it be? He had to work. He would try to get another client, obviously. And that person might travel. And that meant he wouldn't be in Autre.

And her heart sank at that thought.

She wouldn't get to see him anymore. And he might not get to have a dog.

"Your work really is always about the clients and what *they* need and want?"

He nodded. "My job is to make sure that whatever they want to do is safe and secure."

She nodded. She'd had a very close and personal, intense demonstration of his job over the past couple of days.

"And you want a client who is high profile, who would need security on an ongoing, around-the-clock basis, but who you can be close to—get to know and be involved in his or her life?"

Ugh, she hated the idea of it being a "her" if she was around his age and possibly beautiful, and charismatic— because she'd have to be in order to be high profile enough to need that much security, right?—and needing him all the time.

He nodded. "I mean, that's what I've always done." He grinned a *very* cute grin. "I mean, Saoirse's been my only long-term client. But that's what I like. I like to be really involved. I don't want to just come and go. I want to know my people. I want them to trust me, and I want to be a part of their lives."

None of that surprised her. That was Colin. He jumped into everything fully. Whether it was making food for Saoirse's teachers or taking a singer to a little bar to do a free show, he did it wholeheartedly. His job would always be more than a job.

"Come on," Hayden said, rising. She wasn't sure what to say to Colin about his situation, past or present. Or future.

Other than, *don't leave. Stay here. Date me. Be my boyfriend. Even if I don't land a big music deal and don't need real security, stay here and make me feel safe.*

And that was so damned pathetic, it made her cringe to even *think* it.

So she decided to concentrate on *her* present. Today. With Colin.

"See you later, Ben," Colin said to the dog.

They crossed the room to where Bill Lewis, Hayden's grandfather, was sitting next to the window. He was watching the birds flitting around the birdfeeder.

"Hi, Grandpa," Hayden said.

Bill looked up at them. He frowned as if confused. "Hello?" He phrased it as a question, clearly not understanding why she was talking to him.

"Hi. It's Hayden."

He smiled. "I have a granddaughter named Hayden."

She nodded.

Colin stepped forward. "It's a beautiful name. How old is your granddaughter?"

She was grateful. That was the perfect way to find out where Bill was in his memories today.

"Oh geez, she must be eight or nine by now. She's real pretty. So talented." Bill leaned in closer with a conspiratorial smile. "Don't tell the others, but she is extra special to me."

Hayden couldn't help it. She felt her heart squeeze a little. He used to say that to her all the time. The funny thing was her brothers and sister always knew. None of them ever minded, either. Her older brother and the twins had always had plenty of attention. No one had felt slighted in their family.

Bill and Hayden had had a special bond, and whether it was because he truly did enjoy her most, or because of their shared love of music, or his lack of interest in baseball and softball, or because of her lack of athletic ability in a family where that was very, *obviously* important, Bill had always made a point of making Hayden feel special.

"Well, if she's anything like my Hayden I can understand why," Colin said.

Hayden looked at him quickly. The words had rolled off his tongue so easily. Almost as if he meant it and wasn't just trying to relate to Bill. Colin gave her a wink.

"We're just waiting for my music class to start," Hayden said, trying to ignore the riot of butterflies in her stomach. "Would you mind if we sit with you? It's so nice here by the windows."

Bill gestured toward a couple of chairs nearby. "I don't mind. Music class?" he added as they put the chairs closer.

He attended the music class each time she came. "Yes. I'm a music therapist. I come over here a couple times a week and have a class. You should come today."

Bill nodded. "I love music. Been a musician all my life. It's something Hayden and I do together."

"Is it?" She gave him a smile. As much as she missed her grandfather in the here and now, it did warm her heart that he remembered those things. "I bet she loves that."

"She's a natural," Bill said, shaking his head. "Takes to instruments like a fish takes to water. There's nothing I can't teach her. She's also a beautiful singer."

"Does she have a favorite song?" Colin asked.

"'You Are My Sunshine'," Bill said with a smile. "The first one I taught her when she was little. Now we sing it together all the time."

Hayden reached for her guitar case. He was right. That was the first song she'd learned on the guitar. It was one they sang together now too. It always made him smile and he sang along, remembering every word.

"I love that one. My grandfather and I sing it together too. Do you play?" she asked as she pulled her guitar from the case.

Bill nodded. "Of course."

She handed the guitar over. "Would you like to?"

Bill took the instrument and positioned it on his lap. She shot Colin a look. But he was watching Bill, fascinated.

Bill positioned his fingers on the strings and then strummed the first chord. Perfectly.

He played the first stanza and then Hayden began singing softly.

It didn't take long for Bill to join in.

They sang through it twice.

It was always hard for her to keep her composure. It meant a lot to her that her grandfather remembered the song. And as Colin said, the human mind was amazing. It fascinated her that he couldn't remember what day it was, but that he could remember how to play and sing a song from years ago.

Then again, it was something he had done thousands of times.

This time when she looked at Colin, she found him watching her.

She blushed.

This was a very different side of her musically. She wasn't dressed up. Today she was wearing a simple sundress, one that had been washed many times. Her hair was pulled back into a loose ponytail, and she barely had any make-up on. It was a far cry from what she'd looked like at the bar the other night.

She also didn't have the band backing her up and this was not a hard-rocking or sexy-sultry song.

The way he was looking at her was different today too. But it still made her heart beat faster.

At the bar he'd been watching her with heat. Like he wanted to strip her down and put her up against the bar.

217

Now he was watching her with...warmth. It was a much softer expression. Like he wanted to touch her but with more of a hug or something. The look was full of affection.

But both of those looks had something in common—just a touch of wonder.

She was used to people watching her sing. She knew she was good. She'd been told she was talented over and over, most of her life. And objectively she just knew it was true. She was enough of a musician to know that.

And she was sure that people had watched her with a little bit of awe in the past.

Colin Daly's eyes on her did things to her that no one ever had before, though.

She gave him a little smile.

He turned to Bill. "Tell me about your granddaughter, Hayden. What's she like?"

Hayden's eyes widened. Oh really? He was going to learn about her from her grandfather? Who didn't even know that she was sitting right here?

"You don't have to tell us, Bill," she said.

"Oh, I love talking about Hayden," Bill said. He leaned onto the guitar as if he'd been holding it for years. And he had. When she pictured her grandfather, this was exactly how he looked. In a chair, arms draped over a guitar, a smile on his face.

"Hayden is..." He trailed off for a moment, a smile still teasing his lips. "She's like sunshine. She's warm and bright. You just want to be near her. She makes the people around her open up and bloom. Whether it's a kitten she's brought in from the cold, or one of her siblings, or her mom, or me, or a total stranger. She makes everybody feel better when they're near her."

Hayden knew she was staring at him. But she'd never

heard him talk like that before. She knew her grandfather loved her. He'd always told her she was sunny and that she made him smile. She'd heard him say that she made rooms brighter and that she was a nurturer. But she'd never heard it said quite like *this* before.

Colin reached out and put a hand on top of hers on her leg. She couldn't look at him, though. She was studying her grandfather's face. He had a soft, faraway look in his eyes that was full of love and happiness. She wanted to memorize it.

"Our whole family works because of her. She makes things easier for all of us. We don't always realize it though," Bill said, shaking his head. "She's quiet about it."

Hayden could feel Colin's eyes on her.

"She sounds amazing," Colin said.

"Oh, she is that."

"She's only eight or nine," Colin said. "You can already see all that in her?"

Colin clearly understood that even though Bill was talking about Hayden as a child, these impressions of her were based on knowing her for twenty-some years. He hadn't seen all of this in her when she'd been eight. Yes, she'd been taking care of kittens and her siblings and...okay, everyone, as much as she could. But some of what he was 'remembering' and associating with his memories of her were from a lifetime, not just those first eight years.

It still all warmed her from the inside. Like a drink of hot chocolate on a cold, rainy day. She hadn't realized that she'd needed to hear this.

"Oh yeah," Bill said. "Some people grow into what they're going to be. You know? They learn it along the way. But sometimes people are just born with what they're going to be. She was meant to be a caregiver." He frowned. "But people forget to take care of her." He shook his head. "Even a beautiful tree that gives others shade and fruit and provides branches for nests needs water, and sun, and care to live."

Colin was still watching her. She finally met his gaze. The look he gave her made her toes curl and her stomach swoop.

"Do you think she might be a musician when she grows up?" Colin asked Bill.

Bill laughed. "I don't know about that. I mean, she'll play and sing. That makes her heart happy. It makes the hearts around her happy. But she doesn't like to be up in front. She'd be a great teacher or something, though. And a mom," he added. "She needs to have a lot of kids. Lots of people to take care of and love."

Hayden felt her cheeks heat. Suddenly she was thinking about how sweet a little boy with Colin's eyes and smile and dark hair would be.

It was *absolutely not* okay to be thinking about having a baby with Colin.

What the *hell*?

She'd never thought about being pregnant or having babies. Not in specific terms anyway. She supposed she always kind of assumed that probably someday, a long time down the road, she'd have kids. Maybe. Possibly.

But suddenly she had the urge to see Colin holding a baby.

She knew he'd done it. He'd been with Saoirse since she'd been born.

God, she wanted to see him with a baby.

She cleared her throat and tried to think of something to say.

She didn't remember talking about what she wanted to be when she grew up with her grandfather. But no, she'd never dreamed of being a performer. Not on stage. She'd always written songs and she'd assumed she would keep doing that. She'd also always sung. It was just a normal part of her life.

But now that she was thinking about it, she could easily picture herself sitting at a piano or holding her own guitar in her own living room and...yeah, she supposed she'd also always assumed she'd be a mom. That she'd teach her kids to play and sing. That music would fill her house, while they cooked and played and at bath time and bedtime. And that she'd have more kittens and other animals. And that she'd see her parents and siblings and *their* kids regularly. That she'd host the family holidays and get-togethers because everyone else would be busy. She'd keep track of anniversaries, and would plan the summer family vacation, and would teach her nieces and nephews piano lessons too, and when they needed cupcakes for a school party...

She gasped softly, her hand going to her mouth.

Holy shit.

She'd never realized it, but she'd always assumed that she'd keep taking care of everyone. That she'd be the backbone. Even for her siblings' kids. She'd be Aunt Hayden. The one who they'd come to after school and for the extra stuff that her siblings would never think of or be able to handle because they'd be busy doing all the extra amazing stuff they would, no doubt, be up to their eyeballs in as always. Just like...

Her gaze flew to Colin's, and she found him watching her with both eyebrows arched. He was clearly wondering what the hell she was thinking.

We're alike. We do the same things for the people in our lives. We keep it all together.

She pressed her lips together and shook her head to tell him it was nothing.

She wasn't going to blurt *that* out. It was too much. She didn't know him *that* well.

Even if you are thinking about having his babies.

And so what if it was true? It didn't mean anything. She

certainly didn't need him to think that *she* was thinking *we're so much alike. We could kick some major ass and take care of EVERYONE if we were together. God, we could have like six kids and still manage all the nieces and nephews and Saoirse and any kids Cian and Henry and Jonah have too, and we would be like fucking PTA superheroes.*

Yeah, *that* was sexy. And not crazy at all. Especially after knowing each other for two days.

"Do you two have kids?" Bill asked.

Her cheeks grew even hotter. God, Colin was going to be able to tell exactly what she'd been thinking.

Well, maybe not the part about having huge sleepovers with *everyone's* kids, complete with cookie decorating and full-costume singalongs. But...close.

Colin didn't laugh. He also didn't say no quickly. He just shook his head. "Not yet."

Her stomach swooped, her heart flipped over, and her panties got wet.

But worse, her imagination said, *we should do* The Music Man *as a sing-along...the kids should learn the classic musicals.*

Holy crap. She was losing her mind.

"But I agree," Colin went on. "Haydens like ours definitely need to be well taken care of."

She almost moaned. That was so hot. At least in her head, where PTA-cupcake baking and dirty hot sex were getting mixed up into one big I-want-that wish list.

Bill leaned over and patted Colin on the shoulder. "Taking care of a good woman is a blessing. I've been taking care of my Mary Kate for forty-two years and I wouldn't trade a day."

Hayden felt her eyes stinging. It didn't matter that it had actually been fifty-six years. Her grandparents had definitely been a role model for a strong, loving marriage. Her grandfather's condition was extremely hard on her grandmother.

While having him far away was difficult, Hayden thought maybe part of the reason that Hayden's mother—their daughter—had been so in favor of him being in New Orleans was not just the wonderful care he was getting at this facility, but also because she thought it might be easier on his wife to not see his daily decline.

On days like this, Hayden thought maybe she was doing the right thing. Bill didn't know who she was, he couldn't recite the date, or tell anyone who the president was, but right now, he seemed happy. He was thinking about good times, he thought that his granddaughter, Hayden, and his wife, Mary Kate, were nearby and that he would see them soon, and he was playing a guitar. Bill Lewis had never been as happy as when he played guitar.

"Any requests?" she asked, gesturing at the guitar. "What are some of your favorite songs?"

"Do you know 'Jambalaya'?"

She did. Because of this man. "Of course."

They played and sang "Jambalaya" twice. Then she sang "I Love Rock and Roll" for him because he'd always loved that one. Then he requested "Amazing Grace".

She'd been expecting that. He always asked for that one. It was just hard for her to get through.

But when her voice wobbled, Colin joined in.

His deep bass seeped into her and she closed her eyes and was able to keep going. He was even a good singer.

How was she *not* going to fall in love with him?

thirteen

THEY CONVINCED Bill to join them for the music class. Actually, Hayden thought maybe Colin convinced him. But in any case, Bill was a part of the group that sang and "danced" and enjoyed the music for an hour in the common room and Hayden was feeling happy and light as she and Colin walked back out to his truck, hand in hand, afterward.

"So, that's part of what I do," she said.

"It's incredible, Hayden."

She could tell he meant it, and it made her chest feel full and warm. "Thanks. I love it."

They walked the rest of the way to his truck.

Then she said, "You know..." She took a breath. "I'm going to point something out and I want you to just think about it."

"Okay."

"There are some similarities between your situation with Saoirse and mine with my grandpa."

He didn't respond.

"I know you feel like you've lost her. Henry and Cian have shared some things and I know they feel the same way." She took a breath. "I know things have changed a lot between you.

And maybe you have lost pieces. She doesn't live with you. She has Knox in her life now, sharing things with her that you used to share. There are things going on with her you don't have a front row seat to. But..." Hayden thought about how to phrase this. "You're still *there*. You're deep in her memories and her heart. You're a part of her. Even if it's not even consciously all the time. The things that you've shared, the things that helped shape and mold her, are there and they won't leave." She stopped and looked up at him. "And I don't know if I'm making the metaphor about my grandpa and his memories still being there deep down no matter what—the way he can pull those songs out or remember things about my childhood or know things about me as a person when he doesn't even recognize me sitting right there in front of him—or if the metaphor is about me, the little girl who he *mattered* so damned much to that even now that he's basically gone, he's still a part of me but..."

Her voice broke and then Colin lifted a hand and cupped her face, and she felt the tear track down her cheek.

But she was determined to go on. She shook her head.

"*But*," she said stubbornly. "You matter to her, Colin. I know it sucks that it's not the same, but you haven't lost her. And I just want you to know that. You can't lose a person like that. You can't lose a love like that."

"Hayden—"

"And," she said, still having a little more to say and wanting to get it out. "I really hope that doesn't keep you from being important to other people because I know it hurts. But it still really matters. And you're really good at it."

He stood staring down at her. Then he took a step forward, which backed her up against the side of his truck.

"Jesus Christ, Hayden," was all he said before he lowered his head and kissed her.

225

She put her hand at the back of his neck, holding him close.

The kiss started sweet, but it didn't stay that way for long. He groaned and angled his head so that he could more fully taste her. He slid his tongue over her lower lip and in along her tongue. She met his strokes with her own, hungrily. God, she liked him so fucking much.

And she wanted him. So. Much.

Finally, he lifted his head. "You are…amazing."

"Will you…" She pressed her lips together. She knew how this was going to sound and it wasn't *exactly* how she meant it.

"Aye," he said simply.

She smiled. "Will you come over? To my apartment? For a little bit?"

He didn't look surprised. But he looked turned on. And touched, if she wasn't mistaken. "Really?"

"I'd like to make you lunch." That was the truth. She wouldn't mind some more of that kissing in a more private place too, but she really had been intending to invite him over for lunch. She'd love to cook for him. At her place.

"I'd love that," he said, his voice a little gruff.

"And we don't have to get naked."

He smiled. "Oh, I think we do."

She laughed. "I mean…that wasn't why I asked. I'd like to make you lunch."

"I'd love that. I'd love to see your apartment." He leaned in. "And I also really need to get you naked. Soon."

A hot shiver went through her. "Yeah."

"I need to send Matt over to check the apartment ahead of us," he said.

Her eyes widened. "Oh. Well, he doesn't have to—"

"It's fine," Colin said. "If you want to go home, we're going to make it so you can go home."

Right, the letting her do whatever she wanted to safely and

securely.

"But Matt is probably at work, right? I don't want to make him go because I had a whim."

"This is Matt's job. Or part of it. He works for me," Colin said.

"Oh." Hayden thought about that. "Oh. I didn't realize."

"He's part of the team."

"Oh. Well, then..." She smiled. "Great."

Colin returned the smile. "Yeah. Great." He pulled his phone out, sent off a text, then his hands settled on her hips. "Now we have a little more time for this." He kissed her again, sweet and deep.

She let herself settle into it.

The way this man kissed her was addictive. So was the way he touched her. And talked to her. And looked at her.

Ugh, she was never going to get enough.

They made a quick stop at a small market to grab a few ingredients and finished just as Matt texted that everything was clear at Hayden's apartment.

Colin pulled up at the curb. His heart was hammering way too fast for stopping by a woman's place in the middle of the day for her to make him lunch.

But this was Hayden.

She wasn't just any woman.

Seeing her apartment, having her cook for him, after meeting her grandpa, and seeing her at work as a music therapist—something that brought out a glow in her that had reached in and wrapped around his heart in a way that had shocked him—was possibly going to change everything. Permanently.

227

Oh, who the fuck was he kidding?

Things had already changed. Permanently.

Colin climbed the steps behind her, strangely interested in her apartment.

The building was older, but well-kept. It made him fucking crazy to think about her stalker being here. He hated the idea that the other man had found her. Had been audacious enough to come to her door.

He made himself focus on everything from the stairwell to the hallway to the other doors. This was the kind of apartment building where people moved in and stayed for a while. The doorways were decorated, some of them had doormats in front of them, several of the doors had things hanging from the front welcoming visitors, a few had plaques beside the door proclaiming the residents' last names.

Hayden stepped in front of her door and inserted the key, turning it, then pushing the door open. She looked a little shy, and it was adorable.

"Welcome," she said, with a smile over her shoulder at him.

He followed her inside.

The apartment was exactly what he would've expected.

It was small, but incredibly cozy. It smelled amazing. It was definitely the home of someone who liked to cook and bake. There was a touch of vanilla and cinnamon in the air.

The furnishings were colorful and mismatched, yet somehow went together. There were lots of pillows and a couple of throw blankets. The couch and two chairs were over-stuffed. The coffee table was covered with books, mail, a mug, and two candles. A small electronic keyboard was set up along one living room wall and another guitar was propped in the corner.

There were also houseplants.

He wasn't surprised. She was like sunshine. Her grandfather had nailed that. She made the things around her bloom. She definitely had with his friends. They were happier, more open around her. It wasn't that Cian wasn't normally a very happy person, but he had a different attitude when he was around Hayden. He was softer, more caring. It was easy to tell that he adored this woman.

The kitchen was to the right. Directly to the right. Three steps, and Colin was in it. A waist-high counter separated the kitchen from the living area. A tiny table was tucked into one corner. It was also covered with books and some papers, and he could see sheet music.

Colin also liked that she didn't move to start cleaning things up, tidying, or trying to stack things into neater piles as he stepped further into the room. She just let him be here. In her space, around her things.

What did bother him, however, was that it seemed everything was a little worn. Older. Like the furniture had been bought second-hand or was possibly hand-me-downs. It was easy to see that Hayden didn't splurge on herself.

Maybe she didn't want to. That was possible. She seemed very down to earth. But if any woman deserved jewels, fine silks, and the most expensive luxury items, it was her.

Hayden put other people first, and Colin very much wanted to spoil her, treat her, and make her feel like a queen.

And he knew a little something about queens. Or princesses, at least.

"I love it," he told her. "It's very you."

She smiled at him. "How so?"

"Warm. Comfortable. A place I want to get wrapped up in and stay for days."

There was a flicker of heat in her eyes, and she moved closer. "Well, you're welcome to stay as long as you want."

229

He took a deep breath. The idea of staying wrapped up in Hayden for days, barely coming up for air, was far too tempting.

"How hungry are you?" he asked.

"Why?"

"Because I really want to do the naked thing."

She grinned. "Same. But I have to tell you something."

He arched a brow. "Okay."

"It's going to sound cheesy."

"I like cheese."

"While I am hungry, part of wanting to bring you here is that I just kind of want to cook for you. Because I am a good cook. And I feel like people don't cook for you or take care of you at all. And my grandfather was absolutely right—I love to do that. I guess I've always known that but hearing him say it really hit me. That really is me. So I am hungry, but mostly I just want to cook for you. Here in my apartment. And I know that sounds like a lot."

He reached up and tucked a strand of hair behind her ear. Then dragged the back of his fingers down her cheek.

He understood. He did want to get her naked, but he also wanted her to cook for him. And not in the misogynistic women-belong-in-the-kitchen way. But because it felt intimate in a different way. People did not cook for him. He had a lot of friends, all of whom had his back. He never felt really alone. He knew that any of them would help him with anything he asked. But they didn't do caretaker tasks for him. And the idea that Hayden wanted to be the one who did it was a turn on a whole new way.

"I would really like that. Almost as much as getting you naked. And it can definitely come first."

Her smile was bright. Goddammit, he would love to see

that smile over and over again. For a really long time. Like maybe forever.

Jesus.

Speaking of things that were a lot.

He leaned over and kissed her.

On the forehead.

Which also made her smile brightly.

She moved into the kitchen, and Colin set the grocery bag on the counter.

"Want help?" he asked.

"Actually..." She smiled at him as she started pulling food out and collecting ingredients on the counter. "No. Want something to drink?"

She wanted to cook for him. He was going to let her. "Sure."

She washed her hands, dried them on a bright yellow—a sunshine yellow—towel, then poured him a glass of lemonade. He took a chair at her tiny kitchen table. The one that would allow him to watch her move around the kitchen.

He sipped from his glass. It was delicious.

"How long have you lived here?" he asked. There was a short hallway leading off to the left that he assumed would take him to the bathroom and bedroom. But there wasn't much else to the apartment.

"As long as I've been in New Orleans," she said.

"So you like it here? Feel safe?"

"I don't hate it."

She'd already donned an apron and was now tenderizing chicken breasts. He frowned at her answer. When she stopped pounding, he asked, "But you don't like it?"

She shrugged as she sprinkled the chicken with salt and pepper, squeezed an orange over the top, and then brushed Dijon mustard over them. "I just don't like apartment living, to be honest." She transferred the chicken into a pan on the stove.

"Why's that?"

"I like houses," she said, as she seared the chicken. "To me, that's a home." She looked over. "I know that plenty of people make their homes in apartments. I'm not judging that. Just for me...a home is a house with a porch and a yard and bedrooms upstairs and a big kitchen." She paused, studying the chicken. Then she added, "I've purposefully gotten to know my neighbors because it seems so strange to hear other people's noise—their voices, their footsteps—and to have a sense of their routines, and to know little details about their lives, like what they watch on TV and when they get a new purse, but to not even know their names. So I've made a point of meeting them so I know who I'm living with here."

"That way the building feels a little more like a big house with multiple bedrooms?" Colin asked.

She looked shy again, but she nodded.

God, she was so fucking...loveable. "How have you gotten to know them?"

She laughed and held a chicken breast up with a fork. "Food. It's my love language. And I can't cook small. It's impossible for me to cook fewer than six servings of anything. It just doesn't feel right. And it feels even better to cook twelve servings. So, I take food around to my neighbors."

He could have guessed that. "And I'm sure you've gained many fans that way," he commented.

"They do love to see me coming with my containers," she agreed with a grin. "And they bring them right back, washed up and ready to go for the next time."

"Do any of them know that you're a singer?" he asked. He was sitting back in the chair, one ankle propped on his opposite knee. He cradled his glass of lemonade with one hand. He was trying to look casual, but suddenly he didn't feel casual.

"Sure." She turned the chicken. "I mean, they hear me

playing the guitar and the piano and composing and rehearsing."

"They know you sing then," he said. "But do they know you perform?"

She reached to shut off the stove burner and then pulled open the oven and slid the cast iron skillet inside. She closed the door, set a timer, and then turned to face him. "Do you mean, do I think my stalker lives in the building?"

Colin nodded.

"No. None of my neighbors are young, single men."

"He wouldn't have to be single."

"But I would have noticed one of my neighbors at a show. Certainly, at multiple shows," she pointed out. "And we know he's been at my shows."

Colin let out a breath. "Right." Then he frowned. "Is it possible he's a friend of someone in the building? Or a relative?"

She thought about that for a moment. "I suppose. But again, surely, I would have run into him here, right? It's a lot harder to watch someone from afar in a building this size. There are only twelve units. I know them all. We see each other all the time. And I do see their friends and family coming and going as well. I really feel like I would have recognized him at one of the bars if it was someone from here. The shows at the bars aren't huge either."

He nodded. All of that was good and likely true.

She watched him for a long moment. "Is this..." She pulled her bottom lip between her teeth. "Is it a problem we're sleeping together? This whole job thing? Have we complicated everything?"

That was a really good question. A fair one. And it deserved a fair answer. "I've been thinking about it," he said. "And I don't think so. At first, I thought we should keep a professional distance but..."

She just arched her brows and waited.

"No one will ever want to keep you safer than I do, Hayden," he said. His voice was low and firm, and he knew his expression matched the force behind his words. "There is no one who will go to the lengths I will to protect you. And, sleeping right next to you seems like the best place to be if we want to keep you safe."

Her cheeks were pink, and he knew it was from desire. Even from ten feet away, the chemistry between them crackled. She took a few seconds to respond. Her next breath was a little shaky. But he could tell it wasn't because she disliked his answer. Her nipples were hard behind the bodice of her sweet little sundress, and she was pressing her lips together as she stared at him.

Finally, she asked, "And what if it doesn't work out? What if we break up?" Her cheeks got even pinker. "I mean...I don't know if what we're doing is even something that would be a break up exactly. I don't know what...we're doing. Exactly. What we should call it. If you want to call it anything. We don't have to call it anything. But if you would meet someone...or if you want something else...or I would..." She trailed off, squeezing her eyes together. "I'm just curious how this works and just how complicated this really is and if I can still hire you guys if we're involved personally."

Colin stayed in his seat because if he stalked over to her right now, he'd throw her over his shoulder, carry her to the bedroom, and not let her out for a couple of days. He wanted to respect her desire to cook for him. So he gripped his glass a little tighter and said calmly, "I'm not worried about any of that. I've never felt this way about anyone else, and I don't want it to end."

Her eyes snapped open, and her gaze locked on his.

"But that's the personal answer. So, I'm going to give you a professional answer too that will help you feel secure. Jonah or Henry can step in and become your primary bodyguard if any situation would call for that. They *won't* be sleeping next to you." He frowned. "And there's no way in hell they feel the way I do about you, but they do care about you, and they can take over in every other way, so you can still hire us."

She wet her lips and slowly nodded.

"You do understand?" he asked. "All of that?" He really wanted her to get the part about how he'd never felt this way before.

"Yes," she said softly.

"Okay."

She turned back to the lunch preparations. She started pulling bottles and jars toward her, dumping them into the blender without measuring, and then hit the button, mixing it all together.

When that shut off, she tasted what he guessed was a sauce or dressing, then scraped it into a bowl with a rubber spatula, then stored it in the fridge.

She cooked without a recipe or measuring anything.

That was probably a nerdy thing to be turned on by, but he really, really was. She obviously cooked a lot and enjoyed it.

She started chopping vegetables and finally he spoke again. "Do you eat at home most of the time?"

"As much as possible," she said. "There are amazing restaurants here, but I prefer my own food. I'm no gourmet. I do a lot of pretty basic, home-cooking type things. Pot roasts. Meatloaf. Casseroles. But I like it all better than going out a lot of the time. I like everything about it. The warm kitchen, the way it makes the whole apartment smell good. I even like doing dishes."

"Jesus, Spencer will love you," he said without thinking.

She looked over at him, her eyes twinkling. "Who's Spencer?" She had a flirtatious note in her voice.

He shook his head. "One of the Landry boys. A cousin. FBI agent. He lives here in New Orleans. Has a near-fetish about home cooking. Especially casseroles."

"Is that right?" she asked, biting her lower lip, trying to hide a smile as she continued to chop.

"He's very taken," Colin said.

"Hmm," was her answer.

"You think you can steal him from Max with your cooking?" Colin asked, the corner of his mouth twitching. But fuck, she maybe could. Spencer was madly in love with Max, but the feisty redhead didn't cook and Hayden was...fucking amazing.

"I didn't say that," Hayden said, dumping a few ingredients into the large bowl beside her wooden cutting board. "Just thinking I should really make him my chicken pot pies."

"You should *not* make him your chicken pot pies," Colin said firmly.

She smirked at him. "A lot of men have already had my chicken pot pies, Colin. What's one more?"

Was he certain they were talking about actual chicken pot pies? Actually, yes.

Was he still jealous? Yes.

"No chicken pot pies for Spencer. Or any other pot pies. Or any pies at all," Colin told her. "For anyone. But me."

She laughed. "I cannot promise that, I'm sorry."

He gave a little growl. She just rolled her eyes and grinned.

She gave a happy sigh as she turned and bent to check on the chicken.

"You do really love all of this, don't you?" he asked.

How could a woman be so sexy just making lunch? Sure, being fed was one of the most primitive needs. And having a gorgeous woman that he wanted to fuck on every single surface in this apartment doing that feeding was no doubt tapping into some deep, primal area of his brain. But damn, he wanted her right now.

"There's something so satisfying about putting it all together and then enjoying it. And there's nothing like seeing other people enjoying it." She looked over. "Do you get that from cooking?"

He shook his head. "I don't mind doing it, but it's always been more a necessity than anything else. I had to do it to take care of Saoirse and everyone. When I showed up on the scene, the O'Grady siblings didn't know how. Fiona, in particular, was too busy and didn't really want to learn. Torin and Cian just found it easier to go out or have food delivered. That was all fine when Saoirse was a baby on formula and then baby food, but eventually, as she was getting older, I felt it was part of my job to cook for her. It evolved from there. In case you haven't noticed, Cian is more or less a child himself." Colin gave her a wry grin. "He was very happy to eat chicken nuggets and mac and cheese with her, and it was probably the only time he ate many vegetables."

She laughed and went back to chopping.

"I didn't mind doing it," he went on. "But I did want more than kid food, so I learned to make more elaborate meals. The other guys loved it, and I just got good at it with practice."

"It's sexy," she said. "In case you didn't know."

Colin grinned, but he shifted on his chair, her words affecting him. "How'd the love for cooking start for you?"

"Oh, my grandma," she said, dumping vegetables and slices of orange and grapefruit into a bowl. "At the same time my love for music started." She moved to the sink and washed her hands, then dried them. She propped a hip against the counter, facing him. "My brothers and sister would go out to play, but

I'd stay in the house during dinner prep. My grandpa would get out his guitar or would sit at the piano and play and sing while Grandma cooked. Sometimes I'd join him, sometimes I'd join her. But it all mixes together in my mind. The sounds—the sizzling and the clattering in the kitchen, the music and the laughter—and the aromas and the images and the feelings."

There was a faraway look on her face, as if she was remembering it all right then and Colin felt like he was holding his breath, not wanting to disturb that or pull her away from something that was obviously so happy.

"But my favorite part," she said, "was when everyone else would walk in. They would be tired from work and school and practice and playing. They'd be hot, or cold, sweaty and dirty. But they'd all come through that door, and the warmth of the kitchen, and the smells, and the music, and our smiles would hit them, and they'd immediately straighten up and smile and...you could just see them get lighter." She focused on him again. "Does that make sense?"

Good God, he was falling in love with this woman.

He nodded. "Yeah, *cailín*, that makes sense."

She smiled. "I think that's why I can't cook for just myself. It just feels wrong to not make someone else feel good with it too. That's always what it's been like for me." She laughed lightly. "I always have the urge to sing to people when I give them food, too."

He wanted to laugh. Make this light with her. But he couldn't. She was taking his breath away.

He rose and moved to stand in front of her. "Like when you were singing in my kitchen, making my family breakfast."

Her eyes widened. "Your family." She didn't state it as a question as if she didn't understand who he was referring to.

He nodded. "Aye. My family."

She wet her lips. "Yeah. Like that."

He lifted a hand and cupped her cheek, needing to touch her. "You are...incredible."

She swallowed hard. "I'm glad you think so."

"I don't just think it. I feel it. In my soul."

She let out a breath. "God. Colin..."

He started to lower his head, but the timer on the oven suddenly went off. She startled.

He sighed. "Probably a good thing."

"How is it good that you kissing me got interrupted?"

"Because I don't think that kiss was going to end for a very long time."

She smiled, and he traced his thumb over the corner of her mouth.

"Oh," she said.

"Yeah."

"Okay, well, let me finish this up, and we can eat, and then we can kiss for a very long time."

"Yes. Let's definitely do that."

He stepped back and leaned against the counter, watching her put their lunches together.

It was a citrus chicken salad with fresh greens, citrus fruits, cashews, avocado, goat cheese, chicken, and a citrus vinaigrette dressing.

She plated their salads, then assembled six containers of salad for neighbors. She pulled her phone out and texted someone. "Victor and Diane live just below me," she said after sending and receiving a few messages. "I can drop these off with them, and they'll get them to everyone else."

"You don't want to deliver them yourself?" Colin asked, carrying their plates to the table.

"Usually I do, but I think I might be too busy," she said,

giving him a smile that made him want to strip her down and lay her out on the middle of her rug.

"You will be too busy," he promised her.

"Good."

They settled at the table and dug into their salads. Colin groaned after one bite.

"Wow, Hayden, this is delicious."

She looked incredibly pleased. "Thanks."

He took several more bites. Then asked something that had been niggling at him. "You like your own food, and you don't like apartment living. How do you feel about hotels and eating on the road?"

She pushed her food around her plate. "I don't think I'll like it."

That tracked. "That will be a big part of your life when you sign with the label and start touring."

She took a breath and blew it out. "I know."

"Why do you want to do it?" And why was he asking? He wanted her to do it. Hell, he needed her to do it if he wanted the job as her security team. Why put doubts in her mind?

But he wondered if there were already doubts in her mind.

She was an unpretentious, big-hearted sweetheart who loved her family, took care of others almost without thinking about it, loved to cook, made music because it made her and those around her happy, and wanted a home. But she was considering going on the road to perform her music in front of crowds of strangers, live in hotels, eat food from restaurants and convenience stores, far from her family, especially the grandfather she felt responsible for, and her friends.

She set her fork down, pushed her plate back, and rested her forearm on the table. She lifted her eyes to his. "Because it's my turn."

"Your turn?"

She nodded. "To have the spotlight. My brothers and sister got it while we were growing up. Everything in our family revolved around them and playing ball. Our schedules—when we woke up, when we had dinner, what our weekends were like, when and where we went on summer vacations—all revolved around baseball and softball. Our family budget was about that too. Money was spent on camps and special coaches and equipment and travel teams and tournaments. My parents' attention was on them. Our family's last name was in the paper all the time, but it was always attached to Jake, Jared, or Hailey." She took a deep breath. "I'm really proud of them. I'm happy for them. I know everything about baseball and softball. I've sat on more bleachers than probably ninety-nine percent of women my age. I know that all of that time, attention, and money gave them opportunities to travel and choose their colleges and do things most people never get to do. But now...it's my turn. I have a chance to be known for something other than being Jake, Jared, and Hailey Ross's sister."

Colin took that all in, studying her face.

That all made sense.

He reached out and took her hand. He ran his thumb over her knuckles. "And you deserve it. You're so damned talented." That was absolutely true. She had an amazing voice. The songs she wrote were beautiful and fun. She was gorgeous and gifted and she made people happy with her music.

"Thanks. My parents are really excited. My siblings follow all my social media. They're going to come to New Orleans when I perform with Jason next time."

"Right. You're scheduled to be on stage with him when he comes back in a few weeks."

She nodded. "I already signed a contract to join him for those shows. It's kind of a new thing this label has been doing. They've had other new artists who've gotten big on social media performing with him around the country. I guess kind of auditioning? Seeing how the fans respond to them on stage. Sabrina says that everything sounds like the shows here have been the most well-received. Hopefully that means the label wants to sign me as an artist. Sabrina thinks they'll make an offer after these next shows."

"I'm sure they will. You're amazing."

She smiled. "It will be fun having my family in the seats watching me for a change."

"I'll bet." It was interesting that her focus was her family and having them in the audience. It made sense. It *was* her turn. He understood that. But of all the incredible things that would be a part of performing at a huge venue with a big music star in front of a major label, Hayden was thinking about her family being in attendance.

Damn, he could not shake this sudden niggling feeling that she didn't actually want to be up on that stage. Not full-time anyway. Not for the fans or the label or the money or the stardom. Did she just need her family's validation that badly?

"Have they ever seen you perform in the smaller venues? The bars and stuff?" he asked, taking his hand back and trying to seem nonchalant. He started in on his salad again.

"No." She gave a soft laugh. "That's just for fun. A hobby. I mean, I love it. But that's not really big time."

"You do love it though?" he pressed. "You like the smaller crowds and stuff?"

"For sure. I love being able to see the crowd. See their reactions. Hear them sing along. Have them make requests for covers. Or God, when they request a song of mine. That's amazing." Her smile was a lot warmer now. "That's just a lot... cozier. It feels like we're singing with friends. Just hanging out. The big stage with Jason was intimidating as hell."

He took a couple of bites, then asked, "What about your

grandpa?"

She swallowed her bite. "What do you mean?"

"If you're traveling away from New Orleans, who will visit and check up on him? Who will be the emergency contact and everything?" Colin was not trying to make her feel bad and he was sure she'd thought of all of this.

He was just trying to figure out what was going on in her head. Until today, he hadn't thought all of that through. He hadn't known the full situation. Meeting Bill, seeing Hayden with him, had made him realize there was a lot more going on with Hayden Ross than he'd realized.

She nodded. "I...um, have been thinking about that. But my mom said not to worry about it."

"Really?"

"Yeah. Like she said, he's in a great facility that takes really good care of him, and she can answer questions for them over the phone and give permission for things, so it should be fine." She wasn't meeting his eyes though. She sighed. "And he doesn't know me anyway."

Colin felt his gut clench. He could feel Hayden's sadness. He just wasn't sure if it was because of the thought of leaving her grandfather or because she could leave him, because he didn't need her. This girl really loved to be needed.

Colin understood that piece of her very well.

"Your mom said that stuff?" he asked, trying to keep his voice steady.

"Yeah. I mean, you have to understand my family has always believed in going after your dreams and investing in your talents. They've always been okay with having other people taking care of the things they needed help with so they could support Jake, Jared, and Hailey and they saw that pay off. So now, this is what is happening for me. Someone else can step in with Grandpa so I can go after my dreams."

Basically, her parents had always been fine with other people—mostly Hayden—taking care of their responsibilities for them so they could use their time, attention, and energy to push their other children toward stardom.

Of course, they'd be fine with her leaving her grandfather while she went after her musical dream.

He tamped that down. That was not his judgment to make. If anyone deserved a chance to shine, a chance to go after what she wanted, it was Hayden.

If that was what she wanted.

But damn...he was really starting to wonder about that.

What if it *wasn't* what she wanted? What if she just thought she was supposed to want it? What if she thought she had to take this chance to show them what she could do because, finally, for just a minute, she had their attention? What if, because of how she'd grown up, she thought that of course she had to stand in a spotlight if one was shone on her? That being front and center was the only way to *truly* be happy and successful?

But his job was to help her do whatever she wanted and needed to do safely.

He cleared his throat. "Well, I'll tell you what," he said. "You're going to teach Saoirse a few things on the guitar to sing to some sick alpacas, right? One of the guys can take her over to visit your grandpa when you're on the road. I know she knows You Are My Sunshine. That can be one of the first ones you teach her. And I have a *whole bunch* of people who would love to get to know your grandpa. He can have more visitors than he knows what to do with. Hell, we can even get someone else signed up as his Power of Attorney. Juliet *is* an attorney. Or Naomi would be awesome at that. She's sweet and like a mom to everyone and has helped her own grandparents with a lot of health issues. But there are lots of options. All you have to do is say the word."

Hayden's eyes were suddenly glistening. She rose, stepped toward him, and slid into his lap. He gratefully slid his chair back and welcomed her, his hands going to her hips and hugging her back as her arms went around his neck. She put her face against his neck.

"Thank you," she said. "He'll...love Saoirse."

"She'll love him too," Colin said gruffly. "We've got your back, *cailín*. My people are your people now."

She pulled back and looked at him. "I want that."

"I want to give you that," he said honestly. "I want to give you *whatever* you want."

"This is so..." She didn't finish the sentence. Instead, she just pressed her lips to his.

His hand went to the back of her head, and he immediately opened his mouth, urging hers open. She complied with a soft sigh, running her fingers up into his hair.

She tasted like citrus, and he wanted to devour her.

She had just pivoted to straddle his thighs, and his hands were on her hips, grinding her against his cock, when his phone dinged with three texts in a row, then started ringing.

Colin let his head fall back. "*No.* Fuck."

Breathless, she said, "Let it go to voicemail."

He dove back into the kiss. But the phone started ringing again.

She sighed as he pulled back again. "Can't," he said with regret.

"Ugh, I know."

He kept hold of her as he reached into his pocket. "What?" he barked into the phone.

"Hey, good to hear from you too. Missed you," Henry said in Colin's ear.

"What do you want, Henry?"

"Aww, I assume that you're with Hayden and I'm interrupting something."

"Talk faster."

Henry chuckled. "Need you back in Autre. There's a family thing happening in a few hours."

"What kind of family thing?"

"Bennett Baxter is announcing that he's making a run for the Senate. And he's announcing it to the family at Ellie's tonight. He would also like to discuss hiring us to be his security team."

Colin sat up a little straighter. Bennett Baxter had married Kennedy Landry. Kennedy was not only one of the few granddaughters in the Landry family, she'd also been Autre's mayor for the past few years. The Landrys were practically royalty in Autre. But Bennett was from Georgia. Still, he'd been living in Louisiana ever since he and Kennedy had been married. He was not only a millionaire, he was a philanthropist. He'd been working on conservation projects to protect the Louisiana coast. He was well known in Louisiana. And well-liked. Politics was in his blood and Colin had been hearing rumors ever since he'd landed in Louisiana that Bennett would eventually make a run for office. A successful one, according to sources.

This could be huge. Not just for Colin and his friends, as far as work, but for the family. Colin really loved the Landrys. He wanted to be there for them for this.

He looked up at Hayden. Her lips were pink, she was still breathing rapidly, and her hair was tousled.

"I want to tell you to handle this," he told Henry.

"The Landrys would really like you there. And Baxter needs to talk to you personally. You're the boss."

Colin sighed. "Fine. You're lucky she's still dressed."

Henry chuckled again as Hayden blushed.

fourteen

COLIN HUNG up and pocketed his phone. "I'm needed back in Autre."

Hayden ran her fingers through her hair. "So I gathered."

"I can call Matt to come over."

Her eyebrows arched. "Matt's going to take your place here? He's married."

Colin squeezed her hips. "*Absolutely not.*" Yes, he definitely growled that. "He can come over though, if you want to stay here. I know you haven't been home for a few days."

She frowned. "I don't care about being here. Can I come back to Autre with you?"

His heart thumped hard in his chest. He didn't want her anywhere but wherever he was, and he absolutely wanted her in Autre, even if he couldn't be right beside her. She belonged there. She needed to be around her friends, his family, in that house that had become home. "Absolutely. I'd love that."

"Are you sure? I haven't gotten too clingy?"

"I really like you clingy. I'd like you even more clingy at the moment," he said, running his hands under her dress in back where it had hiked up enticingly when she'd straddled him.

"Well, same. But you're being called back. Still, if I'm there at the house waiting for you when you get home..."

Everything in him tightened and heated. The idea of Hayden waiting for him when he got home was everything he wanted.

"Why don't you pack some more stuff?" He paused. "As if you're moving out for awhile?"

She grinned. "Happily." She pushed back off his lap. "I don't suppose you would want to go through my cupboards and my fridge? Grab some things we can take with us and toss anything that could go bad? We can take the trash out to the dumpster on our way to the truck."

He loved the idea that she might be staying with him long enough for food in her fridge to go bad.

"Definitely."

He carried their dishes to the sink and started cleaning up the kitchen while she went to the bedroom to pack. He even grabbed the mug off her coffee table. She also went through the bathroom and grabbed additional things that Cian and Jonah hadn't the other day.

Thirty minutes later, they had the apartment cleaned up, her fully packed, the extra salads delivered to Victor and Diane, and Colin was carrying her houseplants. She gave him a smile as she locked her apartment up. "Thank you."

"Anything you want, any time."

He meant that with everything in him.

It had happened quickly, but it felt completely true.

They headed back to Autre and carried all her stuff upstairs to Fiona's room. It was too soon to move her into his bedroom. Not that he didn't think she'd be spending plenty of time there.

When they were back on the first floor, she frowned and looked around. "Where are the guys?"

"Probably the gym."

"Do you have a gym here in the house?"

He nodded. "It's small. A lot of times we go downtown and work out. Part of that is so the guys can compete against the firefighters and cops. The guys from Bad come over too and it becomes a big testosterone-fest."

"And you never participate in that?"

"Oh, I'm way too mature for that."

She simply laughed.

"But we keep a little bit of equipment here. In case someone wants to work out when the gym downtown isn't open. Henry's probably restless since he just got off the long flight."

"I'm so excited he's back," Hayden said. "Let's go say hi."

Colin led her down to the lower level of the house. Sure enough, the music was blasting, and all three men were there, lifting weights, talking and laughing.

Shirtless.

Colin gave an annoyed growl.

The guys didn't notice Colin and Hayden at first, but Hayden yelled, "Henry!" happily over the music as her foot hit the bottom step, and all three men swung to face them.

Henry's face broke into a grin, and he was across the space in three strides. He wrapped his arms around Hayden and picked her up, swinging her around.

Colin could only shake his head. Of course, Henry was excited to see her. He loved her as much as Cian and Jonah did. She was very fucking loveable.

The other two men grinned and wiped their faces with towels as they watched.

"I'm so glad to see you," Hayden said.

Jonah leaned over and hit a button on the stereo, shutting off the music.

"Holy shit, I'm so sorry I wasn't here, Hayden," Henry said, setting her down and holding her by her upper arms, his eyes scanning her from head to toe. "Are you okay?"

"Of course, she's okay," Colin said with a frown. He reached out and grabbed the waist of Hayden's dress, tugging her back toward him.

The other three men smirked. Colin ignored them.

"Yeah, I mean, I'm still being stalked," Hayden said with a light laugh. "But I'm in one piece."

"We'll get the bastard now," Henry said as he ran a hand over his bare chest. For some fucking reason.

Colin glared at him. "What the fuck does 'now' mean?" Colin asked.

Henry lifted a shoulder. "Just saying, now that I'm back, we can really focus."

Colin scowled at him.

"More hands on deck," Henry added, with a grin. "All of that."

Colin lifted his middle finger at his friend, behind Hayden's back.

"I need to head down to Ellie's," Colin said, changing the subject.

Everyone in the room just looked at him.

Hayden crossed to one of the weight benches and plopped down, crossing her legs. "I'll just hang out here with the guys. I'll see you later."

Cian, Jonah, and Henry simply watched Colin with stupid grins.

"I think that's a great idea, Hayden," Cian said, picking up a barbell and curling it, flexing his bicep.

"Why don't you just come with me?" Colin asked her.

"I'm okay," Hayden said, her eyes on Cian.

"Actually, Bennett and Kennedy want to talk to you with his campaign manager," Henry said. "A serious discussion. It's not just casual. They know you. Us. We've been here for over a year now. They like the idea of hiring people that are close to the family. But they want to talk details. He'll be campaigning all over Louisiana for more than a year. Then, if he wins...D.C."

Colin made himself focus. This was a big deal.

He glanced at Hayden.

Especially if she didn't sign with the music label. If she realized that wasn't what she really wanted. If she figured out that traveling the country, being away from home, being away from the people she cared about and who cared about her for long stretches of time would make her miserable, they'd be out of a job.

Actually *when* she figured that out, they'd be out of a job.

She deserved raving fans. She absolutely did. He just wasn't sure she was going to get what she *really* wanted, deep down, from her parents and siblings. Even if she was up on stage night after night on an international music tour.

Fuck. *He* wanted to give her everything she needed. And he could do that right here. Or really, wherever he and *his* family was.

Could he help her see that? Convince her of that? He'd known her for a few fucking days.

He scrubbed a hand over his face. "Fine. I'll go. But..." His eyes went to Hayden again. She was now watching Jonah do leg curls.

He wasn't *jealous*. These men had known her for months before he had. They were friends. But these guys were flexing their muscles in front of her, half naked, and yeah, he didn't like that.

"Shouldn't you and Jonah come too?" Colin asked. "They'll want to talk to the whole team, won't they?"

"They want to talk to you first. His campaign manager wants to go over a few things with you. Make sure we can handle a couple of upcoming events off the bat. Then his chief of staff wants to really get into it. He wanted you to come to New Orleans for a whole big interview, but Bennett insisted on making the introductions today at Ellie's in a familiar environment," Henry explained. "We'll shower and meet you down there a little later."

Colin sighed.

Hayden was now watching him with a mischievous twinkle in her eye. She sat back on the bench, propping her hands behind her. "Yeah, I'm fine here with these guys. Don't worry about me." She turned her attention back to the other men.

Henry stretched. "Yeah, I haven't seen her in a while. We'll take good care of her."

"Nope." Colin crossed to where she sat, pulled her up, tossed her over his shoulder, and turned toward the stairs.

She giggled.

He climbed the steps with the sound of his three best friends laughing behind him.

"You know I love when you do this, right?" she asked.

He swatted her on the ass. "I'm starting to realize that. And it can be arranged anytime you want without ogling my friends."

She laughed as he deposited her in the kitchen. "I'll keep that in mind."

He cupped her face and kissed her deeply. Then he asked, "Do you need anything before I head out? I don't know how long I'll be gone."

She shook her head. "I'm fine."

"Okay. Well, the whole house is yours. Make yourself at home. Nothing is off-limits." Then he leaned in and put a finger to her nose. "Except my friends."

She grinned. "Your friends were my friends before I even knew you."

"You can be friends with my friends when they...and you... are fully dressed."

"I love when you're jealous and possessive." She stretched up on tiptoe and pressed her mouth to his sweet kiss. "There's no way I could even imagine being with anyone else."

He caught her before she could lean back, his hands gripping her ass and bringing her up against him, deepening the kiss. He tasted her fully. Then set her back. "Very good. But I intend to keep reminding you of that."

"See you when you get home."

"I wish I could take you with me."

She looked surprised. "Don't be silly. I don't even know Bennett and Kennedy. I'll be here when you get back."

He loved everything about that. Well, except for the leaving her here part. But he loved the idea that she would be here when he got home. "I really want you to get to know them. The whole Landry family. They will love you. And you'll love them. I love the idea of giving you friends and family—a bunch of people who will adore you and include you and make you feel loved."

Her face softened. "Thank you."

He kissed her one more time, then turned and headed for the door. If he didn't leave then he wasn't going to. But he already couldn't wait to get home.

Hayden looked around the kitchen. She thought about the books she'd brought. She had some good ones she wouldn't mind diving into. She also had some songs she could go over. She also needed to look at her work schedule since she'd be driving up from Autre tomorrow. She assumed that Colin would keep going with her for now.

But then she thought about the guys working out downstairs. She should make them a post-workout snack.

She looked around the kitchen again and grinned.

Okay, that was actually just an excuse to use this kitchen. It was enormous. She could fit her entire apartment in this one room. It was a dream kitchen. She decided to give herself a little tour and quickly acquainted herself with all of the appliances and the contents of all of the cupboards.

Then she decided that since Colin, Jonah, and Henry needed to be up at Ellie's at Bennett's big announcement, she could help out by making dinner for everyone.

And by the time the guys came in from finishing their workouts and showering, she had three fruit smoothies set out waiting for them and was putting together a lasagna for dinner.

"Holy hell, I love having you live here," Cian told her, grabbing one of the glasses.

"Who says I'm living here?" she asked.

"Well, if Colin doesn't move you in, I will," he said, taking a big drink.

Henry came around the edge of the counter and gave her another hug. "I am very happy to see you. It's super fun to poke at Colin but I do mean it."

She squeezed him back. "I feel the same way."

"About being here or about poking at Colin?" he asked with a smirk.

"Um...both," she said truthfully. Poking at Colin got her thrown over his shoulder. That would never not make butterflies erupt in her stomach and her panties get a little wet.

"I'm glad." Henry was studying her face.

She thought maybe her friend was noticing more there than she wanted him to. Like her gigantic crush on his boss.

Crush? That didn't seem like the right word, but she wasn't sure what else to call it. Was she falling for Colin? Yes. That seemed obvious. And inevitable.

Was that going to end up with her with a broken heart? Maybe. But maybe not. If she signed with the record label and started touring and Colin was there with her, they could just... be a couple, right? They'd be together all the time. Sometimes just the two of them. Sure, there'd be a whole team of people around them, but there would be a lot of down time too. Lots of travel time. They could just be together. Just them. All the time. Just...them.

Henry noticed her frowning. "What's going on?"

She shook her head. "What do you mean?"

"You were grinning and glowing and then suddenly you seemed worried."

Yeah. Because, she was.

Not about her and Colin being together.

He had quickly become her favorite person to be with.

It wasn't the being alone with Colin that she was worried about.

It was that she and Colin both needed more people than that.

While she'd never done it herself, she knew a lot about traveling as a musician. It was different cities all the time. Tour buses. Time on the road. Away from home. Yes, there was a crew, a team, a group of people you were with all the time. But...she would be the one *they* all took care of. She wouldn't be cooking for anyone. She wouldn't be taking care of anyone. The tour bus would be even smaller than her apartment. If she was lying in bed and heard people walking around above her or laughing through the walls it would be in a hotel and those people would probably be strangers. Colin could be beside her and that would be amazing but...he needed more people too.

Did the idea of being in a cocoon with just Colin, wrapped up together, naked, talking, laughing, touching, kissing, and driving each other wild sound amazing? For sure.

Did the idea of staying holed up in Colin's bedroom, just the two of them, lounging in bed, having coffee on his balcony, watching movies, talking, playing, just sitting and doing nothing for days at a time sound like heaven? No question.

But so did the idea of eventually emerging from the bedroom to have pancakes with the guys. Or showering and dressing to go watch Saoirse in a school program. Or heading to Ellie's together to hang out with everyone—a bunch of people she hadn't even met yet.

All of that sounded like more fun than traveling city to city to perform up on a big stage, far removed from an audience full of strangers whose faces she could barely see for all the lights.

Oh...crap.

That was...unexpected.

But the very next thought was a question?

Is it? Is it really surprising, Hayden?

And no. It wasn't.

She'd never dreamed of being a rockstar. Or a country music star. Or a star of any kind. That hadn't even occurred to her until Sabrina Sterling had posted a video of her performing at her bar online and it had gotten a million likes. Sabrina had showed it to her and said, "You could be the next big thing. People love you."

Sabrina had kept inviting her back to sing and posting those videos and Hayden's name had started to spread. Things had taken off from there. Outside of anything Hayden had done. Outside of anything she'd ever thought or dreamed of.

She'd loved playing on the street corners in the Quarter.

She'd loved seeing the people who gathered around to enjoy her music. Watching their faces, seeing their smiles. She loved the small bars too. She could see the crowds there. Meet their eyes. Watch them sing along when they knew the words.

Then she could go *home* at the end of the night. That had always been nice. The balance she loved.

But, over the past couple of years here in New Orleans, home had started to feel lonelier and less…homey. She didn't have family here. The friendships she'd made had never gotten that deep. The neighbors around her served more to remind her of what she *didn't* have than giving her the connections she wanted. And her grandfather, the reason she was here, was slipping away.

Now, suddenly, over the last few days, she'd come here. To this house. To these guys. To Colin. This was her dream. A home. A family. Taking care of people. Being involved in their lives and dreams too.

Fuck.

This was all getting messed up.

Or…was it?

Colin had never traveled with someone like a musician before. Sure, if it was her, it might be different. But he'd miss all of this. These guys. This town. The other people. Saoirse. He didn't really want to be on the road, did he?

Sure, he'd always told himself the job was his focus and he just did whatever it required. It just so happened that his job for the past decade was a little girl who didn't travel and who they actually wanted to keep *out* of the public eye. He thought that his life had revolved around one person, one priority, but that wasn't entirely true. Maybe the house had been Fiona's. Maybe Jonah and Henry weren't related to him by blood. But he'd made it a home and these men were like brothers, Fiona was like a sister, and Saoirse was like a daughter.

It had never just been a job.

It had been a home and a family.

And that's what he'd want again. It's what he'd build, even if he did it subconsciously.

"Hayden?" Henry asked. "Are you okay?"

She finally focused on him. Her thoughts were still spinning, but she nodded.

"I'm fine," she managed. "Sorry. Just a little distracted."

He gave her a wink, clearly assuming she was distracted with thoughts of Colin. Or maybe he thought she was remembering all of *them* half-naked and lifting weights. That had been an okay thing to come home to. She gave him an only-kind-of-forced grin and shook her head.

She looked over and noticed Jonah was shaking his arm. "Hey, what's wrong?"

"Just tweaked my wrist a little bit lifting."

"Here, let me see."

He lifted a brow.

She gave him a come-on-already motion with her hand. "You have no idea how many injuries my siblings sustained over the years playing ball. I've seen a little bit of everything, including bones sticking through the skin. I can massage, bandage, and splint almost anything."

He held out his hand. "I'm never gonna turn down the opportunity to be massaged by you."

"No fun in saying stuff like that when Colin's not even here," Cian said.

Jonah gave her a wink. "Maybe I'm not saying it just to bug Colin."

She laughed as she prodded at his wrist. He winced slightly as she palpated along a tendon. "You sprained it. I have some analgesic cream upstairs. I can rub that in—but it has to be a deep massage that will hurt," she added when he grinned.

"And then wrap it. You should ice it, too. Ibuprofen would be a good idea. You'll feel better tomorrow."

"I can't wear a wrap. I'm a bodyguard. I've had way worse injuries than this."

She rolled her eyes. "I get it, tough guy. But you're just going down to the bar for a family meeting, right? Wear long sleeves and no one will see it. Don't be a baby."

He sighed. "Yes, ma'am."

She went upstairs and grabbed all of her first aid supplies. She should just store them down on the first floor. With all these boys and their training and lifting and just messing around, having the supplies within easier reach would probably be a good idea.

She soon had Jonah bandaged up, and they'd finished off their smoothies.

"Well, I guess we should head out to Ellie's," Henry said, looking down at his phone. "Colin's finished up with his meeting. Bennett's going to make his announcement soon."

Hayden looked around. "Oh crap. Are you all going to eat down there? I didn't even think about that." The lasagna was in the oven and she was buttering garlic bread.

"We are definitely not going to eat down there," Henry told her, eyeing her preparations with appreciation.

"Yeah, we are coming back here for this, for sure," Jonah said, reaching out to grab a pinch of the parmesan cheese she'd planned to sprinkle over the bread.

She felt warmth bubble up inside her. "Okay. Good."

Just then the back door banged open, and Saoirse came through.

"Hey, trouble," Cian greeted her. "What's up?"

Hayden couldn't believe how much she loved how everyone came and went in this house. It reminded her so much of her house growing up that her throat got a little tight.

Not only had her three siblings been constantly coming and going—they hadn't just been star athletes, but had been involved in a number of extracurriculars, and had had busy social lives—but they'd had lots of friends dropping by all the time and the house had been open to anyone at any time.

"What smells so good?" Saoirse asked.

"Hayden's making dinner," Jonah told her.

Her eyes widened as she found Hayden behind the island. "Oh, wow. Hi. Can I stay?"

"Of course," Hayden told her. Then added, "If it's okay with your mom."

"Oh, she'll love it. She loves when I eat over here. She's down at Ellie's anyway and will probably eat there and bring me something home. Or she'll come over here too." Saoirse grinned and headed for the table, climbing into one of the chairs so she could face Hayden as she worked.

"What're you doin'?" Cian asked, pivoting on his stool.

"I'm here 'cuz Mom and Knox need to go down to Ellie's. She said you need to help me with my homework and then start packing the car."

"Why packing the car?" Henry asked.

"I'm going with her and Naomi on a rescue," Cian said. "Something came up last minute and it's too short notice for anyone else to go along." He grinned. "I know it will shock you all, but turns out, I'm available."

Hayden knew that Cian helped out from time to time with the swamp boat tour company the Landry family owned and operated, taking boat loads of tourists out on the bayou, but she could also easily believe that the young prince didn't work full time and had a pretty flexible schedule.

"What kind of rescue?" Hayden asked.

"Some horses," Cian said. "I'm not sure exactly what the situation is, but they were sold from one abusive situation to another. The local authorities are involved, but if the girls don't show up by tomorrow night, they'll get rid of them some other way. She didn't elaborate on what that means."

Hayden's eyes were wide. "You definitely need to go."

"We can do homework later," Jonah told Saoirse. "We've gotta be at Ellie's too."

Hayden spoke up, "I can help. We'll do it here while everyone else is gone."

Saoirse grinned widely. "Really?"

"Sure. I'm just hanging out here. You get started while I finish dinner prep. Are you hungry right now?"

Saoirse looked at the empty smoothie glass in front of Cian. "What's that?"

"Strawberry banana smoothie. I'll warn you that it does have some other extra healthy stuff in it though," Hayden said.

Saoirse considered it. "Hit me."

The men all dispersed—Jonah and Henry for Ellie's and Cian out to get Fiona's truck ready for the road trip the next day—while Hayden mixed up another smoothie and joined Saoirse at the table.

"So tell me more about these rescues your mom does."

Saoirse set her pencil down and reached for the glass. "She gets phone calls from all over. Whenever anybody has an animal in trouble or knows of animals in trouble. Sometimes the state calls or law enforcement," she explained, sounding much older than her ten years. "Then Mom and whoever can go along pack up and head out. Depends on the animals what kind of cages and trailers they take. This time, since it's horses, they have to take two trucks and two trailers. So, Naomi is going with her and they're taking Cian so they have another set of hands and another driver. Once they get the animals loaded up, they don't like to stop for more than a quick pit stop." Saoirse sucked on the reusable straw Hayden had added to her glass.

"Do you know how far away they're going?"

"I heard her tell Knox it's nine hours one way."

Hayden frowned. "That's a really long drive."

Saoirse just nodded, though Hayden doubted the girl really had a concept of how far that was. Hayden leaned over Saoirse's book and read what she was working on. "Okay, so here's what you're gonna do," she said. She quickly explained the first two problems. "You work on those and I'll come check on you in a few minutes."

Then she rose and stepped around the breakfast bar to check on the lasagna. She would let it bake most of the way through but then pull it out before it was done if the guys weren't home yet. Once they got home, she'd bake it the last ten minutes, so it was nice and hot and fresh.

Then she started moving around the kitchen pulling together ingredients for other recipes.

She started to sing as she worked and smiled as Saoirse joined her. The little girl's head stayed bent over her homework though.

"What's all this?" Cian asked when he came back in almost an hour later.

Hayden stepped back from the counter, wiping her hands on her apron and surveying what she had in front of her.

"I made some stuff for you all for the road."

Cian came forward and slid up onto one of the stools. "You made us snacks?"

"I did." She pointed. "These are protein balls. They're chocolate-peanut butter. There's oats, peanut butter, chocolate chips, honey, and protein powder in them. They'll be great to eat on the road and they'll really fill you up. I also cut up veggies and made dip. I made more smoothies, but they're in the freezer. They'll melt down slowly so by the time you want them, they should be ready to drink."

The timer on the oven went off just then and she bent to remove the cookie sheet she'd added to the rack above the lasagna.

She set it on the counter to cool.

"Those look like vegetables too," Cian said suspiciously.

She laughed. "They are. Zucchini chips. Next time, if I know ahead of time, I can make sweet potato chips. Oh, and I can roast chickpeas. Those are really good. I can also make soup that you can just drink so you don't have to worry about spoons. And trail mix. But I didn't have all the ingredients here."

"Hayden?"

She looked up. "Yeah?"

"You realize we can buy our own snacks, right?"

She propped a hand on her hip. "Listen, my brothers and sister and parents were on the road all the time. They ate *so* many meals in the car. It's really hard to eat healthy on the road and that can affect your mental alertness, which is bad when you guys are driving that far at once. It can also be hard on your mood, which I assume can make it even more difficult to deal with an already stressful situation. It can make it really easy to consume too much caffeine which will affect your sleep. Eating poorly is also hard on your digestion—it can upset your stomachs and make you constipated—"

Cian held up a hand. "I'm convinced. And I refuse to talk about being constipated with you."

She smiled, realizing she'd been on her soap box. "I know all about assembling ready to go food that actually keeps you full and is pretty healthy. It will cut down the number of times you need to stop and will make you feel better than anything you can get on the road."

He watched her for a few minutes. "We've been doing this for years."

She shrugged. "And now you can do it even better."

He didn't say anything, but he was watching her. His expression was slightly amused, but there was also affection there.

"What?" she asked.

"You can't help yourself."

"What do you mean?"

"You just gotta take care of us."

She did. "I'm good at it."

"You are." He was quiet for a second. "You remind me of someone."

"Who?" Was he going to tell her something about his parents? She knew that Cian, Fiona, and other brothers, Torin and Declan, had left their home country many years ago and their parents had stayed behind.

"Colin."

She paused. Oh. Yes. Him. That answer made her feel very warm, happy, and tingly.

"Is that a compliment from you?" she asked.

"One of the highest I could give." Cian paused. "But if you tell him I said that, I will deny it."

She grinned. "Noted."

fifteen

"WELL, that sounds great. I think we have a fantastic plan," Bennett told Colin, extending his hand across the table.

"Oh geez," Kennedy said with a laugh, rising from her chair and coming around to hug Colin, rather than shaking his hand.

Bennett just grinned as the men grasped hands while Kennedy squeezed Colin's neck.

"It's going to be so great having people we know around. It's so weird to think about needing to have all this security. I mean, we already have some when we go places, but this will be such a change," she said.

Colin had been briefed on the fact that Bennett's foundation had been targeted by hate mail and threats from groups on both sides of the environmental issues. Bennett's group worked to help save the coastline and, in particular, the barrier islands that acted as a buffer between the Gulf of Mexico and the wetlands and coast, slowing down and dampening storms and waves that could disturb and disrupt the ecosystem in the area. The islands could also work as a barrier between any oil spills or other disasters in the Gulf and the bayou, and Bennett's group was working on improving those protections.

There were groups that hated anyone fighting to protect the environment, usually because they were misinformed about the motivations behind the efforts as well as what was being done, and fueled by the people doing the harm. There were also groups that, apparently, were on the side of environmental issues who had been targeted by propaganda about Bennett and his group, who believed that they were actually doing damage.

Added to that, now Bennett was seeking public office. His policies on a number of issues besides the environment would become public and that would automatically make him a potential target for people who disagreed with him.

This was a big deal. Colin had known it rationally, of course, but now after talking with Bennett, Kennedy, and the people working closely with them, in the middle of Ellie's bar, surrounded by the family members trickling in, it hit Colin that this was what he and the guys had been looking for.

Bennett's campaign would last for over a year and if he was elected, he'd be a senator for at least six years.

Colin had known when his position with Saoirse ended, he wanted something like this, a position where he could really get to know the people he was protecting, and something long term. Something that mattered. *People* who mattered. People who would matter to him, and Jonah, and Henry.

"We're thrilled you thought of us," Colin said honestly.

"I'll see you at the office tomorrow," Jack, Bennett's chief of staff, said.

"I'll be there," Colin told him. "I'll bring the guys."

"Great." Jack rose. "I'm going to return a few calls. You ready to talk to your family?" he asked Bennett.

Bennett took a deep breath then looked at Kennedy. "You ready?"

She beamed at him. "So ready. They are going to fucking

flip. This is going to be amazing!" She leaned over and kissed him. "I'm so proud of you."

Bennett's hand cupped the back of her head and held her close, their foreheads touching. "Thank you."

"For what?" she asked.

"Believing I could be this guy."

She smiled. "You were this guy when I met you."

"No," he said. "I maybe had the potential to be this guy, but you made me believe it. And want it."

Kennedy put her hands on both sides of his face. "God, I love you so much. We are going to rock this, you know that, right?"

"I do. I really do."

She kissed him again, then stood and pulled him to his feet. "Come on. Let's go tell everyone."

Colin watched them head for the tables at the back of the restaurant where the family always gathered.

Yeah, he really fucking liked them. He wanted to be a part of making this happen for them. He could donate money to the campaign. He could put a sign or two in his yard. He could vote for the guy. But if his part could be bigger, if he could help keep them safe and give them peace of mind while they went out and talked to the people of Louisiana and showed them how passionate and smart and genuine they were, then that was perfect.

Kennedy stood at the end of the table and put her fingers to her lips, giving a sharp whistle to get her family's attention. Everyone looked at her, surprised. She took Bennett's hand and pulled him up next to her.

"We have some really exciting news, you guys," Kennedy told everyone.

"Finally!" one of her cousins said.

Kennedy propped a hand on her hip. "Hey! This is the first time we could really do this."

"Girl, I can believe that you needed a lot of practice, but geez," someone else—one of her male cousins—said.

She smirked at them all. "Oh, I see. Y'all think you know what our news is?" She looked around the table. "Ellie told y'all you had to be here tonight, because we were going to announce some really big thing and you all instantly decided that we were going to join you in overpopulating the earth with loud and incorrigible, albeit adorable and smarter-than-all-of-you Cajuns, huh?"

Her cousins all looked at one another, then back to her.

"In our defense," her sister-in-law Juliet said. "Ellie said it was *really* big."

"Swear to God, Kennedy, if you two bring a puppy in here and try to pass that off as your new 'baby', I'm dunkin' you both in the bayou," her cousin Zeke—father to twin adorable, smart, loud, incorrigible Cajun girls —said.

Kennedy looked up at Bennett. "You know," she said. "Maybe we can just do this without them."

"Yeah," Bennett said with a nod. "In fact, it might be better that way."

"I mean, can you even *imagine* takin' them all on a tour of the Capitol?" Kennedy said.

"Someone's gonna end up on an FBI watchlist." Bennett nodded. "They were a fucking handful and a half just in Vegas."

"And even a few of them at a time in Savannah never fail to scandalize your mother," Kennedy agreed. "We can't possibly take this bunch to D.C."

Bennett sighed. "I agree." He started to turn away. "Come on."

There was a beat of silence and then the entire table started talking at once.

Which wasn't all that unusual.

"Wait, *what*?"

"D.C.?"

"Like Washington?"

"Are you running for President?"

"Are you shitting me?"

"Yes! Bennett for President!"

"Wait, maybe it's Kennedy running for President!"

"Why can't you have babies in D.C.?"

Kennedy looked up at Bennett. He looked at her. And they burst out laughing.

"Hey."

Colin pulled his attention from the Landrys, aware he was grinning like an idiot, to find Jonah and Henry taking seats at the table with him.

"Hey." He sat back, feeling suddenly incredibly satisfied.

"I hope you didn't eat anything," Henry said.

"I haven't yet. Why?"

"Hayden's making lasagna and a bunch of stuff," Jonah said eagerly.

Colin felt his eyebrows rise. And his heart thump. And his cock twitch.

Yeah, Hayden cooking for him and his friends made him semi-hard. So what?

"Yep. She also made us smoothies after our workout, and wrapped Jonah's sore wrist—"

Jonah held up his wrist with an Ace wrap around it.

"—and she's helping Saoirse with her homework."

Henry paused, watching Colin's face.

Colin worked to not let on that he was now fully hard. But he had to shift on his chair.

"Oh my God!" Fiona was suddenly beside the table. "I can't believe Bennett and Kennedy are running for Senate!" She dropped into the remaining chair at the table. And *you guys* are going to be their security team! I'm so proud of you!"

"Isn't it just Bennett running for Senate?" Henry asked with a grin.

"Come on, it's both of them," Fiona said. "You don't do something huge like that on your own! And those two? Yeah, they're going to kick all kinds of ass!"

Henry and Jonah both looked at Colin. "So we got it?" Henry asked.

Colin nodded. "Yep. We'll have to hire additional guys, but yeah, they want us."

The surge of satisfaction that went through him as he said it out loud was intense.

"What about Hayden?" Henry asked.

Fiona frowned. "What about Hayden?"

"What about when she goes on tour?" Henry asked. "When she signs the deal, Sabrina thinks they'll make her an opening act right away."

Colin nodded. "Yeah."

"She'll hire us, right?"

Colin felt his gut knot. "Of course."

"I want to go with Hayden," Henry said. "I want to be a part of her detail."

Colin had been expecting that. "I know, but—"

"Jonah can lead Bennett's detail," Henry went on. "And maybe Matt."

"Matt's not gonna want to move his whole family to D.C., is he?" Jonah asked.

"Well, we have to ask," Henry said. "We have to give him the option. He's great. But we can hire others."

"But Kennedy and Bennett are hiring you guys because

they know *you*," Fiona said, sitting forward with a frown. "No offense, Jonah. They'll be thrilled to have you. And they know Matt. But they'll already need more guys anyway and having to replace you and Henry will be a problem," she said, looking at Colin. "Did you tell them that you're going to be with Hayden?"

"No, we didn't talk about—"

"I can go with Hayden if you need to stay with Bennett," Henry said.

Colin gritted his teeth. "That's not—"

"We can't just sign on with Baxter and then bail," Jonah said with a frown.

"I know—" Colin said.

"Hayden needs us," Henry went on. "Not just in the physical security sense, but she'll want friends on the road with her. Familiar faces. People she feels comfortable with."

Colin ground his back molars. "Henry—"

"I know you haven't known her as long as we have," Henry went on. "But she really needs friends. She deserves to have people around her who really care and will protect her more than just physically."

Colin breathed in through his nose. "Henry, stop."

Henry didn't stop. "And I know you're sleeping with her for now, but—"

Henry must have heard Colin's growl because he stopped talking.

"What the fuck do you mean by adding that *for now*?" Colin asked.

Henry, admirably, didn't blink as he met Colin's gaze. "I mean, maybe you're planning for things to change by the time she needs security on the road, but—"

Colin was out of his chair and had one of his best friends by the front of his shirt before Henry could finish his sentence. He'd wanted to get physical with one of these guys over Hayden for days and, if he was honest, Henry was at the top of his list. Yes, he knew Henry and Hayden were close. Yes, Henry had known her first. Longer. Maybe better in some ways.

"Go ahead and finish the sentence," Colin ground out.

"Hey, knock it off!" Ellie yelled at them from behind the bar.

Colin didn't even look in her direction. She had a lot of boys in her family—blood and otherwise—and if she was actually concerned, she'd come out from behind the bar, grab them both by the ear, and give them a lecture. And probably make them do chores in the kitchen after closing time.

"Okay, boys," Jonah said, stepping up, his big hand wrapping around Colin's wrist. "You need him, so you can't kill him and if he gets a good swing in, you'll be no good to Hayden tonight, so let's just calm down."

Colin glared at Henry one last time, then let him go with a shove.

"Jesus, Colin," Henry bitched, rubbing his chest.

"I'm not *just* sleeping with her. And it's not just *for now*," he said. "And I shouldn't fucking have to say that."

"Fine." Henry held up his hands. "I was out of line."

They both returned to their chairs.

Fiona eyed him.

"What?" Colin straightened his shirt with a jerk.

"Oh, nothing. Just you were being *paid* to be worked up over me and I was a freaking *princess*, and I don't remember you ever grabbing a guy for saying something like that about me."

"No one ever accused *us* of sleeping together."

She laughed. So did the other guys. "Yes, they did."

They had. All the time. In fact, they'd *encouraged* the

assumption that he and Fiona were a couple. It had made living together and raising Saoirse together easier to explain.

"You're in love with her," Fiona said with a smile.

"Aye," he admitted.

Henry lifted a brow.

"Fuck off, Henry," Colin said. "You had your chance. If you were too dumb to fall for her first, too bad."

Jonah actually snorted at that.

Henry opened his mouth, then shut it and nodded. "Good point."

"So what are you going to do, though? Seriously?" Fiona asked. "If you've signed on with Bennett, but Hayden signs with the recording label and has to travel, how are you going to manage that?"

Colin frowned. *Hope like hell she doesn't sign.*

But he could not say that out loud. Because that was a horrible thing to think. If it was her dream, and he knew she thought that it was right now, then he needed to support it.

But she didn't want to sign. That wasn't what she really *needed.*

She needed family. Home. She had been searching for a way to feel like she mattered, like she belonged again ever since leaving home and coming to New Orleans for her grandfather. She knew she mattered to Bill, that what she was doing for him was important, but he was fading, and Hayden thrived on seeing the people around her blossom and grow. She was exactly as her grandfather had described her. She was like sunshine. And those little moments when he was brighter and happy and remembering things were so precious to her. But they weren't enough. And they were becoming fewer and farther between. She needed more people. More smiles. More ways to make a difference.

She thought she could get that performing.

Colin really feared she wouldn't.

Not like what she got from her music therapy. And even in the small bars. Definitely not what she got at home, in the kitchen, and helping with hurt wrists, and homework.

God, just thinking about all of that made him smile. She was starting to feel special again, needed...loved and appreciated again. She'd found her *place*. Where she belonged and mattered. *They,* his little family, were what she'd been missing.

But saying *any* of that would be completely out of line.

He couldn't say, 'hey love, you're amazing and incredibly talented and I know you love music, and this is your shot at the spotlight, but I don't think you should take it. I think your very soul will be filled by living with and cooking for the bunch of burly bodyguards I work with, and making snacks for my not-really-but-kind-of-in-a-weird-way-ex who lives next door—oh, and don't forget making the food for her PTA meetings when she signs up for stupid shit she can't handle—and teaching my not-even-really-a-step-daughter guitar lessons in between helping her with her homework, so just stay here, okay? What do you say? Wanna play Snow White and the Four Not Dwarves?'

God, his chest hurt. He needed to go see her. He wanted to hug her. He wanted to see her smile. He'd been away from her for over an hour and he fucking missed her.

"Colin?" Fiona pressed. "What are you going to do about Bennett and Hayden?"

Potentially lose her.

But he didn't have to say that, or even think it long, because thank God, Cian showed up just then.

Which was *not* something that had gone through Colin's mind too many times. Or ever.

"Oh, good, you're here." Cian handed a paper grocery bag over to Fiona. "This is for you."

She frowned at her brother. "What's this?"

"Look at it."

She dug inside. Frowned. Then started pulling items out. "Gauze. Scotch tape. Peppermint oil. Paperclips. Nail clippers. And..." She pulled out a plastic container that held small, brown balls. "What are these?"

"There's a note." Cian grabbed a chair, turned it around, and straddled it, grinning.

Fiona opened the folded piece of paper, frowned, then smiled, then started reading out loud. "Hi, Fiona. I threw together a few supplies for you all for your road trip. I packed so many bags for my family over the years that I learned there are some essentials you never want to be without.

"The gauze and tape can be used to make DIY band-aids, but so many other things.

"Paperclips are incredibly versatile. If you straighten them, they can do all kinds of things. I'll text you the blog I follow. Do you know how to pick a lock?

"Nail clippers because you can never have too many and they can cut other things too.

"Peppermint oil is excellent for upset stomachs (just add a drop or two to your water), it can make almost anyplace smell better (dab it on car upholstery or on pillowcases) and can help you focus and stay alert (dab it behind your ears or on your wrists)."

Fiona looked up. "Whoa."

"The brown balls are protein balls. She made them for us. A bunch of other stuff too," Cian said. "They'll keep us from eating junk. Keep us more alert and...not constipated."

Fiona turned wide eyes on Colin. "Sorry, buddy. I think I'm going to have to insist that you marry her."

Cian laughed. "Agreed. But I want to be a bridesmaid, not a

groomsman. No offense, but I think Hayden will have a killer bachelorette party. I fucking *love* her snacks already."

Colin's throat felt tight and his gut hurt.

Holy shit, he definitely wanted to marry that girl. And he wanted to go to her party more than his too.

"But doesn't Naomi have a purse that has most of that stuff in it?" Cian asked his sister.

Fiona nodded. "Not this exact stuff, but yes, Naomi has a mom purse. Still, with this group? We could absolutely use two people taking care of us. I love that Hayden is this person." She focused on Colin again, pointing a finger at him. "Seriously, keep her around."

Colin could really use Fiona's advice about how to do that. Because everything was getting really complicated suddenly. He opened his mouth to respond, but just then, his phone dinged with a text.

That wasn't entirely out of the ordinary, of course, but most of the people who would be texting him were sitting around the table at the moment.

The stranger thing was that at the same moment, Jonah's phone dinged, Henry's phone dinged, and Colin noticed Spencer Landry and his girlfriend, Max Keller, both rose from their seats at the back table and started toward them.

Colin frowned and pulled his phone out. The text was from Matt.

"Huh," Jonah said, reading the text first.

Colin opened it. The message read, "You need to talk to Spencer."

"Congrats on the new job," Spencer said, pulling a chair from another table up to theirs for Max, then grabbing another for himself.

"Thanks. You have something we need?" Colin asked. Matt freelanced and often helped Max, an investigative journalist, out with research. He even, on occasion, helped Spencer and the FBI.

"Yeah. Stuff relating back to the bomb threat," Max said.

Last summer, Max had been the target of a bomb threat at her newsroom. Spencer had brought her down to Autre to hide out until the guy had been caught. It had all started after she published an article about a company dumping chemicals in the bayou. The men had been caught in an FBI raid, but Max hadn't believed their leader had been caught or even identified and had been looking for him ever since.

"Max actually uncovered some new information recently," Spencer said. "Information that she needed to turn over to the authorities rather than publish."

The expression on his face when he looked at Max was a combination of love, admiration, pride, and worry.

Max's job focused almost entirely on white-collar criminals, and she'd taken down a few high-profile ones. She also routinely poked many others. She got lots of nasty emails and threats.

"Like what?" Colin asked.

It was Max that leaned in. "You know that Bennett has been working on man-made barrier islands," she said.

They all nodded. Everyone who knew Bennett knew that. It was what he talked about most. It was what had given him his reputation as a philanthropist, friend to Louisiana, and job creator in this part of the state.

"Well, he's been doing it as a nonprofit. He's creating jobs and saving the environment and not *making* money at it or lining anyone else's pockets," Max said. "But there are other people who want to do the same thing he's doing but get *paid* for it. In fact, a few also want to award their buddies contracts for materials and labor. One, in particular, has decided that sabotaging Bennett's efforts is the best way for *him* to take over. If he can show that Bennett's nonprofit efforts are 'substandard', he figures investors, or possibly even the government, would be more willing to pay someone else to do a 'better' job.

"So, this person has hired people to interfere with Bennett and to purposefully damage the environment to show that Bennett's islands aren't doing any good." Max looked around. "Like the guys who were dumping chemicals into the bayou that I wrote about. Initially, we figured it was just illegal disposal of manufacturing chemicals, but it seems that it was also supposed to make Bennett look bad."

Colin frowned. "The group you wrote about is also messing with Bennett?"

Spencer held up his phone with the message from Matt. "And it seems like it's the same group Zander's had on his radar for awhile now. They took over some abandoned cabins down deep in the bayou. Game wardens noticed boats with supplies coming in over a year ago. Over time the guys staying there have installed high tech computers and communications equipment. And they're stockpiling guns."

Zander had told Colin about all of this. The men in those cabins hadn't done anything specific that could be acted upon. At least not anything anyone could prove. Yet. But Zander's gut told him something was going on. Colin could understand, and respect, an instinct like that.

Colin looked at Max. "And you found out who's behind everything?"

"I did." Max looked smug.

"Who is it?" Henry asked.

Max looked at Spencer. He nodded.

"Gordon Ridgewood."

Colin should've been expecting that. Max had been convinced the wealthy manufacturing tycoon, who she'd been following for years, had been behind the chemical dumping and the bomb threat but hadn't been able to pin anything on him.

"How did you finally figure all this out?" Colin asked.

Max grinned. "Once I found out that Bennett was even *thinking* about a run for Senate, I leaked it to Ridgewood in an email. He, of course, has one of our current senators on his payroll. The one Bennett is running against. Ridgewood panicked. And it made him sloppy and one of my informants came through. Ridgewood is pissed and worried. He's looking for someone to coordinate an attack on the construction Bennett has going on and..." Max took a breath, her expression somber now. "He's also put out feelers looking for someone to send some "warnings" directly to Bennett to try to convince him to end his campaign."

"Warnings like?" Colin asked, his body rigid with tension.

"Nothing specific. More like a list of options," Max said. "Email or snail mail threats. Spray painted messages on buildings. Bricks through windows. Someone following Kennedy and sending him photos of her being trailed. A fire at his office. Or his house. He was just getting started. Kind of whatever he could get." She looked grim. "But he's pretty desperate. He knows Bennett has a good shot and Ridgewood *not* having his friend in the Senate will make things very hard for him."

All of that hung over the group.

Bennett and Kennedy lived in Autre. Kennedy worked in Autre. If she was followed, it would be around Autre. If someone decided to do anything physical toward her, Bennett, their house, or anyone close to them, it would be here in Autre. They interacted with her family every single day. They were in and out of Ellie's, the Boys of the Bayou offices, the animal park... All of these people would be in potential danger too.

Colin processed all of that. Then he nodded as it all sank in.

Fuck. Their new client had a very powerful enemy.

This job had just gotten a lot more real. And serious.

This was way bigger than anything any of them had done for the O'Gradys. Sure, they'd been royalty, but they'd been the royal family of a tiny country that most people had never heard of and they'd been in hiding. There had never been any serious threats made toward any of them.

This was completely different.

Gordon Ridgewood wanted Bennett out of the way.

Colin spent the next hour making plans with Jack. Now that Bennett had formally announced his candidacy, Bennett and Kennedy needed to stay somewhere other than the little town right by the bayou where Ridgewood's goons were shacking up. Henry and Jonah would go with them and stay at a hotel tonight. They'd also spend time learning everything Max knew about Gordon Ridgewood.

Their job had officially started.

sixteen

COLIN SHOVED a hand through his hair.

He needed to get home to Hayden. He'd been at Ellie's far longer than he'd anticipated.

Fiona needed to get ready to leave tomorrow for the animal rescue, so he headed straight to where Knox was sitting at the Landry table.

"I can *not* believe you're moving! And to Washington, D.C.!" Tori Landry, one of Kennedy's sisters-in-law, was saying to Kennedy. She looked on the verge of tears.

Kennedy was holding Tori's little girl Ella. "It's not for *a while*," she said. "The election is over a year away. We'll be campaigning all over the state for months. We'll be home a lot."

"So you'll be mayor until Bennett is elected, and then we'll elect Knox to take your place," someone called from the end of the table.

Kennedy laughed. "I'll probably need to step down before that. I'll want to be with Bennett on the campaign trail." She leaned over and squeezed Knox's arm. "But I agree with electing Knox in a special election."

He groaned. But he didn't argue with the idea. He was a grumpy asshole a lot of the time. Or pretended to be anyway. But he was a hell of a city manager, and everyone in Autre loved him. He loved the town right back. He'd win in a landslide. Colin doubted anyone would even run against him. Knox probably realized that too. That was probably what the groan was for.

Colin stopped next to Knox's seat. The other man looked up at him. "Need you to go home. Saoirse's at my house, but I'm sending her to you," Colin said without preamble. He kept Saoirse with him as much as he could. He didn't have her nearly often enough these days, and he was selfish with his time with her, so he was sure Knox was surprised by the statement.

But for once, Colin wouldn't mind not having the girl there.

Knox nodded and rose. "Okay." He didn't question it or even hesitate. He trusted Colin with Saoirse and Fiona and, Colin realized, in general.

He was a good man and, not for the first time, Colin realized how glad he was that this was the guy who'd stolen Fiona's heart and wedged his way into the O'Grady ladies' lives. If it had to be anyone, Knox was the right one.

Finally, Colin strode through the back kitchen door. Hayden looked up, obviously a little startled. "Oh, hey."

The house smelled fucking delicious.

She looked fucking delicious.

"Hey."

"Are the other guys with you?" She glanced beyond him and then looked back at him.

"No. Something came up. Cian will be here in a little bit, but Jonah and Henry won't be here tonight."

She wiped her hands on her apron. "Oh." She looked disappointed. "Knox stopped by and picked Saoirse up. I sent some of the lasagna home with them. Saoirse already ate. But there's plenty for you and me and then I can freeze the rest."

"I'm starving," he told her, rounding the kitchen island and moving until he was standing nearly on top of her.

She looked up at him. "Good."

"Not for food."

Her eyes widened as her pupils dilated. He loved that he had this effect on her.

"Oh," she said softly.

"Want me to carry you upstairs or do you want to walk?"

She reached behind her and untied her apron, slipping it over her head. "I do love it when you carry me, but I can walk."

"Walk then. Quickly."

She took his hand and became the one leading the way. They hurried up the stairs and into his bedroom.

He kicked the door shut and locked it before nudging her toward the bed. "Naked. Now."

Without a word, she stripped her dress up over her head and shimmied out of her underwear. She lay back on the mattress, wiggling up until she was right in the middle of the bed, her breasts jiggling and her hair spreading over his duvet.

He stripped, then crawled up the bed until he was braced over her.

"I want you so fucking much," he said, his voice gruff. "You're so fucking beautiful. You're so fucking...everything."

She spread her legs, welcoming him between them, and wrapped her arms around his neck. "Show me."

So he did. He took her lips in a deep hot kiss, tasting every corner of her mouth, stroking his hands over every inch of her body. He played with her nipples, making them hard, then lowering his mouth, sucking on them before biting softly, then a little harder as she writhed against him.

His hands ran over her belly, her hips, down her thighs,

and then up to cup between her legs. He slid two fingers deep easily. He circled her clit with his thumb, pressing then circling, then pressing again until she was bucking against his hand. He finger fucked her for several minutes until she was nearly on edge, whimpering his name, her pussy clasping at his fingers. Then he moved down between her knees, draping her thighs over his shoulders and burying his face in her.

He licked and sucked, thrusting his tongue deep until she came.

As she was still trying to catch her breath, he crawled up her body, kissed her deeply, then pushed himself up to kneeling. He took his cock in hand, stroking it several times as she watched, her eyes heavy, her body flushed, soft, hot, and still so wet and glistening between her thighs.

"I need you like this every fucking night," he said hoarsely.

She simply nodded. He rolled on a condom, lined himself up, then thrust deep, loving the way she cried out his name and arched closer. He thrust into her, not working up to it, his pace frenzied from the start. He cupped her ass and pounded into her, loving the way she wrapped her legs around him and dug her heels into his ass.

It didn't take long until they were both panting and climbing toward the climax.

He put his mouth against her neck, biting gently, and then saying, "Come for me, Hayden, come with me, *mo grá*."

Her pussy clamped down on him as she cried out his name, and he let himself crash over the edge, emptying into her.

As they came down from the high, their breathing slowed, and he finally pushed himself off of her. He headed into the bathroom and cleaned up, then he climbed into bed and pulled her against him.

She took a deep contented breath, blowing it out, the air warm against his chest, making his heart clench.

"That is so good," she said. "Every time."

He nodded, brushing his hand over her hair. "I know, *mo grá*. I know."

"What does that mean?" she asked, her voice sleepy. "I looked the other ones up, but I haven't looked that one up yet."

He paused. Should he tell her? But why not? He meant it. "It means *my love*."

He felt her surprise. She looked up at him. "Oh. Like a casual, friendly..."

He met her gaze. "No. Not casual."

Her eyes widened slightly. "Oh."

He leaned in and kissed her. "Not casual at all."

They lay together quietly, both lost in thought, for several minutes.

Then he took a deep breath. "You should move in here."

He'd planned to bring it up with her, probably over lasagna. But he'd wanted to do it privately. He wanted her to know that this was about his feelings for her, not about her cooking or her safety. Would it be nice to have her here where he could protect her and help take care of her in return? Of course. But he just wanted her around.

"What?" She was clearly surprised.

"It makes sense. You like being here, we love having you here. Obviously, we have enough room. You're comfortable around the guys. They'll be sad little puppies if you leave. You don't like living in an apartment. This is a big house." He tucked her up against his side more firmly. "It's felt even more like a home since you've been here. And I'd very, very, much like to have you in my bed every night." He trailed his finger-tips down her side.

She gave a little shiver. "Well, when you put it that way..."

"You mean it? You'll move in?" The relief that washed over him was surprising.

"Do you still think you'll feel this way after he's caught?"

Colin knew they were talking about X. "Absolutely sure."

"What if...things cool off between us?"

He frowned at her. "I cannot imagine that happening. But... again, the guys love having you here. There's plenty of space. You can be our roommate. Indefinitely. No matter what happens."

She seemed to think about that for a moment. Then she said, "What if you show me one more time about this chemistry that you don't think is gonna cool down?"

With a little growl, he rolled her underneath him. "How about two more times?"

seventeen

A WEEK LATER, nothing about moving in with or living with Colin and the guys was exactly the way Hayden had expected.

She probably should've expected that.

Ever since she'd been tackled off the porch of this house, things had been a wild, unexpected ride. Why had she thought moving in and *living there* full-time would be normal and predictable?

That was on her.

For instance, she'd assumed that Colin would continue going with her to work. She was still being stalked. Presumably.

In truth, she wasn't sure. She wasn't on her social media or checking her email. She was assuming that Henry was still doing all of that.

She might have been wrong about that.

But also, she wasn't showing up at her apartment to unwanted gifts of the teddy bear type, so there was that.

However, instead of Colin accompanying her to her music therapy sessions around New Orleans and to visit her grandfather, Cian went along because Colin was needed at Bennett Baxter's new office. Along with Henry, and Jonah, and Matt. All day. Every day.

Which was fine. Cian was awesome. She loved spending time with him. And her grandfather had enjoyed him immensely. Cian could get along with anyone. He'd been charming, funny, and had taken her to a couple of amazing places for lunch.

At least she'd been able to look forward to getting home and making dinner for everyone and having them all around, laughing and talking while they ate.

The first day, she'd been shocked to pull into the driveway and find Zeke, Mitch, and Josh Landry moving all of her belongings from her apartment in New Orleans into the Autre house. Colin had enlisted their help since he, Henry, Jonah, and Cian were busy.

They'd gone over, loaded *everything* up and brought it back to Autre.

The bookcases, her dresser, her clothes and shoes, and a chair had been moved into Fiona's room.

Everything else had been moved into the basement.

She supposed she didn't need any of that stuff.

And she supposed that it was presumptuous to think that her clothes and shoes would be moved into Colin's room.

But it all felt weird.

What was even weirder though, was that Colin and Cian were the only ones home at night for dinner.

Henry and Jonah stayed in New Orleans at the house where Bennett and Kennedy were now living. That was much more secure and bigger, with more room for people like bodyguards.

At least, she spent every night in Colin's room.

And they'd all settled into a kind-of routine.

Cian went with her to work. They came home and she

made dinner. She, Colin, Cian, and twice, Saoirse, had dinner together. She packed up the leftovers along with extra snacks for Colin to take to Henry and Jonah. Then she and Colin spent the evening together, made love, and fell asleep together.

And she actually loved it.

She got texts from Henry and Jonah telling her how much they loved the food. Henry had called a few times, asking how she was. She'd gone up to the petting zoo with Saoirse twice, with Knox as a fill-in bodyguard, to hold baby wombats and to sing to the alpacas.

She was happy and felt appreciated and...jealous as hell of Colin and the guys' new job.

She loved that she got to be with Colin every night. But he was distracted, and a little stressed, and she missed Henry and Jonah.

And then...*then*...the guys informed Colin that it was *his* turn to spend the night in NOLA and let them sleep at home.

"I get it," she told him.

"*They* don't get it." He was scowling.

"That you'd rather sleep here with your gir...me. And have sex. And be in your own bed. And have me make you breakfast in the morning. And have more sex before you leave? Yeah, I think they get it," she told him with a laugh.

He pulled her into his lap at the table, and caught her chin in his hand. "Hayden."

"What?"

"I want you to say that you're my girlfriend."

A shiver went through her. Yeah, she'd almost blurted that out and then realized they'd never actually used those words. She pressed her lips together.

He pulled her lower lip free from her upper lip with his thumb. "Say it," he ordered, low and firm.

"We don't have to."

He leaned in until their noses touched. "Say it."

"I'm your girlfriend."

"Damn right you are." He kissed her, slow and hot and deep. Then he'd picked her up and carried her upstairs.

Yeah, Henry and Jonah understood.

And Colin had spent the next two nights in New Orleans.

But...they'd gotten to play around with phone sex.

And she'd gotten to make breakfast and dinner for two other guys who *really* liked her cooking and were downright gushy about telling her so.

She liked Colin's hugs best, but Henry and Jonah hugs were great too.

And no, she did *not* tell Colin that.

So ten days in, things seemed like they were maybe, kind of okay.

Of course, her meeting with the record label was coming up and she had no idea what they were going to say to her. Or what she hoped they'd say to her. Or how she felt about any of it anymore.

So, instead of thinking about it, she was cooking. And singing.

She had Adele turned up and was just getting ready to roll out beignets when she heard a knock at the door.

She froze. Shit. Hell. The door? Really? No one ever came to the door and knocked. Everyone who was welcome here just came in without knocking. Was she supposed to answer the door? Did stalkers knock?

She moved on tip toe to the front room, still carrying her rolling pin, then ducked behind the couch. She peeked over the top.

An older woman stood on the front porch.

She wore blue jeans, tennis shoes, and a button-down plaid shirt rolled up to her elbows. Her long gray hair was pulled back in a braid that hung well past her shoulder blades.

Well, surely this wasn't her stalker.

Probably.

And stalkers didn't send their grandmothers to do their dirty work, did they?

Hayden took a deep breath, rose, and crossed to the door. She pulled it open with a smile. "Hi. Can I help you?"

"Well, I figured if you weren't going to come up to my bar to meet me, I was going to have to come here to meet you." The woman smiled. "I'm Ellie Landry."

Hayden's eyes widened. Oh, boy. This was the legendary Ellie.

Why did she feel like she was in trouble?

"Ellie, oh wow." Hayden pushed the door open wider and gestured for the other woman to come inside. "It's so nice to meet you. I'd definitely planned to meet you eventually, but things have been a little...strange around here. I haven't been... getting out much."

"I've never had a stalker myself," Ellie said as she stepped into the house. "But I'd suppose that would put a damper on things."

Hayden sucked in a breath. "You know about that?"

"I know about everything that happens in Autre."

"Ah. Okay. Yes, I'm kind of having to lay low."

Ellie gave her smile. "It's fine. It's good for me to get out of the bar once in a while. And it's very nice to meet you. Colin is one of my favorite people. As are Cian, Henry, and Jonah. You seem to be taking very good care of them."

Hayden relaxed a bit with that. "Well, it's my pleasure. They are some of my favorite people too."

"We already have something in common then."

"Do you want to come in? I was just making beignets."

"It smells delicious in here."

Hayden wasn't sure how to feel about the compliment suddenly. Ellie ran a restaurant. She fed her entire family. She'd fed Hayden's boys for a long time. Yikes. Did Hayden feel confident cooking for Ellie? She wasn't so sure.

Hayden rounded the end of the breakfast bar to return to her dough.

Ellie boosted herself up onto one of the stools across from her. Ellie looked around. "It's kind of strange sitting on a stool on the other side of a bar."

Hayden grinned. "Can I get you something to drink?"

Ellie chuckled. "What do you have?"

"How do you feel about day drinking?"

"I own a bar. I have eleven grandkids, most of them rowdy as hell, all of them marrying people who are just as sassy as they are deep down, and they're starting to reproduce. I'm very in favor of day drinking."

Hayden laughed. "I take you for the adventurous type."

Ellie nodded. "That I am."

Hayden moved to the cabinet where all the liquor was stored. She pulled a few bottles out, then moved to the fridge. She mixed the cocktail on the back counter, added a maraschino cherry, then brought the glass to Ellie, sliding it across the marble-topped bar.

Ellie lifted the glass. She studied it. Sniffed it. Then sipped. Her brows lifted. She sipped again.

"It's good."

"It's a Bijou," Hayden told her.

"That's French for jewel."

Hayden nodded.

Ellie held the glass up and looked at it. "I've heard of them but I've never mixed one. Maybe had one a long time ago. What's in it?"

"I make it the way my grandpa always did. With Grand Marnier, his favorite, instead of green chartreuse, then gin, and orange bitters.

Ellie nodded. "You've just given me something new. That's hard to do."

Hayden felt a curl of pride slip through her chest. "Enjoy."

Ellie sipped again, then leaned her elbows onto the breakfast bar as Hayden went back to rolling out her dough. "So, I'm relatively well known for giving out advice. Mostly my grandkids come to me, but a lot of times, their significant others do too.

"But I realized that you're living here with a bunch of people I have no connection to. It's kind of a first. Colin and the guys here have each other. I mean, they fit right in with us, and we consider them part of the family. I think they feel at home here, in Autre. But they have their own family unit, they lean on one another. I haven't given any of them advice."

Hayden looked at the other woman. "They are very close-knit. I think they've been together long enough and have had to keep so many secrets that they're not used to leaning on anyone else."

"But they let you in."

Hayden felt a flush of warmth, the feeling of acceptance and affection that surrounded her when she was with the guys making her smile. "Yeah. It's been wonderful. They have quickly become my best friends."

"They clearly needed you."

Hayden laughed softly. "I needed *them*. They had my back when I needed protection. They've let me in and have given me a...haven."

"But they needed you, Hayden. It's obvious. You've given them just as much as they've given you."

"I don't know about that." She sighed as she cut the dough

into the small squares she would fry. "Actually, I've been away from my family for a while and haven't had anyone older and wiser to talk to." She gave Ellie a smile that she hoped told the other woman that she meant no offense at the "older" comment.

Ellie sipped from her drink. "That's what I'm here for."

"Have you ever had a chance to do something really, really big? Something...important. But you weren't sure if you should do it. Or rather, if you *wanted* to do it? Because what you would have to give up to do it was so good?"

"Nope," Ellie said, without even thinking about it. "I do my important stuff every day."

Hayden stopped cutting and looked at her. "Really? Every single day?"

"Of course. The bar I run feeds people, gives them a place to come, and is a gathering place for friends and family. It's where my family comes when they are happy, sad, tired, depressed, need help, or need to celebrate. It's where I get to build them up, put them in their place, cheer them on, or just love on 'em. Every single day I do that important stuff."

Hayden nodded. "Yes. Absolutely. I agree. I guess I'm talking about something *really* big. Like...what Bennett's going to do. Being a senator. Something huge. Something in the spotlight where millions of people are going to be looking at you."

Ellie grinned. "Well, Bennett wouldn't be a senator without my bar and the stuff that's been going on there for the past few years that he's been in my family."

Hayden tipped her head. "You think so?"

Ellie nodded without even the slightest hesitation. "I do. Bennett Baxter would not be a man running for Senate right now if it weren't for the Landry family. His own family too, of course. And the love of my granddaughter. He's a wonderful person. His smarts, his charm, his passion—that's all there.

But he needed people behind him believing in him. People who would make him laugh when he was being too serious, tell him an idea was complete horseshit, or that an idea was absolutely amazing. He would have no idea how to talk to the people of Louisiana without us. And that's just one thing that we do.

"We love him no matter what. If he goes on that campaign trail and makes a blunder, he knows that he has a whole bunch of people back here who love him anyway. If he goes out and loses, he can come home, and he's going to have all of us here, loving him, telling him stupid stories, and feeding him gumbo 'til he can't move anyway.

"And that matters. He can go out there and try and take risks and take on challenges because we're back here behind him." Ellie leaned in. "Somebody has to be a senator from here. I'm glad Bennett's willing. I sure as *hell* don't want to." Ellie gave a shudder. "Instead, I get to feed him, and tell him when he needs a haircut, and when he's getting too full of himself, and when I'm so damned proud of him I could bust. Trust me, my job is so much better. But I'm really grateful to the people like Bennett."

Hayden nodded. "Okay, I'm with you. You're a part of Bennett being important."

Ellie studied her. "Have *you* ever done anything big and important?"

"Not yet. But I might have a chance to."

Ellie shook her head. "Try again."

"What?"

"You have done lots of important things, Hayden. Think about them. Let yourself see them."

Hayden took a deep breath. "Okay, I've written a bunch of songs that people seem to like. They've made people happy. I've sung some of them up on stage. I think I've been able to make people happy that way too. Some of my songs are on the internet so people can find them and replay them when they want to hear them."

Ellie shook her head. "There's so much more than that."

Hayden frowned.

"You made food for and encouraged three people who traveled nine hours one way to rescue some animals that had been badly abused. You helped those people bring those animals back to a sanctuary where they can live out the rest of their lives. Not only are those animals now safe and somewhere that they'll be loved, but you took care of the humans. They love their job, and they do it with passion, but it's taxing. And it helps the rest of us who care about them and worry, to know that they had some extra supplies and love along with them."

Hayden felt her heart trip. She had definitely not thought about any of that in that way.

"Also," Ellie went on. "Over the past several days, you have been feeding and encouraging and supporting three men who are wading through the new, confusing, stressful waters of becoming the security detail for a potential U.S. senator."

Hayden pressed her lips together. She hadn't been aware of how much Ellie knew about Colin, Henry, and Jonah's jobs with Bennett and Kennedy, but it did seem that this woman knew everything that was going on with everyone connected to this town and her family.

"And because they have been able to be steady and solid and confident, they are making that someday-U.S. senator and his wife feel more confident and steady and calm. And because *they* are more confident and steady and calm, their grandmother and grandfather are able to sleep better at night knowing they are well cared for and that everything's going to be okay." Ellie gave her a sincere smile. "And that's only a few of the things that you've done in the past couple of weeks, Hayden."

Hayden swallowed hard. "I was talking about maybe being a rockstar," she said softly.

Ellie nodded. "I know. And when you're a rockstar, you're going to be writing songs and singing them for millions of people. Probably making them very happy and giving them joy and making their days better. That's kinda great too."

She said it so flippantly that Hayden laughed. "It's just kinda great?"

"I looked up your brother," Ellie said, lifting her glass again.

"You did?" Hayden was surprised by the sudden change in topic. "Which one?"

"The older one. The professional baseball player."

"Jake."

"Yes. Did you know that Jake happened to be the favorite baseball player of a little boy with cancer named Emmett?"

Hayden stared at her. "No, I didn't."

"Emmett started following your brother when he played at LSU. He went to games with his dad and uncle and would occasionally write fan letters. After he was diagnosed with a brain tumor, Emmett's dad reached out to Jake. Jake signed a few things for a fundraising auction that helped Emmett and his family travel to see a specialist. And then, about two weeks ago, Jake hit a home run in a big game, got the ball, signed it, and sent it to Emmett. He got it the day before surgery."

Hayden felt tears stinging her eyes. She hadn't known any of this. But she was so proud of her brother. "That's...so great."

Ellie nodded. "Emmett didn't wake up from the surgery. It was a very risky procedure. There were complications, and he passed away."

Hayden's hand flew to cover her mouth. She stared at Ellie. "What?" Her hand dropped. "That's terrible. Oh my God!"

"Of course, that's terrible."

"Why did you tell me that story?"

"Because your brother did something really important."

"He helped a little boy get a surgery that didn't even work!"

"No. He gave Emmett some of his happiest days," Ellie said. "All the games with his dad and uncle were some of his favorites. And getting that signed baseball in the mail made that little boy's last day one of his best. Because of who your brother is, because he became a baseball player, he was able to do that. And, with the fundraising, he was able to show Emmett's family that there are people out there who care."

Ellie watched her for a long moment as Hayden processed that.

"I'm guessing that along the way, you had a lot to do with your brother getting to where he is and being able to do all of that."

Hayden felt her chest tighten, and her eyes welled with tears.

"You take care of people, Hayden. You help them be all they can be. *That* is more than kind of great."

Hayden just stared at her. Her heart was pounding and she had so many words tripping through her mind. But nothing would come out of her mouth.

Ellie drained her glass. "Anyway, I just run a bar in a rinky-dink little town on the Louisiana bayou that most people have never even heard of. But that town happens to make thousands of people happy every year by taking them out on swamp boat tours and letting them go through an animal park filled with a whole bunch of different kinds of animals, some that are endangered and others that have been rescued from terrible situations.

"My bar feeds the people who do those tours and rescue those animals. And it's brought together two people who are now going to make a run for the U.S. Senate. If Bennett wins, he'll do amazing things. If he loses, he'll do amazing things. I don't think being a senator is necessarily any more important than doing boat tours or taking care of animals or being an attorney or a teacher. We've got some of those too. I think they all have their place and are making this crazy-assed, what-the-hell-is-goin'-on world just a little bit better. And God knows, no matter what they're doing, they need to be loved while they're doing it. So yeah, I do important stuff every single day."

Ellie slid off the stool and started for the front door. "It was really nice to meet you, Hayden. I can't wait to see you again. I think those beignets are gonna turn out amazing." She paused in the doorway. "And we're going to get along fabulously. Just don't be makin' any gumbo over here, okay? That's *my* thing."

Then Ellie Landry disappeared out the front door.

And Hayden Ross stood there staring after her for a good two minutes before she even managed to close her mouth.

"So, they're going to meet us at Octavia's at two o'clock. Do you want me to pick you up?" Sabrina asked Hayden.

Hayden paced across the living room. Sabrina had just called to confirm the meeting with the executives from the record label was scheduled for the day after tomorrow. They weren't even going to wait until she performed with Jason. They wanted to meet with her *before* the shows. Now butterflies were swooping through Hayden's stomach. It was really happening. It wasn't a *they might want to meet with you*. Or even a *probably*. It was a definite meeting with a time and place now.

"No, I'll meet you there." She still wasn't sure how she felt about the meeting, and she didn't want to be stuck in a car with Sabrina on the drive to New Orleans. Or on the drive back from New Orleans, depending on how the meeting went.

"I know it sucks, Henry. I think it sucks too."

Hayden looked up as Colin walked into the room on his phone as well. They exchanged a quick smile, before Colin went back to frowning about whatever Henry was saying in his ear.

"Do you have any questions?" Sabrina asked.

Hayden tried to focus. She and Colin had been home together, just the two of them, all afternoon. But they'd barely spoken *to* each other. Colin had been on the phone most of the day, and Hayden had been busy working on a new song. Well, after she'd baked three dozen cookies, tried to work off some nervous energy down in the home gym, and taken a long shower.

"Henry, there's nothing I can do about it," Colin said crossly. "Jack wants them in New Orleans. We have to take turns." He paused. "I know that you and Jonah have been taking more overnight shifts."

Hayden felt guilty about that. She knew Colin was coming home to Autre more often than Henry and Jonah got to because of her.

"Well, get a girlfriend and we'll talk about it," Colin snapped.

Yep, she was right.

It didn't make it fair, though.

"Hayden?" Sabrina asked.

Hayden shook her head and focused. She turned away from Colin. Not watching him pacing across the room, clearly frustrated, would probably help with paying attention to her own phone call.

"No, I don't have any questions. I don't think. Do I? What should my questions be?"

Sabrina laughed. "They already love you, Hayden. There's nothing to be nervous about."

"What are they going to expect from me at the meeting?"

"They're going to want to know if you're interested in signing."

"Really? Just like that?"

"It's becoming more and more common for artists to stay independent. A lot of people aren't willing to give up the rights to their music. They're releasing songs on their own. There are pros and cons to both. Social media can give you a platform and you can sell directly to fans. That way you maintain full rights and full control. Of course, you have less financial backing then, and it's tougher to network in the industry. So you have to decide what's important to you," Sabrina said. "Labels are having to pitch to artists more now than they ever did before. So yeah, they'll want to know up front if you're interested."

"Okay. I'll think everything over and I'll call you if I have any questions that can't wait until tomorrow."

"Can't wait to see you."

They disconnected just in time for Hayden to hear Colin say, "You're really getting on my fucking nerves, Henry." Then he disconnected his call as well.

Hayden crossed the room to join him where he was standing behind the couch. "What's going on?"

"Henry and Jonah are bitching because they haven't been home in a few days."

"You can't blame them for that."

"It's part of the job. When they were with Cian and Torin they'd be on the road away from home for several days. Sometimes weeks. Henry sure wasn't bitching when Cian dragged him to Vegas, and they partied on the strip for two weeks straight."

"Partying with your best friend in Las Vegas is probably a

little bit different than being holed up in a house with a bunch of politicians and their staff."

Colin blew out a breath. Then he looked at her. Really looked at her for the first time. "I miss you."

She stepped close and wrapped her arms around him, resting her cheek against his chest. His arms went around her immediately and tugged her close. "I'm right here. You've been home every day."

"Thank God," he said against her hair. "I'd be a real bastard if I hadn't been able to come home to you."

She laughed softly. "We wouldn't want that."

He sighed. "We're just getting used to something new. This is a very different kind of job than what we've done before."

"And everyone's a little on edge."

"And we're used to being more in control. I mean, it's not like Cian's a great listener, but he did respect Henry, and they were friends. Same with Torin and Jonah. Bennett and Kennedy are friendly and respectful, but his campaign manager and his Chief of Staff are calling a lot of the shots. And Bennett and Kennedy are still getting used to all of this too. It's just not the same."

"And you were definitely used to bossing Saoirse and Fiona around."

He gave her a half grin. "Well, Saoirse anyway."

She grinned. "It's just going to take some time."

"Yeah."

"So, I have an idea. Actually, it's just a question, but why can't Bennett and Kennedy be here?"

"Autre's just different. Their house here is less secure. There's a lot more access because of the bayou. The water is harder to patrol. There's a small police department for back up. And they have to be in a lot of meetings."

"Sure, *their* house in Autre, I get that. But why can't they be *here*? In this house? I mean you protected a royal family here. This security system has to be better than even what's in the house in New Orleans. And then all three of you guys could be here all the time.

"And as far as patrolling the bayou, you have Theo, Bailey, and all their people," she said, naming the game wardens that were also family friends. "Not to mention that everyone who lives here knows those waters like they know the streets of this town. And Zander's right here. Plus, you have the firefighters as a kind of backup. And of course, all of the Landrys are going to be watching their backs better than any random New Orleans cops.

"Plus," she went on. "Jack can come down here as easily as you guys can travel back and forth. Seems to me that it's way more important that you guys be well-rested and less stressed than for Jack to be getting eight hours. Plus, Kennedy and Bennett will be way happier staying here in Autre, than in some new random house in New Orleans."

Colin studied her. "What room will we give them?"

That definitely wasn't a *no* or a *that's crazy*.

She pretended to think about that. "Well, there is Torin's room. Though, it would be nice to keep that ready for him for whenever he comes to visit." She sighed. "I mean, I guess we *could* give them Fiona's room. But I'll have to ask Henry or Cian if I can stay with one of them."

Colin growled and pulled her up against him more firmly. "That's *not* going to happen."

She smiled at him. "Or, I guess I could move my clothes and shoes into *your* room."

"We're doing that. Tonight."

Her smile got even wider. "Good. Because if you're all here, then I can cook even bigger dinners."

"So really you're just angling to get more people here under your roof so you can pull out the *big* pots."

She nodded happily. *Your roof.* She loved the sound of that. "Pretty much."

He cupped her ass and leaned in to kiss her, then lifted his head. "You know this is a hell of an idea."

She lifted a brow. "Stick around. I have those once in a while."

The very next day, Bennett Baxter, future U.S. senator, and his lovely wife, Kennedy, moved into Fiona's room. Despite the grumbling from Bennett's Chief of Staff.

Hayden figured the sooner Jack figured out that Colin was definitely going to be calling the shots once in a while, the better for everyone.

Hayden moved her clothes and shoes into Colin's room.

And she made lasagna again, and the guys were all able to eat it hot and fresh out of the oven.

The looks on their faces when they came through the door, the laughter around the table while they all ate together, and the praise heaped on her afterward all made Hayden feel like she was about to burst.

That night after Colin made love to her, and was cuddling her in their bed, he said, "I don't know what I ever did without you."

And Hayden fell asleep happier than she'd maybe ever been.

eighteen

"ARE you sure you don't want me to go in? I love this place," Cian said as he walked her to the door of Octavia's the next afternoon.

Hayden laughed. "If you're in there, I'll be even more nervous."

He scoffed. "Nervous about what? They already love you. You go in there and ask for whatever you fucking want."

She grinned at him. "Thanks. I just have no idea what to expect."

"Doesn't matter. Just remember you're the star. They have nothing without you."

She knew Cian knew very little about the music business either, but she appreciated the vote of confidence. "Thanks. I'll let you know when I'm ready to go."

He shrugged and tucked his hands into his pocket. "Trust me, I can keep myself busy."

The restaurant sat on a corner in the French quarter. It wasn't one of the busier corners, but there were tourists milling about, and that meant pretty girls from out of town who would love to have a handsome, charming guy give them directions to the nearest bar and buy them a drink. She had no doubt that Cian would be well entertained. "I'll text you."

"Sounds good. You've got this."

Hayden watched him walk away and then took a deep breath and pulled the door open. The hostess greeted her immediately. "Welcome to Octavia's."

"Thank you. Hayden Ross. I'm meeting some people."

"Yes. Welcome, Ms. Ross. Right this way."

The hostess led her through the restaurant. This time of day it wasn't busy though there were a few other tables occupied. Octavia's was a white tablecloth, crystal glassware, cloth napkin type of place and even in the middle of the afternoon, short candles burned inside frosted votive candle holders in the center of the tables.

Hayden saw Sabrina as they wove between the tables, and she caught her friend's eye with a little wave. Sabrina's smile was bright and genuine, and she got to her feet as Hayden approached.

"Hayden!" Sabrina leaned in to give her a hug and whispered in her ear, "This is going to be great."

Hayden recognized two of the other people at the table from a brief meet and greet with Jason a few months before. The third was a woman she hadn't met before, but she gave Hayden a warm smile. "Hi, Hayden, I'm Ingrid. It's nice to meet you."

"You too."

They took their seats again, and the waitress arrived with a water for Hayden and to refill the others' drinks.

"Well, we wanted to meet with you because, as you know, we love your music. Jason has nothing but great things to say about you and when we heard you perform with him, we were impressed," Ingrid said. "We would love to welcome you into the Brighton Music family."

Wow, they were just going to get right to it. Hayden sucked in a little breath. "I'm very flattered. What does that mean exactly?"

"It means, we would like to sign you as one of our artists. We would record some more music with you. Distribute it. Get you heard far and wide."

"Does that include any touring?" If they were just going to lay it out there, so was she.

Ingrid nodded. "You're fantastic on stage and Jason's fans respond really well to you. We were thinking we would fly you out to Vegas for his three shows there. Then, if that's well received, add you to the rest of his U.S. tour."

Hayden stared at her, surprise rocked through her. "That's...the rest of the year."

"Yes. You're already contracted for his shows here in New Orleans, but we want to see you outside of your hometown market. See if the response is *you* or just because you're from here. If Vegas goes well, you would join him on the road to finish his tour. If *that* goes well, we think Gretchen Hope's fans would love you. She's heading to Europe next spring."

Hayden sat back in her chair, processing all of that. She looked at Sabrina. Her friend's eyes were wide with excitement. Sabrina reached across the table and took Hayden's hand. "Oh, my God, Hayden. Congratulations."

Hayden's thoughts were spinning.

Gretchen Hope was bigger than Jason. And she had a much bigger cross-over audience from country to rock. *She* was more the next Taylor Swift than Hayden was.

Holy. Crap.

This was happening.

A year ago she'd been writing songs and singing on a street corner. Now she was being offered a chance to tour the country and maybe go to *Europe* to sing in front of stadiums full of people. A recording label wanted to buy her music and record it.

She pressed a hand to her stomach. It all felt unreal.

I can call Mom and Dad tonight and tell them the music thing is real.

Hell, she could bring her family to the concert in *Las Vegas* and take them backstage.

"What...happens now?" Hayden asked.

They spent the next hour going over what would be happening over the following weeks. The contract would take several weeks, so nothing would be official for some time. Her shows with Jason in New Orleans would go on as planned, but no other announcements would be made just yet. Ingrid projected that things would be in place for Hayden to join Jason at his Vegas show.

Hayden and Sabrina hugged in the foyer of Octavia's.

"I'm *so* happy for you, Hayden! You deserve this," Sabrina told her, eyes sparkling. "This is amazing."

Hayden felt so much affection looking at the woman who had seen her on that street corner and recognized her talent. She squeezed Sabrina's arm. "Thank you for...everything."

"Of course. I'll be at your shows here and then I really want to come to Vegas!"

"Definitely! I'll see if I can get you tickets or something!" Hayden laughed. "Can I do that? I don't know how *any* of this works!"

Sabrina grinned. "You'll figure it out. You have a ton of people on your side."

Hayden watched Sabrina leave Octavia's, those words circling in her mind. She did. She had a ton of people on her side.

But she was leaving. She was going *on tour*. That meant leaving a lot of those people behind. A strange sadness swept over her. A few weeks ago, she'd felt alone in this city. She'd wanted more. She'd wanted to feel like she was doing something bigger.

Now, in the space of a couple of weeks, she felt like she had a whole group of friends...a family...she'd be leaving behind.

A shiver went through her as she stepped outside and just stood on the sidewalk for a moment, taking deep breaths. She wasn't quite ready to call Cian. She needed a little alone time before she told anyone about the meeting.

Cian wanted her to be a big star. He wanted to see her on stage and hear her on his satellite radio. He thought she was going to win a Grammy. He'd told her that he would be a much better date to the Grammy awards than Colin would be. She wasn't so sure about that, though Cian would be a lot of fun at a big black-tie party filled with celebrities.

And for some reason, at this moment, she didn't want to talk about all of that. She wasn't sure she could quite match the level of Cian's predicted excitement.

And she didn't want to think about telling Colin either.

She'd be taking him away from...everyone. Everything. His family. This new job that was so exciting.

The job with Bennett was *exactly* right for him. It was important, incredibly so. It was also for someone Colin knew well, liked, and respected. She knew that Colin and the guys would get closer to Bennett and Kennedy and establish a comfortable, familial relationship like they'd had with the O'Gradys. It was already happening. And it was going to be for years to come. She knew Bennett was going to win this election.

It was intense and yes, Colin had been stressed over the past week or so, but she could tell he loved it. It was a challenge. It was bringing the guys together. He'd talked about how much more was involved with this than anything they'd done before, but she could see how it excited him.

Now, he'd go with her on the road, and he'd have to give all of that up. Henry and Jonah and Matt could handle it, she was sure. But they'd miss Colin so much and vice versa.

She just needed to think. She turned right and started toward Trahan's Tavern.

It was the middle of the afternoon so there wasn't much of a crowd. Just a few tourists. But she wasn't here to play for anyone else at the moment.

Gabe looked up as she approached the bar, clearly surprised. "Hayden."

"Hey, Gabe. Mind if I borrow your piano for a little while? On the house."

He chuckled. "It's all yours, anytime."

"Thanks."

"Everything okay?" He looked concerned as he studied her more closely.

"Yeah. I think so. Or will be."

He glanced behind her. "You alone?"

"Yeah."

"Okay, well, you let me know if you need anything."

She gave him a nod and then headed for the piano.

She started to play and sing softly. She didn't want to interrupt any of the conversations going on in the room, but she didn't mind being background noise. She wasn't here to perform.

She didn't really pay attention to the people in the room. People came and went as she played over the next hour. She didn't really make eye contact with anyone or do much more than give people quick smiles as they dropped tips in the jar on the piano. This was mostly for her.

As she played, she thought back over all the songs she'd

sung with her grandfather. And how even now, in the car on the way home from doctors' appointments, when he would be agitated and confused about what they were doing, she could sing and calm him down.

She thought about her siblings and their successes playing ball. She'd called Jake after hearing the story of the little boy with cancer from Ellie. Hayden had told him how proud she was of him. He'd seemed very happy to hear from her, and it had prompted her to look her siblings up online. She'd never done that before. She'd kept up with their careers and successes through her mother. She'd never thought to look them up as an objective observer. She'd found out more about charitable work they'd been involved in with their teams and even a few things they'd each done individually. She'd known nothing about any of that, and she felt bad for not realizing or having it even occur to her that they might've been doing those things.

She was still pretty sick of baseball and didn't have a lot of desire to go watch a game anytime soon, but she was pleased to think that her siblings had something that gave them a platform and a way to reach out to people, kids in particular, who needed a hero and that they were willing to be that person.

And she thought about what Ellie had said about all the great work that was being done in Autre and how the Bennett Baxter for Senate campaign definitely needed a strong foundation. They needed people there supporting them, doing the behind-the-scenes work, and being the people who provided the home base.

And she thought about Ellie's point about how not everyone could be a U.S. senator nor did everybody want to be.

Hayden did *not* want to do the things that Bennett was going to have to do. But man, she was glad he was going to be the one doing them.

And Henry and Jonah deserved to have that big job. They'd be amazing. And Colin...Colin needed that deep, long-term, meaningful relationship with his next client and yeah, she was going to be that 'client'. He needed a bigger-than-a-job job and she was definitely going to be that for him.

But she could probably convince him to let her take Cian to at least one Grammy party.

She picked her fingers up from the keyboard and took a deep breath.

She was ready to go home. And she knew exactly where that was. The place she could come back to when she was in between tours, or when she needed a break, or if things flopped. Just like Bennett, she didn't have to worry about being on the road and going for something big and slightly-crazy... she had a firm foundation no matter what happened.

She texted Cian, *I'm ready. Meet me at Trahan's.*

Then she tucked her phone into her pocket and headed for the restroom.

She took care of business, washed her hands, freshened up her lip gloss, and remembered the last time she'd been here.

It was interesting that when she thought back on that evening, it was Colin and the heat between them and how safe the guys had made her feel, rather than her confrontation in the back hallway that she thought of.

She ran her fingers through her hair, gave herself a smile in the mirror, then stepped out of the bathroom.

There was a man there.

A very tall man with a dark beard.

"Hello, Hayden. Have you missed me?"

She didn't know him. But she knew his voice.

She opened her mouth to yell for help, but he slapped his hand over it, grabbing her by the wrist and tugging her forward.

"Oh no. None of that," he said.

She immediately started to struggle, but he wrapped his arms around her and started carrying her, literally kicking, and at least trying to scream, toward the back door.

"Settle down, goddamn it."

She stopped trying to pull away. And went quiet. It wasn't doing her any good anyway, and maybe if she pretended to be compliant, he'd stop. She did *not* want to leave the building with him. Surprising him might be the best way to stall.

He did stop, letting her feet find purchase on the floor. She dug her heels in, making it harder to move toward the door. He turned her and pushed her up against the wall.

She pleaded with him with her eyes.

He narrowed his eyes. "You're not going to scream, got it?"

She nodded.

He slowly withdrew his hand but kept it right in front of her face in case she'd lied.

"What do you want?" she asked, her voice trembling.

He laughed. Though, it was humorless. "You. Obviously."

"Why?"

"I'm in love with you, Hayden."

"You don't even know me."

"I know enough. You're beautiful, talented, funny, and smart. What? A guy like me can't want a woman like you?"

She swallowed, fear clutching at her throat. But the longer they stayed *here*, the less time they were at some remote bayou cabin doing God knew what? Where the hell was Gabe and his staff? Why did this have to be a slow time of day?

"Of course. I just, I'm not used to guys falling for me when they haven't even spoken to me."

"I have spoken to you. I've sent you several emails." It was clear he was getting angry again.

"Yes. You're right. I know. My bodyguard told me I shouldn't answer you."

"I don't like that fucker."

She nodded. "I understand."

"I don't want to hurt you. You're just making me mad."

"Then what do you want to do?"

Oh God, please don't talk about sex, please don't talk about sex, please don't talk about sex.

"I just want to be with you."

"Be with me where? Do you live here in the city?"

Maybe she could get some information. A confession? Would him confessing things to her even matter? Was that something the police could even use?

She wasn't thinking clearly. But again, they were just standing *here* and not on their way out to a remote cabin. That was a win in her book.

"I live...near here," he said.

"So...are you asking me on a date?" She swallowed against the nausea.

Again, he laughed. "Yeah, something like that." He reached up and cupped the side of her face.

She reacted on instinct and wrapped her hand around his wrist. *Thank you for all the self-defense lessons, Jonah,* she thought, just before she bent his wrist back suddenly while bringing her other hand up hard and fast to his nose.

He jerked back in surprise and pain, howling. The move gave her enough room to punch him in the throat and then lift her knee to kick him in the groin.

She whirled and started down the hall toward the front of the bar.

"You bitch!" He was doubled over and his voice raspy now, a good sign he was in pain.

She rounded the corner and ran smack into someone.

"Oh my God! I'm...sorry! I—"

"Hayden! Jesus!" Strong arms banded around her as the familiar voice and scent hit her.

She sagged against Colin, relief washing over her as the adrenaline coursing through her suddenly made her weak and wobbly.

"What the fuck? Are you alright?" He pulled back, studying her with a scowl.

"No. He's—here..." She pointed toward the hallway.

He seemed to immediately realize who she was talking about. "*Son of a bitch.*" Colin passed her off to someone else and immediately started in that direction.

"Hey."

Cian's voice filtered through the hazy mix of abating fear and shock.

"Hey." Hayden heard how shaky her voice was.

"You okay?"

Cian was absolutely holding her up and he *put* her up on a stool at the bar. Someone passed over a glass of water.

"Need something with some sugar in it," he said to someone.

Orange juice came next.

"Matt," Cian said. "Back hallway. Colin might be killing someone."

"What? What the fuck?" Matt strode past them without stopping, casting only a glance in Hayden's direction.

"Drink," Cian said, pressing the glass of orange juice into her hand.

"I'm okay. Where's Colin?"

"Not sure."

He was in the back hallway with X. "Cian, you have to stop him."

"Nah." Cian gave her a grin. "For one thing, the guy

315

deserves whatever Colin's giving him. For another, no way in fuck would I step between Colin and someone who's messed with someone Colin loves. I'm not the sharpest crayon in the box, but I'm not a total idiot."

She took a breath, and a sip of orange juice, looking worriedly toward the back hallway. "How did he know I was here?"

"I texted him."

She looked up at Gabe who was standing behind the bar. "Oh. Why?"

"You looked like you had a lot on your mind. And you were alone. I was worried, but knew that the person you'd want most was him."

"Oh." He was right.

Gabe grimaced and shoved a hand through his hair. "I'm sorry that guy has gotten to you here. Twice." He was gripping the edge of the bar with white knuckles.

She swallowed and shook her head. "It's not your fault, Gabe. It's *his*." She looked toward the back hallway again.

"Matt will keep Colin out of prison," Cian assured her.

She finally focused on her friend. "I used the stuff Jonah taught me. I might have broken his nose."

Cian gave her a big, proud smile. "That's our girl."

She let that sink in. Yeah. She'd done okay.

Two cops came striding into the bar just then. Gabe simply pointed them toward the back hallway.

Five minutes later, Colin and Matt emerged. Colin's expression was furious. He almost didn't look like himself. "Where is she?"

Cian stepped in front of Hayden. She peered over his shoulder.

"She's *fine*. She's safe, Colin," Cian said, sounding the most serious Hayden had ever heard him.

"I want her," Colin said simply.

"You need to calm the fuck down," Matt said firmly.

Colin sucked in a breath.

The cops came out with X handcuffed between them. His eyes were closed and they were mostly dragging him.

"Oh my God, is he unconscious?" she whispered to Cian.

"Maybe." Cian seemed unbothered by the possibility.

Cian drove Hayden home.

Colin drove himself home. With Matt's words in his head: "If you let your anger get the best of you and you wreck your fucking car and kill yourself, someone else is going to get to marry Hayden. Just keep thinking of that."

That was probably the only thing keeping him under the speed limit and not letting his brain replay everything.

He was lucky that he wasn't sitting in a jail cell right now for murder. Or for anything.

He would have taken that sentence though. Gladly.

His blood was still pumping hard, and his gut was churning the way it had when he'd gotten the text from Gabe saying, *your girl's here.*

Having Bennett and Kennedy in Autre had been awesome. For exactly twenty-four hours.

But that meant he was then twenty minutes away from New Orleans, where Hayden had been for her meeting with the record executives.

Fuck.

He beat his open hand against the steering wheel and swore loudly.

Thank God Cian had gone with her. But why the fuck hadn't Cian been with her at Trahan's? What had happened at the meeting? Thank God Gabe had texted him almost immediately when she'd walked through his door. It had given Colin time to get there from Autre while she'd been singing and playing.

He grabbed the steering wheel, shaking it with another loud *"Fuck!"*

What if he'd been a little later? What if X had dragged her to *his* truck and taken off instead of staying in the building?

And what if Matt had been five minutes later showing up?

Colin would have a murder on his hands.

But he wouldn't have one ounce of regret about it.

Finally, he pulled into the driveway in Autre behind Cian's truck. He got out and stomped up to the passenger door, he yanked it open and pulled Hayden off the seat, and into his arms.

"Colin," Cian said with warning.

"Fuck off," Colin told him.

Hayden cuddled close, clearly not afraid or wanting to be anywhere else. He carried her in his arms up the front steps of the house. The door swung open, and Jonah stood there, his face a combination of worry, rage, and absolute devastation.

"She's fine. Guy's in the hospital. He'll be in jail after that."

Jonah gave a single nod. Then his gaze dropped to Hayden.

Hayden smiled up at him. "Hey."

Jonah swallowed, clearly with some effort. "Hey."

Colin felt his chest constrict. Fuck. He tried to pull in a breath, but it was nearly impossible. Dammit. He wanted to hold her. Tightly. He wanted to take her upstairs, wrap her in all the blankets he had, and never let her out.

But Jonah needed to see that she was okay.

Slowly, Colin let her feet swing to the floor. He sucked in a deep breath, pulling her scent in with it. Then he let go of her.

Everyone inside this house was going to need to see for

themselves that she was all right. And she probably needed to be on her feet for that. She definitely needed to be in these rooms for that rather than up in his bedroom in his bed for the next week. Which the minimum amount of time he wanted to keep her to himself.

She put her hand against his face. "Later." It was as if she was reading his mind.

He pressed her hand against his cheek, then turned his head and kissed her palm. "Yeah."

She was important to a lot of people. They had a family. Everyone needed to see her.

He had no doubt that Cian had called ahead. Or maybe Matt. Someone had filled everyone in.

"Oh my God, Hayden." Kennedy came down the hall swiftly, immediately enfolding Hayden in her arms.

Case in point.

Bennett and Kennedy weren't even long-term members of their inner circle, and they were clearly upset.

Bennett was right behind Kennedy. It looked like he'd been pacing and shoving his hand through his hair repeatedly for the past couple of hours. "Jesus," he said, meeting Colin's gaze. "Everything's fine?"

"If the guy dies tonight in the hospital, I might be in a little trouble."

Bennett arched a brow. "What's the likelihood?"

"Not that good."

Bennett looked at Cian, then at Jonah. "Need me to make a call?"

"Maybe not yet," Jonah said.

There were footsteps on the stairs behind them, and Kennedy let Hayden go as she turned.

Henry froze at the bottom of the steps. He stared at Hayden. He looked like hell.

"Hi," Hayden said, her voice strong and sure. "I'm fine."

Henry came forward swiftly, wrapped her in his arms, and took a huge deep breath, "Holy shit."

Hayden squeezed him. "I'm fine," she said again, firmly.

Henry stepped back holding her upper arms and studying her carefully. "Thank God. Love you."

She nodded. Colin felt his heart clench when he realized that she didn't look surprised. "Love you, too." She lifted her hand to Henry's face. "And I'm *fine*."

Finally, Henry nodded. "Okay."

She stepped out of Henry's embrace and moved to stand in front of Jonah. She looked up at him. "I used the techniques you taught me. I got away from him. And hurt him."

Jonah just stared at her.

"Love you, too," she told him. "And I'm fine."

The big man swallowed hard. Then he grabbed her and pulled her against his chest. "Love you too. I'm glad you're fine. I'm not quite sure I'm there yet."

Colin saw her smile against the other man's chest. "That's okay," she told him softly.

"Hey, I want some of that," Cian said, pushing in between Jonah and Hayden.

She laughed as he enfolded her too. "You already got hugs."

"I didn't get an I love you."

"Well, I do," she said, squeezing him.

He set her back, frowning. "Love you too, but I'm mad at you."

She frowned. "What?"

"You went to Trahan's without me. Not. Cool."

She nodded. "Yeah. I did. I'm really sorry."

He leaned in and kissed her forehead. "Don't *ever* fucking do that again."

"Promise."

And for maybe the first time Colin didn't mind all of these damned people—okay, big, muscley, handsome, charming men—hugging Hayden. He didn't even mind them telling her they loved her.

In fact, he loved all of this.

"Do you need anything?" Kennedy asked Hayden. "Oh! I know! A bath! You can use the tub in our room, Fiona's old room, I mean *your* old room," she said with a laugh. "That's what you need."

Hayden started nodding. Then she looked at Colin. "Will you help me?"

He straightened. She'd known what everyone else needed. To see her in one piece, smiling, hugging, saying she loved them and that she was fine.

And she knew what he needed. Time alone with her. To take care of her. To touch her. To be *with* her.

"Aye," he said simply.

She grabbed his hand and started for the stairs. "We'll see you all in...later."

Everyone nodded with knowing smiles and dispersed.

nineteen

AT THE TOP of the stairs, they turned right and headed for the bedrooms in the new wing. Colin stopped at the door to the bedroom with the claw-footed bathtub in the ensuite.

Hayden tugged on his hand, planning to continue into his bedroom. He shook his head, pulling her up short.

"I don't really need a bath, Colin. Let's go to bed for a little while."

He drew her up against him. "I want to take care of you."

She smiled. "I know. I have some very specific ideas about how you can do that."

He cupped her face with his hands. "You're thinking about ways of taking care of me."

She ran her hands down his back, tucking her thumbs into his waistband. "Well, yes. Both of us."

He shook his head. "I want to do something just for you. Please."

She studied his face, and he let her. Yes, he wanted to make love to her. He always wanted that. And certainly, that would make him feel better. He could feel her warm skin, her steady pulse, feel her heat and her softness, and know that she was whole, and unhurt, and happy. He could give her pleasure. He could reassure himself that she was home and safe that way.

But he didn't need that. Not right now. He needed to pamper her. To comfort her. To give her something that was all about her.

She must have seen at least some of that in his eyes because, finally, she nodded. "Okay."

He turned the knob and pushed the door open. He wasn't sure whose bedroom this was anymore. It didn't matter. It wasn't Hayden's. She was in his room now, and she wasn't leaving.

They crossed to the bathroom, and he ushered her inside. He locked the door behind them. Without speaking, he went to the bathtub and began running the water. Then he went to the cupboard where he knew the bath salts were kept. "Salt, oil, or bubbles?"

"Well, if I get a choice, bubbles."

He glanced over his shoulder. She looked mildly amused. But also touched. That's what he wanted.

He went back to the tub and poured in a capful of the sweetly scented liquid. It immediately started foaming. Then he added another capful. Could never have too many bubbles, he figured.

As the tub was filling, he went back to stand in front of her. He began undressing her. There were no wounds. The guy—he refused to think of the man with a name other than that—hadn't actually hurt her physically. Thank God. And that was all he was going to think about that.

But he was going to burn these clothes. And he was going to scrub her head to toe.

She let him strip her. He couldn't help but run his hands up and down the silky skin of her back. Then he ran his fingers through her hair, gathering it at the back into a ponytail then twisting it up and securing it with his fist. "How should we keep this out of the water?"

She pointed to the counter. There was a big plastic clip lying in the middle between the two sinks. He grabbed it and clipped it into her hair, holding the silky mass up off of her shoulders.

Then he escorted her to the bath and held her hand as she stepped in. She sank down into the water with a long, contented moan.

"Do you want to come in with me?"

"Aye. But that's not what this is about."

"Okay." She wasn't even going to fight him on it.

Her eyes closed and she leaned back, resting her head against the edge of the tub. Colin grabbed a towel off the rack, folded it into a square, and tucked it behind her head.

She let out another happy sigh. He was glad she'd chosen bubbles. The foam covered everything but her bare shoulders and arms, where she rested them on the side of the tub.

He might just survive this with only seventy percent of his blood in his cock.

He reached for a bar of soap. "Let me wash you."

She smiled with her eyes still shut. "I thought this wasn't about that."

"I am actually capable of touching you without fucking you."

"Kind of sorry to hear that."

He just chuckled softly and shook his head. He loved that she wanted more. But he was determined to pamper the hell out of her right now.

He moved down to the end of the tub and lifted one of her feet out of the water. He soaped his hands and started massaging her feet. He ran the pads of his thumbs up and down over her arch, across the ball of her foot, and then up and around her heel, and then dug gently into the tendon along the back of her foot and into her calf. He continued the pattern over and over as she moaned.

"Oh my God." It sounded breathless, but it was a contented, happy sigh versus a turned-on sexy moan.

He wasn't entirely unaffected, of course, but giving her this pleasure gave him a different kind of satisfaction.

He switched to her other foot, then continued up her calf, switching back and forth between her legs until he got to her inner thigh. Then he moved around to the back of the tub and had her lean forward so that he could massage her shoulders and back.

She drew her legs up and rested her cheek on one of her knees, giving him a sleepy, happy smile. "Thought it was going to get interesting there for a minute."

"Later. It will be very interesting. Later."

"This is heavenly."

"I'm glad."

His big hands stroked up and down over her back, then massaged over her shoulders and up into her neck.

After a few minutes, he unclipped her hair and ran his fingers through the long tresses, letting the ends fall into the water as he massaged her scalp.

"Damn, you're good at that too," she praised.

"Okay, dip your head under."

"Get my hair wet?"

"I'm going to wash it."

"My God. I may never leave this bathtub."

She tipped her head back, letting her hair dip under the water. He reached for a bottle of shampoo. He assumed it was Kennedy's, but he wasn't going to be picky. He poured some out into his hand, rubbed his palms together, then rubbed them through Hayden's hair. He massaged the pads of his fingers into her scalp, then down the long strands. He shampooed her far longer than she probably needed. He just loved touching her. She ducked under the water again to rinse the shampoo out.

"Okay, fresh water rinse," he said. He grabbed the glass from beside one sink and filled it under the bathtub faucet, dumping it over her head. He repeated it four more times until he felt her hair was nice and clean.

"Do I want to know why you know so much about washing women's hair?" Hayden asked, squeezing the excess water from her hair.

"I've washed Saoirse's hair too many times to count. She went through a mermaid phase where it could only happen in the bathtub."

Hayden grinned. "Excellent answer."

Colin reached for another towel, rising to his feet. He shook it out, then offered her his hand. Hayden stepped from the tub, and he wrapped her up in the towel.

He dried her off, then wrapped the towel around her, tucking it in between her breasts. He wrapped her hair in another towel, then kissed her nose.

"I love you, *mo grá*. You know that?"

She nodded, her eyes glistening. "I do. And I love you, too."

"And I'm sorry about the record deal." He rubbed his hands up and down her upper arms. "But, you're going to be so happy. No hotels. No food on the road. We'll be here in this house with everyone for over a year while Bennett campaigns. And I promise wherever we live in D.C. will have a huge kitchen and I'll be sure we put in a big bathtub, okay?"

She didn't say anything. She just stood looking up at him, looking a little confused.

He squeezed her arms. She'd had a big day. She probably wanted to curl up in bed. He'd do the cooking tonight.

"I promise to make you happy, Hayden. This is going to be wonderful. By the time we go to D.C., you'll have an even bigger security team to take care of and probably all of his campaign staff." Colin grinned.

There was no way she'd be able to help coming to head-quarters constantly. She'd be making people snacks and helping with events. He wouldn't be surprised if she was the best staffer anyone in Louisiana politics had ever seen.

"Hell, the President will probably eventually hear about your beignets." He squeezed her again with a grin.

Hayden's expression continued to be blank for several seconds. Then slowly her brows drew together

"I...what? You're sorry about the record deal?"

Colin nodded. "Of course. I mean, I'm glad you won't be touring. You would have been so unhappy out there on the road. But I'm sorry if you're feeling disappointed."

She stepped back, and he frowned. She hugged her arms to her stomach.

"Hayden?"

"I got the deal," she said. "They offered me a contract. They're talking about me joining Jason in Vegas for his shows there next month. If that goes well, I'll be continuing the rest of his tour with him."

Colin stared at her, processing those words. Slowly.

"Why did you think I didn't get it?" she asked.

"You...you went to Trahan's. Alone. Gabe said you played for an hour. That you seemed sad and thoughtful. I..." Colin shoved a hand through his hair as what she'd said truly sank in. "I assumed you were working through your disap-pointment."

"No." She lifted her chin. "I was thinking about the big changes that were coming. And how I was going to be leaving people I cared about to tour. And how that was bittersweet.

And how *you* were going to have to leave people you loved." She stopped and took a breath. "I just needed time to process the big change to my life."

Well...

Fuck.

He'd just screwed up. Badly.

He studied her face. She was hurt. He'd assumed they hadn't wanted her. That was bad. And he'd essentially confessed exactly how he felt about this recording contract.

Fuck.

"I'm sorry," he said.

"You said you were glad I wouldn't be touring. That I would be miserable on the road."

He nodded. It would be stupid to deny that. "We talked about that. How you didn't want to stay in hotels and eat on the road."

"Sure. But you make sacrifices for your dreams. I'm sure Bennett could tell you all about that. I'm sure there are a lot of things about campaigning and becoming a U.S. senator that aren't perfect. But he's willing to do them. And what about you?" she asked. "You gave up having any kind of life of your own. You've never even been able to have a *dog* because you wanted to be Saoirse's bodyguard."

"I don't want you to have to sacrifice things, *cailín*," he said gruffly. "I want you completely happy and to have everything you want."

She swallowed. "You knew I was going to do this."

"I thought maybe...things had changed."

"What would have changed?"

"I thought maybe you'd realized that you can have more. Or what you really wanted."

She stood looking at him, confusion and hurt in her eyes.

Colin didn't know what to say. He couldn't take back what

he'd already admitted. He'd really thought she'd turn the contract down. If she got it. But yes, he'd been hoping she wouldn't get it. Then she wouldn't have to make the decision. But dammit, he hadn't meant to hurt her.

She hugged her arms tighter across her stomach. "I'm going to need security," she said.

The words felt heavy in the air between them.

He nodded. "Aye."

"Is your company still available?"

He knew what she was asking of course. Was *he* going to be there for her?

Fuck.

He...couldn't be. Not right now. He wanted to be. He should be. He knew that. But this job with Bennett was huge. Important. Dangerous. He hadn't expected all of this to happen at once. He hadn't thought it all through. Did that mean he was fucking all of this up? Yes, maybe. But he was determined to be what Bennett needed *and* what Hayden needed.

He could keep her safe, if angry with him, *and* keep Bennett protected, *and* give his friends amazing long-term jobs that they could care about all at the same time.

It was just going to suck for *him* for a while.

Or maybe for good if he was apart from Hayden.

So *was* his company still available for Hayden to hire? He actually needed all of his guys for Bennett. In fact, he needed to hire additional men. But there was no way in hell he was sending Hayden off into the world without someone he knew protecting her.

"Of course."

She lifted her chin, and he could see that there were tears shimmering in her eyes. But these were not the same tears that had been there when he'd told her he loved her.

"But it won't be you," she said. *That* wasn't a question.

"Eventually it can be," he said. "After things with Bennett are solid. Right now, I need to lead the team, get people hired, and make sure Bennett and his people feel confident. But I could—"

"No," she said shortly. "I want Henry."

It was as if she'd slapped him across the face. But he should've been expecting it.

"Hayden—"

"It's fine. Bennett's more important. I get it."

"That's *not* what I'm saying."

"Isn't it? He's the big client. The one you've been waiting for."

Colin knew what she was feeling. Her whole life, what was important to her siblings—their dreams and plans—had come before hers. Fuck, fuck, fuck. "*You* are important to me. This is all just bad timing. I can—"

"Colin, I want Henry," she said firmly.

He gritted his teeth and took a deep breath. There was no one else he would send with her. Jonah was awesome, but she'd be more comfortable with Henry and, as great as Jonah would be, Henry would take the job more personally. That's what Hayden deserved.

Colin finally accepted the inevitable and simply nodded. "Okay."

"And you said that I could stay here, no matter what, right? Does that still stand?"

His gut tightened. He'd said she could stay as a roommate no matter what happened between them personally. He did not fucking like where this was going. "Of course. But there's no reason—"

"That's all I needed to know." She turned and left the bathroom.

Colin was right on her heels.

She walked into the bedroom, stopping at the bed to grab her purse. Only her purse. Then she headed for the door, still in only a towel. She pulled the door open and marched out into the hallway and turned toward the staircase.

There was no way he was letting her...

But she kept going past the stairs. Toward the other wing of the house where Cian, Jonah, and Henry slept.

Colin ground his teeth as he watched her walk to Henry's room, open the door, go inside, and shut the door forcefully behind her.

The only thing that kept him from going after her was that Henry was not inside.

Of course, Henry, Cian, and Jonah were up the stairs two minutes later.

"What the fuck is going on?" Henry asked.

"What do you mean?" Colin asked. He was leaning against the railing that would lead to the stairs, arms crossed, staring at Henry's door. Hayden was not going back downstairs without passing him.

"Hayden texted us. She's in my room? She said she fired you."

Colin scowled. "She didn't fire me. We had a fight."

Jonah crossed his arms. "Define fight."

Colin rolled his head, his neck cracking, and reminded himself that he was *happy* these men cared about her. Even if that meant they'd be on his case when he messed up and upset her. "I said something stupid, and she's mad at me."

"You hurt her feelings?" Cian demanded, frowning at him.

Colin counted to ten in his head, then nodded. "Aye."

"Goddamn it, Colin," Henry said. "I knew that you were going to do this."

Colin straightened from the railing and took a step toward the other man. "What?"

331

Henry, of course, didn't back down. "She's sweet. And you're...you."

"Henry, I swear to God—"

Jonah put a hand up between them. "Did you, or did you not, fuck up?" he asked Colin.

Colin looked up at the other, *bigger* man. He pulled in a breath. Then nodded. "Aye."

"Then how about just taking the blame?" Jonah asked. He was scowling too.

Yeah. Fine. He was to blame. He'd made some stupid assumptions and hurt her. But he couldn't *do* anything about it right now. He could only say words and try to convince her that she was the most important thing to him. He couldn't follow that up with action. Yet. *Goddammit.* "I just need to talk to her," Colin said.

"What are you going to tell her that's different from what you told her when you made her mad?" Cian asked.

Colin opened his mouth, thought about the question, then closed it. He loved her, but she knew that. Or, at least, he'd already said it and could only pray that she believed it. He'd told her that he would try to work it out so he could go on tour with her, but he couldn't *right now*.

He'd also told her she could stay here, no matter what, and that *was* going to happen. He needed her here. Even if she wasn't in his room, with him, next to him, *talking to him*, he needed to know she was here with people who loved her and who would take care of her. Make her happy. Make her feel like she mattered.

If *he* couldn't convince her that she was the most important thing to him, at least Henry and Cian could make her a priority.

Letting them do that might kill him, but, as she'd said, sometimes you had to make sacrifices for your dreams.

Hayden, and her happiness, was his dream.

And *he* needed to back off, so he didn't make her want to leave entirely.

"Fine. She's angry with me. For good reason. But I *need* her to stay here. In the house. I need you guys to look out for her." He pinned each of his friends with a serious look. "Got it?"

They all nodded.

"So she's in *my* bedroom?" Henry frowned, but he didn't look angry. Just confused.

"She got a record deal. She's going to Vegas to perform with Jason. Potentially finishing the rest of Jason's tour with him," Colin said.

Cian's face broke out into a grin and even Henry smiled. "That's amazing."

Colin sighed and gave his friend a long look. "I have to stay with Baxter."

"Oh." Henry nodded, catching on. "And I'm going with Hayden."

Colin nodded. "Aye." He looked at Cian. "You both are. You're now her...personal assistant. Anything she needs or wants. Understand?"

Cian grinned and nodded. "Number one fan. I'm on it."

Henry's door opened just then, and Hayden stepped out. Dressed, thank God, but in Henry's clothes.

Colin hated that even more now than he had the first time.

He also assumed she didn't have a bra on again, since all of her bras were still in his bedroom.

He also hated that. *A lot.*

She didn't say anything to any of them. She didn't even seem surprised to see them. She simply walked forward, and they parted down the middle to let her pass. She continued down the stairs and the men all turned to watch her go. When she disappeared from sight, they all turned back to Colin.

"So..." Cian said. "Is she *staying* in Henry's room now?"

"Fuck no," Colin said.

"That did not look like a woman who's coming back to *your* bedroom," Jonah said.

Yeah. Colin didn't think so either.

"She'll take Torin's room," Colin said. "Cian, we're moving her stuff in there so she doesn't feel pressured about coming to mine."

He'd told her that she could stay no matter what happened between them. He wasn't going to make her feel uncomfortable. He was going to give her space. He wasn't going to keep her stuff hostage and he sure as fuck wasn't going to give her a reason to keep going to Henry's room to get clothes, or to shower, or anything else.

He'd give her a room where she could stay by herself with all of her stuff. When she was ready to come back to his, he'd be there.

By the time he and Cian made it downstairs to the kitchen, everyone else was gathered in the room and Hayden was opening cupboards, as if searching for something.

"How about pizza?" Henry asked.

"Or I can run up to Ellie's," Jonah said.

"I could definitely go for some grits," Cian said. "And fried pickles."

"Ooh, I want a burger," Kennedy said. "Or maybe shrimp."

Colin stopped in the doorway and propped a shoulder against the wall, settling in to watch.

"Okay, I'll go up with you to get everything," Cian said to Jonah. "What's everyone else want?"

"Hey, I just realized, we don't have to stay home," Jonah said. "X...I mean, *that problem*, is taken care of. We can go out."

Hayden froze with her hands behind her back, tying her apron.

Colin wasn't sure how this was going to play out. He understood that Hayden felt most comfortable in the kitchen. She would want to cook to show them all that everything was fine, to *feel* fine herself. But they all wanted to take care of *her* right now. They also wanted to celebrate that her "confinement" was over. He loved that they wanted to take care of her and pamper her too. She deserved that.

"We should definitely go to Ellie's," Kennedy said. "She'd love that. She would love it if we came in tonight."

"Damn, we'll need to do a security sweep if you and Bennett are comin'," Jonah said.

Kennedy propped her hand on her hip. "Sorry to put you out."

He grinned. "It's not that. I just realized we'll need to head up first. No problem."

"Well, I definitely want to be there the first time Hayden goes to Ellie's and meets all the Landrys," Kennedy said. "Otherwise, I'd be nice and agree to stay here."

"Hell, her first time up there should be a crawfish boil," Cian said. "That'll really break her in quick."

"Fuck, that's gonna be a security nightmare with Bennett," Henry groaned. "We'll have to get some more guys hired quick. Or we could recruit Michael and Theo and some others for the night," he said, glancing at Colin.

"Everybody sit down!"

They all froze. And turned toward Hayden. Who was standing in the middle of the kitchen, in her apron, hands on her hips, glaring at them all.

"*I'm* going to *cook* for you all, dammit! And you can talk about all of this over family dinner! So sit *down* and shut up for one minute so we can decide what to have!"

They all continued to stare at her. The sweet girl who

baked them cookies and made them smile and took care of them had just yelled at them.

Then they all quickly moved toward the table and scrambled to find a chair.

Colin's chest felt tight, and his heart ached. God, he loved her. They were all going to miss her so fucking much when she was gone touring. And she was going to miss them.

"Okay," she said, her voice back to a normal volume once they were all sitting. "Now, you're not always going to get a choice in my kitchen, so listen up. We've got..." She trailed off. Then frowned. Then moved to the fridge.

She muttered something under her breath, then moved to the pantry.

Then sighed heavily.

She turned back toward them. "Okay, I'm not sure what I have the ingredients for."

"We can still order pizza. And eat it here," Jonah offered.

Just then the front door opened. "Hello? Can I get some help?"

Colin turned to find Ellie Landry striding toward him with a big pot in both her hands. He moved to take it from her and she went back to close the front door.

"What's this?" he asked.

"Gumbo."

Hayden was staring at her. "You brought us gumbo?"

"Yep. I told you not to mess around with it. That's *my* thing."

Hayden nodded. "And I haven't."

"Good. Now you get busy with the salad and some bread. And we're gonna need dessert. I'm thinkin' brownies."

"Ellie, Hayden's kind of had a day," Henry told her.

"I know all about it. Why do you think I'm here with my gumbo?" Ellie asked him as if he was stupid.

Henry looked over at Colin, and Colin gave him a nod. Ellie understood Hayden. The kitchen, cooking for her people, was where she felt best.

She just needed a little direction tonight.

He looked at her. She was already pulling everything Ellie had suggested together.

And she was singing softly as she did it.

Yeah. She was okay, in spite of everything. It might take her awhile to forgive him, but her being loved and cared for was the most important thing.

Ellie pointed Colin over to the stove. "Put that on warm," she said. Then she withdrew a deck of cards from her back pocket and sat down at the table with everyone else. "We'll just have to keep ourselves busy for a bit while Hayden makes us dinner." She held up the cards. "Who wants to lose fifty bucks to me?"

And she proceeded to deal out a game of Texas Hold 'Em.

twenty

THERE WAS a knock on her hotel room door. Hayden crossed to open it. She didn't even bother looking first. No one could get up to the floor where she and Jason were staying without getting past Henry and Jason's security.

"Hi, George," she greeted the room service attendant.

"Good afternoon, Ms. Ross. May I remove your tray?"

"Yes. Everything was delicious. As always."

The older man tipped his head and wheeled the cart out into the hallway. "See you later this evening?"

"I have another show tonight, so it will be past your shift when I get back. Maybe tomorrow for lunch."

"Good luck. See you then."

"'Bye."

She closed the door and sighed. The food here was amazing. She'd already had several things from the menu, and she'd recommend all of it.

She also hated all of it.

Hayden crossed to the gigantic king-sized bed and flopped onto the most comfortable down duvet, on top of sheets that boasted a ridiculously high thread count, on top of one of the three best mattresses she'd ever slept on.

Everything about the room screamed luxury and comfort.

And she hadn't slept worth a shit in the three nights she'd been here.

She lay on her back, staring at the ceiling of the suite. The hotel was in the casino where she and Jason were performing that night. Brighton Music had put them up in some of the most expensive rooms the casino offered. She appreciated the fact that they thought they needed to impress her. That was crazy though. They were making her dreams come true.

She frowned.

They are making your dreams come true. They are making your dreams come true. They are making your dreams come true.

Surely if she kept repeating that over and over, it would eventually feel right.

Probably.

It was all just surreal right now.

That was probably why this all felt so weird.

After the shows in New Orleans, Brighton Music had fast tracked a temporary contract to get her to the Vegas shows. It only covered these two shows. The long-term contract for recording and the rest of Jason's tour was still to come. But the New Orleans shows had been so well-received that Brighton had wanted to get her onstage in Vegas to see how a crowd outside of Louisiana responded to her.

After last night's show, all signs pointed to her being invited to the rest of the tour.

Social media had blown up, and Sabrina had been texting her all day.

Her own family had been absolutely gushy. Her parents and siblings had been there last night, backstage for the whole show. Tonight, they'd be there again but in box seats this time.

It all felt...incredible. She'd never had their full undivided attention like this before.

They'd of course known that she'd been rising in popularity. Her siblings followed her on social media, and she'd shared the news about her shows with Jason Young with all of them. Her mom and dad had watched clips of it on YouTube apparently. But there had been something about seeing her perform in person on a huge stage under the lights with a full band, opening for a major star that had seemed to truly make it all sink in for them. They hadn't been able to stop talking about how beautiful she looked and how incredible she'd sounded and how proud they were of her.

Everything was on track to take this from a hobby to something really...real.

It should've been everything she wanted.

She could be on a plane to Europe to open for Gretchen Hope next spring.

But instead of joining the band and Jason and the record execs for an after-party last night, she'd come back to her room alone. Instead of scrolling social media for mentions of her and the show, she'd reread the texts from Fiona and Saoirse about their visit to Bill at the nursing home two days ago. They'd gone up to see him since she, Cian, and Henry were all out of town. Saoirse had played You Are My Sunshine for him and Bill had taught her the main chords for Amazing Grace. Hayden had also watched Bennett's campaign speeches from both Baton Rouge and Shreveport, and she'd sent Jonah a recipe for a hot drink to help with the cold he said he felt coming on.

She sighed and rolled to her side, cuddling one of the pillows and closing her eyes.

She should be grateful to be in Vegas and so far away from all the tension in the house in Autre.

It'd been two weeks since she and Colin had broken up and

she'd moved out of his room—or rather since *he'd* moved her out of his room.

Torin's room was amazing. It wasn't quite as nice as Fiona's room—Torin clearly didn't have the appreciation for coffee and bubble baths that his sister did—and it definitely wasn't the same as being in Colin's room, but she'd been very comfortable there for the past two weeks. When she was *inside* the room.

Outside of that bedroom, it was a different story.

Colin's presence was everywhere. Even when *he* wasn't.

Fortunately, the day after their breakup, Bennett had started a five-day tour of the northern part of Louisiana, and Colin and Jonah had gone along. Henry had been officially assigned to her immediately, it seemed, and he and Cian stayed behind.

That had certainly lessened the tension. But she'd still felt Colin everywhere. He was a part of everything, every single room, in the house.

Then she had come to Vegas three days early to settle in, meet with record executives, and rehearse on the big stage.

So really there had only been about six days where she and Colin had to act like roommates instead of lovers.

Those had been the hardest six days of her life. Her heart had thumped every time she heard his voice, or passed him in the hallway, and the two times they'd been in a room alone together, she thought she was going to start crying, throw herself into his arms, or throw a plate at him.

Fortunately, living in a house with five other people meant they were very rarely alone, and if they were, it didn't last long.

That had saved her dignity. And all of the dishes.

It also helped that it seemed that Colin had been purposely avoiding being alone with her as well.

She wasn't sure how to read that.

On one hand, she thought he was just giving her space.

On the other, she thought maybe he'd realized just how deep they'd gotten and how quickly, and that it had caused a lot of unexpected complications that he was now happy to have removed.

But even as hurt and angry as she was with him, she missed him. She ached with missing him.

And, worst of all, it was turning out that he was right.

She turned her face into the pillow she had clutched against her chest...and screamed into it.

Colin had been right. About all of it.

She hated being on tour.

She'd been gone for four days and three nights, she'd performed once, it had been everything she'd imagined it would be...

And she was done now.

She'd felt nervous but not excited. It hadn't felt satisfying. It hadn't felt like a thrill. She'd actually felt a little disappointed to find out that everyone was so enamored with her in her performance because that meant that Brighton Music was going to invite her to continue.

It probably would've been better if it had flopped. They could've said, "We changed our minds. This was a mistake. No contract. Sorry. Bye."

Then she wouldn't be faced with all of these decisions.

She tossed the pillow to the side and rolled to her back again.

Maybe she could throw the show tonight.

Was that something people could do? She heard of people throwing ballgames. Losing on purpose. Could she suck tonight on purpose?

Probably.

She sat up. That was not a terrible idea.

There was a *thunk* on the ceiling and she grimaced. See? Noise all around her from total strangers. That felt so weird.

She knew Henry and Cian were around. Nearby probably because Henry's whole job was to stick close to her. She knew her family was still in town. An entire group of people from Autre and Bad were here. Jason had gotten a bunch of tickets for anyone from back home who wanted to come, to fill the front part of the audience with familiar faces. She could call *any* of them, and go have a meal, play some casino games, find a show, have some fun.

But she felt lonely. And restless and a little lost.

Which made no sense. She was in Las Vegas, getting ready to go on stage tonight to perform in front of a huge audience, on her way to being a big star.

She had a path. A goal. Possibly more so than she'd ever had before.

And she felt like she was wearing someone else's clothes.

They might look okay on the outside, and maybe no one else could tell, but to her the whole thing was uncomfortable. Not right. Not her.

So, if she was going to suck tonight on purpose, what did that look like? Would she just flub the lyrics? Would she just sing off-key? She wasn't even sure she could pull that off for an entire song.

She could go to the microphone and say something contro-versial. Celebrities were always getting in trouble for running their mouths.

But she knew she wasn't going to be able to bring herself to do that.

There was a knock on her door. Still mulling over how she could ruin her show tonight without ruining things for Jason and without ending up with a Wikipedia entry that would follow her for the rest of her life, she crossed to the door and pulled it open.

She blinked at the person on the other side.

Several seconds passed.

"Hey, *cailín*."

She blinked again. "Colin?"

"Aye." He gave her that sexy half grin.

"What are you doing here?"

"My job."

Her brows lifted. "I have a bodyguard."

"Aye. One of the best. That's not the job I'm talking about."

She crossed her arms and tried to look annoyed. But God, she'd missed him. Her heart and stomach were both doing somersaults right now, and it was taking every bit of self-control she possessed to keep from throwing herself into his arms.

She'd seen him just a few days ago. In the kitchen. It was always the kitchen that killed her the most. There was something about that room that seemed more intimate. Almost more so than the bedroom. He'd been standing at the island, making himself breakfast, and she'd almost melted into a puddle of I-love-you-I-want-you-I-need-you-please-be-with-me.

"What job then?" she asked.

"Boyfriend."

Her breath caught in her chest, and she had to steel herself against the urge to blurt out *I love you*. "I don't have an opening for one of those."

"No, you don't. It's already been filled."

God, he was cocky. He thought he could just show up here out of the blue, and she would open her door and let him just walk in and pick up where they'd left off?

She studied him for several long seconds.

Dammit.

She stepped back and held the door open. He stepped through.

She let the door swing shut, turning to face him, her arms still crossed.

"But seriously, what are you doing here?"

"I couldn't stay away. This is a big night for you. I needed to be here."

"You don't think I should be doing this," she reminded him.

He didn't step closer, but his expression was serious. "That's not true. I thought you didn't *want* to do this."

"And now you believe I do?"

Now he did take a step closer. "All I know for sure is that you're here. So I need to be here. We can figure the rest out. If you want to sing and tour, then I'm gonna make that happen."

She pressed her lips together as she felt them start to tremble. "You moved me into Torin's room."

"I wanted to give you space. I was afraid I'd make you feel pressured, and you'd leave. I needed you there. Even if you weren't *right there* with me, I needed to know you were with people who loved you and would take care of you."

She took a step closer to him. "But now you're here."

"I don't want to give you space anymore."

She shook her head. "What do you want?"

"You. And whatever you want."

She stared up at him, pressing her lips together. She swallowed. She had to give the tour a try, didn't she? Didn't she owe it to herself, to the people who believed in her—Sabrina, James, Cian, her grandfather who had given her the love for music in the first place—to *try* to make something of this?

But she immediately realized that all of those people, the ones who really knew and loved her, would want her to be happy and would be just as happy if she was singing in the small local bars, and working as a music therapist, and singing to sick alpacas.

They might even be happier for her that way.

Looking up at Colin, the truth came tumbling out. "I want to go home."

His eyes widened slightly, then heat flared in them. "Home? Really?"

She nodded. "I don't want this. You were right. I mean, I did. But I guess...I got what I needed from it. The chance. The idea that I could have it if I wanted it. I got the spotlight. I got to prove that I could. And now...I don't. I want to be at home. In our house. With our family."

That was all it took. He stepped close, backing her up against the wall. His hands came up to cup her face. "You don't have to say that."

"I do if I'm going to get you to throw me over your shoulder and carry me out of here."

He stared down at her. "I will always do whatever you want me to do."

"Take me home."

"Okay."

"Really?"

"After your show."

She blew out a breath. "Oh."

He stroked the corners of her mouth. "Everyone's here. In part to see you. Do one more show. Finish big. Then I'll take you home."

She frowned. "Fine."

"Bill will be disappointed if you don't. I went up to the memory care and watched you last night with him. He loved it. Said you look a lot like his favorite granddaughter. The nurses are going to set it up so he can watch tonight."

Hayden's heart thumped hard against her ribs, and she had to take a deep breath. "You helped my grandpa watch me last night?"

"Aye."

"How? The concert isn't being broadcast."

"Cian called me, and we watched the whole thing on his phone."

"That's not allowed!" she said, but she was grinning as warmth seeped through her.

"Well, there are perks to knowing the security team," he told her with a smile.

"Oh my God, Colin. I love you so much. *All* of you."

He dipped his knees and put his mouth against hers. "But me most, right?"

She laughed softly and wound her arms around his neck. "Definitely you most."

He kissed her, but just as he started to deepen the kiss, she pulled back. "Wait, what about your job? You came here to be with me. Does that mean you quit?"

He nodded. "Aye. But Bennett understood. Turns out he knows all about being crazy in love."

That didn't surprise her. But then her eyes went wide. "So, who is going to take over his detail?"

"Henry. And Jonah until..."

"Until?"

"He got a call from Cara. Torin has gone missing, and they need Jonah to find him."

Hayden pulled back with a gasp. "*What*? He's been kidnapped?"

Colin rolled his eyes. "No. He's basically gone into hiding. He does this from time to time. But I'm sure Jonah knows exactly where he is. It's the dragging him back that will be the challenge."

"Oh my God!"

"Don't worry. Jonah's dealt with Torin for a long time. He'll know how to get the reluctant prince back to his How to Be King classes."

"He doesn't want to be king?"

"He had five minutes where he did. I'm sure he's regretting it now."

"You don't seem sympathetic."

"I'm not. It keeps Fiona and Saoirse from having to be there."

Hayden shook her head. Colin had worked for an actual royal family. And a soon-to-be senator. "This is all so crazy."

"I know."

"All the more reason for Bennett to hire you back." She ran a hand over Colin's cheek. "I'll talk to him. I'll remind him that we're all family and sometimes we'll make stupid decisions, but that we have to give each other second chances."

Colin looked down at her, his expression full of affection and amusement and love. "You're going to talk to him for me?"

"Yes. And make him some pot pies."

Colin growled and leaned in. "I told you no pot pies for anyone but me."

She giggled as he kissed her neck, dragging his beard over the sensitive flesh. "They're only for special occasions. When I *really* need to impress someone. Or get a gigantic favor."

He lifted his head and grinned down at her. "Well, I'm not worried about Bennett. I think he'll take me back. But..." He bent and lifted her, throwing her over his shoulder and striding through the living area toward the bedroom. "I would very much like to talk about the things you're willing to do for gigantic favors and special occasions."

"Special occasions like concerts in Vegas?" she teased as he tossed her onto the bed.

He crawled up next to her, caging her in. "I was thinking more like marriage proposals, actually."

Her eyes went wide. "Colin," she breathed out.

He grinned. "Aye, *cailín*. You be thinking about that. You have a little time."

Then he dipped his head and set about doing her a gigantic favor.

epilogue

A YEAR AND A HALF LATER... *November... Election night. (Bennett Baxter for Senate campaign headquarters) (a.k.a. Ellie's bar, Autre, Louisiana)*

Bennett won with sixty-eight percent of the vote.

The bar was packed full of family and friends.

Hayden wasn't surprised by the results. She didn't really think anyone in the room was, but they were elated.

Well, elated, among other emotions.

She watched Colin across the room with Saoirse.

The eleven-year-old was wiping her eyes even as she smiled at Colin who was crouching in front of her.

Saoirse knew what this meant. One of her very favorite people in the entire world was going to be moving several states away.

They'd talked about this leading up to this night. Everyone had been expecting Bennett to win. The family had been preparing for his victory and for him and Kennedy along with

Colin, Hayden, and the rest of the security detail to move to D.C. shortly after.

Still, now it was actually real.

Saoirse nodded at something Colin said, and he scooped her up into his arms. He gave her a big hug and then carried her toward Hayden.

Hayden gave her a big smile as they drew near. "Hey, Saoirse."

"It's so exciting," Saoirse said, even though Hayden could still see the wetness on her cheeks.

Hayden nodded. "It really is. I can't wait for the party we're going to have for Bennett's swearing-in."

"Mom said we're going to stay for a few days, and you'll go sight-seeing with us."

Hayden reached up to tuck some of Saoirse's hair behind her ear. "Absolutely. We're going to go see the zoo where Griffin used to work too."

Knox joined them just then. "Okay, we're flipping a coin," he told Colin.

"For what?"

"If I win, you take Cian with you. You win, I keep him here."

They all laughed. Cian was coming with them. There was no doubt that all of them would be making many trips back and forth between Autre and Washington, but wherever Henry was, Cian was going to be.

The most important thing to Hayden was that their house, wherever it was, was going to be full at all times.

Jonah had left to join Torin in Cara, but they'd added six more men to Bennett's security detail, and she had no doubt that there would be Landrys visiting their house in D.C. regularly.

She couldn't wait.

Kennedy climbed up onto one of the chairs around the table at the back of the bar and put her fingers to her mouth. She gave a loud shrill whistle to quiet everyone down before pulling her husband up onto another chair next to her.

Colin let Saoirse down so she could get closer to where they were thanking everyone. Then he slipped an arm around Hayden's waist, "Are you happy, *mo grá* ?" he asked with his lips against her ear.

"So, so happy," she told him, honestly.

"Well, there's so much more to come." He kissed her temple. "So very much more."

It was hard to imagine even more than what the past year and a half had brought them.

Her parents had recently moved her grandfather to an amazing memory care unit in Washington D.C., at Colin's insistence.

Hayden and Colin had traveled to visit his family, she'd seen Cara and toured the palace, and had finally met Torin. Then they'd attended the Gretchen Hope concert in London and met Henry's family.

They'd seen Bennett give rousing speeches over the entire state of Louisiana.

They'd seen the birth of Jordan and Fletcher's baby, Sawyer and Juliet's baby, multiple family celebrations, and they'd had a fun yet sad going-away party for Jonah.

And yet standing here in this little bar in this little town with this amazing group of people, she felt a contentment she almost couldn't describe.

There really was so much more to come.

Hayden rested her hand on her stomach. Maybe she could wait a couple of weeks to tell Colin that there would be one more person eventually living with them in their house in D.C.

He looked down at her with a heart-melting smile.

Nah. She'd tell him tonight when they were alone at home.

A loud cheer went up in the room, and she laughed.

Of course, it would be a while until they were home. And even longer until they were alone.

And she loved everything about that and the people that made it true.

She hoped the full house of love, laughter, adventure, and chaos never changed.

Thank you so much for reading Colin and Hayden's story! I hope you loved Rocked Bayou!

Want to know more about the princes (Torin, Declan, & Cian O'Grady) and their bodyguards (Jonah, Henry, and more)? Keep an eye out for **Royals Gone Rogue!** *Coming soon!*

Find all of my books at
ErinNicholas.com
including a printable book list!

And join in on all the FAN FUN!

Join my **email list!**
bit.ly/Keep-In-Touch-Erin
(be sure you get those dashes and capital letters in there!)

And be the first to hear about my news, sales, freebies, behind-the-scenes, and more!

Or for even more fun, join my **Super Fan page** on Facebook and chat with me and other super fans every day! Just search Facebook for Erin Nicholas Super Fans!

more from erin's bayou world!

Want more from my bayou world? I've got so much more sexy fun for you!

Boys of the Bayou
My Best Friend's Mardi Gras Wedding (Josh & Tori)
Sweet Home Louisiana (Owen & Maddie)
Beauty and the Bayou (Sawyer & Juliet)
Crazy Rich Cajuns (Bennett & Kennedy)
Must Love Alligators (Chase & Bailey)
Four Weddings and a Swamp Boat Tour (Mitch & Paige)

*

Boys of the Bayou Gone Wild
Otterly Irresistible (Charlie & Griffin)
Heavy Petting (Fletcher & Jordan)
Flipping Love You (Zeke & Jill)
Sealed With a Kiss (Donovan & Naomi)
Say It Like You Mane It (Zander & Caroline)
Head Over Hooves (Drew & Rory)

Kiss My Giraffe (Knox & Fiona)

*

Badges of the Bayou
Gotta Be Bayou (Spencer & Max)
Bayou With Benefits (Michael & Ami)
Rocked Bayou (Colin & Hayden)

*

Bad Boys of the Bayou
The Best Bad Boy (Jase & Priscilla)
Bad Medicine (Nick & Brooke)
Bad Influence (Marc & Sabrina)
Bad Taste In Men (Luke & Bailey)
Not Such a Bad Guy (Reagan & Christopher)
Return of the Bad Boy (Jackson & Annabelle)
Bad Behavior (Carter & Lacey)
Got It Bad (Nolan & Randi)

*

Boys of the Big Easy
Easy Going prequel novella (Gabe & Addison)
Going Down Easy (Gabe & Addison)
Taking It Easy (Logan & Dana)
Eggnog Makes Her Easy (Matt & Lindsey)
Nice and Easy (Caleb & Lexi)
Getting Off Easy (James & Harper)

about erin nicholas

Erin Nicholas is the New York Times and USA Today bestselling author of over thirty sexy contemporary romances. Her stories have been described as toe-curling, enchanting, steamy and fun. She loves to write about reluctant heroes, imperfect heroines and happily ever afters. She lives in the Midwest with her husband who only wants to read the sex scenes in her books, her kids who will never read the sex scenes in her books, and family and friends who say they're shocked by the sex scenes in her books (yeah, right!).

Find her here:

CPSIA information can be obtained
at www.ICGtesting.com
Printed in the USA
BVHW070137180223
658739BV00008B/939